I0818274

THE MAKING WAR

THE MAKING WAR

BRENDA COOPER

THE MAKING WAR

EBook ISBN: 978-1-68057-111-0
Trade perback ISBN: 978-1-68057-11
Case Lamin Hardcover ISBN: 978-1-680 4-7

Cover
Cover art by Janet McDonald
Kevin J. ages by Adobe Stock
Art Direct

Publi
WordFire P
PO Box 1
Monument CO 8
Kevin J. Anderson & Rebecca Mo lishers
WordFire Press eBook Edition
WordFire Press Trade Paperback Edition
WordFire Press Hardcover Edition 2020

Join our WordFire Press Readers Group for sneak previews, updates, new projects, and giveaways. Sign up at wordfirepress.com

Created with Vellum

DEDICATION

To John A. Pitts, teller of tales, friend to everyone who knew him.

PROLOGUE

A continuation of the story of Chelo Lee, dated December 12th Year 222, Fremont Standard, as brought to the Academy of New World Historians …

I've come to the part of the story that tells of the price we paid. This will be the hardest to hear, and the most difficult for me to talk about.

We were born in war, we grew up as spoils of war, and now we were flying fast across vast reaches of space to join a war.

We left the terraformed moon Lopali grieving the murder of our brother-of-the-heart, Bryan, our strongman and protector. He died at the hands of fliers. Fliers. I know—hard to believe. The gentle 'saviors' of mankind drove Bryan from the sky, forcing him into the ground so hard and fast it killed him. Joseph lost his lover, Alicia, who stayed behind on Lopali, hoping to become a flier. As usual, her selfishness made him feel guilty. I didn't mind that she stayed behind. Not much.

You need to know how things stood when we joined the Making

War, sometimes also called the War of the Five Worlds, before the first clash of fleets, before the meetings, before the undoing and the doing.

Our history is complex, but for this story the most important part is that our blood parents came from Silver's Home, and while we were not born there, we were *of* there. Joseph and his mentor, Marcus, were the two most powerful independent Makers, and even though they entered the war to fight for Silver's Home, they hated its way of life.

I guess that's not comprehensible. Let me explain. Silver's Home depended on the genetic modification of life. Its powerful affinity groups sold enhanced humans, predators, and crops. They made a million things. Eyes and arms and strength and the ability to read data from the air, which both my brother and his teacher had. This story, of course, pivots around the fliers, a made race of beautiful slaves. As the war began, the Court of All Worlds debated their rights. Silver's Home took pride in its creativity, its power, and the beauty of its made things, and perhaps also in its dark side. Marcus battled the dark side of Silver's Home, and he taught my brother to fight it, but he still loved his planet. So when we left Lopali, we were dissidents defending a power we hated. One man had much of that power. The Port Authority's Fleet Leader Andrel Mott had sworn to destroy every Islan ship.

So who did we fight?

The Islan Trifecta Leadership wanted to break the economic back of Silver's Home. Islas's own economy was as big as ours, but controlled rather than chaotic and quick. The Islan government allowed only limited mods, all in service to the Islan government. They claimed a unity of purpose tied to a Higher Power that almost no one believed in, but it made for a convenient fiction. Islans lived under myriad rules and laws.

As the ability of Silver's Home to create powerful mods grew, Islas chose to declare war. I already told you the story of how they tricked us into the first battle, so I won't recount it here. We nearly died. Joseph saved us but damaged himself doing it.

Silver's Home and Islas made up most of the two opposing fleets, most of the power, most of the opposition. But each had a partner as well.

Joy Heaven was a satellite of Islas. While Silver's Home had the threads of its dark side woven into its light like bad blood in arteries, Joy Heaven was an open wound where Islans visited to openly act out their desires. I have seen people from there on Lopali. They dazzle. The terraformed moon is said to be full of pleasures, kind and unkind, and to be so beholden to Islas they were drawn into the war like water falling downhill. Dark humor stories suggested that they brought pleasure ships to provide surcease for the fighters of Islas.

Paradise supported Silver's Home, which had helped them terraform their moon and sold them a working network of cities and transportation.

And Lopali ...

Lopali was the most beautiful prison in the Five Worlds, its fliers the most beautiful prisoners. Seekers came from all four other worlds to worship at the fliers' feet, or perhaps more accurately, at their wingtips. Rumors told how a single feather would grant luck for years, a seat at the Morning Flight would grant peace for decades, and a week in its gardens would change a devil into a saint.

They promised to come with us, to fight for Silver's Home, but at the last minute they betrayed us and refused, declaring Lopali neutral in the Making War.

We went to stop the war if we could, and if we couldn't, to at least make sure we won. The legends about us obscure who we were. Young. Only in our twenties. Three Wind Readers: Kayleen, Joseph, and Kayleen and Liam's daughter Caro. Three planners: me, Liam, and little Jherrel. We lost physical strength when Bryan died, and the courage for extraordinary risks when Alicia abandoned Joseph to stay on Lopali.

As we sped toward the war, our ship carried representatives of both major powers and the neutral party. It carried family and friends bound by history and blood. We grieved, exhausted, and I, for one, wished we were going anyplace else.

1

ALICIA

Running behind an invisible woman exercises the senses. Every once in a while, Induan's mod reacted a beat too slowly and a smear of red petals appeared in a field of yellow flowers or a bit of forest showed at shoulder-height where there should only be sky. Her breathing was an audible tell to her location. Sometimes the salty tang of her sweat hung in the air.

Induan and I ran folded in fields of invisibility, forces that projected our surroundings onto a 360-degree image-bubble that encased us. They worked perfectly when we stood still, and well when we moved.

We passed Keepers harvesting apples and golden-berries, sweet nacks and potatoes. Twice we dodged wagons pulled by squat four-legged animals with thick necks.

Induan's voice floated from ahead of me in a soft hiss. "Alicia!"

I slowed, reluctant. "Yes?"

"You need to eat."

"Nag." But this was her way of telling me she was hungry. We had been running for two hours with no break and needed fuel. I left my mod on. She did too, panting softly as she led me to a nearby bench. My thighs ached and the bottoms of my feet stung. The precisely monitored air temperature cooled my skin while the utter perfection of the gardens crawled up my spine like a thousand ants of irritation.

As soon as we sat down, Induan reminded me how well she could read my mind. "When will you stop running?"

"Are you tired yet?"

"Of course not," she lied. I was tired, so she was tired. We'd been running for three days.

But it felt damned good, and I wasn't sure I *could* stop.

A pile of nuts appeared on the bench between us as Induan laid them out and withdrew her hand. "Bryan is going to stay dead no matter how long you run."

"And Joseph will still be on his way to join a war," I finished for her. She was the practical one, the caretaker, the planner, the queen of politics and logistics. I was the risk-taker. These things were decided for us, built into our genetic makeup. Every emotion Induan felt, I felt harder. If she cursed under her breath, I did it so loudly people turned heads.

"Which you can't stop," she said in her reasonable voice.

I wasn't ready to be calm and logical yet. "Maybe a day or two more."

"We'll run out of food."

"We can always harvest a field."

She snorted. "Don't the Keepers of the Whatever and Everything on Lopali know where every damned apple is?"

"It might be fun to watch the Keepers search for invisible fairies plucking their riches." I drank. My flask was half-empty. We'd need to find water as well as food soon. "They won't care. We're fucking heroes. They'll let us have whatever we want."

"I suspect they won't forgive stealing. It's not perfection."

I reached for my share of the remaining nuts and sucked the salt from them. We could run a few more hours, but then we needed to rest and eat a whole meal. I pulled out my slate. "We can beat the sunset into Charmed for the night or get into SoBright with just half an hour of running in the dark."

"Let's go to Charmed."

I finished the nuts. "I knew you'd say that."

"We can visit Bryan's grave. Maybe they finished his statue."

I wanted to spend another night outside, curled up on a bench or underneath a tree, but my stomach had other ideas. Being a risk-taker was no excuse for complete stupidity. "Okay."

Her hand found mine again, just a touch this time. She whispered, "Look at me now," and left.

"I see you," I whispered to her invisible back. A saying we shared.

A sudden rush of warmth crept through me. Not sexual—we'd never chosen to be lovers. Maybe something more than that, though. Better even than family. She had remained here with me when Joseph and Marcus and Chelo and the others flew off to go get killed in the stupid Maker's War. "I'm glad you stayed."

"If I hadn't, you'd have run all the way around this damned moon."

Good idea. "We could."

I heard the slide of her foot on the path and noticed a slight ripple in the rows of ripening tomatoes behind her. "Catch me?" she called.

Running felt like joy. I'd run in many kinds of gravity, and Lopali's was the one I liked the most—just far enough under normal to give my stride some bounce, but I still had weight to push off with. Practice had made us fast.

Possibly she let me catch her. We ran side by side past fields of lettuce and kale and neat golden-berry vines. We passed through an arbor of empty perch-trees with circles of neatly trimmed grass below them, the bottoms of their branches so low that a few brushed my hair.

We turned a corner and Induan stopped so suddenly I ran into her arm. Or maybe she was trying to stop me. "Amalo," she hissed.

I blinked. Sure enough, the tall flier stood in the middle of the path ahead, arms crossed. He was taller than most humans, and thinner of course. All fliers were thin. His deep gray wings flapped slowly, poised.

I spotted his partner, Marti, just to the left, tucked into the trees to hide her bright red plumage. I should have seen her.

Stupid me.

Amalo was rare—a flier modded to see infrared. Induan and I were as visible as anyone else to him.

Induan and I both turned our mods off, springing into apparent being in a single second as the invisibility fields collapsed around us.

Marti let out a small gasp as she stepped over to the path behind us, effectively blocking retreat.

Amalo's expression made me feel small and petty.

I swallowed and crossed my arms, imitating his stance. "Hello Amalo, Marti. I'm pleased to see you."

"Are you?" he asked.

I had begged him for wings. When he'd finally said yes, I'd walked away, frightened. It had been a snap decision to turn my back on a thing I'd begged for.

Even risk-takers get nervous of really big risks.

Since the battle that had taken Bryan's life had happened moments after I'd walked away from his offer, I'd hoped he hadn't noticed. I tried to look as proud as I could, as steady, as calm. "I'm ready. I had to get over Bryan first."

He raised an eyebrow.

Induan poked me in the side, telling me to stop talking.

I didn't listen. "I did. I ran. I won't be able to run anymore, not when I have wings. I needed to run out my pain."

His face softened, although only a little. "You should be rested and well fed before you begin."

I swallowed.

Induan glared at me.

Marti watched with what looked a little bit like amusement.

A sharp fear of saying the wrong thing settled over me, finally, a sort of awareness of the cusp I stood on. I settled for simple facts. "We are on our way to Charmed."

"Someone will meet you there. At sunset. Run fast and enjoy your last run."

I swallowed, panic knocking my heart. No decision in my life had been this big, or this muddy. But I managed to nod slowly. "We'll see you there."

He and Marti crouched, took a few small steps, and with massive beats of their wings that blew my hair sideways and stole the sweat from my skin, they rose into the air.

Marti's wings were compact, vibrant, beautiful, as if whoever had designed them had been reaching for a work of art. Amalo looked plain beside her, but his larger wings carried him high more quickly than Marti could follow, and he looped in a lazy circle until she caught up. Once again paired, she took two wingbeats to every one of his. She looked like a butterfly while he looked like a raptor.

I shivered, watching them. Longing? Love? Admiration? Abject fear? Were they all one?

Induan turned toward me. "Wings are a horrible idea. They will limit you."

"Because?"

"For one thing, you'll be trapped *here*. You hate this planet."

"Moon."

"This place. You hate it."

"Have you seen the statue of the first flier on Silver's Home?"

"Probably."

Could she have seen it and not been moved to tears? "I saw her the year before we came here, a few weeks after we landed on Silver's Home. She stood in a park, poised for flight. I saw both pain and beauty carved into her face, and I knew deep inside that she was magnificent both in spite of and because of her pain. She looked so alive. I knew then that I needed wings. When Marcus brought us here —here of all the places on the Five Worlds—I knew I would get them."

She looked puzzled.

"Don't you see? That's why I didn't go with Joseph."

She frowned, and for a moment she made me feel the same way Amalo had. "Are you sure you didn't stay because Joseph was too busy saving the world to spend time with you?"

The sting of her words only struck me silent for a moment. "That, too. See? I can be honest. But no, I needed to stay. For wings." I glanced up to emphasize my point. Amalo and Marti had been reduced to small dots of gray and red against a pale blue sky.

She crossed her arms almost like Amalo had, her smaller body blocking me from moving forward.

I could go around, piss her off, but I needed her to understand. "I can change the world here; I know it. I'm already important here, already famous."

"As part of the family that changed everything. Not as yourself."

Induan often said hard things, and I approved. But I did not want to hear this, so I said nothing.

"And that's an end in itself?" she prodded. "Fame?"

Damn her. "I'm tired of being a shadow."

"You've never been anyone's shadow."

"But I haven't ever been anyone by myself, either." She was beautiful, standing there, my mirror, blonde to my dark, her calm a deliberate balance to my love of danger. "Now it's just me." I hesitated. "And you. Now I won't be in Joseph's shadow, and Chelo won't tell me what to do. So I'm going to fly. *To fly.*"

She waited, patient. Sometimes she had an impishness to her, a love of pranking others with her invisibility mod, but right now she just stared at me, calm as hell.

"I'm going to matter here. I don't know how yet, though. How could I?"

She snorted. "That's a matter of politics, not wings. Not your strong suit."

Damn her. I shifted the subject. "Maybe we'll get news of the fleets today."

"We chose to skip the war." Induan shook her head. "We'd best get running, and you'd better love every step."

So she wasn't going to try and stop me. "Is that why you think I'm running?"

She nodded. "I think you know wings are not the answer to anything you need." She turned away from me, clearly not expecting an answer.

I looked up as we stepped out from under the trees. Fliers swooped and rolled through the air a field away from us. Not Tsawo—all of these wings were brightly colored like butterflies—two yellows, a pale blue, a set of orange wings with brown spots near the end, and a bright green pair.

Induan's voice whispered warm near my ear. "Turn on your mod."

I did, and its small spark ran along my skin. I started immediately, each stride just a little longer than the last one until I grew hot with speed. In my imagination, I outran the loss of my family, the loss of Bryan, the pain I had caused Joseph when I didn't show up on whatever ship they flew away from here. I hadn't seen that pain, but I felt guilt for it anyway.

I shouldn't. I should revel in the fact that Joseph was surely happy to be flying away from me, locked up inside a silver ship and enveloped in its data streams. He had left me long before. He took on responsibilities which closed me out, but I never stopped loving him. Once, he had loved me as much as I loved him.

I tried to forget the shape of his face as I ran.

Bryan, my friend. My protector. Bryan who fell from the sky and was buried in Charmed.

I could not give Bryan life any more than I could give Joseph unconditional love. I could not obey Chelo, or help Kayleen. Liam considered me an idiot, or maybe a victim—two things I wasn't.

I was better off without them.

I focused on my stride. Lopali's even surfaces fell behind me and the neat fields blurred.

As we raced into Charmed, sweating and hot, we dodged a group of Keepers as they headed for the fields, walking and chattering amongst themselves. I saw no sign of Amalo or Marti.

We slowed and stopped. "I'm starved," Induan said.

"Me too." We had nothing to buy food with. I stepped behind a building and turned off my mod. So did Induan. We looked like two young women who could have been seekers.

The streets we walked through had been planned to the last detail. The edges of each garden were clipped, the houses clean and painted, the roofs perfectly maintained. Boring. Pretending perfection. I loved and hated Charmed and Lopali at the same time. It left me off-balance. Nothing was so simply good as Lopali pretended to be.

We passed Keepers in flowing uniforms, seekers and pilgrims and tradespeople in a multitude of clothes and body styles. Restaurants filled the air with scents of vegetable soups and mint tea and baking bread.

Fliers glided down from the sunset sky, landing near bars and restaurants and houses.

I expected Amalo and Marti any moment.

Induan had less pride than me, or perhaps she was hungrier. She stopped a Keeper and a flier walking side by side down a street, the flier bent slightly forward to prevent the low sweep of his wings from dragging the ground. "Excuse me?"

The flier turned bright green eyes that matched his wings toward us.

Induan asked, "Please, can you tell us where to find Amalo and Marti?"

I added, "Or Tsawo and Angeline?" They had been there when Amalo had promised me my wings.

"Tsawo shows up when and where he wants." It didn't seem like he approved.

Induan refused to give up. "If you were looking for Amalo, where would you start?"

He shrugged.

"Is there anywhere we can get food now?" Induan asked.

"Anywhere you like. Amalo said you two should be taken care of."

He could have said that to begin with.

Our noses led us to a small cafe with baked nut crackers and fruit salads. The owner greeted us by name as if she had been waiting for us. We gorged ourselves. After that, we walked, watching. None of the primary fliers were anywhere. I recognized a few faces and asked, but no one knew where they were. Eventually, I spotted Chance, the doctor who had helped Joseph and Marcus change the fliers' biology so they could bear children. I walked up behind him and touched his shoulder.

When he turned, he looked stiff, but then he often looked a little stiff. He was a man with almost no sense of humor, a bland man, mousy and unremarkable in every way. A slight but friendly smile touched his lips. "Amalo asked me to watch for you."

I managed to return his smile and say, "Then it's good *we* found *you*."

"He told me you plan to try for wings." He didn't sound happy about it.

I felt my smile grow larger. "I want blue wings."

"You'd better want to live. If you manage that, *then* you can pick the color of your wings."

Induan looked as serious as usual. "What do we need to know about it?"

He kept his gaze on me. "The change is not like any pain you've ever felt. People die of it."

I swallowed, stunned. "People die of pain alone?"

"They do. Or they die of the change. They die from the hollowing out of their bones, or from the lengthening of their legs. Sometimes their organs fail as the changes wrench their insides into new shapes." He seemed to be enjoying himself. "Or they just go stark raving crazy."

"I won't go crazy and I won't die."

"You don't know that."

"Have you seen it?" Induan asked. "I mean, seen it happen?"

He nodded. "I am the current Architect of the Change of Form."

Of course he was something with a silly name. "Really? I thought you hated the idea." I remembered that from some previous conversation in the gold guest house outside of SoBright, not long after we first came to Lopali.

"I hate the way it is forced on children. *You* are making your own choice. I don't have much sympathy for you." He didn't sound sympathetic, either. Maybe amused. Maybe exasperated.

Well.

Induan turned the conversation. "Will there be Makers helping? Like the work Joseph and Marcus did to help the fliers have babies?"

"No. Makers helped create the template, but they don't assist with each change." He cleared his throat and looked up for a moment, then back at us. "Marti asked me to take you to Oshai. They were summoned early, so they couldn't wait for you." He looked at me hard, as if hoping I would back out. "Are you sure you want to do this?"

"As sure as I want to breathe."

Induan sighed. "When will we go?"

"Now. We'll fly."

One last trip on stupid fake wings built for humans. "Let's go."

It was nearly dusk when we landed at Fliers' Field outside of Oshai. I felt like some ungainly half-broken bird wearing the clumsy wings with my shoulder blades screaming and my lower back spasming. I almost fell. Induan made a better show of it, landing elegantly with no bounce.

In the dusky light, the observation perches ringing the field looked like parts of a broken fence. By the time we'd finished racking our wings and cleaning up, the outside lights had transformed the field into brighter greens.

My stomach screamed at me. Flying used as much energy as running, and I'd done both for three hours each today on only one meal. Chance understood. After we hung our wings in the equipment hangar and before we left the field for Oshai, he pulled three seed bars out of a cabinet and handed one to each of us. I inhaled mine so fast I didn't taste it.

We followed Chance to a white one-story building covered in flowering vines. It looked small and unassuming, probably so that the vast pilgrim population didn't mistake it for a place they should visit. He rang a doorbell that hung under a small sign which said, "Center for the Winged Transformation of the Soul."

The name made me wince.

The door swung open. A man in Keeper's clothes gestured for us to follow him down a corridor that opened up into a room so tall a flier would have room to exercise.

Fragrant flowers hung from wooden walls, the red and gold faces of their blooms turned up toward dark skylights. Six fliers crowded on a wooden platform suspended from the ceiling on chains. On the far left, Tsawo's black wings alternately glittered and faded to even darker as he fluffed them, making room for his sister, Angeline. Her pale white wings contrasted with Tsawo's black ones.

Seeing Tsawo brought up a host of conflicting memories. He had kissed me, far more—certain? confident?—than Joseph. Tsawo's kiss was a man's kiss. Before that, he had been distant when he'd taught me to fly in human wings. He had betrayed my family when he'd stopped the fliers from committing to the war. But foremost, the kiss. I looked away.

On Angeline's other side, Matriana stood with her silver, white, and gold wings. Beside her, Daniel stood a full head taller, his pale orange wings glowing in the light. Even though we'd met Daniel and Matriana the first day we'd arrived on Lopali, I still didn't know if they were brother and sister, lovers, co-rulers, or all of the above.

Next to Daniel, red-winged Marti. Amalo wore grey that matched his wings, much like Tsawo wore black to match his.

I had expected just Tsawo, or just Amalo. I hadn't been sure which. Not … everyone.

Marti saw us first. She straightened, startled, and then her face shifted to show pride before she schooled it back into calm. Proud of me? I thought so, and it felt good. She was the only flier in the room who had gained her wings as an adult.

They flowed to the forward edge of the platform, about fifteen feet above us, close enough their wings touched. Flowering vines that hung off the sides of the platform scented the air with a cloying sweetness.

"Come forward," Matriana said.

I did.

Induan and Chance stayed behind me. The light tightened until I stood in a bright circle of it and squinted up at what I yearned to become.

"I understand you have requested the right to become a flier," Matriana said.

"Yes."

"Listen carefully as I read the promise to you. You must respond to each question."

Her words fell onto me like welcome, hard rain. They were going to allow me to do this. I swallowed, the thrill of risk straightening my spine.

Matriana spoke slowly and clearly, almost as if she were

addressing a child. “Do you agree to give up that which limits you to being merely human and to have your soul seared into the shape of a flier?”

“Yes.”

“Do you willingly give up all rights and abilities to have children?”

“Joseph and Marcus fixed that.”

Tsawo glared at me.

Matriana repeated. “Do you willingly give up all rights and abilities to have children?”

“Yes.”

“Knowing that the rights of fliers are different from the rights of other humans, do you agree to be bound by the contracts between fliers and their Makers?”

A bell of warning rang in my head, but I took a deep breath. Marti had talked to me about this. The change made you beholden to the affinity group that created fliers. I glanced at her. She had accepted it. She had survived. Whatever the bond did, I would accept it, too. “Yes.”

Matriana’s voice sounded like benediction and prayer, like permission and fair warning. “Do you willingly give up your right to be called a human and replace it with the reality of being a flier of Lopali?”

“I have never wanted anything more in my life.”

“Yes, or no?”

“Yes.”

“Do you agree to have your bones hollowed out until they are too fragile to run, too fragile to stand in the full gravity of Silver’s Home where you came from, and so fragile that they might break when you try your newly-grown wings?”

A slight frisson of panic made me want to flee and run for another three days, but I stilled my face. “Yes.” Finality and fear shivered up my neck and my fingers tingled.

“Do you promise to keep the work that leads you down this path secret, and to share it only with the people in this room?”

I should have expected that promise, but I hadn’t. “Including Induan? Can I share with her?”

"Yes. Induan has agreed to be your Keeper. She will keep your secrets close."

I turned and looked at Induan. When had she done this?

A wide grin lit her face, a touch of triumph. She had kept a secret from me. It meant she could be with me, and in that moment I realized how much I wanted her there. I whispered, "Thank you."

Matriana's voice called my attention back to her. "Do you agree?"

"I can have Induan as my Keeper always?"

Matriana hesitated for the first time. "Keepers can be given new assignments."

Her hesitation suggested an opening. "We are both from off-world. I request that Induan be always assigned to me."

A short conversation ensued, the words hushed and impossible for me to hear. Matriana looked as beneficent as possible, given that I could also tell she was slightly irritated, the rhythm of her call and question routine slightly changed. "We will not bind her to you, but we will allow her to make that choice any time."

"Thank you."

"Do you want to become a flier with all of your being?"

"Yes."

"To want it with anything less is to guarantee that you will die. Do you understand?"

"Yes."

"Will you honor the Ways of the Fliers of Lopali with all of your heart and to the best of your ability?"

"Yes."

"Very well." Matriana stared down at me, then looked over at Tsawo. "Do you swear to teach her to fly, to teach her to be a flier, and to teach her how to be here?"

He looked at me, met my eyes. Again, I could feel his kiss, and also his frustration.

I stood as tall as possible.

Moments passed before Tsawo said, "Yes."

Matriana looked at Amalo. "And you will do the same?"

"Yes." No hesitation.

Matriana turned back to me. "Repeat every word."

I stood, waiting. I didn't even breathe.

"I promise."

"I promise."

"To endure the change with grace."

"To endure the change with grace."

"To live or to die."

"To live or to die."

"In peace and in balance."

"In peace and in balance."

"To the best of my ability."

"To the best of my ability."

The six of them all stretched their wings as one. In a move as precise as the morning flight, they leapt from their high perch and landed near me so I was surrounded on all sides. They smelled of oils and spices and flowers, of sky and wind.

I trembled, joy and fear all mixed up together, both food for my very soul. A moment meant just for me, for the risk-taker that I was born to be. It was almost orgasmic.

One by one, they touched me, and I them, hand to hand while I turned in a circle to meet each of their eyes. In them, I saw pride, pity, and most of all, love.

The last made me blink back tears.

2

CHELO

Some people love space, while others love the ground. I am the latter. Even horribly, absurdly perfect Lopali had sky and dirt and water that hadn't been recycled a hundred thousand times. Being on a ship again left me unmoored.

Mohami and his helper, Kala, had the rooms next to ours on *Bryan's Hope*. He was completely bald, with merry dark eyes and thin lips. Kala was pretty enough, but quite generic with mannerisms that seemed designed to distance her from people. Their quarters had no sun wall, but Mohami was his own sun. He felt like garden dirt, like dark loam full of promise, nutrients, seeds, and hope.

In Oshai, on Lopali, we had begun each day with a ceremony that Mohami had led. Fliers had spiraled over the town, and then we'd sat and sang songs or listened to lectures or stories about the human heart and hope.

On Lopali, Mohami had ministered to thousands. Here, he practiced for a handful of us. Me and Caro, and often Kayleen's adoptive mom, Paloma. Sometimes other women joined us. The sisters Tiala and Jenna, the Islan Dianne, or even Ming, the dancer who had loved Bryan. Instead of standing in the center of a garden mandala with pathways that held more than a thousand people, Mohami sat in the corner of a small room.

It surprised me that Caro was drawn to the quiet, contemplative mornings. Even at just over five years old, she sat more still than the rest of us, serene and curious. Caro, who easily flushed with fury or railed at us for making rules. Mohami gentled her.

About a week into our flight, Mohami and Kala, Caro and I, Paloma, and Dianne sat in a loose circle on Mohami's floor. Mohami and Paloma both looked of an age, with gray hair and wrinkled faces, although I suspected Mohami was hundreds of years older. Most likely, he had aged past the usefulness of youth drugs. Paloma simply refused to take them. Everyone else glowed with youth, while I was willing to bet that besides Caro and I, Kala was the only other human in the room less than a hundred years old. She might be older, too, but since she was a low-level apprentice, I doubted it. Kala finished singing, her last long high note hanging in the air. We sat in silence for long moments until Caro interrupted us to ask Dianne, "If we are going to war with Islas, why are you here with us?"

Softness from Kala's song filled Dianne's eyes. She said, "Being from a place does not mean you belong there. Kala's song touched me. *If* a morning routine occurred on an Islan ship, I would be forced to attend. Or kept out. Whatever the captain wanted. Here, I can choose." She smiled at Kala.

The girl nodded, smiling faintly in return.

Caro tugged on her long dark hair, a habit she had picked up from Kayleen. She frowned. "But will you mind if we have to shoot people from Islas?"

Dianne looked startled at Caro's insight. "How can I know that before it happens?"

Mohami asked Dianne. "Do you want to tell us your story?"

Dianne stiffened. Mohami waited, his wrinkled hands in his lap. Caro likewise sat still, a mirror of the old man.

Eventually, the silence drove Dianne to speak. "I loved Islas when I was growing up. I did so well in school I was chosen by the Star Mercenaries for my two years of mandatory duty. That's where I met Mad Lushia."

Lushia had killed our father. Although by then Dianne was on our side.

"Star Mercenaries are killers, but killing made me sick to my stomach. I did it, as if killing were homework, but it hurt my soul." She looked to Mohami, who nodded slight encouragement. But then, many of the pilgrims he had ministered to were Islans.

"I wanted to be transformed, much like Alicia wants wings. I went to Silver's Home with two years of savings. It was enough for one of the smaller mods, and I shopped the Street of All Designs for three days, trying to choose.

"I met Marcus on the Street one day, consulting with a booth owner about some shoulder dogs he had helped to Make. I don't know why I drew his interest. Perhaps simply because I came from Islas. We became ... friends."

I had seen Marcus and Dianne greet each other after a long absence and witnessed the joy they felt at seeing each other again. He and Dianne shared more than a casual friendship, if something less than the love Marcus and Jenna had.

Dianne continued. "He taught me I didn't need a mod, that wanting to be different made me different. With Marcus's guidance, I began working for change from inside the system. It took three hard years to become a small part of the corps that managed the diplomacy between Islas and Silver's Home. I travelled between the two places three times." She hesitated, swallowed, and went on. "Eventually I just couldn't go home again."

Caro asked, "Did you get in trouble?"

Dianne nodded but did not elaborate. "Marcus and I travelled the Five Worlds while Jenna was lost on Fremont, before you came back. That is how I knew so much about Lopali when we got there—I had been three times before. I was studying interplanetary economics ..." She broke off and glanced at Caro. "Credit. The movement of wealth."

Caro held a finger up. "And power."

A five-year-old should not understand interplay between power and credit. Dianne appeared to agree; she gave me a questioning look before she continued. "Marcus called me and asked me to go with you. I knew Jenna's story about being left behind on Fremont. I knew she came back with fewer limbs than she'd left with and some extraordinary people she'd rescued. I grew curious, so I am here."

Silence fell for a moment, then Caro followed up on her first question. "Can you shoot at Islans?"

"I don't know." Dianne shifted in her seat, squared her shoulders, her usual calm dissolved into fidgeting.

I felt for her—she was one of us and yet not. "It is hard to shoot at anybody," I offered.

Paloma frowned at me. "You fought the Islans on Fremont."

"To protect the babies. It was almost impossible, even then."

Mohami steepled his hands and looked at Caro. "No one knows what they will do in a war until they are in the middle of it."

Caro must have been saving her questions up for days. This time she asked Mohami, "So why did you come?"

"Because Marcus is looking for a third way. People are fighting over the choice between control and near-anarchy. Islas wants to tell us all what to do while Silver's Home wants no limitations on its Makers. There is beauty and pain in that choice—fliers are beautiful and yet their hearts hurt. We yearn for beauty and it sears us from the inside. Your aunt Alicia is trying to have the power of beauty, although she can't yet really understand how it is bound to sacrifice. It is not," he paused, "altogether healthy."

Dianne asked him, "This third way. Do you know what it is?"

Mohami took a deep breath and let it out slowly. "Keepers create room for change and support growth. Thus, we help the souls of those we Keep. But perhaps we can Keep more than a small population. I came to look for peace for all and, if I find it, to help them accept it."

"Was it your idea to come?" Caro asked him. Once again, out of the mouths of babes.

Mohami looked pleased that she had asked, although he offered no specifics. "Others agreed that I should come."

Perhaps the fliers were helping us after all. I had a question. "Mohami? What do the Keepers Keep?"

A spark of interest in his eyes told me he approved of the question. "We keep physical places that are safe for pilgrims and for fliers, and we keep the secrets that allow them to live. We keep the patterns in land and data that support the peace fliers offer to the worlds. All along, the fliers have been demonstrating the third way *even while they have been slaves*."

Once more, Caro spoke my thoughts. "But they killed Bryan."

Kala spoke for the first time since her song. "Because we failed as Keepers."

"Is that why you left?" Paloma asked.

Kala's lips thinned with what looked like distaste, and she glanced at Mohami. He smiled softly and spoke just above a whisper. "I came because I can do good here."

His use of the word "I" left me wondering why Kala had come. He wanted to be here, but did she? Or was she merely assigned to him, and perhaps unhappy?

3
JOSEPH

I patted Sasha on the head and signaled her to lie down inside her pressurized crate. She gave me a steady look, her brown eyes wide and intelligent, her head slightly cocked.

"You've got to, girl."

She whined softly.

"It's so you can stay with me. Go on."

After one last look designed to make me feel guilty in the way that only a dog can manage, she curled up on the floor of the crate and rested her nose on her paws. I zipped her into the inner lining, closed the outer hatch, and did up the buckles that activated the seal. The crate hummed as its life support systems came on. Marcus had helped me add heat exchange, air supply, and water to a carrier meant to move small cargo loads between ships.

Marcus had bought *Bryan's Hope* outright. It had a good pilot AI, so we were free to sit in the cramped command area and stare at the ships we approached. He'd shown me pictures of the *Maker's Thorn* before, but pictures seldom expressed the power of spaceships well.

Marcus might have tried to prevent this moment, but his intense green eyes seemed even more alive than usual as we got close enough to the three ships to distinguish the *Thorn* from the other two that flew relatively near it, the *Black Star* and the *Highline.* He might not like the war we were going to, but he loved his ship.

The *Thorn* looked true to her name, by far the longest and thinnest of the three. The other two bulked uglier, the *Highline* a barrel of ship that had probably been a pleasure cruiser before it was modified to fight. The *Black Star* had visible armament that looked like a central part of her design.

Pictures hadn't telegraphed the *Thorn*'s true size. I whistled. "I knew you were rich."

Marcus grunted. "I have friends."

"That, too. But I looked it up." I felt a little smug. "The *Thorn* is registered to you."

He turned to face me, not smiling. "She has a captain, Shawna Hill. Shawna's nearly as powerful a Wind Reader as you or I are. She manages the *Thorn* well, and she knows it as if it were her blood. She'll be Captain Hill to you until she says otherwise, but if she takes you into her circle, she'll be Rose."

"Because every thorn needs a rose?"

He laughed. "Exactly."

Marcus had designed the *Thorn*. His pride in her was evident.

"Even if she has a captain, I want to learn to fly her." The first day I saw images of the fleets in the War Room back on Lopali, I had known I would fly one of these ships. I felt her in my bones as we grew closer.

Marcus smiled at me. "If luck is on our side, I'll have time to teach you." He turned to the controls.

I stayed near Sasha's crate, crooning to her, as the *Thorn* bulked above us and a door opened to allow us entry into a dark hold. Light illuminated the noses and fins of other ships, although with so much darkness I couldn't tell how many other ships or how big the hold was. Sasha whined, apprehensive, but I knelt beside her and whispered, "It's an adventure, girl. I'm glad you're with me."

Marcus and I disembarked first. I towed Sasha's crate on a short tether. It rocked as she wriggled. It took twenty minutes to reach the far side of the dark bay, lights beneath our feet showing the path. I pushed the crate through the airlock with me and Marcus. Once I opened the door, Sasha bounded out and raced up and down the small corridor, tail wagging.

Marcus laughed as I gathered her back to me, and said, "Leave the crate with the suits. Someone will figure out what to do with it all."

I did. Marcus led us to an elevator. When it started to move, Sasha became a ring of dog around my leg, her tail tucked and her ears back. Even though she'd been in *Creator*'s elevator, *Thorn*'s was bigger and faster.

Marcus led us amidships and forward through sterile hallways with yellow directional labels and plentiful handholds for low gravity. In Command, busy uniformed staff paid close attention to displays or gathered in small meetings, everyone focused.

I followed Marcus in, keeping Sasha behind me.

The captain stood when she saw Marcus. She gave him a smart salute, a wide grin on her narrow face. "At your service, Master."

Marcus laughed. "At ease."

"Master?" I asked him.

"If I'm not on the ship, I'm merely the owner. But when I am, I become the Master. The captain reports to me, but I do not run the *Thorn*. If I need something, I talk to her. In an emergency, she makes the decisions. She can hand me command, or I can take it, but neither has ever happened."

"They might, though," the captain said, still smiling. "This is not a drill." Tall and rail thin, she only looked about my age even though Marcus had told me she'd been in charge of the *Thorn* for eight years and flown on it for twenty. The dark browns of her skin matched her eyes, both just a little lighter than her carefully coifed hair. A captain's coat hung long over slender and well-muscled thighs. Bright blue and green and silver data threads glittered in a vertical striped pattern that matched up with her almost knee-high boots. Like the old coat my father had passed to me, this would connect the captain closely with the most crucial data about the ship. She bent down and held her hand out to my dog, who went right to her.

"That's Sasha."

"She's beautiful." She looked up at me. "You're bringing her to a war?"

"I took her from a war. She'd have been eaten by something if I'd left her behind on Fremont."

"I wouldn't have been able to leave her behind either." The captain's voice sounded soft and steely at the same time. "I suppose we'll have to keep her safe."

Sasha butted her head into the captain's hand as if to ask for even harder pets. She knew people better than I did; everyone she trusted had turned out to be my friend.

Marcus broke into the conversation. "How are you? How's the ship?"

"Let's go to the communications room, and I'll catch you two up."

He frowned. "Any good news?"

She looked up, still scratching Sasha behind the ears. "It never is, is it?"

4
ALICIA

Pain that starts in the center of your bones radiates slowly from the inside to the outside, cell by cell, layer by layer, burning marrow and bone and vein and blood, so that in the end even your skin burns.

I lay on my back on a hard bed inside a stone room. Walls and floor and windows were stone, the drapery on the window thankfully a thick enough material to dim the light down to near-dusk even at midday.

Each drop of cool water Induan dripped onto my hot forehead felt like it weighed a pound. If I moved, my joints screamed. Even if I lay still, my shoulders and knees were hot points of pain. My legs twitched of their own volition. My hands clenched and stretched on their own, as if they were wholly unconnected from my brain.

Rails around the bed kept me from falling to the floor. Tubes pierced my arms and legs, delivering nanotechnology, food, and fluid, and removing calcium and dead cells.

Machines hummed and clattered.

The room smelled alternatively of urine and sweat and antiseptic and flowers.

Each day lasted a year or more.

Two others were going through the transformation nearby. Sometimes when the door opened, I heard them scream.

Wings rustled around me as fliers came and went. The corners of my eyes caught the black shimmer of Tsawo's wings, the dark blue of the band he wore around his neck, its single indigo feather iridescent when it caught the light. Sometimes I glimpsed Marti's red wings. At least twice I heard Matriana and Daniel speaking softly. Induan slept on a cot on the far side of the room. When she came to cool me with dripping water, she struggled to hide the horror in her eyes.

The fliers chanted and sang. They whispered stories of flight in my ear. I tried to hold onto their words, to let them encourage my new being.

Of them all, only Marti had done what I was trying to do. She warned me that my bones would feel like blades made to cut flesh. She kept her hand on me, gentle as a feather, soothing.

I had attacked her once, trying to escape Amalo. He had seen me even though I was invisible, and I had knocked her down and broken a feather. Feathers had value, but she had let me keep hers in spite of my transgression. Induan had framed it and hung it where I could see it as I transformed. A beacon.

Chance or Induan or both were almost always in the room. They sang and talked, and sometimes hummed. Chance often painted pictures of flowers or sketched fruit, and Induan occasionally worked with yarn.

When they touched me, choking screams filled my constricted throat.

Pain kept me from sleeping. Rarely, Chance dosed me with strong tea—also dripped from the towel. It helped a little. Still, my throat and my bones and the skin under my nails all burned.

My legs grew so long that my toes reached the end of the bed. The metal railing felt blessedly cold, and I clutched it over and over with my long toes, arching my back and extending my legs.

"Be careful," Chance whispered. "You can break."

"I won't," I said through clenched teeth. "I. Will. Not. Break." I stared at Marti's feather. "I. Will. Not."

One day, morning light slanted into the room as I felt my shoulders shattering, my fingers curling into my palms so tightly that if my nails weren't kept trimmed, I would have poked holes in myself. I burned. Surely, I'd melt through the bed and into a puddle on the floor.

Sweat poured from all of my surfaces.

Light hurt.

Chance muttered, "Must you be unique in everything?" He stuck a needle into my arm, leaned over me, and spoke carefully. "We're going to release the spinal targets. You will have to sleep through that."

"Why ..." My throat burned. "Why ..." I swallowed, tried again. "Why sleep now?"

"This is the worst. If you slept through all of your transformation, you wouldn't know the pain of becoming, and you wouldn't pass into being a true flier."

I could have been asleep?

"This is the part of my work that kills people who try to watch it happen to them."

Panic shot through me. *More pain than I had felt as my bones hollowed and my limbs lengthened?*

He continued, relentless. "No one has lived through this part of the change awake."

In that moment, I regretted my choice with all my heart. If I could have, I would have taken back all of my promises and my ability to run. I would have raced all the way around Lopali, and maybe all the way through the sky to Joseph and Chelo and Liam and the others.

"Don't worry," Chance said, "If you are lucky enough to wake up, you will feel the echo of the worst pain of becoming. That will be enough."

I let enough air trickle into my mouth and fill my chest to blurt out a single whole sentence. "Fuck the pain of becoming."

Chance grimaced and did something with his hand, and everything faded to black.

5
JOSEPH

Captain Hill led Marcus and me into a small room off the Command Room, Sasha padding behind. The captain shut the door and turned the window dark. "This is as safe a place as we have. Only the ship's computers will be able to hear us, and they won't talk unless I tell them to, or we get breached."

"Have you ever been breached?" I asked.

"Once. Before I was captain. We reloaded the whole damned ship by hand. System by system. I thought we'd all been downgraded to technicians forever."

I had broken into the Fremont data systems long ago, and the ones the Star Mercenaries from Islas had put on Fremont. I hadn't tried to breach systems on Silver's Home or Lopali, but perhaps …

Marcus began the conversation. "Tell me about the *Thorn*?"

"We've got a few agitators, but they don't seem any more successful than usual. I've been giving people extra cleaning and extra drills."

I wanted clarification. "Agitators?"

"Marcus doesn't hide his views. Being captain confers no right to tell people what to believe. I don't hide the fact that I side with Marcus and hope we never fire a shot. But some of our crew would love to die in the glory of vacuum." She gave an exaggerated shrug. "There's no accounting for some people's goals."

I decided I liked her as much as my dog did.

"How do things stand with the other ships?" Marcus asked her.

She jerked her head toward me. "Does he have any background?"

"Some."

"So you understand that we're trying to stop a war on the way to the first big battle."

"I also know we might still have to fight."

She gave me an acknowledging smile. "The Port Authority paired us with these two ships when we agreed to fly out here. The *Black Star* is a warmonger. It's owned by the Orange Shipbuilder's affinity group. There is nothing but profit for them in a war; they've been raking in credit ever since the rumors of war started."

"Okay," I said. "*Black Star*. Enemy."

The look Captain Hill gave me was so withering that I flinched. "Not that simple. Enemy flying the same flag. If it does come to fighting, she'll be a friend."

Marcus asked, "What about the *Highline*?"

Captain Hill looked back at me. "The *Highline* was a pleasure ship before she joined up—took rich do-nothings to Joy Heaven and back, sometimes took extra cargo from place to place, things that you might not want on manifests anywhere."

"Smuggling?"

She shrugged. "Most of her money came from carrying passengers. Anyway, we thought she'd be like us. The group that operates her—the Celeste Nari—aren't Makers. They only have a few Wind Readers, and those they use as pilots, like me. War is no good for their business. Crew from both ships have been less than friendly. They've asked when you would arrive. They've also asked about Joseph."

He glanced at me, brows furrowed. "I had expected to have a little more time."

She laughed. "For what? To tell them what you already told me, that you've got the brightest boy ever with you?"

She was teasing him, and he knew it. For a moment they both looked at me, their eyes full of laughter and happiness, like two old friends who had been apart a long time. But there was worry there, as well.

Marcus made a face which included an arched eyebrow and a twisted smile. "What do I tell them? That he's stronger than me, or just that I'm teaching him?" He fell quiet for a moment. "Or do I hide him? He's got a price on his head."

The captain's eyes narrowed. "Who wants him?"

"The Authority wants both him and his sister. Something about leaving Silver's Home without permission."

The captain went utterly still, as if she'd just turned the laughter off, and her eyes narrowed. "Something's trying to get in."

"An enemy?"

She shook her head. "It's blunt. Like using a power hammer on a needle." Her eyes closed, her face slacking. She had gone deep. Maybe it was a threat. I glanced at Marcus, hoping he would suggest that I follow her and see what was happening.

He shook his head and whispered, "Let her do her job."

"What do you think it is?" I whispered to Marcus. "The *Black Star*, now that we're here? Islas?"

"You mean who?" He went still for a moment. "Has to be someone local to the three ships."

"Someone curious about our arrival?"

He had a little half-grin. "Or curious about the ship."

Damn. The amusement in his voice told me exactly who he meant. "I'll go check."

"You do that. We'll be here in case I'm wrong. Oh—and the ship will give you directions."

I slid ever so slightly into the skin of the ship's data. After the super-sweet data on Lopali, and the thin, stupid data on *Bryan's Hope*, this ship felt perfect. Complex and professional. Beautiful and powerful. As I dashed from the room, Sasha at my heels, she delivered directions in a warm, gender-neutral voice. When I found our family, Chelo looked alarmed at my quick entrance.

"Is everything okay?"

"Where's Caro?"

Chelo looked puzzled but stood up. “She fell fast asleep as soon as we got here.”

“No,” I said. “She didn’t.”

Chelo led me to the bunk that held Caro’s small form. She was sitting up, looking pissed. “Uncle Joseph,” she asked. “Why did that lady throw me out of the ship’s data?”

6
CHELO

When Caro called the captain mean, Joseph sat down on the floor and held his arms open, laughing so hard that Caro hesitated before she flung herself into his embrace. When he finally stopped laughing, he said, "She's not mean at all. She's protecting her ship. She's a starship captain and you"—he poked her playfully in the chest—"you are a little girl on a warship."

Caro stuck out her lower lip. "I just wanted to know where I am."

"I know, honey." He glanced at me over Caro's shoulder. "I'm going to take her with me. She should meet Captain Hill."

Worry plucked at my breastbone. Caro's powers kept overshadowing her ability to be a child. "Must you?"

He nodded.

"An hour. She needs to sleep."

He raised an eyebrow.

"No more than two. She's a little girl."

He looked Caro right in the face. "And she almost got herself in very big trouble. I'll have the *Thorn*'s AI call you if we'll be any longer than that."

He already had the ship capable of making calls for him? Of course, no matter how awful a spaceship felt to me, it was the inverse for Joseph. He already walked with more confidence and laughed more easily than he had on Lopali.

Joseph stood and took Caro's hand, looking back at me as they headed toward the door. As soon as they left, I went to find the rest of my family. Jherrel bounced on his father's lap. Liam looked so pleased to see me come in that I took over for him, sliding our son onto my knees. Kayleen knelt in a corner, unpacking clothes. There was no large single room with a sun wall here; we shared a connected suite of rooms. "How are you setting us up?" I asked Kayleen.

"The kids are sharing this room. We're in the room next door. I've already requisitioned stores for a bigger bed. I don't know yet if they have one."

"Will we fit without it?"

She grinned. "Spooned."

The three of us shared a glance that filled my belly with longing for our bed, and a few hours of quiet to enjoy in it. I cleared my throat, Jherrel bouncing up and down on my knee. "Your daughter just broke into the ship's data and got kicked out by the captain."

Liam responded before Kayleen. "Really?"

"Apparently. Joseph just took her to answer for her actions."

Kayleen didn't look at all surprised. But then she and Joseph could communicate without words, and she probably knew more than I did.

"We have to figure out what to do with her," I told them.

Jherrel tired of me and went to find a toy. Kayleen sat down on the bunk opposite of me. "Your mornings with Mohami seem to be helping."

"She's quiet there. But she still did this."

Kayleen toyed with her hair. "I spent a lot of time with her on the *Hope* working in the little ship's data streams, but she was pretty stubborn about always going deeper. She doesn't listen to me. Maybe because I'm her mother. She knows how strong she is, and she knows how fragile I am. More than anyone, she knows."

Liam sat beside her and pulled her in close to him. "Shhh … baby. It's okay."

She turned her face into his chest, a tear running down one cheek.

We had almost lost her to data right before we left Lopali. It was dangerous to ingest data directly like she and Joseph and Caro could do, like all ship's captains could do. Some got lost in the data, never returning to their bodies. It drove others into idiots that Silver's Home called *wind burned.* Kayleen had almost died but wasn't crazy. Just fragile. "Maybe Caro should work with Joseph and Marcus," I suggested.

"She's only five," Liam said.

"And I'm pretty sure she just got through at least the first layer of security on a warship."

"Point," he said.

"We'll be on this ship at least six months before we reach the fleet. Then what? Years? I'll take her to Mohami's in the morning. Jherrel can go with Liam. After, I'll work on reading with her and Jherrel both. Then you," I pointed at Kayleen, "can take her with you to your lessons. And Liam, you can do math and mechanics with the children after dinner."

Liam broke out laughing. "Always the organizer."

"Someone's got to be." It would do Liam good to have structure, too. The same worry I'd always had still nagged at me. Liam had been poised to lead on Fremont, and ever since we left, he'd been in shadow. He wasn't capable of flying starships and there had been no wagons to drive or new species of bird to hunt down since we left home.

Maybe Marcus could find a job for him.

Liam held out his free arm, and I crossed to sit on his other side, taking one of Kayleen's hands in my own across his lap. It felt good to be together, touching.

We needed each other. For Caro, for the war, for our own sanity. Joseph had told me he could feel canyon walls full of darkness surrounding him. It was all I could do to squeeze my little family close and hold on.

7
ALICIA

Screaming pain came in waves. It started in my head and neck, spread down through my shoulders and my spine, out through arms and legs, from inside my soul to my toenails. Water dripped onto my mouth and I opened wider, demanding the towel, sucking on it like a baby.

Around me, a soft chanting. I turned my head and paid for the movement with a knife of new pain. I spit the towel out and opened crusty eyes.

Wings everywhere.

Fliers filled the room, chanting softly.

The vibration of their voices tormented my ears.

The pain lessened just enough for me to remember my name and what I was doing. *I am Alicia and I am transforming.*

Above my head, a voice I knew. Matriana. "This is the moment of living or dying. This is the time of choice. This is the threshold of change."

It seemed important to speak my name, to show Matriana I knew myself. But my voice had broken.

I couldn't tell her I could hear her. It didn't seem to matter. She chanted it over and over and the other voices supported her, like a round. Male and female. More than the six.

"This is the moment of living or dying. This is the time of choice. This is the threshold of change."

The chant flowed through me. Sometimes they faded to a river of meaningless sound.

I wanted to leave, to let go.

Living. Dying.

Both were beyond me. Both impossible.

A voice whispered directly into my left ear. "This is the moment of living or dying. This is the time of choice. This is the threshold of change." Marti, who had found a way to live through this.

Pain bathed me.

I floated.

I knew I had to *want* to get through this, to *need* to survive, but I had no will at all. All that I had was this moment, this second, this breath, this pain.

This pain.

Marti's voice sounded higher than Matriana's. The thought struck me as funny. I had noticed something outside my pain.

Something besides the pain existed.

Tsawo nearly sang the words, "This is the moment of living or dying. This is the time of choice. This is the threshold of change."

Memories danced behind my closed eyelids. Being on Fremont, in the East Band. The thugs who had adopted me had kept me tied up when I had run faster than they could, when I had climbed higher than normal humans, when I had jumped all the way up onto a hebra's back and landed in the saddle. They had kept me from showers and combs and made me into an animal. *They'd bruised my soul.*

I had wanted to die then, often.

Once, after a particularly bad beating, I had imagined flying away like the great grassland hunting birds and never coming back. I had felt my wings then, cried for them, for anything to break me free of the hatred and fear Ruth and her band visited on me.

Chanting drew me back from memory, back to looking at the flickering dance of wings against stone walls.

Pain immobilized my limbs.

"This is the moment of living or dying. This is the time of choice. This is the threshold of change." I couldn't tell who spoke. A flier.

They hadn't killed me. I had gotten free of them, free of Fremont. Now I was alone here on Lopali, and I would die alone except for Induan. A tear traveled down my right cheek, the weight of the liquid drop also pain.

As if crying were good, as if they worshipped the tear, the fliers' chants grew stronger. A finger wiped the tear away, the touch painful and fabulous all at once, as much of a dilemma as living and dying had become.

The voice at my head changed again. A man. Amalo. As he led the chant, it became deeper and slower.

My heart began to beat in time with his. Or perhaps my heart tuned itself to his words. Whatever the unfamiliar feeling was, it released itself in tears.

My veins delivered fire to all parts of me, taking the hurt to a new, deeper level, feeding it to each and every cell. I tried to cry out but couldn't lift my head.

Amalo's heartbeat dragged mine with it. He was in sync with me, and he felt what I felt. I knew it. I did not know how I knew it, but it was true.

The others joined, still chanting. Their words had no edges. My whole being opened. I became a heartbeat, a thudding repeating, repeating.

Perhaps I had finally decided to die.

Pain exploded through me, carrying me into some other form, some not-Alicia.

It took a very long time before I finished exploding outward. The pain had become so strong that I couldn't feel it anymore. Overwhelmed, I could only accept.

Tears streaked down my face, absorbed by fingers, by touch. The touches were fire, too hot for pain, almost like light.

Torment.

I imagined Chelo's face, looking out for me. I remembered going back to Fremont for her. I saw Joseph in his moments of power, Joseph tender with his dog, Joseph climaxing while making love, his face transformed with ecstasy. Kayleen chattered in my ear. Paloma. Paloma had helped me when she didn't need to. Mostly, I saw Chelo, felt Chelo even though it was impossible.

"This is the moment of living or dying. This is the time of choice. This is the threshold of change."

I sobbed. Release swamped the pain, a river of light over fire. Each tear, each wracking gasp stripped me of the weight of torture.

A new lightness had entered my bones and my breath and even my toenails.

Tsawo's hands touched my cheeks. Angeline sang over my head, her voice high and clear as the sky. All of them singing, all of them touching, and me sobbing and sobbing and sobbing.

8
JOSEPH

Our third day on the *Thorn*, Marcus, Kayleen, Caro, and I shared berries and melon from the ship's gardens and fresh protein bread spread with rosemary paste in a small galley in the middle of the *Thorn*.

Marcus addressed Caro with a stern voice. "I am willing to allow you to understand the ship's systems. But you must never override the captain or any of her senior crew, or me. You should be able to help guide the ship if she or I ask you to. Do you understand?"

Caro nodded solemnly.

Marcus kept his gaze firmly on her small face. "Do you agree to *never* go into the ship's data without being asked?"

Caro looked still and contemplative—scary still for such a child. She had recently settled into her mother's darker coloring and her blue eyes were a true copy of Kayleen's, including the long lashes. She would be a beauty, like her mom. She smiled and turned up the innocent look in her eyes. "I promise not to do anything you or Captain Hill don't tell me *unless* you aren't around and something needs to be done."

Marcus parsed her words, and then shook his head. Too many

negatives to tell exactly what she meant. "You must wait until you're older to do *anything* on your own with ship's data."

She crossed her arms.

"Or I will show you nothing at all," he said.

I felt her lunge for the data herself, and then felt Marcus's block. He was much stronger—and cannier—than Caro. Hopefully I could learn from watching him work with her. It took a few moments for her to relax. "Are you okay?" he asked her, his voice dripping with patience that didn't quite touch his eyes.

"Yes."

"Are you willing to learn?"

"Yes."

"Very well. Now let's all start at the same place."

He took us all together through the very top layers of the ship's data. Atmosphere, pressure, personnel, maintenance records, fuel status, relative location to the other ships. Data that anyone with crew-level access could have pulled up on a standard terminal. We were doing it with our minds, our bodies, with nanotechnology inside of us that tuned itself to read data streams.

Since I didn't really need the lesson, I watched Caro and Kayleen. Caro was confident and sure of herself, perhaps *too* confident. She knew mistakes could be made—she'd seen us make them. But she'd never made one herself. Not one with real consequences.

With luck, I'd be around the first time she really screwed up. Someone was going to need to catch her, or maybe to clean up after her. Unlike me, Caro had no Chelo, no sibling that steadied her. Her half-brother Jherrel had attached himself to his father Liam rather than to Caro. He loved her, but it was nothing like what Chelo and I had.

Kayleen, on the other hand, felt hesitant even at this simple level of data mining. I scooted closer to her and stroked her back, running my fingers along the ridge of her spine.

Her muscles rippled and twitched, and she lifted her head. "What?"

"Never mind." I didn't try to touch her again. Ever since her experiences on Lopali, she felt like glass that might shatter at the smallest puff of wind.

After an hour, Marcus sent Kayleen and Caro away with a suggestion to rest. After the door shut behind them, I sighed with relief. "I need more time with Caro. Neither of her parents can teach her what she needs to know."

"It will have to wait. You'll be spending the next few days with me." He looked grave. "Are you ready to work even harder than you had to work on Lopali?"

"You haven't figured out how to kill me yet."

He stared at me so hard, I felt yet again that I was being measured. Eventually he said, "Three of the strongest Wind Readers of the war are on this ship."

"You're including Caro?"

He leaned back in his chair, lips pursed. "She might surpass us both if she lives."

"I will kill anyone who tries to hurt her."

He steepled his hands and leaned in close to me. "Do you remember when Kayleen almost died?"

"Of course."

"Who helped?"

"Other Wind Readers. They talked about being of a group even though they are part of others. It sounded like there is a secret society of Wind Readers."

Marcus nodded. "There will be other Wind Readers on all sides of this argument. They came together to save Kayleen because she is one of us. But they won't see sides in the war that simply."

"Of course not."

"I am going to teach you to control all three of these ships without a single other Wind Reader noticing."

"I thought you said that you didn't want me messing with the *Thorn*?"

"I learned some things since we arrived. Sant Robert, the captain of the *Black Star*, is willing to go pretty far to be sure *he* controls this set of three ships."

"Why?"

"He's afraid I'm turning some of his people away from blind support for the Port Authority."

I grinned. "Aren't you?"

"Absolutely." He wasn't grinning back. "I need you to learn things faster than I meant for you to. I've warned Rose we'll be mucking in her data, and I've apologized for it. It has to be done. Sant may try to hurt me, or you, or even kidnap Chelo to control you. The *Black Star* is dangerous. The *Thorn* is designed to sting from a distance. It can't hurt either of these ships as much as they can hurt it, not when we're all flying side by side."

I got up and poured us each a glass of water. I handed him his. "Will we visit the other ships?"

"Not yet." He sipped the water. "We're going to control them from here."

"That's a lot of distance."

"You've done it before."

I eyed the ships on the view screen. They were farther away than the small ship I'd thrown into the sea on Fremont. There had been living people on that ship. I had never forgotten it, never forgiven myself. And now Marcus apparently planned to teach me to kill from a far greater distance. I went cold, and my hands shook. Fear and bad memories mixed, making me gasp. "These are further by far. I can't do that again." I looked at the images of the *Black Star* and the *Highline* in front of me. I remembered the many, many Islan ships. I imagined the number of people on those ships. "I cannot control so much. How could any one person? And I cannot kill."

"You can control without killing."

"But that might not be how it happens, right?"

There was nothing but patient, infuriating love in his eyes. "It might not."

I said something I probably shouldn't. "How is this different than what the Port Authority wanted to train me for? I'd be on one of the Navy ships if you'd let them take me years ago."

He flinched. "You might have to kill in this war. You might even fall under the orders of the Port Authority. The difference is that I've taught you right from wrong. You'll refuse the wrong thing."

In the heat of battle? When people I loved were at risk?

I hadn't refused it last time.

We spent four hours deep in the *Thorn*'s data. As far as I knew, we didn't tip anyone off to our presence, except for Captain Hill who had dived down to say hello. A good thing; I'd recognize her signature in data in the future. She felt intense and curious, very much like her personality seemed in the physical world. She was weaker than me, but stronger than Kayleen. The way she moved through strings and layers of information told me Marcus had trained her.

For the last hour, I'd been trying to use my mind alone to catch hold of the data of a ship I wasn't on. I'd barely been able to read the *Highline's* serial number, which it happened to broadcast every hour to whole local space. I could have just sipped for it on any common data device and done as well.

Marcus stood up and stretched. "Let's come back here in the morning."

He only showed his disappointment by looking away instead of at me. Nevertheless, I felt it. "I'll do better tomorrow."

"Don't spend all night thinking."

He knew me too well.

I did need to think. I found Kayleen in the small galley that we'd been assigned for our family needs. I made myself a weak cup of col and rummaged in the fridge for bread and vegetables.

"There's some pretty good protein paste in there," she offered.

I finished making my sandwich, put everything away, and sat down beside her. "How are you doing?"

"I'm scared."

She didn't usually say things like that. "Why?"

"You know I'm still not myself." Her hands twisted through her hair, and she didn't look at me.

"Aren't you better?"

She shrugged. "I don't lose time anymore. I haven't since just after we left Lopali."

"I'm glad we're nowhere near that data anymore." It had been sweet and sickly data, lies on lies and all of it manipulated. Ship's data was true. It had to be. A planet could run on bad data but not a ship. Life and death rode on its veracity.

"Me too. But I left a little piece of myself down there."

I stopped eating and looked closely at her. She really did look better. Her eyes were brighter, her hair combed. But dark circles still smudged her cheeks. "Are you sleeping?"

She shook her head. "I wake up sweating. I feel like we're all living in a missile aimed at a bad future."

"You always did have a way with words."

She laughed. "I usually use too many."

"You don't do that as much anymore. Maybe you left your extra words behind on Lopali."

"It always helps to see you."

Her words warmed me. I took a deep breath. I could imagine being closer to her, but she, Chelo, Liam, and the children were a family. I could not step into that.

She watched me closely, waiting. Another trait new to Kayleen. Patience.

"I'm worried. You were almost burned out of existence back there. We have a while until we're near the real war. Will you practice going in and out of the *Thorn*'s data every day? Even when we don't work with Marcus?"

"Of course."

I wanted to hold her. She may not be available to me as a lover, but I loved her. "I don't want to lose you. We've lost enough."

Kayleen almost whispered. "Do you miss Alicia?"

If only I didn't miss her every day. "Of course."

"Do you think she's happier? Do you think she's got her wings?"

"I can't imagine any other outcome."

"Will we ever see her again?"

"I don't know." We were flying away from her pretty fast.

Kayleen came over to me and kissed me on the cheek. "Good night."

"Sleep well."

Her smile looked tentative. "I'll do my best."

When she left, the room felt empty of both Kayleen and Alicia.

9

ALICIA

The next morning, Tsawo and Angeline visited. They watched me with great calm, as if meditating in their seats while Induan massaged my scalp, the length and strength of her fingers identifying her.

Her touch didn't hurt.

Someone sat behind me, gently kneading my long, thin thighs and their tender bones. I glanced back to identify him. Chance.

He smiled sadly at me.

I felt their hearts. Not as thoroughly as when Amalo's heart had beat with mine. Still, a soft surprise.

I lifted my head and glanced around, searching faces. I saw pride, and love, and at least in Induan, a touch of awe.

It meant something. The pride on their faces erased the residual pain that thrummed through my bones and blood, leaving me light. I managed a cracking, weak whisper. "How did the others do?"

Tsawo looked away, but his voice sounded strong. "We lost the girl in the bone-shaping. If she'd given up a day or two earlier, we could have left her a life. She could have become a Keeper, at least."

She had been two years younger than me. I had not met her—she started a day before me. But Chance had spoken of her often, and now he looked away from me, too.

"And the boy?" I asked. He had been the youngest of us. At some point on the pain-hazed months of change, I had overheard Matriana tell Daniel that she hoped he could keep his ability to reproduce.

Angeline spoke softly. "We lost him at the end."

"The chanting?"

"The chanting."

No one but me lived? It took a moment before I could speak, and then my words were deliberate. "I almost chose to die in that moment. I don't remember ever crying so hard."

Angeline smiled. "There is no pain like the pain of becoming, there is no loss so sweet, no tears so bitter."

I usually hated words so freighted with ritual, but these beat in my heart like truth as she said them. "I still don't have wings."

"Not yet." She spoke softly, almost reverently. "Now you must lie on your stomach."

"You can't just cut a hole in the bed?"

She shrugged, her white wings rustling. "Fliers have to lie on their stomachs. Might as well get used to it now."

I would never run again. Never lie on my back. I was shedding chrysalis after chrysalis, each a one-way door. I felt dreamy, but I had another thing to ask before I could let myself fall into sleep. "I get to decide what color, right?"

Angeline's spoke. "Choose now. This is the one gift given to people who change themselves, to choose your colors."

I closed my eyes. I had imagined blue wings, pale to bright, folding in all of the colors in the sky. Then I had imagined purples so brilliant you could see me fly from far, far away. So unique that if I joined the stupid morning flight in Oshai, the children would look at me. But neither of those seemed right anymore.

After the pain I no longer wanted beauty. I wanted strength.

"I want black wings, like my hair. Like Tsawo's wings, only an even more intense black. I want violet eyes on the wings, to match my eyes." A concept fluttered around my tired brain, finally coming forward. “I want a tiny bit of red as a symbol of Bryan’s blood. A blood-red teardrop on each wing.”

“That’s pretty complex,” Chance said.

“It’s a good choice.” Tsawo touched my cheek, his finger leaving a fire of pain tinged with hunger for him behind like a brand where he stroked me. “It’ll signify your warrior spirit.” His finger lingered, touched my lips and my forehead, and lifted. His beauty stole my breath the way it had the first time I’d seen him fly down into our group house.

“Thank you.” I took his hand.

He squeezed. “You will be a beautiful flier, a symbol of more than you yet know.”

“Thank you.”

Chance broke the brief spell. “We’ll start to grow your wings tomorrow. It will hurt.”

“Like the other pain?”

“Nothing will ever be as sweet as the pain of the change,” Tsawo said.

He sounded so certain, so earnest. The pale light in the room washed everyone’s colors into duller versions of their sunlit selves. It highlighted the sharp angles of Tsawo’s cheekbones, the twist of dark hair that hung loose by his left ear. In that moment, I wished he and I were alone. “Are you glad?”

“About?”

“Glad I did this?”

“Yes.” He spoke it softly, and while he looked as fierce and protective as usual, I saw the slightest softening of his jaw and a hint of pride in his eyes. I could drift off to sleep on that thought, certain I could handle whatever new pain started tomorrow.

I would have wings.

I lived.

I would have wings.

10

JOSEPH

I stopped in our galley and brewed some col, making two cups of the deep chocolate that Marcus liked. The smell turned my stomach a little—too sweet. But it would make Marcus happy.

I tried to carry it carefully; the hallways in the living quarters had dark plum carpets.

As I passed into the metal floors and scuffed walls of the common areas, I heard footsteps behind me. When I turned to look, they accelerated. Someone slapped my cup. Hot col splashed across my face, and then the wall smashed my shoulder. A booted foot slammed into my gut, crumpling me against the wall.

The cups rolled noisily away from me, leaving dark stains where they'd spilled.

Two figures stood over me in jumpsuits with the insignia torn off. They wore helmets, faceplates down.

Crew.

"Don't send any alarms."

I reached for the ship's data, sending alarms.

A man's voice, muffled by the helmet. "This is a warning."

I found the cameras in the *Thorn*'s data stream. They had picked this spot because the only cam that could see here had been blinded two days ago and not yet repaired.

A foot in my stomach drew my attention. "About what?"

"We're going to fight. Tell Marcus the whole damned ship wants to fight. He can't stop us all."

"Are you trying to take over?" Was this bigger than an attack on me?

"Not yet."

One of them pushed me. I let it happen. They had a physical advantage.

"What do you want?" I asked.

Marcus and Captain Hill were both available to me now, and Kayleen. I managed a quick plea for help across the data nets. *I'm being attacked.*

I'm coming. Three times. All at once, almost together.

Surprisingly, a voice I didn't know. Someone strong and competent. Female. *Me too.* She expected at least one of the other Wind Readers to know her.

I looked up at the masked men. "What do you want?" I hissed again.

"No turning back."

"War. We came for battle. We'll have it."

One pulled on the other's sleeve. They left me slumped halfway to the floor, covered in cooling, sticky col.

The new voice. *I'll track them.*

I managed to stand up by the time Kayleen arrived. "Are you okay?" She fluttered, taking my hand and letting it go, picking up the empty cups. "Did they hurt you?" She stopped for a second, searched my face. "They did. You have a bruise on your face. Are you okay? Does it hurt? You might have a black eye."

"I'm okay."

Marcus jogged down the corridor to me, and at the same time, Caro came from behind Kayleen. Irrationally, I felt more embarrassed than hurt in that moment. "Sorry. I let that happen."

"No." Marcus's voice sounded like ice. "Those were our people." He looked at the others. "We'll catch them."

No one had even acknowledged Caro. I went over to her and picked her up, brought her to my chest. "Thank you for coming."

She looked solemn. "I can find the bad guys for you."

"It's not your job." I pecked her on her cheek and then deposited her in Kayleen's arms. "You must go to your morning ceremony with Mohami. But first you have to tell me how you knew to come find me." I had called Kayleen and Marcus in the quiet world of data, but Caro had shown up as well. She didn't have permission to be anywhere near the ship's data except during our lessons. She knew it, too. She looked completely guilty, but she said, "I saw Mommy coming down after you."

Kayleen clutched her tight.

I couldn't prove Caro was lying.

For now, I just smiled at her and said, "Thank you." I meant that. Even if she was pushing her boundaries, she had been watching out for me.

Marcus gave a signal to follow him, and I did.

When we got to the main control center, the captain looked up. "We caught them."

"I heard another Wind Reader in the ship. She said she'd catch them."

"My mother's grandmother."

Interesting. "She's a member of the crew?"

She shook her head. "She's an … honored passenger."

Marcus looked tickled, the captain slightly chagrined. "She didn't have much trouble. Not two of our brightest. We're interrogating." She looked over at me. "That shouldn't have happened."

"I won't try to carry two cups of col so far in the future."

That got us all laughing, the laughter of survivors when something could have been worse. When we stopped, I said, "They want to go to war."

She shook her head slightly. "People can be stupid. Wait for our interrogators to finish. I'll brief you."

It was a command.

Marcus and I made more col and then returned to our work from the day before. We didn't talk about the attack, but I thought about it when we took breaks. I had been naive.

An hour later, Captain Hill pushed the door open and said, "They were paid by a task-bot. The bot didn't ask them to use violence to deliver the message." She frowned. "But they were willing. They're looking forward to being shot at." She sat back, her arms crossed.

"What did you do with them?"

"For now they're in the brig and under extra guard."

Marcus's jaw clenched. "Keep looking for who sent them. We'll do the same."

I shook my head. "Have any of them been to a real war?"

"There hasn't been a war to go to." She narrowed her eyes. "Except on Fremont."

I looked at Marcus.

He shook his head.

So Chelo, Kayleen, Liam, and I were the only ones in this entire fleet who had seen death through war? I had no words.

11

CHELO

The day after the attack, I invited Joseph and Marcus to join us for the morning ceremony. Everybody else from Lopali, too. We filled the room.

Kala sang, a wordless chant with a background heartbeat rhythm that she played out on her knees. By the time she finished we were clapping and chanting with her. As the last beats stopped, we felt unified, nearly transcendent.

Caro sat on the floor next to Mohami, her expression serene. Jherrel leaned against me, and while he didn't look at me during the song, he looked up afterward, a sense of wonder on his face.

Mohami raised his head after the chant, looking around at each of us. He wore a blue robe under a soft white shawl. "Today we will finish refining our message. We have a beginning, which we have been working on for days. Caro will present that to you, and then I ask for silence for a few moments so you can reflect on what the child says."

Caro looked up and around at the group, her face young and wise and impish, her blue eyes bright. She had expected to do this; her hair lay in neat black ringlets around her shoulders, and the front had been clipped back with some barrettes I'd gotten from my friend Sky on Fremont during one of the best parts of my life.

Not that I'd given her permission to wear my hairclips.

She stood up, so her eyes met ours as we sat. She looked like a practiced speaker instead of a five-year-old terror. "We have been told there are only two ways. The Islan way, which is to do what you are told. Only a very few people have the power to choose." She looked at Dianne, waited until Dianne nodded. "And the Silver's Home way, which is to do whatever you want."

It was quite a simplification. Not far from true, though.

Mohami smiled at Caro and she continued. "There is a third way. People can create whatever they want, but they must take responsibility for it, including helping whatever they create become independent."

She paused. For a five-year old, she had an uncanny sense of timing. Or maybe Mohami had trained her.

"We've been trying to build a simple message everyone can understand. The idea is that Makers are parents of their creations instead of owners."

An even longer pause. Caro working her audience. A child asking for a parent. "This would have freed the fliers years ago," she said.

Truth.

"We came up with an idea about what to call it. Making of and for the creation." She repeated herself. "Making of and for the creation."

She bowed her head, and Mohami bowed his, and Kala beside him. Soon the rest of the room followed; a long silence enveloped us all.

I had seen the phrase built. It sounded sincere and powerful in Caro's small-child voice.

Mohami whispered into the quiet room. "What do you think?"

"It takes away profit," Jenna said. "Hard sell."

I closed my eyes, listening to the conversation without worrying about who said what. I let phrases roll over me and thought about them as they passed through me.

"Perhaps the created would willingly support payments to the creators?"

"Maybe. In trade for freedom?"

"For example, the fliers could pay a portion of what they earn through tourism to their creators."

"Who have almost all of it now."

"No choice will make Makers as rich as ownership. Silver's Home wants what it wants."

"An Islan win will ruin it all."

"Do you think they can win?"

"I like the idea of letting the fliers get free."

"How do you decide which creations *can* be free? For example, if I let every butterfly I created out into the wild, some would never make it." Marcus. The best Maker in the room. "Some are intermediate. There has to be a way to define a finished and sentient creation, and to separate it from a simple one. Every blade of grass does not need a voice, but to steal the voice from the fliers is reprehensible."

"We must define sentience."

"Let's look for a more active way to say it."

Now I opened my eyes in time to see Paloma say, "Creators of and for the Creation."

Liam countered, "Two for creation."

Marcus looked at Liam and said, "That's good. It could be made into a logo."

Liam needed something to do. Maybe he could run our campaign to infiltrate first this ship and then the others with new ideas.

Maybe I'd make him my spy.

In another hour, the slogan had morphed to, "Creators for creation."

It wasn't perfect. It would do. The basic ideas turned on innovation and fairness. I liked that—it had always seemed to me to be the strength of Silver's Home. It had created my brother.

In addition to innovation, the talking points demanded freedom for the created to make their own destiny after a time. We couldn't decide on a timeline, so we left that for later.

Liam—who had become quite engaged—looked up and asked, "What should we call this? The slogan is great, but we also need a name."

Kayleen burst out with it before anyone else had a chance to speak or raise a hand or jot down an idea. "We should call it the Doctrine of New Making."

Mohami looked pleased.

Caro said, "Yes, like the ship."

Liam said, "Yes, because what we need is a new way for Makers."

Even Marcus looked happy.

The meeting ended with another chant from Kala, which felt like a benediction on our efforts.

We were likely to need it.

12

ALICIA

My growing wings seemed to pull from my heart, pain spreading through my shoulders and along my spine like a great cross. I lived in the same stone room, belly down on a new bed that hugged my torso while straps held my lower back immobile. Induan rotated the bed so that I sometimes lay on my stomach, sometimes stood, bearing weight and leaning into the padded bed.

Intricate scrollwork painted on the stone floor had been modeled on the mandala-like gardens that covered much of Lopali. Even prone, I could turn my head enough to see most of a tapestry of bright blue sky dotted with birds that covered one wall. A single flier with red-gold wings rose up from the bottom left, angling toward the top.

One afternoon, I asked Induan, "When is Tsawo coming?"

"It's foolish to be obsessed with him." Her fingers flew back and forth in a complex fight with silken yarn that was slowly resolving into a yellow and gold scarf.

I still remembered his kiss. "He's more fun than Amalo."

She shook her head, looking bemused.

"Isn't it time? I feel done." My wings felt like a second set of shoulders. Some contraption I'd never quite been able to see separated my back from the fine bones and feathers. They had weight and heft and *felt* finished. If I twisted even a little bit, the long new muscles in my shoulders pulled and bunched.

I wanted to *see* my wings.

Induan's fingers didn't miss a beat as she started a new row. "I am not the Keeper of the proper time to see your wings."

She spent a few hours of every day at the School for Keepers of the Ways of Lopali. Her lessons there had bathed her in ethereal calm. Active calm. The calm of a coiled snake, perhaps. "You've changed as much as me," I said. "The old you didn't have all this patience."

She smiled. "You've changed more."

"You are a completely different person."

"Bah."

"Truth." She knew it, too. Her old sarcastic self had drowned in her new calm waters. "What else do they teach you at Keepers school? Besides how to make baubles for seekers?" I pointed at the scarf. "And how to be deadly serious?"

"Patience." She smiled softly and whispered, "Soon. Soon."

"I miss your laughter," I told her.

She merely shrugged.

Not ten minutes later, she did laugh—a little—as Chance opened the door and held it open. Tsawo and Angeline, Amalo and Marti, Daniel and Matriana came in together and surrounded me, murmuring gentle greetings.

Finally.

Matriana waved Induan back, and she leaned against the wall, watching.

They stood three at each side of the bed, humming as they fussed with whatever held up my wings. They moved and shifted them. The stretch felt like heaven punctuated with the foul surprise of pain in places I didn't recognize as part of me.

As the fliers worked, I began to feel their heartbeats, then their movements before they made them, to understand when a gentle pull would come, and what response they expected. They shared the same heartbeat and wanted me to share it as well, to become one with them. I fought the eerie sense of blood rushing in and out of all of our hearts at once.

They overwhelmed my resistance until I tumbled into the connection, unable to sever it, no longer even willing. A guilty, frightening pleasure.

When the fliers stepped back, the desperate closeness thinned until I could breathe easily again.

Tsawo tilted the bed up with a lever. My wings tugged at my shoulders as the bed shifted to a vertical position.

Straps still held me tight. Good. My stomach felt sure I would fall if I were allowed an opportunity.

Induan took my right hand, Chance my left.

Tsawo stepped behind me and did something gentle and painful with the masses on my back, stroking them so they rustled.

"Can you stand by yourself?"

I nodded, determined.

Daniel and Matriana slipped the bed away and against the wall.

My legs shook, but with Induan and Chance still holding me, I managed.

Marti held a mirror up to my face. The changes in my features shocked me. My cheekbones angled up above hollows. My eyes seemed too far away from each other and bigger, although the pupils remained the same pale violet. Wider nostrils would allow new breathing I didn't quite understand, even though Chance had explained it twice. Breathing didn't feel different standing still, but the change would matter for flight. My mouth remained almost its original shape, wide and full, but it looked more prominent in my new face. I still looked human, but not entirely. More like Tsawo.

I blew out a long breath, totally unbalanced.

I strained to see my wings in the small mirror. Glossy purple and black rose behind my black hair. Marti held the mirror too close for more.

Then Amalo and Marti took two steps back and to the left, angling the mirror to show my reflection in a wall sized mirror that had been hidden under the blue wall hanging that now lay pooled on the floor.

I stared.

They had made me an angel of dangerous beauty.

My wings arched up above my head and curved outward and

down, the pinion feathers hanging in the air below my feet. Near my head, the shorter feathers glimmered with a deeper violet than my eyes, then darkened to a deep purple and then to black as rich as the ebony between stars. A drop of crimson centered in the bottom quarter of each pinion feather symbolized Bryan's blood so well I choked back a sniff.

Wings were an unfamiliar and strange weight.

I tried to flex them, but they barely responded … just the slightest rise and fall that I felt more than saw. Tsawo laughed. "Wait. You need training."

When he had taught me to fly with the fake wings I hated so much, it had been one tiny bit of a new movement after another, a flex, a balance point, a way to strengthen a particular muscle. This was going to be like that. "How long?"

He shook his head. "Weeks or months."

I took one more glance into the mirror.

"Would you like to look longer?" Amalo asked.

I wanted to look forever. I stared at the great curving black truth of my wings. Tears ran down my face and turned to sobs. After about fifteen minutes, the weight of my wings began to drag at me. Marti signaled to Induan, who pulled the bed back, and helped me back to horizontal.

I immediately wished I were still standing. Lying down without the scaffolding sent ripples of pain through my shoulders and lower back.

The fliers shuffled out, walking with their wing-shoulders hunched to keep their feathers from trailing on the ground. I wanted Tsawo to stay and touch me, but none of them looked at me as they left.

Induan whispered, "Are you all right?"

I nodded and reached for a handkerchief and wiped at my face, disregarding the pain in my shoulders as I moved my arms. The pain came because of my new wings.

Satisfaction fell over me, tinged with both fear and elation.

I had become what I was meant to be.

13
JOSEPH

A week after the two men attacked me, Marcus shook my shoulder, pulling me out of a deep sleep.

"What time is it?" I mumbled.

"Midnight."

"What do you want?"

"Caro's about to get in big trouble."

His tone of voice suggested *he* was about to get her in trouble. "I'm coming."

We found her in her bunk with her eyes squeezed shut. Marcus picked her up, and I looked around for a parent to bother. Chelo seemed the most versatile. Her eyes snapped open the minute I touched her, and she followed us back to a small common room Marcus and I often used.

He sat Caro down on the couch and stared at her, waiting.

She gazed steadily at him, defiant, although her hands twisted in her lap. "I get bored."

Chelo knelt beside her. "What did you do?"

Caro mumbled, "I did the right thing."

"Marcus will tell us if you don't," Chelo said. "Whatever it is, you might want to use your own words to tell me."

Caro looked down, and one hand crept up into her hair to twist it around her index finger. I smiled. The gesture reminded me of Kayleen. "I sent our story out. That's all. The movie we finished."

I didn't understand what she meant, but Chelo clearly did. "To who?" she asked.

"To the other ships." Caro stared past Chelo, at Marcus. "We're running out of time. We're getting closer to the Islan ships and there will be a war."

Marcus knelt down beside Chelo. They looked more like they were offering Caro obeisance than punishment. "What was the video about?"

"The Doctrine of New Making."

He glanced at Chelo. "A documentary?"

Her lips were thin and her eyes full of concern and fear. "More. A call to arms, kind of. We didn't plan to broadcast it. We planned to show it to people who had already come to agree with us."

Caro stared at her. "You didn't tell me that."

"And you didn't ask." Chelo sighed.

Caro crossed her little arms over her chest. "It's a good video."

Marcus glanced at Chelo. "How bad is it?"

She swallowed. "It won't reflect well on the Captain. It's not quite insurrection. Not to us."

Marcus nodded curtly, then spoke to Caro. "If it's interpreted wrong, this could be very bad."

Caro went quiet.

"How did you catch her?" I asked him.

"Lou."

"Lou?"

"Rose's great-grandmother." Marcus shrugged. "Lou keeps odd hours. She has a special passion for watching what comes in or out of the data shell around the *Thorn*."

"So she saw Caro send this?"

"She saw it go out, chose to watch it, and as soon as she did, she contacted Rose and told her to wake up and prepare the *Thorn* for battle."

"Really?"

"Lou has been known to exaggerate. But she could be right. No telling how that video will affect ship to ship relations." He looked at back at Caro. "Why was sending that out wrong?"

"It wasn't. People need to know. I promised not to do anything with the ship. Not the video."

And asking her not to manipulate data with her mind was like asking other people not to breathe. I picked her up and looked into her eyes, forcing her to pay attention to me. "You have been doing things we didn't give you permission to do."

She bit at her lower lip. For a moment, I thought she felt remorse. Then she said, "I knew you wouldn't like it. But I did the right thing."

"I don't think so."

"I do."

"You're too young to know that."

"I'm not."

Marcus had been following our little side conversation. He broke in and touched Caro on the forehead. "I've never been tempted to shield a five-year old before, but I can cut off your access to data. And if you do anything more complex than playing with your toys, I will. Do you understand?"

She gave him a long level look. "I hate you, Marcus."

My cheeks flushed red with embarrassment, but Marcus just laughed. "No, you don't. I've raised many children, and you just hate it that you need me."

If her look could kill him, he'd be dead. Somehow he managed not to laugh.

"It's okay that you're strong," he told her. "I'm proud of you for it. More than you can know. But I own this ship. Captain Hill runs this ship, and Joseph is your uncle and responsible for you. You *cannot* make the decisions yet. Do you understand?"

"I understand what you mean."

She was dodging him yet again. She wriggled in my arms. I held her a little tighter, demanding her attention. "Caro?"

"Yes."

"Will you promise not to do anything we won't like for the next eight hours?"

She nodded solemnly, and I thrust her back into Chelo's lap and looked at Marcus. "Now what?"

"We put Caro someplace safe."

Caro started to object, then sat back and fell quiet.

To my surprise, Marcus kissed Chelo on the cheek. "We're taking her to Lou. She can watch her. Wake Liam and meet us in the Command Room."

I wasn't surprised to find the captain with her great grand-mother. Lou had grown too old for anti-aging treatments to stop wrinkles by her eyes, thinning hair, and the occasional age spot. She used an assist on her chair to stand and shuffled to meet us. When she saw us, her eyes widened. "This is Caro?"

Marcus nodded. "Yes. She has promised to behave for the next eight hours, at least some of which she should spend sleeping."

Caro stiffened, eyes wide. Marcus put a hand on her tiny shoulder. "Remember," he said, "I can force a shield around you. I can also teach you things you need to know. But right now, I have to repair the damage you just did. Lou will show you how to shield yourself. After she teaches you, you are to stay shielded." He knelt down and looked her in the eye. "Before Joseph knew so much, I made him stay shielded so that no bad people could find him. That's what you're going to start doing."

She glared at him.

"I mean it. You must exist without data flows to manage yourself in them properly. We'll play a shield game later, kind of like hide and seek."

She smiled faintly but remained a few steps away from Lou.

"Lou can handle her," the captain said. "Let's go."

Marcus turned to the old woman. "Call us if there's any trouble."

I glanced at Caro, who looked back at me with hope in her eyes. I couldn't rescue her. I didn't even feel particularly sorry for her.

On our way to the Command Room, the captain asked Marcus, "What's in the video?"

"I haven't seen it. I suspect all of our main talking points. Silver's Home is wrong. The war is wrong. Islas is wrong, too. We need a new way. The new way means everything is free."

Captain Hill's voice almost broke as she said, "You're kidding."

"No. The political theory is called the Doctrine of New Making, and we were going to leak the ideas slowly, use them to get people talking."

She sounded incredulous. "And you thought that would work?"

"Maybe. This won't. Caro is smart but not wise."

"Hey!" I said. "She's five. She's wise for a five-year-old."

We watched the video. It made a decent case for the Doctrine. A little over-zealous. But the lead-in was a pretty tough takedown of both Islas and Silver's Home.

"Marcus," I asked. "What exactly did Caro do? Just add the video to playlists somewhere?"

He laughed. "I wish. She's more thorough than that, our Caro. She sent a copy to each of the crew's mailboxes."

"She got through that much security?" I wasn't sure I could have done that.

"She convinced the mail AI it's a mandatory training video from the Port Authority."

"Both ships?"

"All three ships."

"Can you delete it?"

"Not without a trace. It will have been watched by some people by now. Our better bet is to hope no one knows we created it."

The captain stood up. "A five-year old? A five-year-old did that?"

Marcus laughed. "I believe this particular five-year-old could be one of our back-up pilots."

The captain's eyes narrowed. "How do you know that?"

"We've been training her."

"You trained me. But you refused to even start until I was twenty-one." She sounded a little put out.

Marcus sighed. "It's for our safety, not for her convenience. Caro is strong, and we've needed her skills. But she's a child, and far more capable than she is wise."

The captain interrupted. "Let's try to mitigate the situation. Caro's safe enough with Lou, unless the Authority decides to arrest her."

I winced.

Marcus told me, "You take the *Highline*. You already know how to breach her systems."

"Okay."

Marcus chose the *Black Star*, leaving the *Maker's Thorn* to Captain Hill. At least we were breaking and entering at a good time: most crews were asleep. On the *Highline*, I found an AI that had watched it, two bored cargo movers who were arguing heatedly over whether it really came from the Authority, and three senior officers who were oddly diligent about consuming messages with their morning col.

Caro had pretended to be Port Authority. Hopefully no one would believe a five-year-old could do such a thing.

Which meant they would suspect me, or Marcus.

A second senior officer watched it, an older woman with perfect regulation-cut hair and a spotless uniform. She immediately sent an email to the captain:

Watch the new training video. Not what it seems. Pure propaganda. Permission to wipe from systems except one copy to test further for new security challenges?

It turned out that all three ships managed it the same way. Security officers on each ship went into the crew's information boxes and deleted unwatched copies. Across all three ships, a few hundred copies had been watched, fewer saved. Reactions were mixed. Most of the people who had been awake in the wee hours were either officers or the bottom of the crew barrel—people who worked maintenance or fixed engines or collected trash.

The security officers hadn't figured out how the video got in there. At least Caro had sent it around the *Thorn* as well, so we wouldn't be immediately suspect. She had her moments.

14

ALICIA

The sun warmed my face as I perched on the roof of my new house. Induan sat just below me, clutching a cup of hot tea and watching for the first fliers to kiss the morning sky. I had water in one hand and a cup of nuts on a tray in front of me, but I touched neither.

My wings still felt awkward. Not heavy, not like they had when they were brand new, but not yet part of me like a hand or foot. I was always aware of them.

Below us, light started painting the fields of food and flowers with bright colors. Keepers began to move among the rows, some splashes of bright color and others in blacks or whites.

"There." Induan pointed at the sky and I squinted north.

Red wings fluttered against the pale sky. A flash of gold confirmed they were Marti's.

I raised my water glass in a toast and stretched my back out, fluffing feathers. Induan had groomed my wings the night before, and they felt loose and flowing. My shoulders rose toward my ears and I forced them down, still struggling to control the new muscles as well as the old.

As I drank, Amalo's gray wings joined Marti's. I watched for

Tsawo's black wings, but of course they didn't appear. He had sworn to be my teacher, but he had been absent since the first day I'd come home. Damn him.

Amalo and Marti played in the air as they flew toward us, swooping and rolling, near each other and then far apart. I imagined their hearts beating as one, connected. They slowed and backwinged, landing lightly on the edge of the roof with perfect balance, nearly close enough for their feathers to mingle.

Amalo was a study in grays. Gray eyes, long silver hair caught in a braid, pale skin, gray clothes, gray wings. A few of his jewels were black, a few white, none had any color. Marti stood a head shorter than Amalo, and never wore even a scrap of gray. Her short hair and wings were red, her face a pale white splashed with freckles, her eyes as gold as the gilt-colored edges of her pinions. Her black pants and shirt fit close to her body.

Induan stood and bent her head to acknowledge Amalo before she headed down the human stairs to the kitchen, two stories below us. Amalo and Marti came almost every day. Induan knew what to serve them.

Amalo opened the conversation the way he always did. "How are you sleeping?"

He didn't need to know dreams woke me often. "Well enough."

He looked at the place Induan had been, but she wasn't there to contradict my story. "Stretch."

A thin platform beneath the perch allowed me to stand so the perch touched the back of my thighs. I lifted my arms, and my wings followed. It had been a necessary gesture once, although I had learned to raise just my wings. I liked the way the long muscles in my back felt with my arms raised. Many fliers took off this way, arms reaching for the sky and pointing in the direction they wanted to go. Some wore bracelets of beads or jewels that fluttered softly against their forearms, dramatizing the gesture.

Amalo sighed and counted to thirty loudly while I held my arms and wings up, my belly tight, my knees slightly bent. By the time he got to twenty, my wings started to flutter slightly with the effort.

We did this thirty times, which meant I held myself ready to take off thirty time-counts of thirty, and by twenty sweat stung my eyes and dropped from my chin.

Induan appeared with a tray of fruit, nuts, and energy teas for the fliers, as well as a bitter tea Marti had prescribed to help me recover from my exercises. As usual, Marti watched the cup until I took some, and then smiled.

An hour later, I had finished three more exercises, including one that had me standing on one quivering leg for almost five minutes. Five times.

When we finished, Amalo looked grudgingly pleased. "In a few weeks you can begin short flights."

"You told me that last week."

"It's still true." He turned, bent his knees, and leapt up into the sky, his movement so natural it made my eyes sting with longing. I craved flight, but couldn't risk losing the ability to fly forever by shattering a wing.

Induan picked up Amalo's abandoned cup and plate and disappeared down into the house, leaving me alone with Marti.

I could tell her more than Amalo. "I dreamed of falling again."

She put a hand on mine, a gesture of friendship. "I still dream of falling some days. Maybe every flier dreams of falling."

"Did you ever fall?"

She shook her head. "A crazy girl knocked me down once."

That had been me, trying to avoid capture. She referenced it from time to time, always with warm amusement in her voice. A way to tease me. I asked her if she had any news.

She stared out over the fields, and I felt sure she was sifting through events and deciding which ones to share with me. The longer it took her to start talking, the more important the news.

I fidgeted.

She noticed, set her cup down, and turned to look at me. "There is a three-way knot of tension on Lopali now. Traditionalists like Matriana and Daniel are owned by the Wingmakers and beholden to the Keepers of the Ways. But they are peaceful. Rebels are willing to kill to keep Lopali from changing. Tsawo and his generation want both freedom from our Makers and to keep all of the magic and secrets of who we are."

She was framing background. When I nodded, she continued. "Matriana and Daniel have power. It is based on the myths that fliers are spiritual objects. Matriana and Daniel believe these myths."

"That they are spiritual or that they are objects?"

She smiled, apparently approving of the question. "Both."

"Why that word? Objects?" It offended me. I wasn't an object.

"Because they are not free. They'll tell you how being in pain and owned while being beautiful makes them into gods."

I laughed, not without bitterness, and maybe a little fear.

"They would never hurt a flower, much less another flier or a human. But to keep their power, they must prop up the common myths. There is another group, also beholden to the Wingmakers, who would like to be little godlings themselves. They were induced to fight, but as sacrifices."

"Sacrifices?"

"Tsawo told me three of them have been executed." Marti hesitated, again being careful. "I suspect they didn't know the stakes when they volunteered to fight."

I stilled. "Executed? By who?"

"The ringleaders were killed. By the Wingmakers. They are here, you know, our Makers. Enough of them to ensure we continue to be what they made."

I could not imagine a world where a flier could be killed. "Executed?" I repeated the word; it still made no sense. Humans did not kill humans for punishment, not on Fremont, nor on Silver's Home, at least as far as I knew. In war, sure. We'd been in a battle on Fremont and many people had died. But there was nothing even remotely approaching a visible disagreement on Lopali, much less a war.

She looked directly at me. "Executed. Two days ago."

"Is that legal?" There had been a conversation about that, and about the Court of Five Worlds, and I had a vague memory of that conversation. "Angeline told me that we had a voice on the Court now, that Marcus had arranged it."

"There has been no vote to give us the rights of humans. There isn't enough proof yet that we can reproduce. Until we can—" she shrugged in such a way that I knew she cared deeply about the topic. "Your brother and Marcus changed one woman who bore one child. And all of that is basically hidden. I could not bear children now, nor could you."

But to *kill* fliers? "I want someone to be punished for Bryan's death, but not killed for it."

"They cut the wings from everyone but the leaders. There are twenty new Keepers now."

I shivered.

"Tsawo believes the Makers killed the leaders because the Makers started the fight. This isn't information they would want out. If they kill the people they induced to fight, no one can track the fight to them."

A deep anger settled in my chest. "Are you telling me the Wingmakers killed Bryan?"

"I'm telling you Tsawo thinks they might have."

"You've seen him?"

She nodded. "Last night, but he is already gone again."

I swallowed a twinge of jealousy. Marti was the only flier who told me much of anything, and I loved her for it. I had no idea why Tsawo was avoiding me, but it probably wasn't because of Marti. "No one will hurt him, will they?"

"He's strong. And clever. I'm telling you this because you risked your life for your wings." She picked up her cup, sipped the last of her tea, surely cold now, and then stood and looked at me. "You need to understand the stakes of becoming. You are associated with Joseph the liberator and Chelo who created the war."

She was getting them both wrong. "Joseph is the fighter. Chelo hates war."

She shrugged as if the truth didn't really matter. "Wings will not make you one of us. I want you to be my friend."

Without waiting for me to answer, she crouched and leapt. The wind from her wings fluttered through my feathers before she was too far away to hear me reply.

I stared after her until the incredible red-gold of her wings began to dip toward the ground.

15

JOSEPH

Marcus made me keep up a running commentary as we walked the *Thorn*. I didn't mind. I did well enough to feel proud of how well I knew her. "We're coming up on the bays where small ships are kept. It's just past the repair bays. *Bryan's Hope* is in there, of course, and others."

Marcus said, "I included fast ships meant to travel across and inside the fleet. Assume you can travel for a day and then you'd have to turn around. I also designed haulers and carriers. All of them—even the slowest and smallest and ugliest—have the best security I could buy. If anything happens, any of these ships could serve as a lifeboat."

He meant if the fragile peace between ships broke. "I heard you went to Mohami's morning meeting. How many people showed up?"

"Seventy. We had to open a crew briefing room."

Chelo and Liam must be happy with that. "I'll go tomorrow."

"Don't." He paused. "Let Mohami—and thus Lopali—take the credit. It says one thing for Chelo to work on what is essentially a protest, and something else entirely for you to do it. Or me, for that matter."

"So Mohami is a target?"

"He came to be a target."

That surprised me. "You knew he was going to come before we left?"

"I suspected. I think he knew Tsawo's intentions, and he wanted to keep Lopali ideas in the fight for peace."

"Aren't we all part of the Doctrine?"

"It was built from lessons learned on Lopali." Marcus stopped at an airlock. "Let's take one of the ships out, give you some flying practice."

"You bet." I hadn't piloted anything fast for a long time.

On the far side of the airlock Marcus said, "Pick out the fastest ship."

I stared at them, thinking. "It won't look fast, will it?"

He smiled. "You know me too well."

"And it won't look the slowest, either." I named a few ships, and he shook his head over and over.

He eventually told me that he had modified *Bryan's Hope* after we had reached the *Thorn*, and I struggled not to burst out laughing.

He spoke in very low tones. "There are records of how fast this little ship can go. Now it is a third again as fast, and much more agile. That may give you the seconds you need to save your life."

"And I already know how to fly it."

He smiled. "Let's take a different one." He headed straight for one of the smaller ships, a two-seater named *Stinger*. After we passed through a lock, a doorway in the hull irised open for us, and we left the *Thorn* behind. I flipped *Stinger* right and left, did a roll, and tested her speed. Flying her felt like the moment just before orgasm when all is about to become perfect with the world, when nothing else matters but the single moment that you are part of.

"Don't get too cocky."

I burst out laughing at the way the word he chose tangled up with my thoughts. "I've never flown anything quite so much fun."

He took the controls from me and pushed the *Stinger* even faster than I had. When he finished a last full roll that pasted me to my seat, he smiled in a way I hadn't seen for a long time, as if the flight let him leave behind a whole ton of worries. He handed me control. "Now, be a little slower and nicer so we lose some of the attention we just got and take us out where we can have a conversation."

I chose a spot equidistant between the *Thorn* and the *Black Star*, and a bit ahead.

Three other ships now strung some distance from us, on the far side of the *Star*. "Can we go look at the *Unicorn*?"

"Go wherever you like."

The *Black Star* kept itself between us and the new ships, as if its presence walled off the flow of ideas.

Since Caro's video stunt, the crews had polarized. The *Highline* and *Thorn* had far more crew who showed an interest in at least talking about the Doctrine. Some loved it. Those seventy people came from somewhere, anyway.

Just yesterday we had heard that three proponents of the Doctrine had been locked up in the brig. It was illegal to restrain or constrain people for ideas; that's what Silver's Home was founded on. Ideas and freedom. But they had been locked up for something, and it probably wasn't coincidence that they were the most active in spreading the Doctrine on the *Star*. "You're getting more worried every day," I told Marcus. "Is it mostly the *Black Star*?"

His features relaxed the way they did whenever he thought hard, his face turned forward so I could see him in profile. His hair had grown long and curled down his shoulders. On Marcus, the look was neither feminine nor soft. He stared out the bubble window, which, at the moment, showed the front of the *Black Star* blotting out some of the stars. "Caro had it right the day she sent out the video. Wrong action, but the right idea. We're too slow. Instead of stopping at Lopali, we should have been out here with the ships, talking to the people who can make a difference. We were hunting for allies instead of doing the work here."

"Hindsight."

"It was never the only plan, anyway." His tone of voice resonated with my own feelings, sharp and acidic. He took a deep breath and continued. "For example, we have groups working out talking points like ours in other ships on their way to join up with the fleet."

"Are they any more successful than we are?" I asked.

"Hard to tell."

I considered. "There is some counter-messaging. They wouldn't bother if we weren't making some difference."

Marcus smiled in his *I'm proud of you* way. "They're reacting. There are people who see their whole future fortunes riding on this war."

"Are those the people who tried to arrest us on our way off Silver's Home?"

He burst out laughing. "If you only knew how many things they've tried. But the stakes are higher now, and there's no hiding. Not out here." He sighed and sat back, then sat forward again, then back. "Don't be surprised if I disappear."

"To do what?"

He shook his head. "Not on purpose. But I'm a clear and easy target out here."

Marcus? An easy target? "You're a ship's owner. No one can throw you in the brig."

"Which makes me far more dangerous. I will try to stay free and alive. I have friends, some of whom are on these ships." He pointed vaguely at the three ships that had joined us, and then widened the gesture to include the ones we were already traveling with, even the *Black Star*. "More friends are coming on ships that will join us before we get to the main war. Other friends are already with the fleet. But there's no easy way for you to recognize them. It's not like we have codewords."

Did he expect to die? "Are your friends also trying to make a third arm of the war?"

He fell silent for a second. "Out of the mouth of a child."

"I'm not anymore."

He shook his head. "That's a point of perspective."

"Isn't that what you're doing?"

His shoulders relaxed a little. "I had been thinking we were creating an insurrection within the Silver's Home fleet. But if I use your perspective, we can work on the Islans as well, and they wouldn't be betraying Islas quite so directly. If there was ever a system ready for revolution, it's that one. Talk to Dianne someday."

"Chelo is friends with her."

"Good."

We were past the *Black Star* now and heading toward the first of the new ships. The *Unicorn* was similar to the *Thorn*, thin and beautiful, if a little wider. Like the *Thorn*, she looked capable of landing butt-down in an atmosphere if she had to. I liked her. "She's as pretty as the *Thorn*."

"She's owned by Master Skulla. He is a friend if you need one." He glanced down at one of the smaller monitors below the actual window. "Look behind us."

Three ships had detached themselves from the *Black Star*.

"Get closer to the *Unicorn*, see if they follow."

They did. They also spread out, as if making sure we wouldn't be able to get past them easily.

"Hail them," Marcus suggested.

I did. They answered normally. "We hear you, *Stinger*."

"Nice day out here."

"Yes, it is. How long do you plan to stay away from your ship?"

"I'm practicing," I said. "It might be a while."

There was a long enough silence for them to talk to someone else and get a reply. "Carry on," they said, as if we needed their permission.

They backed away. I said, "That was too easy."

"They didn't actually go away. They just gave you a little more room."

I took a breath and checked. He was right.

"Maybe you should drop me off on the *Unicorn*," Marcus said.

"And act like that was the plan all along?"

"Sure, we're out visiting."

"I'm supposed to go back and help Chelo and Liam get ready for a ship-to-ship chat they've been promoting."

"You'll be late. Open a communication channel with the *Unicorn*."

As soon as we got permission to land and drop Marcus, he looked at me. "I'll catch a ride back with a pilot from here."

"I can come get you." I grinned. "I'll bring *Bryan's Hope* over really slowly."

He looked me full in the face, turning all of the energy of his gold-flecked gaze on me. "We should never both be in the same small ship again." His face had gone thoughtful again. "In fact, I may try to rent a room on the *Unicorn*."

"But the *Thorn* is your ship," I protested. "You should be there!" Did he know something he wasn't telling me? It wasn't like him to be spooked by three little ships. Surely we could … what? Destroy them?

"You can sit in on the dailies on the *Thorn* anyway. It will be good practice."

Practice for what? "I don't like it."

"I'll come back if it's safe. I'll know in a few days."

"I could come with you."

"Your family is on the *Thorn*."

"So's yours."

He turned his face away from me so I wouldn't be able see his reaction. He wasn't quite fast enough. His eyes were wet.

16
ALICIA

Oshai spread out below me, the great mandala in the center surrounded by housing for tourist seekers and the Keepers who trained them, parks for humans and fliers on two sides, houses on the other sides, ring roads, then straight roads heading out to Fliers' Field, to the spaceport, to the University, to the farms. It was, of course, perfectly neat, perfectly dressed in flowers and lawns.

From up here, the mandala looked even more complex, walkways looping back on each other and linking in ways I hadn't noticed from the ground.

It had been a full year since I'd promised Matriana everything in trade for the ability to fly. Getting wings had taken half a year, strengthening them a quarter, and learning to fly another quarter.

I had become good at feeling the wind, and banking and twisting and riding in the upward thrust of warm thermals.

Flight demanded attention. It drove away every thought except the power of breath, the almost effortless sweep of wingbeats, the glory of wind, and the freedom of reaching any height you wanted. In moments I could go from a perspective that showed me five streets and the small people on them to one that outlined the entire city and included the traffic to and from the spaceport.

Wind flowed between my legs, hardened my nipples, and blew the long braid of my hair along my back.

Today, I would finally be introduced to the society of fliers on Lopali as one of them. The thought threw little disturbed winds into my stomach. I had been isolated from the city for a full year. I had started to fly alone a few weeks ago but had been forbidden to land anywhere except at home.

Pilgrims began emerging from their lodging under the hills. A few of them looked up at me and pointed. They *saw* me, the wild girl no one had loved on Fremont. Me, the risk-taker who had chosen wings. Me, Alicia the Black Flier of Fremont. Marti had told me she'd heard me called that, and I loved it.

The mandala was nearly full, so I dropped down and down, shrinking my perspective from city to ceremonial ground to the roof of my house and the glorious back-wing of a perfect landing. Which I nailed.

For a fleeting moment, I wished Joseph could see how well I did. But I couldn't afford to worry about him, so I focused on Induan, just emerging onto the roof patio with a great wide grin on her face. She walked up to me, tipped up on her toes, and folded me briefly in her arms. I allowed it, although human touch had faded to something far less glorious than the touch of the air.

But Induan had helped me from the day I'd met her walking through the Street of All Designs on Silver's Home. I tilted my wings toward her. They didn't flex forward enough for an actual hug, but she knew my intent, and looked up at my face with a wide smile.

All was right with the world.

Induan's fingers pulled at my hair as she strung bright white and violet jewels into eight short braids that left the long ends of my black hair to flow into the black of my wings. From time to time she added a red jewel, the same blood-red that looked like eyes on the end of the long pinions on my feathers. "You look magnificent," she said. "Are you nervous?"

"I'm worried about flying with so much finery."

She tugged so hard I almost tipped from the perch. "Sorry. You had a tangle. This would be easier if you modeled yourself after Tsawo."

Who wore only a single jewel at his throat, and otherwise clad himself in black to match his all-black wings. "I can't imagine looking that stark."

She shook her head, laughing. "When I am done, you will be the brightest patch of black in the sky."

As if he'd heard us talk about him, Tsawo landed at the edge of the roof, then fluttered slowly down to the open kitchen where Induan stood on a stool to reach my hair. Tsawo's dark was followed by Angeline's light. Her skin was as pale as Induan's, her wings off-white. She wore a pastel blue bodysuit that clung to her perfect figure. At the moment, I was dressed in a simple wrapped cloth, but later I would wear a black outfit similar to Angeline's, and soft purple and red shoes with black soles that trailed ribbons decorated with tiny jewels.

Tsawo looked me over and gave a low whistle. "Excellent, Induan. You should dress us all for the next ceremony."

"There wouldn't be time." But she blushed at his compliment.

"We brought you a gift," Angeline said. "For luck with your introduction."

"Your feather was already a gift," Induan said.

Angeline held her hands out, and I plucked a small package from them.

The sky-blue ribbon matched her dress, and it took me three fumbling tries to free the small wooden box and open it. Inside, a dark onyx teardrop brooch held three jeweled heads and the hint of three sets of wings. A man, woman, and child, all fliers.

"It's a symbol of what you mean to us, to Lopali. Of the gift Joseph and Marcus gave us."

It was beautiful, finely wrought, and lightweight. A twinge of pain tried to cross my face and I forced it away. The jewelry reminded me of Joseph, and the loss that had earned my wings. I would have had both, but if I could only have one … well, already I had chosen flight over my lover. Surely Angeline didn't mean the gift as a rebuke.

Tsawo explained, "These will be sold all over the commons today, and available to the pilgrims. We thought you'd like to wear one."

I turned it over in my hand, feeling its edges.

Angeline whispered, "The first true child was born last week."

So the change had been transferred to another woman, probably by Chance. Or by the Wind Readers of Lopali. "All they … we … needed was the blueprint?"

Tsawo nodded. Flier women lost the ability to bear children when they were transformed, a process that started when they were very young. If the Wingmakers could make humans fly, they could have made them mothers. Keeping them sterile gave them control.

Chance and the others had been working on the eggs and sperm, successfully altering basic genetics to remake the babies before they were born. The re-Making of the women as adults had been beyond simple human doctors and geneticists, which is where powerful Makers like Joseph and Marcus came in.

While the babies weren't born winged, they were far more ready for the transformation than random human babies. Most would live. *And* they were the genetic children of their parents. Truly a huge gift to the fliers, even if some spit on it for its newness.

Induan took the brooch from me and set it on her tray of jewels. "And Paula's baby girl is still well?"

"Yes."

Induan reached back up for my hair. "When will she know if the babe can fly?"

"Her wings will be grown, but while she is young. She'll learn to walk before she can learn to fly. But she came from the womb with the bones and structure to support the change. Her transition will be easier than yours."

I asked, "She's in hiding?"

Angeline smiled. "Both are safe."

I glanced at the brooch. "I'll wear it today."

Angeline smiled broadly. Tsawo looked more serious. "This is your first introduction to the society of fliers and your first opportunity to help us bring peace to pilgrims."

Funny, I had never thought he cared about that aspect of flier life. "How so?" I asked.

"Look at how much you've overcome. We'll tell that story—how your family came here to help and how you lost your brother Bryan. Don't worry about listening for it. Just fly as beautifully as you have been." He leaned in and brushed my cheek with his lips, one hand caressing my neck for just a moment.

Heat shivered through my center.

Angeline took my hands in hers and brought them to her face, so that her cheek touched the back of my right hand. "We'll talk after," she said. "Good luck. Daniel and Matriana will escort you to the field."

They climbed back to the roof, both slightly awkward on the ladder, and then they became a black and white tumble of wings and hair and blue sky, lost almost immediately from our narrow field of view through the opening.

I glanced at Induan. "Where should I wear this?"

Induan took it from me and set it down on the table. "Let me finish your hair first."

"I need to eat." I reached for a handful of nuts and berries, craving the protein and fat.

After fifteen more minutes of pulling and twisting, Induan held up a mirror.

I barely recognized myself. "So beautiful."

"Don't expect this much fussing over you every day. You'd get a big head."

She already thought I had one. I grinned at her. "Thank you."

Induan finished wrapping my body suit around my torso before Amalo and Marti flew down. Amalo's blood-red belt and headband matched Marti's wings. She wore black accented with cobalt. A little too choreographed, although no one asked me. They were not light and dark of each other like Tsawo and Angeline. Instead, they seemed like two pieces that made up a kaleidoscope.

As soon as they settled on perches, Marti held out a long, slender gift box. It lay across my outstretched arms while she untied the grey and red ribbon and pulled a long, lightweight sheath from inside. The first day we'd come to Lopali, Matriana had pulled a pinion feather from a similar container and given it to Marcus on our landing. "You shouldn't molt for a year. But it's hard to be certain until the first time it happens."

"This will hold only one feather?"

"A few more." She smiled. "But unless you're in a fight, you won't lose more than one at a time."

Laughing felt really good. I leaned in and kissed Marti's freckled cheek. "Thank you for forgiving me."

She looked pleased and glanced at Amalo, who gave a sharp and slightly begrudging nod of approval.

"Now, carry that all the time," she said. "It fits on your back. Induan knows how."

I glanced at Induan, who simply took it and set it along the top of her tray, still wearing the eerie calm that becoming a Keeper had draped over her like a cloak.

Marti continued. "Your feathers will be worth more than most. I'm certain of it. For what you are alone—like mine. There are only a few of us who have transformed as adults. Humans value our feathers, as if ours alone might let them fly."

"I believe it. I know how much I wanted to fly."

Amalo cleared his throat, drawing my attention. "I have one more gift for you."

He gave me a wristband made of violet ribbon with a clear resin decoration the size of my thumbnail. A tiny grayish-white feather had been trapped in the resin. It appeared to float there. "This is a small-feather from the down on my back. It's meant to wish you luck and to honor you for your becoming." He paused for a moment, a flash of pride in his eyes. "I'm pleased you succeeded."

My throat thickened. He had warned me away from wings more than once. I held my hand out so that Marti could tie it around my left wrist. "Thank you."

Marti leaned forward, whispering so softly that I wasn't sure Induan or Amalo could hear. "Remember your tears. You will spend more of those before you are part of flier society."

Her look and tone were so solemn that I shivered.

She withdrew and returned to standing so close to Amalo that she could touch him. I thanked them both for the gifts and watched as they went to meet the sky.

Induan found a place to pin the brooch near my heart before Matriana and Daniel joined us.

I was beginning to feel important. Or something. Maybe just nervous. "Hello!" I greeted them. By now, I expected the gift, which came from Daniel this time.

"We want to honor the amount of change you endured to become one of us, and to remind you that you will always live under change. A flier's life is neither simple nor static."

I nodded. Most people here didn't know what I'd been through on Fremont.

Matriana smiled softly and—perhaps—sadly. "Marcus told us that you were designed to be a risk-taker."

My cheeks heated. "I try not to let it get me into trouble."

"It may be something we need here," she said as she gestured for me to take the box from Daniel's hand.

It filled my palm. I carefully lifted a soft, protective fabric wrapping. In the middle of that, an elastic band with a shell on it. I held it up, puzzling over the significance. It wasn't even particularly pretty.

"This is a shell from the top of a mountain on Silver's Home," Matriana said. "Lopali was created in whole, of course. But Silver's Home was once a wild place. Over long times, places that were seabeds became mountaintops and mountaintops became seabeds. If planets change, how much more do hearts and minds?"

Induan plucked it from my hands and worked the shell into the front right braid. "We'll take good care of it."

"I'm sure you will," Daniel said.

"Are you ready?" Matriana asked.

"As ready as I could ever be."

"The wagon is on its way."

"Is there any danger?" Induan asked. "Anything I should watch for?"

"Not that we know of."

"It will be the first time she's been exposed to Lopali natives since the change," Induan fretted.

"Tsawo is setting guards. You two should focus on the ceremony and on Alicia's job. Make a dramatic first impression." Matriana fluttered up to the top of the roof and stood on the perch-bar looking down. Human fliers usually do not look at all like birds, but in that moment if she would have cocked her head and cawed, I wouldn't have been surprised.

Daniel glanced apologetically at us, and said, "I'll see you in Oshai."

The wagon reminded me of a roamer's wagon from Fremont, except that it was only two colors—pastel green on the sides and the pale blue of early morning sky on top. Like the roamer's, there was room to ride inside, although I perched on top. Flowers in small pots lined the front and back of the roof. It should have looked ridiculous, but of course since it was on Lopali it simply looked too damned perfect. An older Keeper drove. I sat on the top, angled so a bench supported my back while my wings flowed neatly alongside the sides of the wagon.

Two draft animals as tall as hebras but with shorter necks and sturdier legs pulled the wagon. Necklaces of yellow flowers draped over their gleaming black necks and along their tails.

Something pinched my foot, pulled at it, and I heard the scrape of a knee on top of the wagon.

Induan, with her mod turned on.

I had lost my ability to turn invisible, but Induan had kept hers. I wondered if the other Keepers even knew about it.

My knees bumped her back from time to time. Her presence comforted me.

Simply being on a conveyance that swayed behind the ample bottoms of draft animals reminded me of being in the East Band, where nearly everyone hated or feared me, and where once I had been chained inside a wagon for days.

"Be watchful," she hissed.

"I will," I pressed out through teeth clenched in a smile. We started up a street lined with pilgrims. Lopali drew the rich disaffected or depressed from all of the five planets. It was still neutral in the war. While most of the pilgrims were from Silver's Home, I spotted people from Joy Heaven, Paradise, and even Islas. Their clothing gave them away. People from Silver's Home mostly dressed in flowing clothes made of fine material, Islans in severe and simple uniforms, and people from Joy Heaven in colorful and quite incredible outfits, the alter egos of their parent planet. Paradisers were harder to separate from the pilgrims that came from Silver's Home. Their primary identification was that they dressed somewhere in-between everyone else. Human natives of Lopali tended to be thin and tall, and to a one they all looked perfect. If you lived on Lopali and forgot to brush your hair one morning, would they exile you?

Children waved at me, and I waved back.

Adults looked curious, and a few even reverent. My eyes slid away from those. Curiosity was understandable; reverence disturbed me. I craved being liked, being loved, being beautiful, and perhaps even being powerful. But I wasn't going to save anyone from themselves, ever.

No fliers were allowed to be in the air until after I flew this morning, but some stood or perched along the route.

A chant started, low and even, a close cousin to the chant that went with the morning flight. As we approached the center of town where I had escaped from Chelo and Liam and Mohami, the chant grew louder yet. Induan tugged at my arm and hissed, "Look to your right."

Mille. She stood on a block that put her above the crowd and stared. No reverence there, but then she had mistrusted me before I grew wings. She had followed me and Bryan around town and was known to disagree with Marcus's and Joseph's efforts here. She was close enough for me to see the disdain on her face.

"She looks like she wants to eat you," Induan said.

"She does."

"Have you seen her since you were a human?"

I shook my head, suddenly overcome. *Since I was a human?*

We were past Mille now, and I could worry about her later. I would probably have to. But in that moment, in the reflection of

Induan's simple question, I felt not only what I had become, but what I had left behind. *Since you were a human.* I felt for Induan's invisible hand and clutched it. I waved the other hand, drawing the attention of the watchers to the wave and drawing strength from the warmth of Induan's hand.

By the time we came near the garden mandala the fliers rose above every morning, the streets were so choked the driver struggled to keep the wagon moving.

Induan whispered, "They came from the other worlds for this moment."

"There couldn't have been time."

A hint of irony laced her whispered laugh. "Some left home before they knew if you would live or die."

I swallowed at the wonder of that idea. Our stories had been told, but I had always seen them as about Joseph and his incredible abilities.

Did they come to see me succeed, or to watch me fail?

The wagon stopped. The Keeper who drove it turned to look up at me. "It's almost time. When you hear the bells ring, fly."

So simple. I breathed. Again.

Bells pealed, high and bright.

I hadn't expected flight to follow so quick after the instructions.

Induan hopped down so that I wouldn't knock her off. I knew how to see the barest hints of her when she wore the invisibility mod, but others would think her a speck of dust in their eyes, or too much sun.

"Go!" the Keeper urged.

I lifted and shook my glossy black wings and pulled the sky toward me.

The crowd gasped.

The chanting continued.

I rose and rose, circling above the mandala, now filled with faces looking up at me like so many flowers.

The pilgrim's chant lightened my wings.

A twist of my feet shook the black and blood-colored ribbons on my toes loose. I flapped my wings in full slow beats while my heart raced, the blood pumping up and through my back.

I fought to gain speed and height, the first few wingbeats painful and slow. Then, far enough up, the pain and labor of flight dropped away.

This was my dream.

Here in the sky, people could see me, but they couldn't cut me with words or put me in a cage.

This flight followed a ritual choreography that criss-crossed the grounds of the mandala and previewed the route the larger morning flight would follow. I disobeyed my Keepers slightly, adding five minutes of free flight at the end, low enough to see features on faces but not read the subtleties of expressions. Children gasped and cried out. One baby cried.

When the ache in my muscles made lifting my wings hard and my throat felt parched, I landed in the center of the mandala where the Keeper of the Ways of Lopali stands during the morning flight.

Since Mohami had gone with Chelo, there had been another, and now a third Keeper of the Ways, a brown woman from Silver's Home with black hair and coal eyes named Jagruti. She stood at the edge of the circle, her arms up in the air while I landed. As soon as my feet were solidly on the earth, she stepped toward me, looking into my eyes with a raw innocence colored by love which sparked a similar response in me, like the look a dog gives you when you have no choice but to pet it. It shook me. The hairs on the back of my neck and forearms rose.

I spoke the ritual words. "I have flown into Oshai, and I have become."

Her voice was higher than mine. "And what have you become?"

"A Flier of Lopali."

"Do you promise to follow the Ways of Lopali?"

Their laws. "I do."

"Do you forsake the ways of all other places?"

"I do." A twinge at that. But Fremont had expelled me, and Silver's Home had tried to arrest my family. Perhaps Lopali would keep me.

Jagruti hesitated as if sensing my slight misgivings. She looked around and then back at me and swallowed as if some bitterness stuck in her throat. "You are welcome here. You are one of us."

"Thank you."

"Drink of our water and eat of our food." She held out a glass of water and a small ceramic tray with nuts and seeds on it.

I took the water first, and then ate. Someone refilled the water and I finished that glass, too.

Refreshed, I stood while a last chant began with Jagruti and flowed out through the mandala and up into the rolling hills and around it. I felt as if I stood in the center of something bigger than me, and yet also about me. At the end of the chant, I thrust up and back into flight, only far enough to land on a perch that had been set aside for me atop the closest low hill. Induan waited for me there, her mod turned off and her face and features ethereally pale. "You were beautiful." She smiled, satisfied and perhaps relieved, and sat down at my feet. Her face reflected discipline and composure as she looked up and waited.

The morning flight commenced, a flowing stream of wings and color that danced on the air, fliers so close they could touch wings or hands if they wanted to, and so aerobatic as they rolled and flipped and sped and slowed.

I had despised it, seen it as showy and way too perfect. I still felt that way, except now the flight beat in my heart and bloomed in my stomach as if a thousand butterflies fought there. While I watched, I was no longer myself, but rather an observer of magic and—even though I could not fly it yet—a participant.

This was the feeling that drew people from the other Four Worlds to Lopali. I admired it and hated it. Surprisingly, on that morning, it drew tears down my cheeks.

17
CHELO

While I struggled to convince the AI that I really did want blue lettering on a meeting invite, Liam stared at a wall display, reviewing requests from *Thorn* crew members to help spread the Doctrine. Over a hundred people had showed at the last meeting, almost a quarter of the *Thorn*'s crew. But since some had come to heckle the others, Liam had started cross-checking requests against other available data. He looked over at me, brow furrowed. "Honey?"

"Yes."

"Joseph sent a note. We can see the Authority ship."

Captain Hill had told us to expect an official visit from the Port Authority. The *Opportunity*'s image filled the screen Liam had been using. Ugly. Broad. Big. Imposing. While those words flew around in my head, I looked for more details. Her gun turrets pointed in multiple directions. Huge rail guns were mounted on the sides. I pointed. "She could destroy us with one good shot."

Liam whispered. "Yes."

Opportunity made me want to hide the children.

Marcus wasn't with us. He had been away for months. There had been attempts on his life, and Joseph's. Another reason we vetted people coming to meetings. Joseph had ingested poison that would have stopped his heart if he couldn't read the data from his own body as well as he read ship's data. He'd still spent two days in the hospital complex. Marcus had been shot at in transit. His ship had a life pod he'd designed himself, so he had been back on the *Unicorn* in time for dinner.

Things had just gotten worse. The Authority had a price on Joseph's head, and Marcus's. *Opportunity*. My head filled with words to slip behind the name. Opportunity for death. Opportunity for hatred. Opportunity for repression.

If one Port Authority ship scared me this much, how would a whole fleet of them make me feel? I was designed to be a mother and maybe to help run a small town, not to carry out a whole revolution.

Liam slid beside me and folded me in his arms. We breathed together, in and out, as slowly as possible. "I never imagined," I whispered.

"I'll take paw-cats and demon dogs for enemies any day."

Which reminded me; we had ridden hebras and won hand to hand battles with packs of demon dogs. I had killed a cat longer than I was tall on the rough plains of Islandia. I could stand up to anything.

By the time inspectors from the *Opportunity* boarded, all traces of pro-Doctrine posters, videos, and lists had been put away. We hid some in common areas, shredded others. We shoved a few in secret places.

Fourteen Authority crew boarded us. They wore formal blue uniforms. They toured from stem to stern, searching random dressers and desks, finding nothing.

They called all of the civilian passengers together in one place. There were about fifty of us, including Lou in her wheelchair, Mohami and Kala, and all of our family. Caro sat on Joseph's lap, and he whispered in her ear so she laughed and—largely—sat still. Jherrel watched the soldiers with a very solemn face, and I felt sure he'd be able to recite the details of each uniform, each rank insignia, and maybe even the scuffs on boots.

Three were strongmen, another had a second set of arms, and a woman with an extra pair of wide-set eyes seemed able to look in all directions at once. Knife-shaped fingernails and the ability to Read the Wind wouldn't be visible, nor would a host of other mods.

We could not have hidden. They had too much access to the ship's systems.

I wondered what Ming thought, and if she was wanted by the Port Authority. Probably. She had abandoned an active Port Authority post to accompany Joseph to Fremont. I was a little hazy on how she had changed sides, and she never talked about it. I searched her face for a clue, but she merely sat and looked bored, her long limbs at rest and her dark hair swinging softly against her slender shoulders.

A strongman, clearly the leader, spoke. "I am Kym Minister." No title. I wasn't sure what that meant. His uniform pulled tight across the shoulders and the width of his body made his flat face and small ears look out of place. He looked carefully around the room, demanding attention. "This is your last opportunity to depart before the war. We will be meeting a transport ship that will take civilians away. Anyone not actually part of a crew will become part of a crew and wear the uniform of their ship. They will then be considered by extension a part of the volunteer Navy for the remainder of this exercise."

In other words, if we left, no consequences. Maybe. This was one of the moments I wished I could Read the Wind. I whispered to Kayleen. "What does Marcus say?"

She made the kind of stay gesture that Joseph used to tell Sasha to be still.

Kym Minister said, "If you want to leave, stand up."

No one stood. Mohami sat on the floor, watching the soldiers with a peaceful gaze that demanded as much attention as Kym's loud voice.

Kayleen leaned over and whispered in my ear. "Marcus says they're bullies. He suggests that we behave so they leave the ship as fast as possible."

The strongman noticed the whispered conversation and bellowed, "Do you have something to say to all of us?"

Kayleen twisted her hair in her hands, hesitating.

Caro wriggled free of Joseph's grasp and stood on the bench next to him. "We're staying."

I wished she showed a rational fear of strangers even once in a while. I didn't want their attention on her. I didn't want anyone's attention on her.

"Is that true for all of you?" the man asked.

"Yes," I said.

"Yes," Lou added.

Kym looked like he suspected we were lying. "Very well. I guess you'll all be going to war then."

We already had been. Except suddenly it felt real and immediate.

Kym gave us one more long look. He appeared to be enjoying himself. "You'll join the main fleet in a few months. Make sure your affairs are in order."

18
ALICIA

Induan's long fingers massaged my neck, peeling me awake from a running dream. "Nap time is over. It's almost time to be a sage."

She sounded serious, but a small smile crept up her face as she pulled the pillows that held my wings free. She crouched over me and lifted me by the waist from behind while I pushed up with my arms. When I balanced enough to climb free of the bed without damaging my feathers, she said, "We really should figure out a way for you to get up on your own. What if I'm not here one day?"

I swallowed, unable to imagine her absence. "Maybe I'll try to sleep sitting up again."

"Do you know how Marti sleeps?"

"I'll ask." I hated being dependent. At least Induan felt more like comfort than chain.

She glanced at my face, maybe seeing my need for her. "Are you all right?"

"Yes. I'm very sleepy."

"You didn't sleep much last night. Did the flight this morning tire you out?" She handed me a tray of energy cakes.

"Yes. How do you know I didn't sleep?"

"You moaned all night. Eat."

While I picked at the cakes, she tucked escaped strands of hair back into place and groomed my wings with her fingers, her touch light and satisfying. After twenty minutes, she stopped. "Perfect. Time to go."

Afternoon sun slanted across the tops of the perch-trees surrounding my house and threw long shadows from my wings across a wide patch of grass. Induan ran smoothly and easily below me, her white dress slapping her bare calves.

I landed on my assigned perch with reasonable grace. A small crowd had gathered. Once more, adoration. The words Matriana had coached me with came back to me. *Be yourself. Be authentic. Show the pain and glory of who you are. Show your soul. Be vulnerable.*

Pain and glory were easy. Fremont had taught me vulnerability sucked.

I fluffed my dark wings. People drifted away from other fliers and drifted toward me. Two young women ran, and the senior Keeper stepped gracefully in front of them, slowing them, guiding them to edge of the growing crowd.

Induan helped me start. "I'll take a question."

A young girl's hand shot into the air. "How much did it hurt to grow wings?"

Not *did it hurt?* I took a deep breath, looking into the girl's eyes. She was about fifteen, tall. I wondered if she wanted to fly as much as I had. "The physical pain was worse than any pain. It took me away from myself. It absorbed me, but I overcame it and I lived." I swallowed. Vulnerability. "I was frightened." I paused, then added, "Two others died in the attempt."

She blinked up at me, eyes wide with contemplation.

I had never been asked about myself before. Not this way, not by strangers. It felt … good. Marti had told me every flier felt this differently, but that they all developed a bond to the pilgrims.

Another hand, an older man from Islas. "Was it worth it?"

"Yes. I wanted wings more than anything in the world. Every time I saw a flier, I wanted my own wings."

"Why?" the man asked.

"Flying makes me feel safer than anything else." After I said the words, I realized how true they were.

"Tell us about it!" a compact woman from Paradise begged.

I did. I had expected to hate this new thing that would be a part of my new life. It made me tired. Me, who almost never tired before my transformation. But I didn't hate it.

A tall woman asked, "What do you think about the Making War? Was Lopali right to stay neutral?"

I swallowed. No. They weren't. But spending my first morning as a part of flier society taking sides? Too much risk even for me. Induan stepped in front of me. "Alicia will not answer questions that belong with policy makers."

"But her family . . ." someone blurted out.

Induan calmly accepted another raised hand, rejecting two questions before accepting one about what I had lost with the change.

A half-hour later, the Senior Keeper gave a hand-sign and Induan offered the crowd a deep bow. "That is all. Alicia the Black will return another day."

I smiled, pleased to hear that name.

Now, the party. For the first time since my transformation, I would be part of Lopali's community of fliers.

I flew. Induan jogged beneath me, keeping up as we neared the rest of the fliers in the Park of Gathered Wings to celebrate my inclusion into the daily lives of the fliers.

At some point, she disappeared.

Amalo and Marti met me at the metal gate at the north entrance to the park. Behind them, the perches were already half-full and string music spilled out from the crowd, just loud enough to turn conversations to background noise. "Where's Induan?" Marti asked.

"She'll be along soon," I replied.

As if I had called her, Induan's hand touched my arm on the side farthest from them. I barely managed not to flinch. She had been fast.

I smiled at Amalo, daring him to challenge Induan. Most fliers wouldn't see her with her mod turned on. But Amalo's infrared vision meant she was visible to him. I held my breath. Surely, he wouldn't disturb this event.

Amalo's exasperated stare made me feel young and slightly stupid, but he extended a hand to welcome us in.

He stayed at the gate and Marti led me to a long table piled with untouched food. The scents of chocolate col and fruit and fresh breads mixed in the air, tickling my stomach.

People noticed me and drifted close.

I had probably been drilled about this, but all of my focus had been on the tight choreography of the flight earlier and then on the unexpected intimacy of the questions. I was supposed to give a speech but had no idea what I should talk about.

The fliers watched me, expectant. Beautiful. Slightly intimidating.

Outside of the fliers, in a great circle, Keepers stood watch.

Amalo's instructions slid back into my memory. "Please consider me one of you. I offer myself to you, to be your family."

Here and there I caught an occasional smile, while others remained neutral and one or two faces looked away. I looked for a sign of Induan, but she must have been too still to give herself away.

I bowed my head, then raised it and spoke the ritual words, "Please come and partake of my feast of becoming."

Fliers approached me one by one, starting with Matriana and Daniel, then Amalo and Marti, then Tsawo and Angeline, and then others in apparent rank order. Most offered small words of welcome or gave me a little information about themselves. One made jewelry, another loved to sing, another to plant gardens in trees that only fliers could see.

Mille was about thirty fliers in. Important, but not one of the most powerful. Her pale lavender wings with large blue circles on the bottom were quite unique; I saw her while there were ten fliers in front of her.

I struggled to focus on each of the ten, but Mille's cold expression kept pulling me to glance at her. When she got to me, she nodded stiffly, not touching me, her eyes and face expressionless and cold. "Welcome, my sister, to the house of heart and hope, to the skies of Lopali."

"Thank you."

She offered nothing else, and I moved past her, disturbed by her presence. She hated my family and everything they wanted for the fliers. Her job included brokering the assignment of newly changed flier children, so she would lose significant status if that career no longer existed.

Finally, after I had counted and greeted seventy-two fliers, I was able to pile my own plate with seed breads, berries, and honey. Last in line of the fliers. Starved. And noticeably, followed by the first of the Keepers, Jagruti.

I took my plate and moved to Amalo's side. He leaned over and whispered, "Sit with your peers."

I swallowed and looked through the line of Keepers queued up for food, laughing and talking amongst themselves.

"There," Amalo pointed to a table with perches occupied by the last few fliers who had greeted me.

"Isn't this my party?"

"It is."

So they thought that *I* would fit into flier society the same way that any new flier would? From the bottom? I bit my lip to hold in the words I wanted to say.

A hand touched my arm and I turned to find Jagruti. "I will eat with you," she said.

It was all I could do to curb my anger enough to nod. At least I was doing something different from what Amalo wanted me to, taking a small risk.

Jagruti's dark hair was plaited into a series of braids not unlike mine, although hers mostly wove up and around her head. Three thin braids decorated with golden beads fell down her right shoulder. She tugged on them absently, twisting the plaits between her fingers.

The thick, seeded bread with the honey tasted fabulous, and I made enough of a mess to lick my fingers.

Her silence unnerved me.

After a few moments, I asked her, "Is everything always this scripted? I didn't know Amalo wouldn't want me to eat with him, for example. Everyone I've been working with since the change is ignoring me here."

She cocked her head at me, as if deciding both how and whether to answer. "Each flier has a role here. You do not, yet. That will have to be earned." She ate a few more bites, watching me slantwise, then continued. "There are the leaders—you know them. We have a vast number of scholars, of artists, and a whole cadre of protectors."

"What do protectors protect?"

"The stories fliers do not tell the seekers or the Makers. The secret things that help keep us strong."

Again, the secrets I didn't know.

"And then there are air dancers—the ones that lead the morning flight. They have status. Every town has a pair that leads it."

"Mated?"

"Not always. Matriana and Daniel are the best of friends."

That cleared up one point of confusion. Music began to play—a flute, and somewhere close to that, a stringed instrument. "So how do people get status?" I asked her.

"As Joseph's family, you're very important to the pilgrims. That makes you important to the economy, and that will matter for you."

"But they're gone. And you broke your word to them!"

Her smile was gentle. "Your family did not break their word to the fliers. They will have children. That is more freedom than most fliers dreamed of."

"But they killed Bryan!" A deep stab of longing made me shut my mouth and work to hold in tears. "I'm never going to understand Lopali."

"If you don't, you will die."

I thought of the executed fliers. "How?"

"Haven't you promised to follow the rules over and over?"

I only hesitated a moment. "Yes."

"If you do not, I will take your wings. This is one of the Ways of Lopali."

And she was the Keeper of the Ways of Lopali. Her words knocked a tight, surprised breath from me. Where would I be safe from people with too much power? Anywhere?

Once more, I wondered where Induan had gotten to.

As the sunlight faded, party lights blinked on in a multitude of colors. Some of the fliers had braided glow-in-the-dark beads and threads into their hair, which brightened as night fell.

Jagruti had fallen silent, maybe watching the night descend like me. "Tell me about the role of Wingmakers," I asked her. "Are you one of them?"

She narrowed her eyes, looking past me for a long moment. "They can take away my power the same way that they can take yours. So we both work for them."

"Are there Wingmakers here? Have I ever met one?"

"I do not know who you've met."

She dodged questions as well as Marcus. "How do I know what all the *Ways of Lopali* are?"

"You ask." Jagruti shrugged, as if threatening to destroy me was unimportant, and then she smiled. "There is a school for new fliers. You will attend."

"Will you be the teacher?" I chewed on a small seed cake, looking around for a flash of invisible Induan. Surely she would join me soon.

"You will have many teachers," Jagruti said. "Sometimes I will be one."

"So back to how I get off the bottom rung of the ladder. . . ."

She looked like she was choking back a laugh. "Time and choices. Flier and Keeper society is a complexity of favors and opinions, and it depends highly on relationships."

"Are you saying Marti has power because Amalo does?"

She frowned. "Marti is a spokesperson for adults who change. *And* she tweaked the system so that it takes longer … she survived a change that only took months, but one in a dozen survived. That made her angry, so she worked with Chance to improve the system. Now more survive."

"I was one of three …" I smiled, amused. "So I shall hold her in high esteem."

Jagruti gave a long, low laugh that sounded genuine. She stood gracefully. "I have a meditation session to lead."

Two women followed her through the crowd, just far enough behind they didn't interrupt others who stopped her in greeting.

Acolytes? Bodyguards? Both?

I wandered from perch to perch, eating and talking. Most conversations were polite but awkward. Three fliers thanked me for the work Joseph had done and talked about maybe having children.

Did Joseph miss me? I hadn't missed him much, but tonight I felt his absence like a cold place beside me. I didn't see Tsawo or Angeline except from a distance. It seemed like every flier I knew well was avoiding me, forcing me to meet new person after new person.

Induan stubbornly stayed away, which I found just as galling except when it worried me.

The night began to cool, and fliers took off one by one, flying low over the crowd so they would be visible. The bright party lights made them look almost garish with their wings spread wide.

Fliers didn't often fly at night, but here in town the roads had been lit up so that they served as snaking beacons we could follow.

Maybe Induan was home waiting for me.

I needed her comfort. I had expected this to be a triumphant party, and to spend it with Marti and Amalo, and Tsawo, with Chance. At least some of it.

She would be happy to see me, and just for myself. She didn't care about my status.

As if in tune with my thoughts, the bells for the night's rain began to fill the park, a warning for fliers to get home. One by one, each began to break free of conversations and leave.

I looked for Induan again. Nothing.

While rain wouldn't hurt her; it might ground me. I looked around, thinking that with all this ritual someone would want to escort me home. But the park had nearly emptied, and no one appeared to pay special attention to me except a very young Keeper waiting to scoop up my dishes.

I gathered myself and leapt into the air, the initial downbeat causing an empty cup to rattle and nearly fall over.

I flew low above the brightly lit path to my house. My shadow changed shape and size as the angles between me and artificial lights changed. My shoulders were tight and sore and my wings heavy by the time I landed at home.

The roof entrance to our houses shut in the time of rain. I landed on the lit path and started waddling toward the front door. I nearly tripped when my right toe caught in the dead weight of an invisible body.

A dark stain soaked the path in two places.

I knelt, breathing hard, using my hands to feel along Induan's shoulders and waist for the switch to turn her mod off. When I found it, the illusion of empty path flashed away to reveal her lying in a crumpled heap. Her legs were both bent at the wrong angle and blood soaked her pale hair and white dress. Her eyes were closed. Rain washed dried blood down her cheek like red-stained tears.

I pitched forward and caught myself hard on my palms.

Bent this close over her, I saw that her chest rose and fell. Barely.

Relief filled me. I pushed to a crouch with stinging hands and slapped her cheek.

She moaned but didn't open her eyes.

Someone had left her here for me to find. On purpose.

I couldn't leave her to find help, so I screamed.

19
ALICIA

I stood screaming over Induan's broken body until the furious beating of wings told me I had been loud enough.

Dark wings in a dark sky.

Tsawo, his face a fury. He bent over Induan and touched her back as if hoping she would flinch. "She's alive?"

"Barely." Anger made the single word hard to choke out.

Other wings beat wind around my face and hair as three fliers landed close to us, then five more. Most were strangers to me. They murmured one to another, their words a blur. The light from the road illuminated the bottoms of their wings and their legs and showed their chins more brightly than their eyes.

Chance raced up, panting, almost falling to kneel beside Induan. He ran his hands expertly over her wounds.

Tsawo stood and pulled my attention back to him with a question. "Did you see who did this?"

"No. I tripped over her. She was alone and just like this. What if I hadn't? What if I hadn't found her?" My voice shook. "Bastards."

Tsawo's hand crept to my neck, his thumb caressing my cheek. "I will get you justice." His tone left no room for doubt.

"I want to kill them."

His face softened, perhaps in approval. "I will find them."

A hand on Tsawo's shoulder pulled him away and Chance replaced him next to me. "She's been beaten. Her legs are broken."

No kidding. "Is she okay *inside*?"

Chance's cold and professional voice had pulled me through some of the pain of becoming in the middle of long nights. "She's probably concussed. In addition to her legs, one or two ribs are broken. She has two shattered fingers."

Shattered. How would she knit?

Chance wasn't finished listing injuries. "Bruises and contusions. Maybe internal bleeding. I need to take her to the hospital."

"Is it safe to move her?"

"I need an operating room. Now."

Tsawo touched my shoulder again, a small consolation. He glanced up at the sky and then focused on the other fliers, his voice measured. "Thank you all for coming to be protectors of those who need safety."

A chorus answered him. "We serve and protect."

"And the protected thank you," he responded. A ritual call and response. Then he changed to a more intense voice. "Hans, Kassy, stay. Search the perimeter, report, and watch outside. The rest of you go *now*. Find whoever harmed a Keeper."

A brief chaos followed as all but two of the fliers pulled themselves up into the rain.

Two men I'd seen around the hospital jogged up the path with a stretcher. They rolled Induan onto it and strapped her down. She looked like a corpse, face translucent and eyes closed. Blood flowed sluggishly from a cut above her right eye. Surely it took a heartbeat to drive blood from the body.

I started to follow them, but Tsawo grabbed my arm. "Stay."

"I need to be with her."

"Chance will take care of her."

"What if she dies?" I pulled away from him, but he held me hard, a demand.

"He'll send word back after he knows she'll be okay." He glanced at Chance.

"I'll see to Induan," Chance said.

I panicked. "I *need* to go."

"I can't let you," Tsawo said. "There is no wagon to take you and you don't have the strength to fly."

He had no idea how much rage powered me right then. I'd make it.

Tsawo rested a hand on my chest and leaned in. "You *may not* go. What if this is an attempt to get to you? There's no other reason I can see for anyone to hurt Induan."

"Who would want to hurt any of us?" I pushed back.

The look he gave me made me feel small, almost like a child. I hated it and pursed my lips tighter. He glanced at the men. "Go."

As they hurried Induan away with Chance following, the night rain mixed with tears on my cheeks.

"Go inside," Tsawo urged.

Kassy sat on one of the perch-trees just outside, shaking dampness from slender brown wings tipped with paler brown. Her soft blue eyes shaded almost to white. Eerie. She whispered, "Your home is clear. Hans is watching the back door." She cocked her head at me. "What was she doing before you found her?"

"She was scoping the party, listening for dangers."

Tsawo's jaw tightened, and he leaned down and whispered in my ear. "It's *our* job to keep you safe. That is not a Keepers role."

As we stepped out from under the perch-trees, I told him, "Induan and I have always protected each other."

He pursed his lips and stared at me for a long moment. "We are trained."

"You didn't protect her."

He glared at me, but I spoke truth. He flinched and said, "Keepers should be safe anywhere on Lopali."

I had hurt a Keeper once. "Is anyone safe right now? Bryan died here. People were killed for killing him." Anger curled up my spine and draped my words with knives. "Seeyan died, and she was a Keeper. Admittedly, she was trying to harm us, and she died because someone landed on her. But she died here where *no one* dies an untimely death." My voice rose. "People just lost their wings. And the new Keeper of the Ways of Lopali just threatened to take mine if I acted out, which

I'm likely to do if people keep dying." I stepped toward Tsawo, coming so close I smelled the musky odor of his sweat. "How were any of those people *protected*?"

He blinked at me and stepped back, hands up. "Stop. Just stop."

"I'm speaking truth."

I saw the moment he chose not to engage, when he breathed and looked away, and gentled his voice. "Focus on Induan. You just found her there, invisible, and tripped over her?"

I had forgotten he knew about her mod. I took a deep breath, utterly spent. "I said that."

He held the door open and I entered the house, heading for the kitchen. He followed and asked, "Do you know who hurt her? Or why?"

"No idea." I climbed up on one of the tall stools that surrounded the thick block of wood. He sat across from me, rainwater dripping from his wings, his face serious. Chiseled and beautiful, but at this moment, aloof. I thought about his question. "The bounty hunters were never after me. They wanted Joseph." I tried to erase the bitterness in my voice. "I could never be a Maker or a Wind Reader. Before I became one of you, I was nothing except maybe bait. Induan … Induan is not a Maker. Not important."

"Could you be bait now? Would Joseph come back for you?"

I blinked at Tsawo. "He's off stopping the war. Or fighting the war. Or something. He doesn't love me enough to stop doing that."

"Even if someone harms you?"

"Even then. This isn't about Joseph. But what is it about?" Tsawo knew more about the secrets of Lopali than I did. "What do you think? Mille hates me, but I don't see what she'd get out of hurting Induan."

"Some people hate what your brother did, and they might want to hurt you."

"That's a done deal now. Bryan died for it."

He reached a hand out and covered mine on the table. His hand drew heat in me, but as much as I usually craved Tsawo's attention, I didn't want his touch tonight. I drew my hand free. "I'm a lousy host. Can I get you water or food?"

"Both."

I had to hunt through the kitchen to pour two glasses of water and pull out two cookies that Induan had made the day before from grains and dried fruit. "Could this be about the war?"

He took the water and the cookie but didn't drink or eat. "What makes you ask that?"

"Someone wants me to do something. They thought they'd killed her, maybe. Maybe … maybe someone thinks I'll go catch up with the fleets if I lose everyone I love."

He put his glass down, his face softening. "We are being hard on you, aren't we?"

I wasn't about to admit it. If he left—when he left—I was going to go to Induan.

He glanced at the door, as if Induan or Chance should be coming through it. "You're alone." He spoke as if he were gentling a wild animal. "I'm sorry this happened. We'll do our best to find out what happened."

"What will that look like? Will it be pretty and perfect like the rest of this place, only poison?" I fisted my hands and beat on his chest.

He stood and let my rage wash over him.

After a while the anger left, and I began to feel sorry I had lost my temper. I stopped, sobbing, and brushed at my hair with my fingers, pulling the braids out as fast as I could. Induan should be doing this, and she couldn't, and it had to be done.

Tsawo watched me, silent. After a while he said, "I'm sorry."

"For what?"

"We have our own problems. We're fractured as hell."

"About the war?"

"About who we are." He paced slowly around the kitchen, nibbling on a cookie. "You've got power in who you are. In your family's feat here. In your legends from Fremont and the beginning of the war." He looked away from me. "In your beauty." Another turn around the small kitchen, the oddness of a flier's walking gait accentuated in the small space. "We kept you in the traditional place for new fliers tonight because of that. To show people you need to earn your powers in spite of your family."

Talking to him felt like conversing with a cloud. "My powers?"

"In our society. Your place."

"You're all about order, aren't you?" I took an exhausted breath. "The vaunted peaceful fliers, the most beautiful beings in the universe, and at the core you're all about who's ahead of who?"

"You're oversimplifying."

The import of his words was still sinking in. "You refused to talk to me tonight because I've lost so much that I might belong somewhere besides the very bottom of your society?"

"You're twisting my words."

"Try again."

"There is an unusual and frightening beauty in you. We value loss here and you've lost everything. More than any of us. Bryan. Joseph. Chelo. Marcus. Kayleen." He looked directly into my eyes. "Everyone you came with but Induan."

I shivered. "Do you think someone hurt *Induan* to make *my* suffering more complete?"

"More loss might make you more powerful."

That felt like a knife blade in my back. "How insane." He had to be wrong. "Did you do that? Did you hurt her?" I stared into his eyes, searching them.

He looked back, his gaze level and even. "Never. I would never hurt you."

I felt the usual pull between us, and I wanted him to step into me and kiss me. But was he jailor, friend, possible lover, or enemy?

Rain poured down the window in slender runnels. On Lopali, the rain came every evening at the same time, for the same amount of time. The perfect fucking planet, everything controlled except the human heart.

The Time of Rain and Inward Thoughts was designed for meditation, and between the rain and the darkness, no one would fly to see us, and I wouldn't be allowed to leave. My dark *protector* would make sure of that.

I thought of Induan and her warning about becoming a flier, and how right she had been.

I had well and truly jailed myself, finally risked too much and lost.

When I slipped into fitful sleep, I dreamed of Induan. Of her hands plaiting my hair, of us hiding together in plain sight a hundred times, of us saving the babies on Fremont and running for days across the surface of Lopali. I dreamed of the shape of her face, the fall of her hair over her pale eyes. She had been beside me on *Creator*, on Fremont, on the flight back, and every day here at Lopali, every step of my transformation.

Tsawo slept on his stomach on a bench. In the dark of the night, his presence offered sparse comfort.

The first blush of light drove me to open the roof and let the damp morning air rush into the house so that my fingers and nose felt the bite of it. "Wake up," I demanded.

Tsawo shook on his perch, instantly searching for danger.

My stomach demanded food. I frantically spilled nuts and cakes into a bowl. "Eat. Then we're going to see her."

Tsawo whistled, and Kassy and Hans flew up onto the roof-edge, reporting that everything appeared normal. I added more nuts and found berries in the cooler. The four of us ate quickly. "You should stay here," Tsawo said.

"I need to see her."

"We don't know if you are in danger."

"I don't care."

He stiffened, apparently surprised.

"Playing protector?" I asked, knowing he would hate my tone but not really caring in that moment.

He gave me the sharp look I had expected. "Lopali is dangerously close to losing its reputation for peace."

"Didn't I tell you that last night?"

He didn't react to my barb. "We could lose our ability to be a refuge. There is … a faction that wants that to happen. They want us to gain anger."

"I am more than a little angry." I wondered if he were really talking to me, or if he was talking to his two followers. Although they hadn't joined the conversation, they were clearly listening. "Aren't you angry?"

"I am. But I don't want to live in anger. That's not who we are. We are beauty and spirituality and hope. We are one of the Five Worlds, and I want our voice to be equal to the others."

"Really?" I wasn't any of those things right now. I was pissed. "Why didn't you go to war? Wouldn't that have helped? Your ships are so nimble Marcus lusted after them. He also thought if you stopped being neutral, we might have forced a peace."

"*Our* ships. And *we. You are of us now.*" He spit out his words. "We didn't go to war because it would have been fighting on the same side as those who created us and keep us slaves."

"And on the same side as Joseph and Marcus, who gave you part of your freedom back," I snapped.

He glared at me. "You know nothing. This fight has been building for years, and *it will happen.* Why die to stop the inevitable?"

I had no answer.

Induan would hate it if I left the plates out. I set them in the sink. "I'm going." Before he had time to protest, I waddled over to a good spot to take off from and flew up past Kassy and Hans, noticing the startled look on their faces.

Tsawo joined me moments later, trailed by the other two protectors.

When we reached town, Tsawo surged ahead of me and led me down to a small scrap of lawn near the hospital. Kassy and Hans stayed in the air, circling.

Tsawo stalked toward a smaller building beside the one where I had undergone my transformation.

Inside, an old man in Keeper's robes sat behind a simple table. Before I could ask him anything, he pointed toward the right. Three doors down, I found a room with two Keepers posted outside as guards. They allowed me to enter, also silent. Their silence was terrifying, the silence of people with nothing good to say.

To my surprise, Tsawo didn't follow me in.

Chance looked up from Induan's bedside, his face ash white. I looked past him to her. She lay very still, her eyes closed, pale hair damp around her head. Tubes led into the veins of her right arm and her legs had been straightened under her long, pale blue gown. The gentle hum of music I had heard in Mohami's rooms played in the background, the flutes and low drums dolorous in this place.

"Will she be okay?" I whispered.

Chance shook his head.

"She has to be."

"No, Alicia. Nothing has to be."

I stepped over to her and ran my hand along her forehead. My fingers shook. "Did she say who did this to her?"

"No."

Her hand reached up suddenly and clutched mine, and she whispered sharply, urgently, "Alicia!"

"Yes." I bent down.

Her grip tightened. "I wanted to stay with you."

"I'll stay beside you until you're better. You did that for me. I can do it for you."

"I'm not."

I leaned closer to her.

"Don't take power here." Her voice shook as much as my hand, and she sounded as desperate as I felt, or more. She took two deep breaths that sounded harsh and ragged. "Go to Marcus."

"Who did this to you?"

"The Makers."

Makers? "Like Joseph?"

She threw her head side to side, and her breath rattled again. "The ones who made you." She gripped me even tighter as she fought for breath.

I screamed at Chance. "You *made* me. You took me through worse than this. *Save her*."

His eyes were damp, his expression stoic.

Her hand fell from mine.

"Induan." I shook her. "Induan! Come back."

Her breath had stopped.

I screamed at Chance again. "Do something!"

"There is nothing to do." A tear ran down his left cheek.

I clutched Induan to me, her body lifeless and small.

20

JOSEPH

I sat alone in the galley near our family quarters, sipping bitter chocolate col and thinking about Caro. She was at least as strong as me, and I had been hunted all over Silver's Home because of that. I had given her instructions to shield whenever we told her to, and we had been telling her to do that a lot lately.

The *Opportunity* still bulking near us worried me. If the Port Authority had wanted me, they would want Caro worse. Either working for them or dead. Did they know about her?

I should tell her to shield all of the time. Then she'd be invisible to other Wind Readers. But that would cut her off from the moment-by-moment breath of data from the *Thorn* and make it impossible for me to reach her in an emergency.

I also suspected she might not do it.

The bottom of the cup tasted too sweet. I set it aside, closed my eyes, and let the *Thorn*'s giant heartbeat calm me.

Caro screamed.

I couldn't tell if the scream was from inside the data or something I heard with my ears. Nor could I tell if she was screaming anger or pain or both.

The sound stopped.

I wanted to pelt down the hallway, but instead dove deeper into the data, searching for Kayleen or Caro. Nothing. I tasted the ship's data. Normal.

I had to find her. I hurried through the ship's corridors.

Chelo and Liam held Doctrine meetings in one of the big recreation rooms. I broke Marcus's rule about attending and slipped into the meeting. Twenty or so people sat in front of Chelo, who stood, pacing, talking with her hands, going on about the cruelty of owning thinking beings. Her audience was primarily off-duty ship's crew who probably saw themselves closer to the enslaved species than to anyone likely to create sentience.

Liam sat near the back taking notes.

No Kayleen, Caro, or Jherrel. I leaned down near Liam and asked him where they were.

"With Lou."

A long way across the ship from where we were.

"What do you need?" he asked.

I didn't want Chelo left alone. "Caro cried out for me, but now she's quiet. She may have just been calling."

Liam frowned. "That means she's not shielding."

"I know," I whispered. "I'm going to go find her. I'll let you know if I need anything. It might be all right."

It took twenty minutes to get to Lou's room. All along the way I held the ship's data inside me, testing for anything wrong.

Perfectly normal, all of it.

When I knocked, Caro opened the door. A tear track stained one cheek. Her hair was a mess. "Thank you for coming."

"What's wrong?"

"Mom."

Kayleen lay stretched out on the couch with her head buried in Lou's lap. Her hair covered most of her face, but one bright blue eye regarded me as I came in.

"What happened?"

She pushed herself partway up, which revealed just how miserable she looked. Her eyes were rimmed in red, although she wasn't crying at the moment. "I lost it, got mad at Caro."

Caro sat by her mom, looking both contrite and concerned. "What did you do?" I asked her.

She sounded poised, almost like an adult in spite of her tiny body. "I sent Marcus a message and told him about the people from *Opportunity* coming here. I asked the other Wind Readers here to help me watch out for people trying to break into our data."

Lou added to Caro's story. "Her mom told her not to do this, and to stay shielded. She argued, told Kayleen it was too boring to stay shielded. Said she could protect herself." Lou shook her head, as if in disbelief. "Kayleen got mad and started yelling at Caro." Lou's hand stroked Kayleen's shoulder. "I would have done the same."

Kayleen sat up and pushed the hair out of her face. Her voice came out weak and shaky. "I blacked out. I lost my temper with Caro, and I blacked out. I lost about ten minutes. It felt like being lost on Lopali had felt, like I was nowhere near my body."

"That's when Caro screamed," Lou said. "I saw Kayleen fall, and then Caro screamed out loud and fell on Kayleen, and a moment later I realized she was screaming through the ship's data—probably looking for you. So I made her shield."

"How?" Kayleen hadn't been able to do it.

"I told her she had to shield to protect her mother."

Caro adored Kayleen. "Good thinking. That was true." I turned my attention to Kayleen. "Did Caro somehow make you fall?"

She shook her head. "That's what's scary. I think my head just couldn't take my being angry."

"Have you been angry since you were lost at Lopali?"

"Just the normal amount of frustrated with the kids. I was a little scared when the Port Authority was here. But not like just now." Her cheeks reddened. "I shouldn't get that mad at my own child."

I glanced at Caro. I could imagine getting that mad at her. I folded Kayleen in my arms and held her. "It's okay. It'll be okay. You're doing great." I didn't have experience with parenting, but I'd been watching Kayleen and Chelo, and they were fabulous. "Caro presents special challenges." I smiled at Caro to make sure she didn't take that wrong. "Are you okay now?" I asked Kayleen.

She whispered, "I'm scared."

I put my finger under her chin, tipped her head toward me, and looked as deeply into her eyes as I could. It's hard to really know what you see in the eyes, no matter what people say. She looked more afraid than insane to me, but I saw both things, and shivered. Right after the incident on Lopali, I'd watched her carefully. Here, far away from the siren song of Lopali's over-sweet data, I had relaxed.

Maybe that hadn't been such a good idea. Losing Kayleen couldn't happen. I wouldn't be able to bear it.

It would be worse if we also lost Caro. I released Kayleen and bent near Caro's small, elfin face. "No one but family can know about you."

"Why not?"

I struggled for an answer, and one came. "You are our secret weapon."

Caro nodded solemnly. "Yes, Uncle."

A small weight lifted.

21

JOSEPH

Every day I took one of the little ships in the bay of the *Thorn* out. There was danger. If anything broke, I could be left behind given how fast our small fleet moved. But I loved being by myself, controlling my own speed and direction and eating risk. Maybe I was channeling Alicia.

I missed her. Not for any good reason—she was too rash to be helpful here. But I still missed her.

Flying gave me time to be alone and to think, or to not think, to just be one with a machine and forget about the politics of war and the pseudo-religion of the Doctrine and the subtle power games that happened on any ship with hundreds of crew.

I had been trying to get Marcus to join me ever since Kayleen's blackout three days ago, and he had ignored me. After two sleepless nights I sent Marcus a coded message to meet in space. I added urgency with a second code word we'd agreed on long ago. There were two more levels, so hopefully he would understand this could wait if needed.

He agreed to meet the next day.

I took a fast ship named *Dispatch*. Marcus met me in the *Twin Sister*. We paced each other while I told him about Caro and Kayleen.

When I finished, he went silent for a minute, then said, "Extreme emotions can trigger psychotic breaks. If we didn't need her to help manage Caro, I'd tell Kayleen to stay shielded for six months and get extra sleep."

But we did need her. "I should be able to take Caro a little more often so Kayleen can sleep."

"That might help, but Kayleen's got to build a better defense system. Spend some time with her; help her see how you do it."

"She told me she feels too fragile to practice anything right now."

Even on the small comm screen, he appeared worried. "Tell her she needs to work on defense. I can't come over there right now. I'm in the middle of a few things."

"Want to talk about it?"

"Someplace more secure."

Where could we possibly be more secure?

He continued. "I may need to be able to reach you on short notice. We're all being watched, but mostly me and you. If anyone is planning to try anything, they'll do it before we match up with the rest of the fleet. Maybe before we match up with the next group of ships. Stay alert."

"What do you expect?"

A long silence. I was just about to check and see if he was still there when his voice came over the radio, his face quite serious. "If anything happens, you'll have to drive our plans forward and fill my place."

Laughter burst from my lips. "I can hardly handle my own family."

Another silence. "You're doing fabulously well."

"Right. Chelo and Liam are working themselves to death and skirting the edges of authority as if it couldn't bite them, Kayleen might be going crazy. I have almost no control at all over Caro, who might be a stronger Wind Reader than me. In fact, as far as I can tell, Jherrel is the only one in the family with any decorum at all at the moment."

At least that made him laugh. But then he sobered. "I'm going to disappear for a little while. I'll show back up."

"Hey, I don't like that plan."

"It's necessary."

Whatever his problems were, they were bigger than my own. A five-year-old and a friend in need didn't compare to efforts to stop the whole war.

"Now? You're leaving now?" I wasn't ready to do without him.

His rich, lovely laughter reassured me. "No. But before we catch up with the rest of the fleet."

"That's only about six weeks from now."

"We'll meet next week. I'll introduce you to more of the people you need to know. Right now, we should not be together. I'm sorry." He sounded sorry, too, and like he missed me as much as I missed him. "The stakes are too high."

"I understand." I still felt alone. "Take care. I'm looking forward to meeting whoever you think I should meet."

"I'm looking forward to introducing you. You do know how proud I am of you? How much like a son you are?"

This wasn't something he called me. I was still trying to think of a reply when he turned the *Twin Sister* away and punched it up.

I saw the moment when Marcus's ship bloomed with light for just a second, the brief flash of the fire of his death. The fragments held the light for just a moment, and then they were lost in the darkness of space, far behind me.

22

CHELO

Kayleen and the children and I sat together in the common room in our suite, on a low blue couch the color of Kayleen's and Caro's eyes. Caro sat on my lap. Jherrel sat between me and Kayleen, holding a slate in front of him and reading a story I'd written for him about Fremont out loud. He was just starting to become a confident enough reader to add real inflection to his small, high voice. A slight smile touched the edges of his mouth from time to time. Caro bounced incessantly on my lap since it was always easier for her to be the reader than the listener.

Sasha curled at Jherrel's feet.

Jherrel touched the slate to demand more words. "'The boy crept up the hill toward the djuri herd. They—'"

Kayleen screamed. Caro stiffened and went away from me in an instant, going limp.

Kayleen rolled off the couch and landed on the floor, holding her head and panting.

Jherrel dropped the book, worry and confusion on his face. He touched Kayleen's cheek. "What happened, Mama?"

She went still. Not so much as a finger twitched. Jherrel stared at her still form as if frozen. Sasha crept silently over to her and lay with her back to Kayleen's as if protecting her.

Caro twitched twice and sat up straight, panicked. "Marcus!"

"What about Marcus?" I asked.

"He blew up. He's gone."

What? Joseph! Ice filled my muscles. "Where's Joseph? Wasn't he with Marcus?"

"He's in a different ship. He's mad."

I bet he is. "Me, too." We had multiple problems. "Is Kayleen in the data?"

Caro blinked for a second as if needing to clear her head before she could think about a new thing. She closed her eyes and then opened them again and stood up. She went to Kayleen's side and stared down at her.

"Is she okay?" I asked. A lot to ask a five-year-old, but no one else on the ship would be able to answer my question.

Caro stared down at her mom. "She's lost. Like when I made her mad at Lou's."

I had heard about that, but only in passing. Kayleen had brushed it off.

I looked directly at Caro, whose blue eyes were only half-full of her, the rest already gone somewhere else. "Your mom came back from that. She was okay. How did she come back?"

"Joseph helped her. I'm going to do that now." She sat down and fell forward, snuggling into her mother's still form. Their hair blended, dark on dark, and both twitched slightly.

I gathered Jherrel into my arms. "Did you hear that Marcus is probably dead?"

He nodded solemnly, clearly fighting for self-control. "Are you okay?" he asked. Thinking of me, in spite of his own pain. He loved Marcus. Had loved.

Pain dizzied me. "I think so. There's nothing for us to do now but wait for Joseph to come back and to try to help Kayleen." I wanted to scream and cry and rend my clothes and take a ship out to find my little brother, who had to be devastated. But everyone needed to see me be calm. I watched Kayleen breathe shallowly, lost wherever she was lost, and hugged Jherrel tighter.

"Caro will help her," Jherrel said. "She's good at it."

How much did these children hide from us? Sorrow split my breastbone and stuck in my throat. We expected so much of the children. Needed so much. It wasn't fair.

"Would you like me to keep reading?" he asked.

No matter how much we asked of them, they kept delivering. I kissed his downy hair before he climbed off my lap. "Good idea."

He picked up the book and sat back down on the couch where he could see all three of us. I remained on the floor, guarding my lover and her child, and my brother's dog.

Jherrel's voice started out shaky. "'They didn't hear the boy come close to them. He sat on a rock. Near him, a paw-cat also watched the djuri herd.'"

Sasha got up from her place by Kayleen and lay next to him, looking up at his face.

His voice steadied as he read about the boy saving the grazing djuri from the paw-cat, and then saving himself from the big predator. Helping Jherrel sound out a few of the Fremont words for animals kept me from going stark raving mad with worry.

Lou showed up just before the end of the story, wheeling into the room with an angry face. She stopped when I put a finger up to quiet her so Jherrel could finish the last few sentences. "'The boy came back home. His mother asked about the scratch on his face. He told her he fell.'"

Maybe I should have re-written the story with an ending where the boy told his mother about the paw-cat.

Jherrel closed the book.

"Do you know?" She surveyed the room. "You must." She noticed Caro sitting silently beside her comatose mother. "Poor baby."

I didn't ask which one of them. It didn't matter.

"I need to sit closer to them, on the couch," she said.

Jherrel hopped up and held her hand as she took three unsteady steps toward the couch, relaxing into it next to Sasha and closing her eyes. I wondered if the captain had sent her here, or if she'd come on her own.

Jherrel brought me his favorite picture book about spaceships.

Liam burst through the door. He took in the scene almost immediately, and just stood there for a long moment looking back and forth between the three female Wind Readers all in nearly-catatonic states, and me and Jherrel reading. Then he did the only thing he could possibly do and sat down on his son's other side. "Show me the biggest ship?"

I loved Liam with every cell, every part of my being.

23
JOSEPH

Space eats light and fire, swallows it whole and replaces it with the dark black of a midnight scream. Marcus's death had barely made a light at all, and now whatever atoms of him remained were part of empty space.

When the *Dispatch* started beeping about low fuel, I realized three hours had passed. I had flown the ship on course to stay near the fleet, but I didn't remember a single command I'd given it. I didn't care, not really.

He had told me he would be leaving soon. I wanted to imagine this was a sham, a way to fake his death. But no escape pod had jettisoned from the wreckage. I had been in a perfect spot to see everything.

The *Dispatch* had been watching, too. I reran the recording and clipped out the visual of the brief, violent explosion, saved it in two places so it couldn't be accidentally erased.

Calls came in and I ignored them.

I stared at the sky and the stars all around and the unfriendly ships.

The fuel monitor began to screech more loudly. I stared at it, unable to quite comprehend its message, or how time passed.

The comm beeped at me. My hand rose slowly to push a button

and allow the incoming message. Captain Hill's voice filled the small cockpit. "Master Lee. We have a berth available for the *Dispatch* and I'm here to debrief you."

The word *Master* jolted me into the present.

I couldn't answer. I realized I was panting, and that Captain Hill could certainly hear me. I wanted to just stay out in the stars and stare at them until there were no more choices left, until I ran out of fuel and watched the lights of the war ships fade away.

If it weren't for my family, I could. I had come out here to find help for Kayleen. Did she know? If so, was she okay? My voice sounded high and strange as I pulled it out of the fog of my shock and said, "On my way."

The captain met me at the airlock door on the far side of the ship's bay. She wore her dress uniform: blue and black with white stripes, pressed smooth. As I stepped through the lock and shut the door properly behind me, she saluted me. "At your service, sir."

I leaned against the wall to keep from falling.

"I'm sorry for your loss, sir," she said.

Her eyes were red although she showed no other sign of emotion. "He's a loss to us all."

"Yes, sir."

We stared at each other. Her chin quivered. Just a little. It made her beautiful.

An awkward silence confused me until I realized the cause and told her, "At ease."

Her shoulders relaxed visibly. "Thank you."

I took a deep breath, realized I felt as tense as she had looked, and took another. "What do I need to know?"

"Marcus's death is being called an accident. It has been verified that no life pod escaped the accident."

"It was no accident." I was certain of that.

"Do you have proof?"

I shook my head. "I have a recording of the explosion that we can look at later."

"Very good, sir. I can report that there is no apparent additional threat from outside."

"How is my family?"

"They would like your company, sir."

"Please don't call me sir."

She took off down the corridor, obviously expecting me to follow. I found Kayleen in her bed, surrounded by Caro and Sasha. Lou looked as if she had passed out on the couch. Jherrel, Chelo, and Liam sat together just inside the door.

Sasha glued herself to my leg.

Chelo folded me in her arms. "I'm so sorry."

Marcus had guided us all. "How is Kayleen?"

"I can't tell."

I brushed a fingertip hello to Liam as I passed him, noting his worried expression. Kayleen lay on her back, covered up with a blanket with her eyes closed. Her breath stuttered, slow and shallow. Caro lay beside her, one small hand across her mom's shoulder. She opened her eyes and looked up. "I can't find her."

She sounded small and dispirited.

"I'll help." There wasn't room to lie down, but I managed to sit on the bed and put a shaking hand on Kayleen's shoulder.

Chelo appeared at my elbow with water. My sister, my angel. My oldest memories were almost all Chelo helping me. Chelo offering water or a cookie, watching over me when I sped away from the guild hall on Fremont and lost myself in the colony planet's data. Chelo holding me when we lost our second set of parents, and again during the later deaths on Fremont. I reached up for the water, took it, and stood for a moment, hugging Chelo, smelling the sweet silky scent of her hair.

We were skin to skin, almost like lovers instead of sister and brother. Perhaps we were closer than lovers could be. I drew strength from her, and her from me, both taking and giving. Eventually, Chelo pushed me back. She whispered, "Save her. Save Kayleen."

They *were* lovers—all three of them. Liam and Chelo and Kayleen and the two children were a single family that had bonded out of despair and—maybe—destiny. I gave her a harder squeeze and swallowed the water in a single long gulp like drinking air. "One more."

After I drank, Chelo took the cup and whispered, "Good luck."

I slid down next to Kayleen, scooting as close as possible on the narrow bed. Sasha curled at my feet. Chelo stood beside me, her thighs against my back. She would be there to keep me from rolling off.

I let the world fall away from me. The ship hummed and reported. Life support, fine. Hydroponics, fine. Navigation, fine. Last course check three seconds ago.

There was nothing of Kayleen in the data. A soft steady personality that monitored and waited for something to do: Lou. Diffuse and far away, Caro. A nearly unconscious trace of Captain Hill, the same trace that was always there.

In between and all around, the endless multiple heartbeats of the *Thorn*'s data.

Instinct demanded I rush after Caro, after Kayleen, but I waited, letting the situation clarify. I was already ragged. Marcus had told me to watch these moments, that anger or loss or fear drive every case of insanity among Wind Readers.

Lou watched me as well as Caro, now. I found a voice that spoke to her and said, *Help me support Caro.* I told her what had happened on Lopali, how it had been Caro who brought her mom back while I had supported Caro.

She said, *I will focus all of my love and attention on Caro if you will do the same.*

Love was a word I had felt in the places of data, but never said.

It was not a thing Marcus would have said.

But Lou was an older woman who knew women, a successful Wind Reader.

I surrendered to the idea, and it took me.

I joined with the old woman, folded into her steadiness. She didn't have Caro's strength, or mine. But she had a sureness about her that transcended both. I felt strengthened by her.

Very well, I told her, *I will wait here with you, and we will hold onto Caro ourselves while she searches.*

Yes.

At first it was easy enough to keep track of Caro as she wandered down pathways of data, gulping statistics and information and searching for traces of Kayleen's energy. As she went further and further, I showed Lou tricks to help her stay in place and also stretch. That wasn't exactly what we did, but there are no better words. There are no words for much that we do as Wind Readers.

Caro began to slip further from me than I wanted. I started to follow but Lou held me back. *You must stay where you can be retrieved if the ship needs you.*

No! I must save my family.

You must do both. If you cannot do both, you must prioritize the Thorn.

I can never.

You must. It was a command.

I hesitated, testing the thought. If I died, someone else could take the *Thorn*. I would not lose Kayleen. *Let me show you how to do with me what I am doing with Caro. Together, we can stretch a little closer to Kayleen.*

She resisted until she realized that I would not bend. Caro and Kayleen were family, and family was life.

Lou learned slowly, and I had to show her a few times. Like the older people at home on Fremont, comprehension came slowly and with repetition. But Lou had strength, and a steadiness I couldn't match.

As I worked with Lou, my link to Caro grew thinner.

As soon as Lou felt grounded, I dove further, strengthening my bond to Caro while still connected to Lou, as if the old woman and I held hands.

Caro sent back, *I feel Mom!*

She surged away, and I struggled to keep the threads we needed to follow backward to our bodies and hold my tenuous connection to Caro open. *Can you bring her with you?*

I'm trying. She gave me a gentle push, a request not to be tampered with.

I held still, tasting where we were, rolling as many of my senses as possible around the long streams of data that pulsed between us all, holding as tight as I could to the traces of Caro's path so she and her mom would be able to find me. Data is not truly sensual of course, but some of the tricks that Marcus had taught me engaged the senses, allowed more of me to come into play than just my brain. It was like the child's rhyme I had learned with Chelo way back on Fremont when I had been smaller than her: *Blood, Bone, and Brain.* A chant. *Blood, Bone, and Brain.*

Master!

I jerked. Lou.

Master. You MUST return. My great-granddaughter calls you.

I can't leave Caro.

Go! Caro sent. *The Captain would not call you for no reason. I'll be okay!*

I addressed Caro. *Come back. We'll go back later and find your mom, when I can help.*

Caro didn't bother to reply to that. I wouldn't have either, if I were her. Nor would I have obeyed me. And of course, she didn't.

I understood.

What is it? I asked Lou.

Go up. Talk to your captain.

Her great-granddaughter.

I swallowed, afraid to stay, afraid to go back. Caro mattered more. But the *Thorn* was mine now, and so was her captain and crew.

What would Marcus do?

I knew, but something bright and deep shattered inside me as I turned away from Caro.

When I surfaced, light slammed my eyes shut again as soon as I opened them. I blinked, put a hand up, grunted. Chelo still supported me, but now her back had turned as she looked at Captain Hill, who stood in the doorway with widened eyes. "The *Opportunity* is sending a ship to come and collect you. The Port Authority is calling your warrant."

24

ALICIA

I woke in the hospital rather than at home, instantly aware of loss. No Induan. I had left family and friends and lovers, but Induan and I had been more than any of those things.

If only I hadn't helped her get into the party while invisible.

The bed was similar to the one I had lain on when growing my wings, comfortable and constricting at once. I had been strapped to it. I stared at the floor, struggling to breathe, then slid my hands around the bottom of the bed, looking for a lever to pull.

If only I could have her back. My eyes watered.

"Good morning."

Chance. I didn't want to see him. Not one bit.

"Let me help you."

I felt along the bed's legs. "I can find it, damnit."

"It's locked." He put a gentle hand on my shoulder. I tried to shrug it off as he leaned down and pushed something that started the bed's upward tilt. My vision tracked along the floor and up the wall until I squinted at bright light spilling onto the floor.

"Is it afternoon?"

"Afternoon and an extra day. I gave you something to sleep."

"Damn you."

He spoke calmly. "I'm a doctor. You were exhausted even before you found Induan."

"Why did she die?"

"A beating."

Ass. I didn't ask him how she died. He must not have noticed the look on my face, since he kept cataloguing her injuries. "She had internal injuries. By the time she came in, her stomach and intestines were full of blood. Two ribs punctured a lung. Her heart was bruised."

Each thing he added felt like a slap. I interrupted. "Who did this? The same people who killed Bryan?"

He shook his head. "They've been dealt with."

I knew. Executed and stripped forever of wings, turned into low-level Keepers. "But they might have had friends. Someone had to know her. She was invisible."

He cocked his head. "Invisible?"

"She wore a machine from Silver's Home. It was part of her. It changed what people saw when they looked at her, showing what was behind her always. It was perfect when she sat still, and almost perfect when she moved. Maybe she overheard something someone killed her for."

He raised a hand to his chin, looking thoughtful. "Unstrap. You need to eat."

My stomach felt like a cavern. But I stayed still. "Her mod was turned on when I found her. If I hadn't tripped over her, I would have walked right past her. She could have laid there for a day before the mod's power faded so we could see her."

"So whoever beat her turned it on after they left her?"

I reached for the strap around my waist, fumbled with the big, easy buckle. My hands shook. "No one but me and her would have known how to turn it on." I hesitated. That couldn't be true. "Maybe someone from Silver's Home, but they'd have no reason. It was on when I last saw her. So someone found her invisible and beat her that way and left her that way. Amalo could see her. It had to be someone like him, who can see in the infrared."

Chance seldom gave any emotion away, but now I could see a

disturbance in the calm that usually rode him, a widening of his eyes, a tight line to his jaw.

I bent over the straps that held my thighs to the bed. I snapped a question at Chance. "How many are there?"

"Fliers who can see infrared? I don't know." He ran a hand through his hair. "I didn't even know Amalo could do that." Chance shook his head as if clearing it of some thought he wanted to banish. "It could be humans with the right equipment. Even mods from Silver's Home."

"She said Makers. The Wingmakers aren't fliers themselves." I stepped out from the bed.

"Follow me. You must eat." Chance led me to a small kitchen with three perches and three human chairs. I sat on a perch, legs dangling one way and wings the other, too empty to stand or crouch like we sometimes did. He was right. Anyone could have killed her.

Word of Induan's funeral must have leaked into the population of pilgrims. Humans lined the hilltops, standing or sitting in small groups, watching. I stood near her body. Keepers wrapped it carefully in white linens and murmured over it in ritual words that were undoubtedly full of capital letters like the Keeper of the Winged Black Flier or something equally stupid. I didn't want to hear what they said. When they lit her bier, I nearly doubled over, the flames tightening around my heart.

I stayed until the flames went out, until there was nothing left of her, until she was forever invisible.

I flew to a small, empty hilltop just outside Oshai, landing easily now with only one extra step. Only then did I let tears fall. I had no words, but I had tears.

Wings announced a visitor. More. I looked up.

Tsawo and Marti, black and red-gold.

They landed, looking carefully at me as if assessing whether or not it was safe to come near me.

I managed to smile.

Tsawo came forward with water and Marti with food, and the

three of us stood together on the hilltop, eating and drinking, until I had calmed enough that I was completely empty and no longer leaked tears with every breath.

Tsawo gave me a long, searching look. He must have been reassured by my control, since the next thing he said was, "I found out more."

I followed Tsawo and Marti to a large blocky building outside of Oshai. It looked plain and unassuming, with no stupid name painted on the outside.

Marti flapped down into the large open roof. I followed, Tsawo coming in last. Because we enter buildings feet down, I didn't see who was in the room until I was toeing for my perch. Amalo, as well as Matriana and Daniel. Then I noticed pale lavender wings with blue circles.

Mille.

The one flier who had let her hatred of me show from the day we landed.

I nearly blew my landing, one foot slipping off the platform, so I had to lean back and put a hand out, pulling hard enough on my muscles that my side and shoulder both screamed at me. I found a balance-point and looked over at Mille, hoping bonds tied her to her perch.

Surprisingly, she offered me a small smile and her words sounded sympathetic. "I'm sorry for your loss."

Others had said those words to me as well, over and over, as if there were a ribbon with the words *Sorry for your Loss, Sorry for your Loss, Sorry for your Loss* printed on it, wandering through the air asking everyone with a mouth to pick it up and repeat the meaningless words. Nevertheless, I nodded. A nod made the words go away faster than any other response.

I had no idea how to respond to Mille, so I looked around. Almost everyone in the room had power. In addition to the various leaders among the fliers, Jagruti leaned against a wall with her arms folded.

Her long black braids rested across her arms artfully, so it appeared she had carefully posed herself. The Keeper of the Ways in all her glory.

Silence fell, as if everyone waited for something.

The door opened and Chance came in.

Matriana cleared her throat.

My stomach felt like it was full of bees.

"Alicia? Do you remember Mille?"

I kept it simple. "Yes." If she had hurt Induan I was going to break her wings.

The look on Matriana's face suggested I wasn't doing a great job of hiding my animosity. "Mille brought us news that helped us learn what happened. She is a respected member of our society, and we chose to let her tell you the same tale she told us."

They were reminding me that even Mille outranked me. I stared at her, then nodded. "Thank you."

Mille was blocky for a flier, her jaw square and her eyes an unassuming gray that faded toward the lavender in her wings. She was beautiful in the air, but on the ground she was nowhere near as striking as Matriana or Angeline, or even Marti. She started out haltingly. "The ones who made us. The Wingmakers. You frighten them. You know they sent the young ones who attacked your brother Joseph and killed your other brother, Bryan."

"Murdered."

She nodded. "They sent the young fliers they had complete control over in that fight, and then killed or maimed them. They are our Makers, but they are not always kind."

"I know that." Although I had thought she supported them. "So what did they care about Induan?"

"They want to unbalance you."

"They would kill a Keeper for that?"

Daniel answered my question. "No flier would kill a Keeper. That part of the story makes sense to us."

"But then how did they deliver her? She was dropped in front of my house."

Tsawo looked tense. "Let Mille tell her story."

I took a deep breath, looked back at Mille.

Mille said, "They are from Silver's Home. They are rich. Most of them have many mods. And of course, since they watch over us, they have ways to be invisible."

I settled down lower on my perch.

Tsawo flapped his wings once, slowly. "They have the money for better mods than you or Induan had. It is a thing we know, but we don't often think about, other than to make sure we never say anything we don't want them to know unless we are in a place like this."

"Like this?" I asked.

"Buildings with no doors. Or the caves."

Caves? I wanted to ask, but Matriana was glaring at Tsawo as if he should stuff the word back into his mouth. I turned to Mille. "Did you see Induan's killers?"

She nodded. "I am like Amalo. I can see heat. This means that the Wingmakers cannot hide from me any more than you or Induan could. There are only a few of us. It was an accidental capability, given to a single generation, a genetic change meant to allow us to fly at night but so inconvenient for the spies among us here that it has been removed. You cannot do it, for example, and you carry the latest flier code set."

I wanted to ask her a million questions. But I wanted to know what had happened even more.

As if Mille had heard my thoughts, she began to speak so fast her tongue tripped over words. "They found Induan listening to Tsawo. They were also listening to him. He is *interesting* to them."

I glanced at Tsawo. He watched Mille closely.

"They trapped her," Mille continued. "It took three of them. They were quite forceful. You need to understand that when I see heat, I don't see details. So I watched the fight, and I could tell who was on what side, and that everyone landed and took blows. I was surprised it was a physical fight at all, that they didn't just kill her some easier way, or even spirit her away and put her on a spaceship."

If only they had. If only she were still alive even in captivity.

"They took her outside of the fence. Then she slowed way down. I think they gave her something, maybe a drug transmitted by touch. At any rate, she became docile and followed them down an alley. I saw them go, but I didn't do anything more. I don't want to get in trouble. But she was a Keeper, and one of my Keepers spoke well of her." Furrows marred her brow and she took a deep breath and fluffed her wings. "It is hard for me to hide with my wings. I flew higher than usual in the dark and caught a glimpse of all three of them moving toward your house."

"Then?"

"Then I went back to the party. I did not expect them to do her harm. I thought they were just angry with her for using their own tricks, and that they would try to teach her a lesson."

My voice trembled with anger I could hardly control. "What time was this?"

"Just before we all went home. Maybe half an hour. Some people were already going home."

I swallowed. "And you didn't choose to tell me?"

She looked away. "I didn't think there was any real danger."

Chance walked over and looked up into my face. "Calm down. Mille did not have to tell us any of this. She has taken a risk. Only she, Amalo, and one other flier at the party have heat sight. Suspicion will fall on all of them. You should thank her."

My words sounded clipped and angry. "We could have saved Induan!"

He stepped up on the bottom rung of the ladder to the perch, bringing his face close to mine. "Fliers are beholden, and they know it."

"I am not beholden to anyone."

He whispered. "You swore the oaths."

My hiss was soft, only for his ears, and full of anger. "I can unswear them."

"Do not say that out loud," he hissed back. "You will lose your wings."

I hated Lopali in that moment, and I swore, right then, that I would leave it. But as far as Chance knew, all I did was smile at the woman who could have saved my only true friend hereif she had bothered to try. I swallowed and told Mille, "Thank you."

25
ALICIA

Jagruti sat on a high stool that placed her eyes even with mine in spite of my comfortable perch. The schoolroom was meant for twenty or so students. With just the two of us it felt quite large. The open roof and high windows let light fall on either side of us, although Jagruti's thin face lay in pale shadow, inscrutable. "Tell me three ways that seekers who come here attain what they are looking for."

By now, the words came easily. "They use our pain to see their own is small, they use our beauty to see their own potential, and they find the best of themselves in a place with no distractions."

"You say that so easily. How do you know it?"

"My friend, Chelo, loved the morning flight. She lost her worries here, even though that is not what we came here to do."

She nodded. "How did the rituals of Lopali affect you?"

I hated the words she wanted me to say. But I needed to survive this hour and the next. "As a human or as myself?"

"Both."

"I didn't trust the rituals as a human." Thus, she heard what she wanted, and didn't know I still found Lopali's pretense at spirituality silly and frightening.

Jagruti waited for me to continue.

I shifted uncomfortably on the perch and shook my wings. "Now, they provide me with a framework within which to lead pilgrims to what they seek."

"Deeper."

A command. I liked her more than Mohami, but that was saying very little. "The rhythms of Lopali and the rules of Lopali structure time. They structure movement. They structure the ways that we interact with seekers."

"All true. Do they make you a better person?"

The word *no* tried to spin up my throat, but I pursed my lips to keep it in. "They tell me how to please you."

The look on her face told me she didn't like that answer.

"They guide me to learn what the Wingmakers are trying to make me become."

She stretched a long leg out. "If you let ritual guide you, you will learn to move in harmony with us. You need that harmony before you attempt the morning flight."

I didn't quite manage to keep the sarcasm out of my voice. "The most beautiful thing on Lopali, but to be part of it I have to give up my sense of self?"

Her face hardened. "Meet me in Fliers' Field just after dawn tomorrow."

That startled me. "Won't you miss the morning flight?"

She didn't answer me. But then, she almost never answered direct questions that were about her. She climbed down from her stool and left me to fly up through the roof and back home.

The next day, I woke before the sun came up. Loneliness made it hard to crawl from bed and take a cup of flier's col from my new Keeper, a nearly silent woman named Felicity with a hunched back which had once borne wings. The bitter smell made me hesitate, although drinking it gave me energy.

Felicity and I seldom talked. She didn't smile or laugh or share my history. She had never run beside me. Her presence reminded me of Induan's absence.

The first week after I'd lost Induan had been sharp with anger and pain, but a numb emptiness had fallen over my moods like a smothering blanket.

It wasn't better than the pain; it was worse. It slowed me down.

But this morning woke a spark of curiosity. Jagruti had never given me more time than the prescribed two hours of lessons, three days a week, that were part of the scripted plan for turning me into a real flier.

Whenever I was with her, I felt I was being tested. I had the impression she didn't think much of me, that her teaching me was a dismal duty. So what would cause her to miss a morning flight?

I handed my cup to Felicity, took a few bites from the bowl of nuts she had set out, and rose up through the roof.

The soft light of morning bathed me and the fields with gold, and a slight wind carried the scent of watered grass.

Induan had loved first light. A brief spear of loss caught in my throat. I bit it back and then soared, the rising sun drawing heat from the ground and offering it to me.

Jagruti stood in the middle of Fliers' Field, holding human wings. The pressure and gravity of Lopali combined to allow normal humans to fly awkwardly with such wings, even though they looked like a paper costume pasted to thin wood. Jagruti's, of course, were a brilliant, blinding white. Watching her single-handedly strap herself into the complex contraption reminded me of how hard I had found the same work.

Jagruti took three graceful running steps and launched herself into the air.

Only then did I realize she had barely acknowledged me.

I took off after her, working to catch up.

She led me away to the top of a hill outside the city, to a clearing full of perch-trees. To my utter surprise, she landed in one.

I managed to land gracefully in the same tree. Perch-trees were art created to look vaguely like trees, but mostly designed to hold us with our wings off the ground. Their wood and metal branches seated one to three fliers each, with support for wings and feet and backs. I had a good view of the city, although the mandala itself was blocked by buildings.

Jagruti cleared her throat. "Good morning."

"I hope so."

She unstrapped her wings and lay them on a flat surface near the top of the tree. It was meant to hold food carried up ladders by young, agile Keepers, and it was wide enough to hold Jagruti's pure white human wings. "Do you know why I brought you here?" she asked me.

Another test? "You wanted a more private place."

"That is so." She pointed back toward Oshai. "We can see the morning flight, and you can speak alone with the Keeper of the Ways of Lopali. No one but me will know what you say here."

A reminder that wasn't necessarily true in the school, even when we seemed alone. "What do you need to say to me?"

She smiled. "That I am not ready to see you killed."

Again, she reached for shock. This time I was more ready. I kept my voice calm and low, carefully conversational. "Am I failing?"

She reached into a pack tied loosely around her waist and brought out two pieces of orange fruit, handing me one. "You have some time until I consider you a failure. One thing worries me. I do not see any surrender in your eyes."

"Why should you?"

"If you do not surrender, you cannot become what you must. You would not have gotten your wings if you could not demonstrate the ability to surrender. Perhaps you need to remember that moment and let go, let this place take you, let yourself become one of us."

The fruit had a thick skin, and I stuck my thumbs in to peel it. It smelled more savory than I had expected, the juice sticky.

"No need to do that," she said. "The rind gives you strength. Eat the whole thing."

I stared at the fruit, searching for words. "I *am* one of you. I swore the oaths; I fought for my wings. I've learned the things you want me to say. I've even learned to manage my own questions when you surround me with sweet little pilgrims. What more can you want from me?"

"What do you love?" she asked.

I searched for the words she wanted. "Flight. Freedom."

"Watch."

I had learned the routines here. There would be nothing to see for a few minutes yet. I bit and chewed and wiped juice from my skin. It tasted salty for fruit, with a sweet aftertaste. Different. "This is good."

She didn't respond. She seemed lost in herself.

I finished the fruit just as the flight started. We were so far away the fliers looked more like butterflies than humans. With very few exceptions, I could not make out who was who. The flight's beauty lay in precision—fliers rising up straight like a column of water and then falling away and back down in circles to catch the bottom and go up again. From here, they were almost a blur. They were inches from each other, harnessing the drafts of air they created to help each other. A delicate and difficult thing.

Even from here, it mesmerized me. It seemed brighter than I expected it to, the colors richer.

"What happens if one of them falls away?" Jagruti asked.

"There is a hole. Or they hurt others. Or both."

She nodded. "Or die. It happened seven years ago. An older flier lost the rhythm, and the wind of his wings shook a younger one free. They kicked another. The last in the line, a woman in her prime, a friend, ended up with a break in her wing that made her plummet to her death."

"I'm sorry."

Jagruti's features had stilled to stone. "Her death made the Wing-makers rich. More people came the next year than ever before."

"That's horrible." I hadn't really seen it as risk. Maybe I would like it.

She smiled. "I'd like to see you lead the flight, but you must learn to surrender first."

The flight fascinated me—how could it not? But it also repelled. Anything so perfect repelled. Besides, I liked my risks solo. "I don't want to join the flight, much less lead it." I still planned to leave. I had no idea how, but this place didn't feel like my place, not even now that I could fly in it. "I'm happy enough watching the flight."

"What does it mean to you?" she asked.

The ceremony was almost half over. By now, I had watched it so many times I knew it was on target to finish well, that our visitors would be impressed, that a few would even claim they had reached a step on their path to enlightenment. The flight usually left me feeling like I was watching a great manipulation or an empty show, but today it grew in my breast like a flower full of wonder and awe. Had there been something slightly psychedelic inside of the fruit? "It's a symbol of perfection."

She glanced at me, her face neutral except for a touch of disappointment in her eyes. "Not perfection? A symbol of perfection?"

She made tripping in my words so easy that I just told her the truth. "It's a lie."

"That's what I wanted you to say."

"You don't believe it."

"Don't believe the flight is a lie? That the perfection of Lopali is a lie? Of course I don't. I am the Keeper of the Ways, and the ways are my truth. Why do you believe they are a lie?"

"We're owned. Every one of us. You can take away my wings, so you own me. The Wingmakers and your duties own you."

"That is true."

"How can anything owned be perfect? If I am under threat—from you, from whoever killed Bryan and Induan—I cannot be perfect. I can only be angry."

She tugged at one of her braids. "To succeed at the flight is to be connected to every flier in the flight, and to me, and to the Keepers of Lopali. It is to be so much more than yourself that who owns you is not a question. Ownership is not a question. Time is trivial. Connection is truth."

Her words made me dizzy. Not dizzy enough to fall, but I gripped the railing in front of me nonetheless.

She continued, hot with conviction. "The moment is all there is, and all of the beings whose hearts beat with yours. Now. This moment is all, this conversation, this flight."

She fell silent. The silence stretched. Awkward. Then she continued, her voice a little softer. "That is Keeping, as well. Keeping is knowing when a flower needs water, when to pollinate, the exact moment to harvest. For those lucky enough to Keep fliers, it is knowing what they need. This is what we were teaching Induan and what Felicity already knows."

"Felicity barely talks to me."

"Isn't that what you want?"

Damn it.

"I feel your frustration."

Damn her. "Why does becoming a flier mean you can feel my feelings?"

"The pain of becoming made you surrender. If you had not surrendered, you would have died. Because you surrendered, you can reach into yourself. Others can also reach you. If you allow walls to rebuild around your heart, you will fail and I will take your wings."

I was getting used to that threat. So matter-of-fact.

The flight had started the last movement, the fliers spinning off the column in all directions, making a wide spiral of color before they landed at the same instant in a circle around the mandala. Chelo had cried the first time she'd seen the morning flight. I had wanted to laugh at Chelo for letting these people make her cry.

"Anger feeds walls, and so does loneliness and fear. These are yours. I cannot fight them for you."

I wanted to get up and fly away, but her threat was probably real, and I still felt dizzy. "What fruit was that?" I asked her.

"The fruit of truth."

I wondered why she'd told me that, and what it meant. But then, she had also eaten one.

"Success," she mused, "is all about connection. And connection is about truth. Not justice. Not fairness. Not anger. The truth of the moment."

The skies were clear by rule before the morning flight and for fifteen minutes after. Jagruti and I sat silently watching other fliers take off, some to practice, some for joy, some to teach. A few minutes later, the first awkward human wings rose unsteadily from Fliers' Field.

No one came near us, which seemed so strange I asked Jagruti, "Are people avoiding us on purpose?"

"There is always room around me when I want it."

"How?"

"Connection."

Her silence told me she was waiting for me to tell her some truth, or to surrender to her view of the world.

I held my tongue and heart in check and let the connection exist without feeding it or pulling away. She would have to be content with that. It was all I had in that moment.

I had been closer to Induan than to anyone, ever. I had found her on Silver's Home, which was the first place I had felt like I belonged. We had built our friendship over years and across adventures. When she'd died, I'd broken.

When Jagruti finally picked up her wings and strapped them back on, I felt a great sense of relief and flew after her, keeping some distance.

26

ALICIA

Colors still seemed too bright as I flew home, each blade of grass below me appearing individual, each tree or path perfectly outlined. I felt each pull of my wings, and the flow of air through feathers and against bone.

I didn't want to go where Jagruti pushed. Whatever change she was after, I didn't want it. Not yet. Maybe never.

I found my house unexpectedly full. Marti and Amalo sat in the kitchen, Tsawo and Angeline in the living room, and Felicity had clearly been sent outside somewhere.

I wondered if they knew about the truth fruit talk.

Their faces looked so serious that the first words out of my mouth were, "What happened?"

Amalo spoke. "Chance has disappeared."

"What? How?"

Angeline put a slender pale finger to her perfect pink mouth.

Tsawo wore his protector face. "We will stay with you until time for the afternoon flight, and then we will fly with you."

They thought it took all of them to protect me? Wouldn't a warning and one watcher be enough? But I remembered Angeline's finger and I nodded.

"You should nap," Angeline said, her white wings blinding. "We all should, although we will take turns."

"Is there room for five of us to sleep?"

"Three," Marti said. "Come lie down with me. There are two sleeping benches in your room. Amalo will rest out here."

Any day I flew in the morning, I had to rest if I wanted strength to fly again that afternoon. Tsawo was the same. He had napped the days he was teaching me to use human wings at Fliers' Field. I had thought him rude before I understood. A morning flight usually exhausted me enough that sleep demanded me even when I tried to stay awake.

Even though the bench and the wing-rests felt more solid than usual, and the incense smell that permeated the walls seemed twice as sharp as usual, I passed out.

The only good thing about waking was that the strange enhancement of my senses had been lost to sleep. Marti had already woken, and the soft murmurs of low conversation drew me to the kitchen.

A feast had been laid out on the table. I was so hungry I filled a plate before I realized that Jagruti was in the room, sitting quietly by the door, watching me.

I ignored her until after I had finished most of the food on my plate. Everyone was silent, as if her presence suppressed conversation.

After we ate, Felicity came in to clean the kitchen. To my surprise, Jagruti helped. I glanced at Marti, who picked up a plate and handed it to Felicity. I joined Marti in passing plates and glasses. Tsawo wiped the table up after us.

Jagruti glanced at Felicity. "Leave us."

Felicity immediately obeyed her.

The rest of us, five fliers and the Keeper of the Ways of Lopali, sat around the table in silence.

We did not share a single heartbeat.

Amalo's eyes narrowed in a way that suggested he hoped I would maintain silence. After I nodded at him, he said, "We will take her for initiation into our secrets. We will take her tonight and return when we are finished. We will be finished when we are finished."

Another fucking ritual.

Jagruti nodded and spoke slowly, as if the words were hard for her to say, "You will be finished when you are finished. And then we together will choose her place in our world."

"And then we together will choose her place," Amalo answered.

Each face looked so still and serene I knew they were hiding something.

Jagruti had apparently concluded her business. She turned and left the room.

"Now," Amalo said, "we fly."

We rose, Amalo, then Marti, then me, with Tsawo and Angeline following. We flew for a long time. My shoulders ached long before we came to ground near the entrance to a cave. A stream flowed loose from near the mouth, winding through rocks and low-growing mosses. It was well kept, but not the way Keepers did such things. Here and there death could be seen as plants past their season were stained with tan or gray, and bloomed-out flowers maintained their grip on browning stems.

A wild place. Here, on Lopali. A place where weeds grew, and plants were allowed to die in the ground.

Still gardened, though. A fall of orange flowers too pretty and too perfectly placed to be utterly natural lined both sides of the cave mouth.

"Your brother came here," Angeline told me. "He and Kayleen and Marcus did much of their work in this cave. It is a place where Wingmakers do not go."

That explained how Marcus and Joseph had accomplished so much without being stopped. "Is Chance here?"

Tsawo had overheard. He looked over his shoulder, twitching one wing down so that I could see his face. "I hope so. But we think the Wingmakers have him."

"Why?" I asked.

"They don't like fliers created from adults like you two," he nodded at me and Marti, "or fliers who can suddenly have children. It might damage the economics of their affinity group."

Amalo gestured for us to follow him. The source of the stream was a waterfall that came down just to the right of the dark entrance, the sound of the water like birds singing and small bells. Inside, the cave opened out into a vast room that was clearly created, or at least shaped, with heavy machinery. The cave walls had been squared off in some places and shored up in others. Whole buildings existed inside, on the vast floor. Locked rooms that might have been storage or meeting rooms or even schools. There were also exits and, in some cases, closed doors in the cave walls. A few ladders lead to doors set higher in the walls.

Amalo led us to a small meeting place where the seats were comfortable rocks just tall enough to keep our wings from dragging the floor. As soon as everyone settled, I asked, "What was that about?"

"We are allowed to take every flier here. This was brokered by our ancestors, before Lopali became as—" Amalo searched for the right word. "As ordered as it is now. One of the earliest fliers indentured us to the morning flight in return for the ability to have our own private place. We reap ten percent of all the money paid by all of the seekers as a group, and it goes here. The Wingmakers know about the caves, but they don't know what we do here. We pay for good security, and we keep the secrets here, all of us."

Ten percent of a fortune. "This place needs that much investment?"

"You can only see a part of it from here. Besides, we make more than the Wingmakers pay us. That is one goal of this effort. It took four generations."

I nodded, impressed.

Tsawo said, "You must stay here until we tell you you're safe."

"I won't miss flier etiquette school," I said. "And I'm ready for secrets."

Amalo smiled at me. "Good. The secret is everything you see here. All of it. Every word. Every deed. Every face. From the moment you walked through that door until the moment you leave by any means, all of the things you are exposed to are the secrets of fliers and can only be spoken of here."

"What else is here?" I asked. "Do you have ships, stores; is there a spaceport you can use?"

"Will you keep our secrets?"

"I will." I had known of this. Not exactly of this, not that there would be a cave full of secrets with a stream outside, but I had known secrets existed.

Amalo looked pleased. "There is a penalty if you do not keep our secrets."

"I will lose my wings?"

"You will lose your life."

Oh. Well then.

Angeline spoke, her melodic voice welcome after Amalo's deep and demanding one. "You would not be here yet if Chance had not disappeared. But he is nowhere. Normally we can all find each other. He is dead or captive or has been taken off-world."

A shiver ran up my spine. "Why?"

"Because he is needed to help the babies grow their wings."

Oh. I didn't like Chance much, but I owed him a great deal. "I hope he is okay."

"So do we," Tsawo said. "Like the rest of us, he is beholden to the Wingmakers. Now that you have promised, I will take you on a tour."

"Is there a restaurant on the tour?"

"There is food." He smiled. "I need some, too. That was the fastest flight to here I have ever logged."

Sleeping and eating. My new fascinations. Who knew that a single little thing like adding wings and length to a girl would make her like an infant? "Will I ever stop being hungry?" I asked.

Marti laughed. "No."

The laugh broke some of the tension of the little gathering, and we got up to follow Tsawo.

I was well fed by the time we waddled into a room full of screens. I stopped just inside the door, staring. Half the screens showed ships. The others mostly displayed trajectories and system-wide maps. A few were news streams. Three teenage humans sat rapt in front of an image of a sports game of some kind. There were no other fliers in the large room, and maybe seven or eight adult humans, all of them quite intent on watching the readouts. A woman with severely-red hair pulled back from her face and tall black boots that matched a black belt hurried over to us. "Amalo! What brings you here?" Her eyes widened when she saw me. "Alicia."

I saw her bite back the end of that and smiled. "The Black" had almost escaped from her lips.

Other than the people I'd arrived with, everyone here was a stranger.

Amalo told her, "We are showing Alicia around. She may be here for awhile and must be kept safe."

The woman nodded as if she needed no explanation and extended a hand. "I'm Elopha. I run this room at the moment."

Somewhere in those screens, there had to be a picture of Joseph. Or whatever ship he was on. Suddenly I was starved for my family. Maybe because I had been thinking of them in the tree with Jagruti, still sticky with the juice of the truth fruit. "Can you communicate?"

"Excuse me?"

"With the ships. With Joseph and Chelo and Marcus?"

"The message delay is a few days, and we can't count on anything being secure."

Oh. So they were far away. "How close are the fleets? Are they fighting yet? Is everyone okay?"

"They are still weeks away from being in range of each other." She glanced at the screens and amended her comment. "At least for the bigger warships."

I blinked. The war had seemed so very far away. But here it was, visible just a few feet from me. "Can you show me which ship he's on?"

"We don't know that. They didn't leave here in a fighter. But they caught up to the fleet some time ago. We are getting some of their communications traffic, but it's only the open comms and thus only information the fleets aren't horrified to share, even with each other. All secrets will pass via Wind Readers."

"Don't we have Wind Readers?" Joseph and Kayleen had talked about how the Wind Readers on the whole planet had come together to save him, and there had been one woman who helped little Caro.

"They can't communicate with each other over this much distance." She slowed down, as if she addressed a child. "Wind Readers have to be in data that is tangled together, so they can talk anywhere across a planet like this, or across a single ship. Sometimes between ships that are close. Strong ones can reach ships in orbit. Marcus could cross to other planets or moons, but the fleets are further away than that. Impossible."

I should have known that. Would have, if I'd been thinking. "Show me what this tells you?"

"Of course. They are all at least two days behind except for a few that are simulations, and they are probably wrong." Elopha looked happy to be asked though. One of the few people here who actually seemed to want to tell me things. She began going through each screen. The information fed a hunger I hadn't known I had, and I forgot about the others, except for Amalo, Marti, and Tsawo, who followed close behind me and occasionally asked questions.

I had not imagined so many ships. "How will he live through this?" I asked.

Tsawo answered. "Many won't. Why do you think we didn't go?"

I turned to him. "I thought it was because you couldn't pick between the people who control you and the people who might free you, so you chose the easiest thing."

He flinched but said nothing.

"We have plans to free ourselves," Amalo said. "We don't need the help of anyone from outside. That's what this place is about."

I looked around. "Information will free you?"

"We are building more than that," Amalo said. "We should continue the tour."

I turned to Elopha. "Can I come back? Have you show me more?"

She looked to Amalo.

He nodded. "But you may not send any messages. We can't risk letting anyone know this is here; we cannot lose this access."

Joseph suddenly seemed close enough to touch. "Can you send messages?" I asked Elopha.

Amalo answered, speaking to her and using his command voice. "She will not. Not with Chance missing, which every flier will notice, and you missing, which every pilgrim will notice. We will send nothing from here."

Elopha stiffened but didn't answer him directly. She looked at me and said, "You may come back. Any time."

I glanced at the screens again. Being in this room wasn't as good as leaving Lopali would be, but there was at least some ability to see places where danger was clear-cut instead of hidden.

Surrounded by data, I understood that I had not let myself see what Joseph was flying into. There were many ships on both sides, maybe even hundreds, and they all had weapons.

I should have gone with them. What was it Jagruti had said loneliness did? Built a wall that would take my wings?

27

JOSEPH

Captain Hill's announcement that the Port Authority intended to arrest me stunned me back into my body. I stretched, blood rushing to my fingers and toes. The scent of stale sweat hung in the air. I opened my eyes again, still stretching, and looked at the captain.

She looked back, her face as serious as it had been when she'd met me in the airlock.

Chelo perched beside me, steady in the face of two impossible things at once. My rock, my anchor.

Captain said, "Repeat after me."

I blinked. "What?"

"Do it," Chelo said. "Listen to her."

I nodded.

"I, Joseph Lee."

"I, Joseph Lee."

"Accept command and responsibility."

"Accept command and responsibility."

"And agree to obey the Navy of Silver's Home."

I hesitated. It didn't sound right. Chelo squeezed my arm, whispering, "Do it."

"And agree to obey the Navy of Silver's Home."

"For the period of declared war with Islas."

No. "Did Marcus say those words?"

"Marcus was not about to be boarded," the Captain hissed. "This might keep you safe."

"Say it again," I told her.

"For the period of declared war with Islas."

"For the next year, or for the period of declared war with Islas, whichever is shorter."

Captain Hill looked startled, angry, and then approving in quick succession. She closed her eyes for a moment, then opened them. "That worked. You are verified. They cannot arrest a ship's owner with no process. It is one of the terms of the agreement the Port Authority struck with the collected affinity groups joining this war."

"Now can I go back and save Kayleen?"

She looked firm. I might suddenly own the ship, but the *Thorn* was *her* command, and she cared deeply about it. "We have to save your ownership *now*."

I stood and looked back at the bed, at the still forms of Kayleen and Caro and Lou.

"They are vulnerable if you let the ship be lost."

I'd just promised to protect the *Thorn* and all that lived inside of her instead of just those I loved. I brushed my lips across Kayleen's cheek, whispering, "Come back."

She didn't even flutter an eyelid.

Liam and Jherrel bent over a slate playing games in a corner. I asked him, "Will you and Jherrel tell me if anything changes?"

Liam looked at Jherrel, as if he were allowing him to make the decision. They were one and the same, father and son. Serious as all hell and always around when you needed them. Jherrel nodded solemnly. "We will."

Chelo squeezed my hand. "We'll be okay."

She couldn't know that. The look on her face and the single tear gathered in her left eye told me that she understood Kayleen's peril. I leaned down and kissed her cheek as well. "I'll return as soon as I can."

Captain Hill filled me in on the way to Command. "I used the feed from your ship to verify Marcus's death, with a little help from the *Unicorn*."

I closed my eyes for a moment, still able to see the flash of the explosion.

She continued. "About thirty minutes ago, the *Opportunity* hailed us and demanded that we yield you, Chelo, and Kayleen up. When I told them that you were now Master, they demanded proof. That's what we just created. The *Thorn* now knows you have been sworn into the position. Its systems will obey you."

"Will that stop the *Opportunity* from boarding?"

"No. But it may stop them from taking you away."

"May?"

"Power doesn't always obey rules when it's pissed off."

She spoke those words so formally that I laughed even though there was nothing funny in our situation. Maybe I laughed because that was all that was possible in that moment, laughing or giving up. "Marcus disobeyed the Port Authority the day I landed on Silver's Home, and I think he's done so ever since."

She smiled. "I know. I'd like to hear that story someday."

"How much time do we have?"

"Half an hour. I've ordered a uniform for you. Breakfast will be served in the room where we watched the video." She stopped right in front of me, turning, asking me to stop. "It's possible that Marcus was killed so the Port Authority could get to you. You are a powerful asset to have in a possibly rogue position in the back of the fleet. They might be very insistent. Don't give them a reason to take you in."

It was all I could do to swallow and nod. I was so empty, and so worried about Kayleen, it was hard to think. The uniform was in a room near Command. It fit perfectly. The shoulders had the same insignia on them that she wore, the bars and stripes of a captain, plus an extra bar above that in bright blue. One chest pocket was decorated with the logo for the *Thorn* embroidered in data threads. The other sported a copy of Silver's Home's flag. I was smaller than Marcus, so this had been found for me since his death or made before.

I didn't want to know which.

Wearing it helped. Nevertheless, when I met Captain Hill, I still felt thin and lost. She looked pinched and yet somehow regal. A leader ready to lead.

She sat sideways by our food and col, her long thin legs stretched out in front of her and crossed at the ankles. "I have issued an invitation to a few of the other masters and captains to join us and wish you well in your new position." She handed me a cup of col.

I was beginning to understand why Marcus had valued her so much, and why he had trusted her enough to leave her with the *Thorn* while we were all on Lopali. The drink tasted like heaven and braced me. "Have you spent all of your life in space?" I asked her.

She handed me a plate with a single slice of bread and protein paste on it. "My grandmother and my great-grandmother were both captains. My mother was a chief engineer."

So that's why Lou had such calm control, and why I had obeyed her with so little question. "Where is your mother now?"

"She and my grandmother were flying together when they collided with something, destroying the engines and most of the life support. By the time a rescue crew arrived, everyone on the ship had died." She fell quiet for a moment, as if trying to decide how much more to tell me. "My grandmother sacrificed herself early even though she was the captain. She left my mother alive to try and string together enough working machinery to keep the ship going. Obviously, she failed."

I choked down half the bread. "It sounds like a situation where anyone might have failed. How long did it take for the rescue to arrive?"

"Three months."

"They must have been far from developed systems."

"They were surveying another moon, like Lopali, to see if Silver's Home could expand."

Like our parents had been exploring Fremont. So far, every world had its own single government. The bigger worlds exerted influence on the smaller ones, but no one world controlled another. "I bet Islas didn't like that idea."

"I don't know if they knew about it."

And unsaid, she didn't know if Islas had anything to do with the disaster. We finished eating in silence. As soon as I put my plate and cup down, the captain stood up. "Let's go prepare our reception. My staff would probably like to see you."

I checked for messages. The only one from Liam said, "No change."

Captain Hill led me to a large conference room. A single black table dominated the room. The *Thorn*'s logo splashed across the table's center in bright blue and silver. Six other officers lined the table. Four well-armed strongs stood behind them, against the wall.

She introduced me to all of them, but between worrying about being plucked from the *Thorn* at any moment to be incarcerated aboard the *Opportunity* and fretting about Kayleen and Caro, I only managed to remember two of them.

Commander Lin Juong was a serious dark-haired man who stood about three inches shorter than the captain. I had seen him before and wondered who the always-serious man could be. He nodded when the captain introduced him, but a smile was apparently beyond him. He had no obvious mods, and I didn't see any sign that he was a Wind Reader, either. However, something in his eyes radiated extraordinary intelligence.

The other officer who took watches had clear physical mods. Paul Greene's wide-set eyes could probably see behind him as well as in front of him, his shoulders were almost as wide as a strong's without the bulk, and he had an extra set of arms which were folded against his chest at the moment I met him. They looked as strong as his primary set. The extra arms explained the shoulders, as both arms seemed to rely on one fairly complex shoulder joint.

I sat beside the captain at the head of the table. Lin and Paul flanked us, and the others sat down on both sides. From time to time people cast me furtive, short glances. Sizing me up.

The thought jolted me. On some level, the promise I had made to the ship and to Captain Hill managed to jostle its way past my loss and my worry.

I had uttered words that were going to change me.

A thousand questions I should have asked the captain went through my head.

"Captain Hill?" I asked.

She looked … patient. "Yes?"

I ran through possible resources in my mind. Chelo would be here, except not with Kayleen in crisis. That left out Liam. Paloma wasn't strong enough. "I would like to have two of my own people here."

She pursed her lips. No response.

I didn't have to ask. But I should tell her what I was doing and why. I was going to need to know those things from her. "Ming. She is an effective fighter and she knows the Port Authority. She used to work for them. And Jenna, who has been an advisor for years." And who had survived what amounted to an attack by an entire colony of people back on Fremont.

She looked pleased. "At once. I'll send someone for them."

Taking action made me feel more prepared to meet whatever was coming. But only a little. Once more, I wondered how Marcus had made all of these contradictions look so much like water flowing along the stream of his strength.

28

ALICIA

I lay in the darkness of my room in the cave, listening to Marti breathe. The others had all left the night before. Apparently Marti was the only one with low enough status to stay away from Lopali for days.

A slight resentment tugged at me. They had left without telling me all of their secrets. I had seen schools and small ships that went between here and the stations in low orbit, and been back to the room of screens one more time. Angeline had shown me gardens. But there was more. I could feel it in the way the others sometimes glanced from one to another when I asked a question.

They didn't trust me.

Jagruti wouldn't trust me until I bared my soul for her, and I suspected she wouldn't trust me then. Not if she saw the anger and frustration that had always followed me.

My stomach rumbled. There were Keepers here, but no one Kept me or Marti. I pushed myself up off my chest and staggered to my feet, taking two steps to find my balance.

A quiet, friendly laugh told me Marti had watched me bobble the simple act of standing. "Eventually, your wings do become part of you."

"They are!"

"Not yet," she said. "You still have to work around them." Then, as if to mollify me, "But you fly quite well."

"Thank you."

She spoke softly. "I'm sorry about Induan. I can't imagine how alone you must feel."

I swallowed and turned away. "Thank you."

"If I can help …"

"I'll let you know." I offered the closest thing to truth I could get. "I don't even know what help to ask for. You can't bring her back. Maybe just being here and talking to me from time to time is all you can do."

"I can be a friend."

Not like Induan, she couldn't. Not yet. "Thank you." I forced out a small smile.

We walked side by side until we found a common mess hall. Cooking oat-cakes, heated syrups, and warm bread combined to make the busy kitchen smell fabulous. This morning, we were the only fliers here, so we filled our plates and shared a tall table. After I'd downed enough chocolate-flavored col to feel competent, I asked her, "What is your story? Where did you come from?"

She cocked her head, considering.

"You know mine," I offered. "My parents are from Silver's Home, but I grew up on Fremont, where the damned war started, and now I'm here. I've only spent a little time on Silver's Home."

She stopped with a fistful of nuts on the way to her mouth. "I'm from Paradise."

"Why did you come here?"

"Same as everyone." She stopped for a sip of col. "I wanted to get away from the craziness. I know Paradise is supposed to be a place for escape, but those of us who spent our lives helping tourists reach their hearts' desires …"

I struggled to focus on my col and stay noncommittal.

She must have seen the look on my face. "I wasn't in the seamier parts. We helped people become winning athletes. Better bakers. Painters. Things like that."

"That's good."

"I was getting burned out and I didn't know what I wanted, so I came here to find out. Then I saw people fly, and I wanted that."

Before I could ask her a follow-up question, I felt a hand on my shoulder and turned to see Elopha, her red hair swinging loosely around her shoulders and her clothes looking rumpled from sleep. "Come to see me after you eat. I'll be in the situation room."

She meant the room with all the screens. Even though I knew it was too early for the fleets to have clashed, my spine stiffened with a cold shiver. "Is everything all right?"

She licked her lips and nodded. "Yes. But there are things you might want to know. Is Amalo gone?"

"Yes."

Marti took my hand. "I can go get him. Should I?"

"No." Elopha dropped her hand from my shoulder.

I turned so my wings were a little out of the way and looked at her. "Is anyone in danger?"

She hesitated, then shook her head. "Not immediately."

"Then we'll both come. Now?"

"Give me half an hour."

We used our half an hour to take sponge baths. With no Keeper, we had to wash each other's feet. It felt more sensuous to have Marti touching me than Felicity. More like Induan. For a moment, the feeling caused the emptiness to fall back around me, but as we dried each other's backs, curiosity about Elopha's cryptic invitation crept back.

I chose a clean red jumpsuit and Marti a black one with a short skirt. It made us look like we had planned our wardrobes together, although we hadn't. The red I'd picked was more like the blood-drops on my wings than Marti's bright red plumage, but the colors did complement each other.

Without Induan or Felicity, I settled for catching my hair in a simple black braid.

Elopha met us in the situation room and took us to a conference room I hadn't seen before. The seats weren't meant for fliers, so we stood. None of the three screens on the wall were on. Elopha looked hesitant. "Are you well?"

"We are," Marti crossed her arms. "What did you want to tell us?"

"We get information from many sources," she said. "We have spies. From fliers in the flyspaces on Silver's Home, merchants who owe us favors or hope for some from us, people who traded us for information."

"Like what?" I asked.

She shook her head. "We got something yesterday. I've been trying to verify and so far, I can't. So it might not be useful. It came from Silver's Home, from a contact at the Port Authority."

Marti looked curious, so I told her, "That's the police on Silver's Home, and more. Also the people who started the war."

"Thanks."

Elopha nodded at me. "Supposedly—not certainly, but probably—there is a spy with Joseph. One of the people who was here with you."

29
ALICIA

The sheer weight of the mountain above us felt like a trap, so Elopha allowed me out by the mouth of the cave. Cascades of flowers sweetened the air. Sunshine glinted off the sliding surface of the bust stream. Small fish made streaks in the surface as they nabbed smaller gliding insects for breakfast. Most of the fish were dark, but from time to time a golden fish as long as my hand bullied the smaller fish aside to nab a particularly fat morsel.

When I looked up, the sky was full. Marti and Amalo, Tsawo and Angeline, even Daniel and Matriana.

So many? Why? Dread made the morning lose some of its brightness.

For the first time, I actively tried to connect with other fliers, to feel what they felt. Connection had come over me with force when Amalo had wished it, and it had snuck up on me in groups, but I had never wanted to initiate it.

I slowed my breathing and listened to my heart, and thought of the others, watching them.

They were connected to each other. They had to be to fly so close.

Now that I wanted to feel them all, I couldn't tell if I felt them or merely myself.

Either I wasn't getting it right, or they were filled with apprehension. Which was exactly what I felt. Or maybe that was the point.

They landed in a line on the path, Daniel in front.

Interesting. When I tried to read him, he looked more angry than apprehensive. But then, I didn't know him as well as the others.

Daniel and Matriana led SoBright, and thus were a formal part of the government of Lopali. Daniel was as tall as Amalo, maybe taller, and barely slighter. His cropped dark hair framed a light-skinned face, almost as pale as Induan had been, his eyes closer to the color of his skin than his hair—white tinted with summer-sky. For the first time, I noticed the maroon tips of his orange wings matched the blood-colors on mine.

As he came close to me, he reached his hands out and took mine. His were warm from flying, and larger than mine, but I did not feel captured. Rather, folded in.

When he looked into my eyes, the anger had faded from his face, taken over by the need to say whatever he was about to say.

I took a deep breath and another, matching him.

His eyes widened and a small smile touched his lips.

I smiled back, feeling our heartbeats.

He did not feel apprehension. Curiosity. Anger, but not with me. A little fear maybe. About me, or for me. I couldn't tell which.

"I have bad news," he said.

A lump formed in my throat. "What?"

"We found Induan's killers, and their reasons. There is a plan to sacrifice you, and we believe she learned it. A death trying for something too fast, a lesson for other fliers, a martyrdom. Maybe also a message to your family, although we aren't sure about that part."

I swallowed, struggling to stay connected to Daniel while absorbing this. Was every planet determined to destroy me? I had threatened to kill the leaders of Fremont after they abused me. Islas had tried to kill me in a battle on Fremont many years later. I had made enemies on Silver's Home by taking up with Joseph's rebel leader and teacher, Marcus. *I had been so careful here.* I hadn't done anything risky, not really. Not except stay behind to beg to become one of them. So *why?*

If Daniel weren't holding both of my hands, I would have doubled over.

He let me breathe, let me feel him. Strength and power. Acceptance. I looked into his eyes, trying to drink in the acceptance.

Matriana slipped in, offering the same thing. Acceptance. This was nothing like Wind Reading—Joseph and Kayleen could have a conversation—but it was connection.

And I would lose it.

Connection slipped away. We still held hands, but our hearts beat apart, mine racing ahead of his. He looked down into my eyes, demanding nothing. After a number of gasping breaths, I asked him. "How did you find out?"

It took him a few moments. "Jagruti … she was part of it, but she also told us. Said she couldn't help, not anymore."

I went cold and spoke very slowly. "Jagruti had Induan killed?"

"No. No." His hands squeezed mine. "Jagruti got in trouble for letting you get away. Amalo suspected. That's why we took you here early. Jagruti could have stopped him—there are tests you haven't passed which are required. But she didn't."

He paused. It took a while before the shape of his words settled into my being, and I could hear the stream again, feel the breeze, feel Daniel's fingers in mine.

His fingers tightened and he said, "She came to me and told me the Wingmakers decided you are dangerous. They had expected you to fail the transformation, slow the numbers of humans who try. When you didn't, they waited a while to evaluate. And then they decided to kill you. One of them saw Induan too near a conversation about that."

No wonder I had never trusted the beauty here. Every flower sipped from poison soil. Induan's last words had been truth. *The ones who made you.*

I bowed my head to escape Daniel's gaze and to let a tear fall unseen, but he touched my cheek with his finger and waited for my eyes to meet his. "You are not safe. Not even here. You must leave."

I tensed and my eyes stung. I had wanted to leave because I wanted to, not because I was being kicked out. I swallowed, breathed.

I could allow this; I could own this. Eventually I spit a word past the lump in my throat. "Okay."

"You are not afraid?"

I stood as straight as I could, still a head shorter than Daniel. I smiled at him. "I am a risk-taker. I like fear."

He smiled back. "If only I were so strong."

"Most people consider it a weakness. You heard there might be a spy aboard Joseph's ship?"

"Yes."

"I think I know who it is. One of two anyway. Dianne or Ming. Dianne is an Islan after all. But that might be too obvious. Ming worked for the Port Authority." I was babbling. This was not their business. I stopped for a breath. Daniel squeezed my hand again, and I squeezed his in return. I couldn't recall if he and I had ever touched before.

Tsawo stood beside Daniel now, Matriana on his other side. Amalo and Marti slid behind me. I stood in a circle of fliers, and it reminded me of the moment I had known I would become one of them, and in that instant my heart beat with theirs and all of them were precious.

Of course. This was the moment I would lose them.

The bitterness of that thought freed me from the feeling of oneness, and I reached for the empty blanket of despair I had felt after Induan's death. Only it wasn't there. Just anger.

Induan had died because she'd heard someone planning to kill me. I had been certain it was my fault, and now I knew for sure.

"Snap out of it," Amalo told me. "Focus. There's not much time, and I won't risk this place to keep you here."

I blinked at him, unsteady. "I'll go." Then I stood a little straighter. "I want to go."

Matriana cleared her throat. "We can't send you to Silver's Home."

"Of course not. Surely it's almost as infested with Wingmakers as this nightmare."

Matriana flinched.

"Sorry. Lopali is a bad dream for me. Especially now."

She swallowed. "I understand."

"I'm going to the fleet. I have to warn Joseph anyway. I can do that, right?"

Tsawo nodded. "We have a ship. You can leave tomorrow. Jagruti and Marti are going with you."

"Jagruti?"

"She is not safe here either. Not now that she told us these things."

I wondered if she would bring the fruit of truth and tools to clip my wings with her. "Tell her no more lessons."

Marti told me, "I will. I have to bring her back your permission."

My permission. That was sweet. "Tell her she can come if she stops threatening to take my wings." I hesitated. "And tell her thank you."

A laugh started to escape Marti's lips, and she closed her mouth over it and managed a simple smile, "I will."

"Everyone else is staying?" I asked.

"I haven't decided yet," Tsawo said.

I laughed. "You could be my protector."

He did laugh.

I wanted him to go with us. Maybe we'd finally have time to be lovers.

Daniel said, "We'll go back tonight to talk. Stay here. Felicity will keep you safe, and some of Tsawo's protectors are almost here."

I nodded.

"Are you okay?" Matriana asked. "Will you be okay if we leave you?"

"Yes."

"We'll go now," Daniel said, his voice edged. "We have to. It is appropriate for all of us to be gone, but only for some small time. Each of us has a part in the conversations tonight."

I watched them leave, sadness washing through me, and anger, and resolve. I stayed outside until they had gone so far I couldn't see them.

When I turned toward the cave, my emotions settled. A clear, glorious, and incongruous happiness lifted my wings. The joy of risk. I was finally going to leave this place. I had my wings, I had my freedom, and I had a way back to my family.

After all, what was one more planet that hated me?

30
ALICIA

I woke early, surrounded by silence and a closed door. I stretched, every muscle stiff from sleeping on the conference room table. The lights flicked on in response to my movement, and I covered my eyes. Elopha and I had been up late, talking through battle strategies.

As if she knew when I stirred, Elopha came in with a tray of col, bread, berries, and fruit. She wore the same clothes she had worn last night. I still wore the red jumpsuit, now slightly wrinkled. She handed me a cup of col. I warmed my hands with it while slowly flapping my wings to loosen them after the uncomfortable night.

I felt unsteady, ready to fall, my flier family on one side and my family from Fremont on the other. I wanted them both.

We had just finished breakfast when Elopha said, "They're here."

"How do you know?"

"We have sensors." She lifted her wrist, where a small button on a bracelet glowed green. "I asked to be notified. Your things will be brought to you."

"Brought where?"

She smiled, a nearly intimate smile that implied she had enjoyed answering my questions the night before, or at least that she liked me. "Follow me." She led me into an adjacent, empty conference room and through a door concealed behind a quilt hanging on the wall.

Flier secrets.

Elopha hurried down a long hall. I hurried after her. Down steps. Through a huge door that opened at her command. On the other side, Tsawo, Marti, and Jagruti perched on a large motorized cart stacked with boxes. Jagruti drove it. She gave me a long, level look, and I hesitated, evaluating. I had never trusted her. But now? I mouthed a "thank you" at her.

She nodded.

Elopha squeezed beside the Keeper on the small bench seat, and I climbed up next to Marti. Behind us, Tsawo held a stunner loosely in his right hand. The tunnels smelled of stale water and were featureless except for pale blue lights built into the floor and ceiling, and here and there a box on the wall with an unknown purpose. Cameras? Communication devices? Jagruti drove so quickly I had to clutch Marti and a rail when we turned corners, but still we rode for an hour.

I whispered to Marti. "Are you coming with me?"

"I am."

"And Tsawo."

"Yes. The others said to wish you well. They stayed to make the day appear normal. Tsawo is often gone, and I don't matter as much as the others."

"You matter to me. I'm glad you're coming."

"Thank you."

The cart rose up a steady slope, slowed, and stopped in front of a door.

Tsawo climbed down. "There will be a few people to help load the boxes, so just bring yourselves and get into the ship as fast as you can. It's already preparing to leave."

The door opened onto a vertical hallway with a ladder. Climbing hurt my sore back. The weight of my wings wasn't meant for this kind of exercise. Muscles screamed as I pulled myself up through the hatch.

The shadow of a ship hid us from the midday sun. It looked smaller than I'd expected, and squatter. Scars from high-speed impacts marred her side.

Shouldn't a flier ship be beautiful?

Jagruti pulled me after her, helping me traverse the ramp into the ship quickly, the others close behind us.

The door closed us away from Lopali. I hadn't told Elopha goodbye, or thanked her.

The deep rumbling of engines drove me up into the ship, and a human directed me to a special crash couch. If we got into trouble, it would not save my wings, but it did take me face down, and cradled my torso, limbs, and head. The man who led me here had to strap me into it.

I wondered briefly what fliers did for environment suits. Then we were away, free of Lopali.

The weight of movement drew my wings back uncomfortably. I had to work to find a way to hold them so the forces felt like a strong wind.

This would not do for long.

After what must have been at least a few hours, the man came back and unstrapped me. "Stretch out and get ready."

"For what?"

He sounded gentle, concerned. "You'll be transferring to a ship built for you." He helped me stand and massaged my shoulders a little, as if he were a Keeper. I stretched, drank a bulb of water that he brought me, and washed my face.

The door opened onto the ship's hallway. "Hurry!"

My nameless helper pulled me through an airlock into the docking hold of the station, down a long branching tunnel, and then a cargo airlock.

On the other side, a few hallways and turns led to a large open space with decorative perch-trees that also served as scaffolds for flowers and tomatoes. Tsawo flew from the edge of the lock to a seat on a branch near the center of the ship. We joined him, except for Jagruti, who sat cross-legged on the edge of the airlock, apparently not caring that she couldn't follow us.

As soon as Marti and I found seats, Tsawo told us, "We're on the *Sky Anvil.* Two ships just took off from the surface and one from another station, hoping to stop us. We'll leave as soon as the *Anvil* finishes prep. Twenty minutes."

I told him, "I like the name."

He laughed. "Follow me. I'll take you to your rooms."

Clearly he'd been here before. That raised a number of questions, but I kept them to myself.

When I looked back, Jagruti was gone.

My room looked large for a spaceship. My boxes were already stored in a locker. The corner held a … bubble. A crash couch like the one I'd just been in nestled inside the bubble, with padded supports that would cushion my wings during acceleration thrust. There were also tubes and a mask and a few other things I didn't recognize. "Is that a crash couch built for fliers?"

"I'll help you into it."

It held my wings the way the scaffolds in the hospital had. My stomach and legs strapped to the bench with fastenings I could reach. "Under thrust," he said, "your hands rest here." He took one of my arms and showed me how to turn it, exactly how to lay the hand down. "It's important that you get it right. Can you do it?"

I showed him.

"Okay. Wear this." He lifted a mask and slipped it over my face. "This is how you will breathe. If you take the mask off, you will suffocate within an hour. The couches had to be made airtight to protect them well enough to guarantee you won't lose your wings the first time we go over two G's. The whole bubble will be protected. So you have two layers of protection for everything except your wings, and they have one. Stay here until I come for you. If you feel the *Anvil* jerk, that will be evasive maneuvers. Stay put. You'll be okay if the ship is okay."

"All right."

He hurried from the room. He must have barely had time to climb into his own crash bubble, since I felt the weight of thrust shortly afterward.

Then the *Anvil* jerked sideways.

31

ALICIA

The *Sky Anvil* stopped twitching shortly after she got underway, although she kept thrusting for distance for at least a day. The mask let me breathe easily, and there was water to drink. More than water, based on the tinny taste and slight thickness in my mouth.

When the thrust stopped, Tsawo and the same man who had helped me between ships came to pull me out. I nearly fell from the bubble. My cheeks hurt where the edge of the mask had dug indents in my skin.

"That was close, wasn't it?" I asked.

Tsawo said, "Yes. We're safe for now. The Wingmakers have repudiated us, and the fleet from Silver's Home knows we're coming. They probably all know we're coming." He smiled wryly. "I'm not sure if they care, but they know."

"Joseph knows?"

Tsawo shrugged. "The admirals know. It will probably be in the fleet feeds. But I haven't requested any special message be sent to Joseph."

"Can we?"

He frowned. "I'd like more information first." His frown turned to a forced smile. "It might not be smart to call attention to Joseph."

Questions tumbled out of my mouth. "When can we all meet up? What happened in Oshai? How did Marti get here? Did Amalo mind?"

He held up his hand. "I'll see you in the comm room in an hour." He gestured toward the man who had helped me on the other ship. "This is Anak. He will help you."

None of my Keepers had been men.

As if he read my thought, he said, "There are no Keepers assigned to fliers here, but there are two people, Anak and his brother Tanti, who will teach you what you need to know to take care of yourself. We'll groom each other's wings."

Oh. "Okay."

It felt like heaven to be clean. After the sponge bath, Anak led me to the *Anvil's* Command Room. It had stations for ten or so fliers, and room to actually fly, up and around in circles. Marti was demonstrating, doing basic flight maneuvers like simple loops in space that made them look dramatic.

Good. We could fly in the wide corridor of tree-perches as well.

The *Anvil* was truly huge.

Two of the stations were manned by fliers I had never seen before. A man had deep navy wings with white tips, and the other was of indeterminate sex from here, with wings the color of the summer sun.

Tsawo pointed at them. "That's our pilot and co-pilot."

"Don't pilots have to be Wind Readers?"

"They are."

And they must be good to fly a ship like this. "Since when do fliers Read the Wind?"

He gave me a serious, deadpan look. "Since we Made them."

"You're kidding?"

He grinned. "It was necessary. Chance helped."

Tsawo was starting to remind me of a ten-year-old boy showing off a science project. He pointed toward human-sized desks at floor-level. "Those are for the crew. Some of the weapons are run from here, too."

This had truly been built primarily for fliers. "How many more fliers are there?"

"Half the crew."

And two people designed to help them. "How many is half?"

He shrugged. "I don't know for sure. Between twenty and thirty. There's an almost equal number of humans, and one of the backup pilots is human. For safety.

"For safety?"

"We're more fragile."

Oh. Of course. "Speaking of humans, is Jagruti coming to this meeting?"

Tsawo shook his head. "We took her aboard for her own safety. But she is not one of us. We'll welcome her at the dinner meals, but otherwise she'll be confined to her quarters, the library, and the gym."

I felt lighter hearing it. "That's good. Maybe I'll visit her in a few days."

Tsawo grinned.

"Is this the ship Marcus wanted?"

"We have a fleet of five. I suspect he wanted all five. The *Anvil* is the newest."

"Did we steal her?"

Marti landed near us, listening.

"No. We own her."

"What? *We* own her? *Who is we*?"

"Fliers. All of us. You, too." Tsawo looked quite proud of himself. "This was a trick Amalo pulled off a long time ago. We aren't supposed to be rich, but we are. You saw the operation in the cave? He used a shell company that appeared to be aligned with the Wingmakers to build all of the ships. This one has not yet been turned over to them and won't be now."

I still didn't understand. "So how did you betray us? The Wingmakers never seemed to be in the deal with Marcus, and you promised to join us in the war. Then you betrayed us. But you only had one ship?"

Marti must have seen the anger on my face. "Surely you were on Lopali long enough to learn the many ways the Wingmakers control us there? They were doing the bargaining. Not Tsawo. Not Amalo. Remember, they thought they controlled all five ships."

Tsawo's smile was wide, almost gleeful. "We just explained that we own this one when we started getting it ready to fly yesterday. Given that they just tried to shoot us down, I suspect they weren't expecting that little lesson."

Marti added, "They wanted to trap Marcus on Lopali. Amalo's guess is that they didn't think he would succeed, and it would keep him out of the war."

An anger which had been tied up tight inside me began to unravel, and a different anger crept in to replace it. I swallowed, looked at Tsawo, and told him, "I'm sorry. I've been mad at you since they left. I shouldn't have been."

He nodded. "I couldn't tell you."

"I understand." I did. They had been saving themselves long before Marcus and Joseph came to save them. "I kind of ... I think I'm a little happy that Marcus was wrong. You didn't need him."

Marti was close enough to reach for my hand. "We did. We could not have done the Making. Remember two things: No one thing will free us, and we're not free yet."

I stared at what I suspected was the front of the ship, toward the war we were heading directly into. "Not yet," I said. "Not yet."

32

JOSEPH

Jenna and Ming swept into the room dressed in simple dark clothes with their dark hair caught back and up, illuminating the difference between Jenna's angular face and Ming's slightly elfin look. Jenna moved with the wary grace of a predator, and by the time she reached the table she appeared to have decided on strategy, assessed dangers, and identified exit points. Ming walked in with precise steps, an erect carriage, and a directness that put her at the table a moment before Jenna.

As they stood in front of me, Jenna narrowed her eyes, something in her look reminding me of how she had protected us on Fremont. Her voice was measured and a little cool. "That's a Master's uniform."

They might not even know. Marcus had been gone forever to me, since each hour that had passed took a year, but it hadn't been a full day.

Marcus had been at least a mentor to Ming. A teacher once. Maybe a lover. Jenna was certainly his lover, and more. She and Marcus were often together, holding hands, drinking and playing games, lifting weights. Her face and stance reminded me of a fighter bracing for a blow.

Pain caught in my throat, and when they came out, my words were knives. "Marcus's ship blew up."

Ming gasped. Jenna flinched and then stood straight, looking as feral as she had in her one-armed days on Fremont.

I continued as soon as I thought they could hear me again. "The *Opportunity* is sending a small ship here. Rumors suggest that they intend to arrest me. I need you by my side as we tell them they cannot do that."

Jenna gave me a look full of questions.

"I saw him die."

Neither of them said a thing. I spoke. "Thank you for coming."

"Of course," Jenna's voice quivered. Even though she gave no outward sign, I felt her anger and loss match mine. But then, I knew Jenna very, very well.

Ming never lost her composure, and didn't do it now, either. She kept her eyes fixed on the doorway. Serious.

Captain Hill directed them to chairs close to us, on the other side of two strongs that bulked beside us.

A monitor screen showed two uniformed junior officers from the *Thorn* leading the delegation from *Opportunity*. Two strongs in *Opportunity* uniforms flanked a tall man with bright red hair and two other less noticeable people, one man and one woman.

I closed my eyes and allowed the slightest brush with ship's data. At least one was a Wind Reader. No, two. One of the strongs as well.

I had hoped for low-level uniformed thugs like the first boarding crew that we had encountered, but these were officers. I couldn't see all the ranks, but there were many bars and significant-looking insignia.

Before they arrived, the ship's AI spoke quietly into the room, calm words that caught everyone's attention. "There are ten small ships close enough to board. Three will land shortly. These are from the *Highline*, the *Black Star*, and the *Unicorn*."

A small smile touched Captain Hill's lips. Our invited guests, then. "And the other ships outside are all from *Opportunity*, right?" she asked the AI.

"Yes."

"If any of the small ships from *Opportunity* boards without permission, take the crew to battle attention. Invite the three who have hailed to board. Have Julianna escort them here as soon as they arrive."

Even though I needed to stay present in the room, I kept a soft hold on just enough data to watch Kayleen or the ships outside.

So far, the foreign Wind Readers weren't trying to read the *Thorn*.

The captain and I stood as the door opened. The crew around our table stood with us. Julianna led the delegation into the room. I knew the man who stood in front. Red hair. Blue eyes. A stiff demeanor. Lukas had tried to conscript me into the Port Authority the day I'd landed the *New Making* illegally at Li Spaceport. Ming had been there then, standing behind Lukas and protecting him.

Had he ordered Marcus's death? Or was he simply taking advantage of it?

Lukas gave no sign that he saw Ming, or that he recognized her if he did. But he did glance at me and narrow his eyes briefly before addressing Captain Hill. "Thank you for welcoming me on board your ship."

The captain inclined her head, but gave no other sign of welcome.

"I'm pleased that you have made this job easy for me."

She raised an eyebrow. "Surely you know we are in mourning for our Master, who was just lost in an accident in space."

He bowed lightly, the gesture far more a formality than a mark of respect. "I forget my manners. I am sorry for your loss." His words were cold and clipped. "I will complete my business as quickly as possible, and I will leave you alone."

"Very well. Tell us what you need."

He turned to me. "Joseph Lee. I have orders to place you under arrest and take you into my custody. This is for fleeing Silver's Home against our direct orders, and for leaving when I forbade it."

He had chosen the word "I," made this personal. I swallowed, forced myself to stay calm.

Marcus had never been outwardly worried about the Port Authority. I'd best try to at least sound as confident as he had when speaking to authority. "The flight was cleared, and we left from a private port. I left legally and anticipate that when the war is over, I will be welcome to return to Silver's Home as a resident."

Lukas continued as if I hadn't spoken at all. "Additionally, you are also under arrest for war crimes. It is illegal to use your powers as a Wind Reader and a Maker against a foreign power. You acted aggressively against a ship from Islas, causing death."

A ghost of the old and deep guilt crept up my spine for a moment, cold and cruel. But I had seen so many of our people die before I'd killed any of our enemies. "I defended my family."

Jenna spoke up, her voice a low snarl. "The Star Mercenaries broke the rules of engagement long before we did by using nanotechnology weapons. They murdered our people by eating their blood vessels from their feet up. They tried to poison our water."

Lukas raised an eyebrow at her. "Our? Did they kill us?"

"They killed innocents. They killed people Joseph saw as family."

"The same people who tried to kill you?"

"Don't oversimplify," she snapped. "This isn't about who the damned Islans killed. You want to control all of the strongest Wind Readers. You were afraid of Marcus's powers, and you're almost as afraid of Joseph."

Lukas flinched, then recovered, a sign that her words had hit a nerve. "Joseph Lee, you destroyed a ship on Fremont with the powers of your mind." He paused for effect, looked over the captain. "Only the powers of your mind. You turned the skills of a powerful Maker into those of a Destroyer. This was an illegal use of force, and you are a subject of Silver's Home and will answer for violating her laws."

I was still trying to absorb the word *destroyer* when Captain Hill said, "This is all very entertaining, Lukas Poul, but you forget yourself. As captain, I welcome you aboard the *Maker's Thorn*, and Master Joseph Lee, who is our owner and Master in truth and name, and registered in those roles, welcomes you aboard as well."

Lukas's mouth thinned into a red line and his eyes narrowed. "The *Thorn* can't be in his control. He's a child."

I stiffened. Maybe I had lived barely twenty-some years, and maybe he had lived hundreds, but I hadn't been a child since Steven and Therese died years ago on Fremont.

"It can be owned by anyone," Captain Hill said. "That is the power of *our* independence and *our* right of choice. You can't arrest the

Master of a volunteer ship unless he commits a crime while he is serving under your contract." I almost imagined her laughing inside as she said that last bit.

Captain Hill stood just enough taller than Lukas for the difference to be obvious. She wore her rank well and spoke with all of its authority. "The *Maker's Thorn* is serving at the behest of the Navy and the Port Authority, but that does not give you the right to assign crew or to take Master Lee's ownership from him. You may order the *Thorn* to fight alongside you and tell us when and where. Out here, your jurisdiction is limited by the agreements we made before we came to fight for you."

The edges of Lukas's lips curled into a brief, snide smile.

I couldn't hide behind the captain. I spoke loudly. "I *am* the owner and Master of this ship, Lukas Poul, and I will gracefully accept appropriate orders that fit the capabilities of the *Maker's Thorn* if this war comes to physical conflict."

"The fleets are not moving all this way to stare at each other," he said. "It will be a war, and we will need to have seasoned veterans on board all ships."

"Most of *us* have never seen war," the captain snapped.

"I have," I said. "We were attacked by Star Mercenaries on Fremont and many of us died. We defended ourselves successfully. My family and friends who are with me have seen battle." I took a deep breath. "There may be more seasoned veterans on the *Thorn* than on the *Opportunity*."

Lukas smiled coldly. "You broke the law during the one small skirmish that you were part of, on a small planet far, far away and not under the protection of this system. You may have caused this war."

Jenna looked at Lukas the way one might look at a child having a temper tantrum. "His father might have, although Islas does choose which jobs its mercenaries can take. It's much more likely the Islans used this family to start their war."

Lukas glared at her. Before he could respond, the door opened and Julianna led in a tall gentleman with long grey hair caught back in a ponytail. He was sharp and spare, his cheekbones small shelves in his face and his dark eyes like the black coal of a tightly banked fire.

"Announcing the presence of Master Edward Skulla of the *Unicorn*."

Marcus had admired Skulla. "Welcome," I said. "Thank you for coming."

"You must be Master Lee. I offer you congratulations on your inheritance and condolences for your loss."

"Thank you. I'm pleased to meet you." Hopefully I would have time to talk to him.

The ship's AI spoke quietly via the data streams. *The other small ships from the* Opportunity *are coming closer. Wind Readers are looking for entrance to the ship's data.*

Captain Hill's jaw tightened, a sign that she had heard what I did.

I risked closing my eyes to focus on the data for a short moment. The ships from the *Opportunity* were forming a circle around us. Even if I didn't understand what they wanted to do, I didn't like them in formation.

I stole a second to check on my family. I could sense Lou, but barely. She felt more focused than panicked. But reading a person's mood inside of data is far less of a science than reading the data itself. The longer it took for them to be successful, the less likely we were to pull Kayleen back whole. Kayleen had slipped into wind and air and I wondered if she wished to die.

In the room, Lukas had stepped back and was subvocalizing something.

"Lukas." I waited for him to turn his full attention to me. "Surely there is no need for the *Opportunity*'s small ships to set up a circle around us. I don't plan to go with you, but we will not harm you. We are both bound by oaths."

He stared at me for a long time, and then looked back and forth between me, the captain, and Master Skulla. I could feel his anger and see him trying to control it. He took three additional breaths, and then spoke quietly and firmly. "Ming Li On left our employ illegally. She should return with us."

I glanced at Ming. She had stiffened, but maintained control of her fine features.

Captain Hill looked surprised, but quickly shot back, "She is a valuable crew member aboard the *Maker's Thorn*. We have need of her."

"I believe my authority is sufficient in this matter."

I had no idea. That must have been clear on my face as Captain Skulla offered quiet counsel directly to me. "If Ming is an officer, then it is in our right as Makers to retain her services. If she is not, then Lukas is correct."

I lied through my teeth. "Ming is in charge of our security here. She is a ship's officer."

Captain Hill glanced at me and then looked back at Lukas. "Is there anything else that we can do for you or for the Port Authority at this time?"

This time Lukas glanced toward Master Skulla before he answered, but when he did, he spoke to me. "You have chosen to take on a very big responsibility, Joseph Lee. See that you perform flawlessly, and that you obey us to the tiniest detail. If you use your abilities to destroy without a direct order from the Port Authority, I will make you pay for it."

"And what will happen if I kill at the fleet admiral's command?"

He hesitated, and then snapped, "That will be acceptable."

I swallowed. "Very well. I shall serve the fleet admiral and the Port Authority as well as I can in this battle."

Lukas looked like he wanted to punch me. He leaned in and snapped, "See that you do," glared at Captain Hill, and then he and his retinue left the room.

I held my hand out to Master Skulla. "Thank you. I believe you changed the balance of power for the better."

"Lukas is a dangerous enemy. And you just made him very angry."

I nodded. "He isn't a new enemy."

He laughed, deep and hard, and Captain Hill joined him. When they regained control, he said, "There is no love lost between the Authority and most of us. We value our freedom. The Alliance is made only out of mutual fear of the Islans."

"Marcus told me a little about that, but some of the ships, like the *Black Star*, seem quite invested in going to war."

"This war isn't two sides," Master Skulla said. "It's a circle of stupidity."

Jenna laughed bitterly.

Our new friend continued. "Marcus's loss hurts us all more than you can know." He surveyed the room. "Is there someplace we can talk more quietly?"

Captain Hill answered. "The others are arriving now, and they do not all agree with us. Perhaps we can take food and drink all together, and then you can stay for a few moments at the end?"

He smiled. "A plan."

"I want a moment to check on my family." Best to send Jenna to handle the immediate diplomacy; I trusted her the most. "Can Ming escort me to the gathering a bit behind you?"

Captain Hill did not look pleased, but she nodded. "The food is laid out in the small ballroom."

Shortly, the big conference room was empty of everyone except me and Ming. I watched for a moment as she unwound herself from her chair and stood nearby, her face becoming slowly less guarded. She flexed her hands, her nails turning to small knives, which she admired. "I never liked Lukas," she said.

"Me either."

"Thank you." She curled her hands closed again and took the chair next to me, close enough for me to smell her minty perfume. Her features were small and precise, every part of her muscle and grace. She had joined us during the same event Lukas had cited first, when we'd left Silver's Home to retrieve Chelo. "Why did you leave Lopali with us?"

"I was a student of Marcus's once."

I sighed. "Like everyone else on Silver's Home."

"And *you* are his best and brightest, the one he believed would carry on his legacy."

"What do you think that is?" I asked.

She frowned. "Don't you know?"

I laughed. "I'm supposed to bring world peace, to change the way both Silver's Home and Islas thinks, and to free the fliers of Fremont. I'm sure there are a few things I'm missing." My hands shook. The adrenaline from chasing Kayleen had been followed by the shock of seeing Lukas and becoming the *Thorn*'s Master.

Ming whispered, "At the heart of it, Marcus was teaching us to be responsible."

"Perhaps. Will you watch over me for a few moments while I check on things?"

"Am I really your head of security?"

"Personal security. I can't speak for Captain Hill about the security of the ship."

"Then can I be your personal bodyguard from time to time?"

I startled at that. Marcus had never needed one. But we would be in actual combat soon. That was the truest thing Lukas had said. "When I need one. If I need one."

"You will."

"I'll see that you are listed as a ship's officer."

"Thank you."

If I weren't tired and sore and overwhelmed, I could have remained aware of Ming and gone deep into the data all at once, keeping split focus. I looked at her, sitting with her dancer's legs and perpetual wry look, and asked, "I can trust you, right?"

"Why do you doubt it?"

"You used to work for the Port Authority. I need to know you don't support them now."

Her lips thinned, and she stared at her fingertips, the ones she could turn to knives. "I could never say that. You, too, must support the Authority. You are going to fight for them."

I swallowed. "I am. But I can't be caught by them. If Lukas or people like him limit me, I won't be able to become what Marcus wants me to."

"You're safe with me."

She looked sincere. I braced my feet against a table leg and slumped in my chair and closed my eyes.

The room disappeared as I fell deep into the ship's data, noting the passage of the ships from *Opportunity* as they left.

33
CHELO

Sasha lay in the corner of the room, twitching softly in her dreams. Small yips floated from her from time to time, barely louder than a whisper. I wished Caro would do as much, or Kayleen, or even Lou. All three of them were so still that I suspected their very souls had left their bodies and travelled somewhere else.

At least they still breathed.

Jherrel lay asleep on my lap, his limbs soft and awkward. I stroked his slightly sweaty skin, offering him comfort.

"We should put him to bed," Liam said.

I nodded.

"After, why don't you go see Mohami? He always helps you feel better."

"Maybe." I carried Jherrel to his bed, lingering to feel his velvety cheek and brush his tiny forehead with a kiss. Then I went to find Kayleen's mom.

Paloma stood in a small office, her back to me, staring at a star chart projected on the wall in front of her. Her grey hair hung loose down her back, and she wore a simple white shirt over drawstring pants and comfortable shoes. She was a miracle; even though she never spent a moment trying to look pretty, beauty seemed to surround her, and grace. I hated to disturb her with bad news, so I stopped in the doorway for a moment, just watching. "What do you see there?"

"I know about Marcus," she said without turning around.

"How did you find out?"

"Jenna messaged me. How is Joseph?"

"I don't know. Kayleen needs you."

She turned to face me, her eyes red from crying. "So she went away again." A statement. She started flipping lights and displays off, putting the room away neatly, her movements studied.

"Caro is with her, and Lou. And us. But Liam needs a break. Can you watch Kayleen?"

"Yes."

"I'm going to find Tiala, too, in case you need a runner."

"Jenna?"

"Is with Joseph, who is helping the captain." I couldn't repeat the threat to her; it seemed like just too much.

Paloma looked around the room once more and picked up her bag. "Where is she?"

"In her room."

"I'll be there in five."

She passed me with explicit grace, her head bowed.

I found Tiala alone in a game room watching three virtual armies with men the size of fingers trying to take a five-foot tall castle. She turned, staring at me for a long time. "Jenna is with Joseph."

"I know. Can you come with me?"

The figures froze in mid-battle, then winked out. "Of course."

Liam looked up when we came in, eyes wide.

"Come on," I told him. "Time to move. Paloma is on her way, and Tiala will come get us if anything changes."

He stared at Kayleen and Caro. "I don't want to leave them."

I loved him so much. And he needed to move. "Me either. But I don't want to be alone, and I need exercise." It truly would break my heart to just stare at them much longer. He must feel it, too. "Maybe Mohami has a secret for dealing with Wind Burned minds."

He stared from Kayleen to me and back again.

"Go on." Paloma came through the door, carrying an extra blanket. "I'm here."

Liam hesitated for another moment, but when I held my hand out, he took it with fingers like ice.

We found Mohami and Kala together in one of the galleys, studying a tangle of circles and lines covered with words and displayed on a wall. Mohami turned to face me and stopped. Perhaps the dread I felt showed. He gathered me into his arms, and I breathed in the smells of incense and calm.

After I felt like I could talk, I told him about Marcus's death, Kayleen's collapse, and how Caro and Lou had gone out in the data fields to try and gather her back into herself.

We all sat, and Mohami held out his arms and let me sit inside the circle of them while I clutched Liam's hand.

Mohami spoke to Liam. "You don't know how long it will take for Kayleen to come back?"

Bless him—he hadn't said *if.*

Liam said, "We don't."

"Well then, perhaps you can help us for a while."

Bless Mohami for knowing I needed touch and Liam needed work. He gestured toward the convoluted drawing. "We're trying to track values across the ships we know about so far."

"Values?" Liam asked.

"Yes. We're trying to separate belief from value. Belief can be changed. When pilgrims came to us in Oshai, we helped them strip away beliefs they no longer needed."

"That would have been a handy trick back home," Liam mused. "We could have given people a belief that we weren't dangerous."

Mohami smiled. "It's very hard to shift a belief that makes us feel good. We keep those even when they hurt us. But we can shatter a false belief with experiences that break expectations."

"Like the morning flight?"

Kala spoke for the first time since we'd come in. "The morning flight strikes people dumb with its beauty and precision. It's like a triple rainbow. A thing so full of grace that you can't pull your eyes away from it. When pilgrims start every day struck dumb with impossible beauty, they have an easier time shedding uglier beliefs later."

Mohami went on. "That helps with beliefs. For example, if you only see fliers walking, you believe they are ugly. But if you see them fly, you know that your belief was wrong." He studied Liam. "Values go deeper. You value family very genuinely. I suspect it would be hard to teach you not to."

"You couldn't."

"Our usual methods could not, anyway. Wars are fought over values or over fears, or both. Value conflicts start wars, and fear fans the conflict until it blows into hatred. People who start wars always say they are about resources, or about fairness, but really they are about values.

"Silver's Home values the ability to create whatever it wants; its economy is built on that. Islas values order and sees beauty in tight control."

Mohami moved me gently away from him and stood, pointing at the diagram. "The authorities on Silver's Home say they value independence, so we have a bubble for that. But we also know they value credit and power. We have bubbles for those things. Not all values are even things that people or governments or affinity groups will admit to. That adds complexity."

His words surprised me. I asked, "Are you saying Islas and Silver's Home are fighting over something so buried that they don't see it?"

Mohami pointed at another circle. "Marcus valued independence, but he specifically hated concentrated power. Islas values power over its economy, its education, its people's available choices. So, people like Marcus and people from Silver's Home value independence enough to both fear Islas. But people like Marcus also dislike the way Silver's Home is run."

"We know most of that," I observed.

"Of course we do," Mohami said. "But if we want the Doctrine to spread, we need to be sure we align it with values and sell it based on values. We need to make sure that we don't try to tell an Islan that the Doctrine requires complete freedom for all. It is a middle way."

"Dianne would buy that."

"Are you sure? You heard her story. She went from Islas to Marcus, so she changed who she took her orders from. But is she as independent as you or Jenna?"

I didn't have to think very hard for that answer. "No."

Liam looked thoughtful. "That's how my father led. He understood his people, and he treated some differently than others. Not better. Different. His band ran far better than the other roamer band."

Mohami smiled. "Let's look at the way these value systems function on the *Thorn*, and then move out to the other ships. I think we've got it mapped out well enough, but two extra sets of eyes would help."

Liam glanced toward the door, but Tiala wasn't coming through it right then to get us.

"We'll help," I said.

Even though I suspected we were interrupting them, I fell into the process. Mohami was good enough to ask us both deep questions designed to make us feel like we mattered, even though we only suggested small changes in the data. Seeing how it all mapped out fascinated me. The value bubbles helped me understand how our Port Authority and the Islan Navy shared more than it seemed. They both wanted to fight. The Port Authority was slightly more interested in the safety of Silver's Home than the Navy was in defending Islas, but then it had more planetary defenses. Neither was likely to become a hotbed of believers in the Doctrine of New Making. But among the civilian ships, there were some possibilities, and even some converts.

Lopali may have refused to provide us the help we had expected—ships and fighters—but perhaps they had given us something of even more value in Mohami.

Did Tsawo send Mohami to make up for betraying us?

34
JOSEPH

I fell into the data, searching for Lou or Caro, for threads to Kayleen. Perhaps I was too exhausted to find them. My brain kept conjuring pictures of Marcus's ship blowing up, of Lukas racing after me, of Captain Hill as a great savior, of the fleets coming closer and closer together, bristling with weapons and impending death. I passed out into an unwanted and fretful sleep.

A hand on my shoulder and then my cheek drew me to sit up. I blinked, then remembered the circumstances that had left me alone with Ming in the uncomfortable chair with my head on the table.

Ming whispered, "I think you need to go see the captains and masters. It has been almost an hour."

I owed Captain Hill far better than that. So much lost time! "Do I look presentable?"

"You look like your father just died and you haven't slept in six days."

"Half right. I did sleep last night. Is there a sink?"

I splashed water on my face and stuck it in front of a dryer meant for hands.

"That's a little better." Her expression suggested I still looked like I'd been asleep on a desk.

In the ballroom, three men and Captain Hill stood around a nearly empty sideboard. Others, including the strongs and Jenna, stood in conversational groups. Ming went to Jenna's side. A page refreshed the table, his movements filling the room with the heady scent of fresh col, the sweet underlying tones of fruit from the gardens, and bread, hot from the ovens.

The smell of food soured my stomach.

I winced as Captain Hill frowned at me, a clear reproach for being gone for so long in her eyes. I gave her a little bow, maybe born out of my grief and lack of sleep. "I apologize for being tardy. I was busy trying to solve a family emergency."

She softened a little. "Were you able to make progress?"

I shook my head. "I'll have to return to it after this. I've met Master Skulla. Would you please introduce me to our other two guests?"

She nodded at a man in a perfect uniform with a matte-black star insignia on the pocket. "This is Sant Robert, Captain of the *Black Star*."

"Pleased to meet you," he said.

Every starship captain is also a Wind Reader. A strong one. He had short-cut hair almost as black as his uniform and a square face with frown lines surrounding his mouth. His handshake was sharp and fast. I sensed he wouldn't be a good friend, but would be a worse enemy.

Captain Zusak from the *Highline* stood tall and thin, with sandy hair and a freckled nose that hung over pale, thin lips. His pastel blue eyes looked almost white when he turned his face toward bright light.

Master Skulla did not seem like a Wind Reader, but then a Master wouldn't have to be. I wasn't sure, though. Maybe he could shield well enough to hide his abilities from me.

Ming brought me a cup of col and a piece of bread and told me to eat in no uncertain terms. I glanced toward Jenna, who seemed to have put her up to it, and raised the cup of col up and then to my lips. The entire cup barely scraped the edge of exhaustion from me.

The conversation drifted to Marcus. After condolences went around, each man said something about him. Captains Zusak and Robert had platitudes and stories about his skill, but nothing truly personal to say. I thought of Akashi, now long lost to me. He would have said they spoke with no heart.

Master Skulla raised a glass, "To the best and most interesting Maker to have ever lived."

I blinked back a tear.

Sweet lemon-cream pies were served and eaten, the talk small and awkward. I managed to circulate past Jenna and to ask her to check on Kayleen. I had to explain, so here was yet another worry for her. She hurried off, and I imagined she must be glad for even a moment of time alone to soak in Marcus's loss. At least I had stayed out in the stars and *felt* for a while. She'd been on display ever since I'd told her.

I had made so many mistakes today.

After twenty awkward moments, Captain Hill asked Master Skulla if he would stay for a few moments, and he nodded. The others gathered their things, looking relieved.

Marcus would have done something useful. I should at least try. I held my hand out to Captain Robert. "Thank you for coming," I said. "It's good to have support in our time of need."

He took my hand hard enough to flatten my fingers and send a spear of pain up my arm. "My pleasure. We'd like to have you visit in a few days."

"I'm sure I'd like that." Although I certainly shouldn't go and wouldn't like it. "But it may not be immediately. There will be a lot to take care of here for a while."

When I shook Captain Zusak's boneless hand, he managed soft polite words while looking utterly unimpressed.

When Lin Juong came to escort them back to their ships, the room felt better without them in it.

Master Skulla took a glass of water. "You'll have to do better next time. I understand you are grieving, but starship chess is won with cunning and strength. You showed neither, in spite of all the good words Marcus had to say about you."

His words stung. "I will learn." I chose my next words more carefully. "Marcus told me we had good friends on the *Unicorn*."

He laughed. "I knew Marcus for a hundred years. We both loved the idea of screwing with the power structure, and so do many of our friends. He wanted you to lead us, but of course, you're ..." He hesitated. "young. Why did he put such store in you?"

Captain Hill busied herself with the plates of leftover food, rearranging and keeping herself out of the conversation, so I answered honestly. "I don't know."

"Me either." He stopped for a few breaths, examining me like the other captains had, but with more open curiosity than animosity. "Marcus planted what amounts to legends about you throughout the fleet. He said you are stronger than he was, that even the first time he met you he was bested."

"I met him deep in ship's data aboard our family ship on the way into Li spaceport. I was landing without permission, and he was supposed to stop me." I didn't say that I was sure he could have stopped me if he wanted to, or that to the end he had been stronger than me, and more driven.

Marcus had advised me to meet his friends. As much as I wanted to go to Kayleen or to sleep, I couldn't waste this opportunity. "How did you meet him?"

He raised a bulb of deep red wine. "Marcus was a legend before I ever saw him. He taught at Foral University, which is a school for Wind Readers."

I raised my empty cup of col, clinked his wine with it a little too hard. "I've been there."

He smiled. "I was Marcus's student. I have the skill, but only a little, and I don't use it much. Our captain is much stronger."

Apparently every Wind Reader in the known universe had studied with Marcus.

Master Skulla continued. "Marcus also taught us about Making. He was working on that garden of his and had just finished the light-link butterflies. Did you ever see one?"

"Yes."

"Beautiful. Anyway, he talked about responsibility and caring in ways that I liked. Marcus had a sense of morality about him that others don't. Not religion—religious affinity groups have the morals of thieves. Marcus lived a long time, taught a lot of people. Spread common sense and political smarts everywhere he went."

I laughed and reached for more col. "Almost everyone I've met was his student once."

"He was old. I suspect he touched about ten percent of Silver's Home. In another couple of decades we would have been ready to change much there."

"Would have been?"

"The rich and powerful were starting to follow him." He glanced around at the *Thorn* meaningfully. "But you might have noticed a little problem. There's a war in the way."

"What happens to Marcus's plans if Silver's Home wins?"

He walked over to Captain Hill and took a handful of small cookies. "It will be taken as evidence that the current crop of idiots who run the place are right."

Marcus had never been that crass.

He continued. "There used to be a ton of room on the planet and only a few people with real strengths. A few Makers, a few Wind Readers, all of them weaker than Marcus. Many went crazy when they tried to do too much. These were new mods, and the people who got them were, by nature, willing to be stupid. A lot died."

I winced, thinking of Alicia and Kayleen.

"We didn't think very hard about the responsibilities that come with acting like gods."

I spit back some of the Doctrine of New Making at him and then added, "We've got slogans going through most of the ships. My sister spends a ton of time making fliers and setting up ideas. Makers for Creation."

He laughed and then got serious all over again. "That's right. But do you believe it all the way in your bones? Is that what drives you?"

I thought about that. "If I Make anything sentient, I want it to be free."

"But would you die for it? Marcus just did."

I didn't have an answer for him.

He took a step closer to me, kept pressing. "What will happen if the fliers get enough power to break free of their masters? Or the fliers and a few others—they're not the only intelligent race in thrall today. There are predators bred to match the sentience of the hunters on

Water Lily. If we don't fight for the fliers, they will have to. That's another kind of war, and a lot of them would die. They're fragile as hell."

"We were just on Lopali. They didn't seem fragile, and they betrayed us."

"Marcus and I had many long talks about what happened on Lopali. It may be the first sign of the fliers testing their own power."

"They killed my friend, Bryan. He was much stronger than them, and they killed him." Anger flared; I paused to regain control. "And they seem to have stolen my girlfriend. She's trying to earn wings."

"I heard. Marcus didn't think it likely she would help talk sense into them."

"Maybe not." His comment irked me, so I changed the subject. "Is the *Unicorn* on our side?"

"I am. But even the *Thorn* has crew who hold beliefs across the whole spectrum. You should try and befriend the men who were just here." His voice softened. "You've been through a lot. I should go, and you should rest. I'll come back in a few days and start teaching you what I can. For Marcus, the art of persuading people was like breathing. It's possible he was never able to break that down for you."

Chelo and Liam and even Jenna were the leaders of people. I hadn't been designed for that, but here I was. I would need this man's help.

"Thank you," I said. "I look forward to spending time with you."

He stared at me for a long time, still assessing.

I was falling short, maybe very short.

"I will return in three days." His promise sounded like a threat. He stepped away from me, and I breathed deeply.

In that moment, I needed to be with Kayleen. I also wanted my sister, and I wanted to be alone. I wanted them all at once. Master Skulla would come back, and I could solve the problem he represented then. I held out my hand. "I'll see you in three days."

He took my hand and shook it, his grip friendly enough but his face impassive.

What else could he have expected? I'd just lost Marcus, I might lose Kayleen, and I was falling-down tired and heartsore. What I had found to give him was just going to have to be enough.

I already hated the term 'Master.'

Except for the feral look that tainted Jenna's eyes, Tiala was a near carbon-copy of her sister. At the moment, she was concern bundled in black hair and warm arms as she practically caught me reeling in the door, exhausted.

Sasha looked up, tail thumping, but didn't leave her post by Kayleen's side.

Chelo and Liam and Jherrel were nowhere to be seen. "Where's Jenna? I sent her to you."

"She and Paloma are rounding up Chelo and Liam."

"Any change?"

"No. You look like hell. What happened?"

"Nothing good, and nothing that matters more than Kayleen." I glanced toward the bed. I'd been away for hours, but the only one who had shifted even a little was Lou, who now lay with her head on her long arms on the end of the bed. One of her fingers twitched from time to time.

"Lie down," Tiala said. "There's room."

Not really, but I collapsed onto the edge of the bed next to Caro. My eyes closed and refused to open. I surrendered and fell spinning and dizzy into the data streams. I scented Lou because she was steady and heavy. She was also focused far away from me and growing tired.

Sasha curled around my legs, her nose on my knee.

Good girl. Such a comfort. I didn't have the strength to pet her for her help.

Before long, my breathing calmed and my hold on the tenuous world of information split into dreaming.

Marcus had warned me not to sleep unless I fully inhabited my body.

I tried to push up and out. It's a strength thing, a force of will, and usually I could do it easily.

This time, a fog of threads—of information—pulled at me from all directions. The beating heart of the ship's oxygen, the swell and call of her past logs, the libraries of data that belonged to kitchens, to repair bots, to the small ships that rested in the bay.

Maybe it was instinct, but I noted that one or more of these had been disturbed. I couldn't focus down on that, though. The *Thorn*'s weapons systems were even more beautifully complex, and I needed to know them. After all, I was the *Master* of the ship now …

I spluttered and choked, resented being pulled away from the data.

A small foot kicked me in the stomach and again in the upper thigh.

I rolled into it, trapping it, the effort of moving almost impossible, my brain fuzzed between the real and the more real, the physical and the bright, simple world of choices based on rules and math.

Caro bit my ear, and her warm breath tickled it as she whispered, "Come back to us, Uncle Joseph. If you get lost like Momma, I will be too mad to save you."

I opened my eyes. The captain was beautiful, standing there full of her power and yet worried about us all. I wanted to wake up enough to talk to her, to thank her for keeping me from the Port Authority, to apologize for being such an idiot that I hadn't made a good impression on the captains.

It didn't matter what I wanted; there wasn't enough energy in the physical world to pull myself awake. I couldn't even lift my head.

Caro scrambled out from between me and Kayleen, and then a blanket fell over my shoulder.

"Will he be okay?" Caro whispered.

"He's strong," the captain replied.

No, I thought as I drifted. No, I'm not strong enough for all of this. The only man who was strong enough for all of this just died.

35
CHELO

Caro stirred and then stretched her chubby arms up over her head. "I'm hungry."

Liam scooped her up. "Me, too." He gave me a questioning look.

"I'm fine."

They left, and I kept watch. Joseph and Kayleen slumbered side by side. From time to time one or the other of them moved. Sometimes he cried out. When he did, his dog crept up beside him and nuzzled him until he stopped, and afterward, Sasha lay down near his feet again. Kayleen moved less often, and when she did it was languid and soft.

They had slept a full twenty-four hours, and it looked like they were going for another twenty-four. Joseph had woken twice to take care of physical needs, but Kayleen's body didn't seem to need her.

It felt good to have everyone else in the room—even the dog—asleep and dreaming. The ship creaked and moaned all around me, like all starships do. Like a house does, only the inner sounds of a ship are electronic and metallic and cold.

I fretted. When we'd moved Kayleen here, she had been able to walk with Liam on one side and me on the other to support her, but had barely seemed to recognize us. Joseph would be fine, and Caro had looked as much like herself as possible given her mother had been—perhaps still was—in mortal danger. We were so much more fragile in this big world than we had been on Fremont. We'd lost Bryan. Marcus. We kept coming close to losing Kayleen.

It felt like being punched over and over.

That was my job. To lead. Me and Jenna and Liam. We needed to stay strong enough to survive. I took my succor from Mohami, lapping at the well of peace that he offered. He kept me strong. But that was also selfish. Me feeding me. I needed to feed the others.

We were going to have to convince Kayleen that she had to take a real break. To sleep. To stay away from data. To leave managing Caro to Joseph if he could handle it, or to me and Liam and Lou if he couldn't. I walked over and took her hand, which felt slightly cold. Her fingers tightened around mine. I whispered to her. "It will be okay. Stay with us. Stay close."

She let go of my fingers and turned away from me.

An involuntary moan escaped my lips. I sat down on the edge of her bed and stroked her shoulder and rubbed her neck. She felt like butter under my fingers.

Paloma came in and sat down in the chair I had been using. "Any change?"

"Not really. She hasn't shown any sign of real consciousness. I'm worried. What if she left part of herself someplace we can never go?"

Captain Hill poked her head in the door. "Good morning."

"How is your great-grandmother?" I asked her.

"She hasn't woken up. The doctor and the medical robot are arguing about whether or not she's in a coma."

"I'm sorry," Paloma said.

The captain shook her head. "It's okay. The robot is right—she's not in a coma. She's responding to my voice from time to time."

"I'm sorry."

The captain swallowed. "She's strong. She'll be okay."

I didn't tell her she was protesting too much. This was a scary-smart woman. She knew.

"How about Joseph?" she asked. "Is he awake?"

"Yes," he said from across the room, his voice gravelly with sleep.

"Good," she said.

"Is it an emergency?" he mumbled.

She laughed. "Not quite that bad. But if you are awake, I'd like to debrief you on the most recent orders."

Joseph pushed up from the bed with a soft grunt. "Let me eat something."

The captain's smile was so thin I wondered if she had slept. "Of course. I'll meet you both in the war room in twenty minutes. You can bring Sasha."

That didn't seem long enough, but Joseph managed to use the time to down two glasses of water, eat a tube of vitamin paste and a real sandwich, and change into his old captain's coat from the New Making. I hadn't even been sure he still had it. He looked so good I couldn't help but tease him. "Don't you need a Master's Coat now?"

"Let's just call this that, okay? Marcus gave it to me."

"Testy?"

"Sorry. Distracted."

I wondered if he was distracted by the captain, or by all of his worries, or by Kayleen.

Sasha refused to leave Kayleen's side. Given that she was Joseph's furry ghost, I took it as one more bad sign about Kayleen. Before we left, I kissed her and whispered, "I'll be back."

Joseph led me to a room that I'd never seen. I'd been in one like it, back in the cave on Lopali. Every wall was a visual of the fleets—our small group of ships converging on the larger fleet from Silver's Home, the Islan Fleet coming toward us. Ship's outlines ghosted across the walls, flying left to right, followed by statistics about crew and weaponry.

The captain and Joseph shared a somewhat intimate smile as they greeted each other. They weren't lovers. I would have known that. But he was falling into her orbit and she was either attracted to him or felt protective of him or both. I could read him; I couldn't read her.

Perhaps it was harmless; he needed to learn to be a Master and he'd just lost his mentor.

There was genuine disappointment in her voice as she said, "You didn't bring Sasha."

"She wouldn't leave Kayleen."

"I'm sorry."

"So is something different in our orders?" he asked her.

"No. I'll review them with you later today. I needed to get you both in here, where we have extra layers of shielding. I don't want anyone but you two to hear this. Yet."

She and Joseph shared a glance, communicating at a level I couldn't hear.

The walls began to dance with pictures, to zoom in and out, to simulate one type of ship in combat with another and then a different pair.

They could see this without me—read the raw data. They were both Wind Readers. Joseph was one of the most powerful ever seen on Silver's Home, but Captain Hill must have formidable skills for Marcus to have left her in charge of the *Thorn*. So the visual display was all for me.

Apparently, they were waiting for me to say something.

"How certain are you that the fleets will actually engage?"

"Do you remember Lukas?" Joseph asked. "He was here. Tried to arrest me for fighting back on Fremont."

I shivered. He had tried to *buy* Joseph from Jenna once. He had tried to stop Joseph from saving us on Fremont. "But he didn't?"

"He's sure the fleets will engage."

"Lukas is on the *Opportunity*?"

Joseph nodded.

The captain said, "Even if Marcus had lived, the chances of the fleets getting into real combat were good. Now they're better. You two are both trying to stop it, and so are others. Maybe we can gather enough allies to slow it down. Maybe we can't even do that."

I had been thinking about this for a long time. "We're trying to make a third idea. That's what the Doctrine is about. Aren't we making a third fleet?"

"That's treason," the captain snapped.

"And who would lead it?" Joseph asked.

"Okay. Don't think of it as a third fleet. Think of it as a third force. Think of it as a counterforce if you will."

The captain had folded her arms across her chest. Her look told me she hated the idea. On the wall behind her, images of huge ships flew by one by one, sometimes two at a time. The Islan ships looked more uniform than ours, much more martial. There was no doubt they were built to fight. Hearts and minds and dreams of glory drove those ships as much as the propellent matter of stars. "We can protect ourselves from our own—I could stop *Opportunity* from boarding us. I can protect us from Islans. But I cannot attack our own. And I cannot disobey a direct order during a battle. I have sworn those things." She looked at Joseph. "You swore those things, too."

"I know. We can't disobey, but if we can change the orders they want to give us? If we can change the fleet's consensus? If we can help them to think differently?"

Bless him. I spoke up. "Right now, fear is driving every one of those ships on the wall behind you."

She shook her head. "No, Chelo. Not fear. Power. They want to tell us what to do."

I thought of Mohami's map of beliefs and values. "Are you saying we want power over them?"

"We don't," she said. "We want them to leave us alone. They're the ones starting this war. We just have to stop them."

"We're afraid of them."

"Aren't we always afraid of our enemies?"

I took a step toward her, made sure Joseph was watching me too. "Is it possible they're coming for us because they're afraid of us?"

She turned around and stared at the images of the Islan ships. They weren't real time, of course. But they were modeled on the real ships; they were what we would face soon.

"And why are they afraid?" I thought of Mohami's exercise. "Because we value different things?"

She shook her head. "I value my skin. But even more, I want the world to be better. I want the fliers to be free. I want a sense of right to come back into what we create. I want us to have integrity. We had that once, and it's all turned to power and credits. To games of politics."

The more time I spent with Captain Hill, the more I liked her. She was wrong … it did matter that the Islans—and us—were driven by fear. It meant we could use Mohami's ideas about values to change things. But Joseph didn't trust Mohami as I did. He had not been with us in Oshai, and he hadn't seen the morning flights.

He had really only seen the betrayals.

I let it go. As Marcus often said, there weren't really just two sides. "We'll join the larger fleet soon."

"I've been dreaming of fighting," Joseph said. "I've dreamed of being on the *Thorn* in battle, but I've also dreamed of me flying some of these other ships. Even a lot of these other ships. The dreams feel so real they almost have to happen. I knew this all the way back on Islas, and the closer we get to the war, the more realistic they seem even in my waking hours." His voice dropped to a whisper. "I don't want these dreams to be real, but I think they must be."

Captain Hill gave him a long, measured look. "That's part of why I brought you here." She glanced at me. "And your sister."

"Because of my dreams?" he asked.

"Because you own more ships than the *Thorn*. And have an interest in even more."

I swallowed. Everything about this week was getting worse. Like a slide down a mountain with a cliff at the edge, and almost nothing left to grab onto but prayers and thorny redberry bushes.

Joseph was not as single-minded in his opinions. When he was a child and all we had was a silver ship that had sat on the plains for so long that it looked derelict, he had drawn it and made stick figures to represent it and hoped and dreamed. And of course, he had eventually flown it.

The captain said, "Let's start with the pieces. There are a hundred and twenty ships aligned with Silver's Home. Seventy of them are owned or completely controlled by the Port Authority. Piloted by Port Authority pilots. There are thirty-one ships that are wholly owned by various powerful space-going affinity groups or—in five rare cases—by individuals. The *Thorn* is one of those five. So is the *Unicorn*."

"Who are the other individual owners?" I asked.

"I'll get to that in a moment." She furrowed her brow. "That leaves fourteen ships that are owned in common by people who share our feelings. The fourteen and the five are all spreading the basic message that you folks further refined as the Doctrine of New Making. It's slightly different on each of the ships, with the same main message. We have been led to believe there is an Islan version as well."

Joseph watched the wall as Captain Hill brought up fourteen ships, all looking slightly different from one another, and over half clearly adapted for war rather than meant for it. No matter what the captain thought, as I looked the fourteen ships, I saw the beginnings of a third fleet.

We stared in silence for a moment, and I kept turning over the implications of a three-way split in power.

"Who owns those?" Joseph asked.

"A coalition. I even have a piece of them. But so do you, now. Marcus passed his part of the ownership to you. Twenty-one percent."

So much? "Out of how many owners?"

"Ten."

I kept drilling her. "Does anyone else own more?"

"No."

I felt as if I'd been punched in the gut. Joseph was the majority owner of fourteen ships and of the one we sat inside right now. "How much do you own?"

"One percent. It was a gift from Marcus, too."

"Just now? A bequest?"

"No." She smiled sadly. "It came through my mother. She and Marcus worked together years ago."

Marcus who knew everyone. "There's more you have to tell us, too." I could feel that in her, that she wasn't done with basic reveal.

"Marcus had ownership—entire—of two other ships. You are the Master of those ships as well, as soon as you say the words for them. They are the *Peacemaker* and the *Sun's Orbit*. They're part of the fleet we'll be catching up to soon." She nodded toward the far wall, where the images of two ships shimmered in silver and gold, brighter than anything else we'd been looking at. They were both bigger than the *Thorn*. The *Sun's Orbit* was a fat ship designed to carry cargo. There were no obvious weapons, but Captain Hill said, "Inside, the *Orbit* is carrying a whole fleet of small ships that have formidable weaponry. Enough for a small Navy."

"Was she built for that?" I asked.

"No. For flying close to stars and collecting data on planets in close-in orbits, such as mining data. She hasn't been used much lately —we've learned to make almost any material out of its raw parts. So Marcus picked her up for a little over the cost of salvage about twenty years ago. He used her to carry cargo between space stations. She's got excellent shielding. Very few of the Islan weapons can penetrate her hull easily."

"And the *Peacemaker*?" Joseph asked, his gaze already directed toward the bigger of the two ships, and the most beautiful of all three. The *Thorn* was a dagger, the *Orbit* a bucket, and the *Peacemaker* a full-scale war machine. She was long and thin, and riddled with what looked like guns and shields and instruments. Perhaps that was a trick of the wall, or the way the captain was showing her off, but I swear she glowed. Everything about her whispered trouble to me, although you'd have thought Joseph was admiring a naked girl.

"How did Marcus end up with that?" he asked.

Good question. We'd always known Marcus had money and power, but this wasn't a casual starship. If there even was such a thing.

The captain laughed. "Someone gave it to him."

"What?" I asked.

"He had … supporters. The Master of the *Peacemaker* died twenty years ago. She willed the ship to Marcus. It wasn't even finished then. But it's all her design."

Marcus had always had a way with people, and particularly with women. Even so, this was hard to take in.

Didn't anyone give away nice little planets, with skies and the heat of the summer sun? That, of course, isn't what I asked. "Didn't Marcus have other heirs?"

"Not that he gave spaceships to." She looked directly at me, and spoke slowly and clearly, as if she thought it would be hard for me to understand. "If anything happens to Joseph, by law, all of this goes to you as long as you are his next of kin."

I had always loved Marcus, always would love Marcus. But this was too much for us, too much for Joseph. If he would have ever been ready for so much, it wouldn't have been now. I was suddenly furious with Marcus for dying.

When I looked over at my brother, tears ran down his face.

36

JOSEPH

Captain Hill left me and Chelo alone in the war room. Chelo came up beside me and I pulled her close, trying to fill some of the empty place where Marcus should be. We stared at images of the *Peacemaker* and the *Sun's Orbit*. I turned them round and round in 3D. This moment felt like the first time Jenna had led us up the ramp into the *New Making*. It would change us forever. Finding Marcus had done that, losing Marcus had done that, and now the gifts he left me had done that, too.

"It's hard to know what to think," I mused.

She whispered, "I'm very, very scared."

Chelo often claimed war followed us. Now we raced toward battle. Toward Islans I might kill. With two ships. No, three. Some of another fourteen. People I was responsible for. Captains I should meet.

Her weight felt like safety. "The *Peacemaker* looks like the ship I've flown in my dreams."

Chelo laughed softly. "I don't know of any mod that helps you tell the future."

"I don't either. But these ships feel like destiny. I'm as scared as you are. But we can't show that."

"I know." She glanced around the room slowly, as if trying to memorize every ship on every wall. "I need to come back here. But we need to go check on Kayleen."

"Your work with the Doctrine matters more than my memories of ships I'll fight in." I turned the walls all off with my mind. A little show of power I didn't need to use, the kind of thing that was merely a brag. Marcus would hate it. But after all the horror of the last few days, it felt good to display a tiny bit of control.

Kayleen lay tangled in her sheets, Sasha lying across her feet, nose on her thigh. Paloma drowsed in her chair.

Sasha came to me and nosed my thigh. "What?" I asked her.

She nosed me, and then Kayleen. "Sasha thinks Kayleen is doing better."

Chelo raised an eyebrow and began sorting the sheets, lifting one white limb after another free. Kayleen's long feet looked funny sticking up in the air. Kayleen the climber.

She wasn't waking up.

"I'll be right back," I whispered. I found Captain Hill with Lou, who was sitting up in bed talking.

"Glad to see you're with us again," I said. "I thought maybe we'd lost you. Can I borrow your wheelchair?"

She arrowed her eyes. "For how long?"

"An hour. Maybe less."

"If you bring me and the captain a glass of col first."

"Are you supposed to talk to your Master that way?" I teased.

"Age over beauty."

"Only since I'm the one asking the favor."

"There is that," she observed.

We wrangled Kayleen into the oversized wheelchair. She moaned and opened her eyes but shut them again. It was enough progress that I felt a bubble of hope light in my chest. "What are we doing?" Chelo asked.

"Giving her a shower."

Chelo raised an eyebrow but didn't argue. We stripped her to her underwear, ran lukewarm water over her, and washed her hair. She put her head down to her knees and mumbled, "You're pulling."

I pulled a little harder. She put a hand up in protest.

"Can you stand up?" I asked her.

She bit her lip, and then leaned her head farther back so I could rinse her hair. It felt good to touch her, to massage her scalp and feel her respond normally.

When I finished rinsing, I held my hand out. "Now can you stand up?"

"If you give me a towel, I might consider it. How long did I sleep? What happened? Did Caro have to bring me back?"

I handed her the towel.

Her eyes rounded as she took it. "Oh—Marcus! Marcus died. That's what happened." She looked at me, her green eyes bright with concern, as if we hadn't all been worrying about whether or not she'd ever wake up. "Did I miss anything else?"

I don't think she understood why I laughed so hard, or why Chelo joined me in laughter until we both almost fell down.

37

ALICIA

A few weeks into the flight, I knocked on Jagruti's door.

When she opened it, surprise bloomed across her face for just a moment, and perhaps pleasure as well. She stepped back and invited me in with a sweeping gesture. Her rooms already felt like the home of a Keeper of the Ways of Lopali: An electric candle burned on a shelf, low instrumental music played, and a thick black rug good for meditation covered the floor.

I chose a pedestal chair with a soft cushion on top and two pegs for flier feet.

"Would you like anything?" she asked.

"Water."

"I have tea."

"Great. Thanks for seeing me." I felt awkward, the roles between us suddenly unclear. Surely she had no power over me now? I took a deep breath. "I hear that I owe you my life. Thank you."

She poured water into self-heating cups. "Mint? Or Green?"

"Mint."

"I couldn't take your life," she said. "Or let them do it. You were right about the lie. They wanted to destroy you for being inconvenient. I couldn't keep working for them after I saw what you showed me."

She paused, took a slow, deep breath. "I did not save your life. You saved mine. How could I be a spiritual leader and lie?"

"That's seems rather common on Lopali."

She winced but didn't add anything

I stepped back, giving her a little room, and made sure she was looking at me. "Thank you."

She chose a soft voice to say, "You're welcome."

Now that I had told her I was grateful, twice, I could leave, except she had just poured us tea. I wanted to flee. But she still knew things I didn't. "Does that connect us? The shared truth that Lopali is a lie?"

She handed me my cup. "Lopali is a great truth. It is what the Wingmakers worked toward. They failed because they chained the fliers, and how can a thing in chains be a truth?" Her voice softened. "They wanted to make the world better."

"Do you really think they believed in the story of Lopali? They used it to get rich while they treated you like a slave as much as they treated fliers like slaves. They used that story to rip the wings from the people they sent to kill Bryan."

Her eyes widened.

"You knew about that, right?"

"I knew they turned them to Keepers. Not that they sent them."

"See?" I said. "Lies."

"Surely they were doing their best."

She wasn't ready to go where I had gone long ago. I blew gently on the surface of the tea. Steam bent away from me and little ripples decorated the hot water.

She continued. "It is not *all* a lie. Travelers to Lopali find peace. Connection brings new, inner power. Healing. The Ways of Lopali create harmony. If you ever get back, ask Matriana and Daniel to tell you their favorite seeker stories. They will tell of enlightenment."

The tea was pale green. It tasted fresh and smelled almost as bracing as good col. "Some fliers don't believe in enlightenment."

She gestured at the *Anvil*'s walls. "Is there truth in this war? Is one side right and the other wrong? Don't they all believe they are right?"

She was still good at trapping me into agreeing with her. I told her, "Yes."

She smiled. "Why did you choose wings?"

"How could I not? But it was for freedom and beauty. Not enlightenment."

"Did you get freedom?"

"When I'm flying."

"Tell me your story. I didn't greet you, Mohami did. I don't know your origin story."

I told her about the statue of the first flier that I had seen, and how the combination of pain and ecstasy on her face made me want to be her.

When I finished, she rinsed her cup and filled it with water and came back to sit. "You are a risk-taker, right?"

"Yes."

"Transforming into a flier was a great risk, right?"

"Yes."

"Was it worth it?"

My answer was instantaneous. "Of course."

"Even though you cannot have children, cannot run, cannot be measured as a full human under the law."

I refused to cringe. "I plan to change the law part."

She looked curious. "Do you miss being human?"

I stiffened. "I'm still human."

"Not in the eyes of many."

Anger curled along my limbs, forced muscles to stand out and my heart to beat faster. "My parents left me behind on a planet that hated me. The roving band of scientists I lived with locked me up when I displayed my abilities, which were *nothing* compared with what I can do now. If they saw me fly, they'd use arrows to pull me down."

She looked at me, swallowed.

I tried to choose words that would scrape the calm off her face. "They weren't my parents, or my foster parents. They were my enemy. They were afraid of everyone like me, or even like you."

"Ah." She paused, finished her water, crossed her legs. "No one who comes to Lopali is afraid of fliers. They want to be you, they want to feel what you feel, they want to grow on the back of your pain.

They want to thank you for what you have gone through and pick your soul apart looking for wisdom. That is not fear."

I hadn't thought of it that way. "But is it truth?"

She looked down at the ground and then up at me. A supplicant more than a teacher. "Can you try not to destroy everything Lopali is, all of the truth of Lopali, when you expose the lie of it?"

I didn't know what to say. I set my cup down on the table. "I don't really know what I'll do."

Her voice was a whisper. "Thank you."

38

CHELO

I rearranged flowers I had already arranged in the room where we would receive Master Skulla of the *Unicorn*. Such pretty things for a spaceship. Their delicate scents lightened my mood. Neither Captain Hill nor Joseph had said anything good about Joseph's performance the previous meeting. But with Marcus gone, we desperately needed friends. It had taken weeks to arrange this meeting, long weeks that we used to study and fret. Long weeks of feeling alone.

Hopefully Master Skulla liked flowers.

Joseph came in with Caro wriggling in his arms. Her dark hair fell in fresh curls around her face. Even in a fancy blue dress, she looked out of place for a formal meeting. I raised an eyebrow at Joseph.

He shrugged. "I wanted to bring Caro or Sasha, and Caro dresses up better. We need to make Skulla smile."

"I was hoping the flowers would do that." I wanted to say so much more, like *Caro should be a secret*, and *Caro might say the wrong thing*, and *What were you thinking?* But I didn't.

Joseph smiled as if he were totally innocent. "Caro asked to come."

"And you always let five-year-olds dictate their own schedule?"

Caro gazed at me with her unique solemnity. "I turned six yesterday."

Joseph and I shared a glance. What an awful parent I had become.

He ruffled her hair and kissed her cheek. "Here's a birthday kiss."

She slid free of him and raced to the far side of the room where she climbed up on a stool to smell the bouquets of flowers.

Joseph watched her, deep fondness on his face. "You must have decimated the gardens."

"This is important."

He hugged me. "Thank you. You've made it look like a party." He leaned down and whispered in my ear. "Caro is less likely to dig around in his data if she's here."

She turned on her stool. "I heard you. *I promised*."

"Yes," he said, smiling at her. "Yes, you did. And I trust you to keep your promise."

"You don't, but I will."

At least they were talking out loud.

A chime notified me that Master Skulla's ship had docked with the *Thorn*. I was out of time to do anything about Caro. She'd just have to behave.

Ten minutes later, Captain Hill brought Master Skulla in, then left, saying, "I've got to attend my shift change meeting."

He stood taller than me by a head, and slender. A long grey ponytail trailed down his back to his hips, tied simply with a red beaded twist at the bottom. It contrasted with his severe black uniform.

We had chosen our everyday uniforms. I cursed myself, made a mental note to dress up next time, and held out my hand. "I'm Chelo Lee, Joseph's older sister and his Deputy Secretary." We had made the title up, and then Joseph had made it real.

Master Skulla's hand felt bone dry and cool, his grip strong but not overbearing. I indicated my brother. "Of course you remember Joseph?"

"Yes." His face gave nothing away, placid and neutral.

They shook hands, each looking friendly and awkward.

I finished the introductions. "And this is Caro, one of the children in our family. She wanted to meet you."

Caro tilted her head up and offered her hand to him.

He looked like he wanted to laugh. He didn't, but he bent down and took her small hand briefly in his long fingers. "Pleased to meet you."

I ushered him and Joseph to a couch and asked Caro to help bring them wine and plates of snacks.

We had rehearsed questions for Joseph to ask. He had spent hours poring over specifications for ships and searching for details about Master Skulla's background. None of that prepared us for when he looked at Joseph and asked, "Why are you here?"

Joseph, of course, blurted out the first thing he thought. "Marcus brought me."

Skulla looked unimpressed. "Why did you come with him?"

"First, he saved me from the Port Authority. Then he saved me from myself."

Joseph fell silent for a moment, and I hoped he was thinking hard. What he'd said so far made him a follower, and Skulla needed to see a leader.

"He taught me that power needs to be used for freedom."

Skulla's frown turned to a slightly curious look. "What does freedom mean to you?"

I thought of four or five good answers. *The ability to choose for oneself. Enough responsibility to help others. Shared rules that people follow out of respect. The end of slavery.* But impressing Skulla was Joseph's job, so I kept my mouth shut and hoped.

My brother leaned back and spoke casually. "Responsible creation. You mentioned you'd seen the light-link butterflies? They are a vastly improved design, and live healthy lives, like regular butterflies. But the fliers? They could have been made more independent and healthier. Marcus and I studied their genetics, and there are flaws built into them *for the express and only purpose of making them controllable*. They could live free. Instead, they are effectively handsome spiritual slaves."

Master Skulla's thin lips twitched into a faint smile.

Joseph added, "We came here from Lopali. The fliers believe the spiritual part. They think they can save the world, even though they're slaves. That feels wrong."

It was an answer skewed for Makers, but a good one.

Master Skulla sipped his wine. "Go on."

Joseph tapped his fingers on the table, hesitated, and then said, "Wouldn't it be more responsible if we required that the freedom to create be combined with a requirement to create *for the good of the created*?" He waited for Skulla to nod. "If I create a shirt and sell it to you, and it falls apart, then it's not really fair, right? But if it's a good deal and I make money and you have a good shirt, you're happy, right?"

Master Skulla again sipped his wine and nodded for Joseph continue.

"But if I modify a sentient being, or make a sentient being from scratch, then I shouldn't be able to sell it, or to own it."

"Then why would you Make it?" Skulla asked.

Joseph leaned back. "I might not. Or maybe I would do it for the love of the art. Or because that being needed to exist. We're not weaker because we don't create a slave."

Caro crept in between the two men and slid onto Joseph's lap. Her presence worried me. So much rested on this meeting, and on Joseph. I could have satisfied the Master's questions more quickly, but it wasn't me who owned three starships—no, warships—and parts of fourteen others. It wasn't me who Marcus wanted this old, canny man to follow. He had to follow Joseph, willingly, and so Joseph had to perform.

My little brother, who had no practice leading men.

Master Skulla changed the subject. "What do you know of war?"

Caro held up her hand.

I held my breath.

Master Skulla looked down at her, his brows drawn together. "Yes?"

"We were all caught. My parents and Joseph and Chelo were left behind on Fremont after the first war, and then, after they got free and flew to Silver's Home, they had to come back because me and my brother Jherrel were caught by Islans. There was a war about that, and Joseph made sure we won."

Wow. I knew she knew both stories, but not that she had put them together.

"How old were you then?" Master Skulla asked Caro.

"I was a baby. I don't remember it."

He smiled at Joseph. "Maybe you can tell me the story."

Joseph had paled; he took a sip of wine.

I handed him a plate full of food, but he set it down. I sat beside him and pulled Caro into my lap.

"You know the war started on Fremont?" Joseph asked.

Master Skulla nodded. "Star Mercenaries. From Islas. They killed some natives."

Joseph managed not to wince.

He chose to tell the story short and straight. "My father sent the mercenaries. He thought we were dead, that the *natives* had killed us." Joseph pointed at himself and at me. "Sending Star Mercenaries back to kill everyone was attempted genocide. The *colonists* had adopted us. Many were our friends and our family. They raised us. So it was utterly unfair when the mercenaries were sent to wipe them from Fremont."

Caro stiffened in my lap.

Joseph looked at her, the two of them clearly sharing a moment of communication.

Master Skulla glanced at her and then back at Joseph. "She's a Wind Reader?"

Joseph nodded as if it were only a small thing, and continued his story, keeping it simple enough for Caro to follow. "My father was sure we'd been killed at the end of the first war for Fremont. His affinity group had left a ship behind on Fremont, the *New Making*. Every day I breathed, I dreamed of flying it to find my parents."

I felt proud of him for keeping it simple.

"I got my dream. I found my father on Silver's Home, just in time to learn he had hired Islan mercenaries to wipe my family from the face of Fremont." He looked at me. "Chelo was there. Liam and Kayleen, Caro's other parents. All in danger because of my father." He swallowed. "He planned genocide. He almost killed his daughter and granddaughter as well."

Caro sat still in my lap. I stroked her stiff back to comfort her.

Master Skulla looked at each of us in turn, clearly assessing. Most disturbing of all, his gaze rested for a long time on Caro. "What happened next?" he prodded.

"My father came back to Fremont with me and a few of our

friends, and we beat the Star Mercenaries."

Skulla's already pallid skin paled further. "Islas didn't send the Star Mercenaries? Your father sent them?"

He had just learned that from us?

Joseph picked up a cracker, twirling it in his fingers. "To avenge us. I didn't know about the babies until I got there. And well, we had to save them. To do that, we had to beat the Star Mercenaries. My father died in that fight." Joseph's face had gone stony. He'd left much out but included the bones of the story. The cracker stayed in his hand, a toy more than food.

Master Skulla sounded incredulous. "People don't just 'beat' Star Mercenaries. Trained soldiers can't do that. How did you?"

Joseph offered up one of the bits he had left out, his voice wooden. "To beat them, I had to control their ships." He paused, looked directly at Master Skulla. "I learned to control Islan ships on Fremont. Smaller than these, of course. But I might be the only Master in this fleet who has ever controlled an Islan ship." He swallowed, stopped, drank some more wine, and finally ate the cracker. I could see the moment he decided to go all-in. "I killed a ship. So I guess I can kill some of these if I have to. But I don't want to. I want to end this without blood."

A long time passed.

Captain Hill came in; I gestured her over with a finger on my lips. I wanted to hear what Skulla said next without an interruption. She nodded and sat quietly.

Skulla took some time to answer, as if he were turning Joseph's words with a spade and checking for worms. "You know most of the crew on most of these ships wants to fight?"

Joseph nodded.

"*Desperately* wants to fight. Credit has been spent to outfit the best warships we've ever seen on these planets. Careers will be made, affinity groups will gain or lose power, Islas itself will gain or lose even more. They are betting their way of life."

Joseph nodded again.

I held my breath.

Caro sat still, her fingers clenched tight on two of mine.

"There will be a fight," Master Skulla said. "Perhaps we can make a peace out of the aftermath, perhaps not. But there will be one hell of a battle."

Joseph blanched. "I know."

All of our lives had been arrowed toward this fight, and we were going to be in it, probably in the next few days. And we weren't ready. I hated it.

Skulla addressed Captain Hill. "I'll tell the others to give Joseph his chance."

The Captain's expression looked lighter than I'd seen it since Marcus had died. She hadn't heard most of what Joseph had said, but Skulla's words apparently buoyed her.

Personally, I found it insulting that he addressed the captain instead of Joseph. But it didn't look like Joseph had the common sense to be disturbed. He had impressed Skulla. But he hadn't made a friend.

Two hours later, the flowers and snacks had all been put away and I'd sent notices to the captains of the *Peacemaker* and the *Sun's Orbit* announcing Joseph's ascension to Master, his promises to follow the fleet admiral's commands, and his directions to his new captains to do so. We also affirmed their contracts, and at my suggestion, added a two percent increase to the entire payroll, as well as a modest one-time bonus to both captains. I'd seen the bank balances, and it seemed a wise expenditure. They needed to go to battle confident.

I had added the same bonuses to the *Thorn*'s payroll.

I went home. It felt like heaven to land on the couch next to Liam and fall into his arms. He looked tired, and I touched his cheek, admired the curve of his lashes. "We missed Caro's birthday."

"Oh, no!"

"She was philosophical about it."

"I'll make her a cake tomorrow," he said. "I'm sure the kitchen staff will help."

"Thanks."

"How did it go?"

"Managing all these ships will be a full-time job. And then some. You should sign on. We need two hands."

"Someone needs to watch the children. Better me than you."

"That might be the harder job." I told him about Caro's turning the conversation, and about her insight, ending with, "I wouldn't have put those things together so succinctly until I was a teenager."

"It's going to be hard to stop her from trying to play war games," he mused.

"Sedatives?"

He knew I didn't mean it, and he told me so by leaning down and kissing me as if we were on our way to bed, sending a thick shudder of desire through me in spite of my tired brain. "Are the kids in bed?"

"Caro went to Lou, and Jherrel has been asleep for an hour."

"Kayleen?"

"I think she's off making protest signs."

I puffed out a breath and climbed out of my comfortable spot to pour us each a bulb of good red wine from Silver's Home. "Can we keep Kayleen happy? Can we even keep her sane?"

He took the bulb from me. "She likes Lou's company. I worry more about Joseph."

He always knew my deepest fears before I did. No wonder I loved him so completely.

Liam nodded, and raised his glass. "Here's to no one, ever, being lonely."

He had the right of it. Joseph was alone. And he'd just become very, very rich. That would make him a target. He was spending more time with Ming, who now ran his security and sometimes stalked the halls beside him as his bodyguard, a job she took quite seriously. I wasn't sure she had any training, but she looked the part. Then there was Captain Hill, who he *almost* seemed to have a crush on. She was probably too smart to fall for her Master, but who knew? He was no boy any more. He was wickedly smart, powerful, and now he was rich.

I looked Liam in the eyes. "I remember when we first left Lopali, and he said he didn't know if he could kill again. He said it might destroy him if he did. In the meeting just now, he told Master Skulla he could destroy Islan ships. What will happen to him if he does?"

39

JOSEPH

I slept drenched in bad dreams and sweat. I chased ships down and *thought* them dead. Lines of data forced me into decision after decision, all deadly choices. I screamed at my sister about leaving politics out of it, swearing at her that hope doesn't stop torpedoes. I twisted in my sheets as ships burst into the light of death over and over, just like Marcus's had, death on death on death, all of it because of things I chose.

I buried my face in the soft fur on the back of Sasha's neck and whispered in her ear, "Does being a Wind Reader give my dreams more reality than anyone else's? Or just more cinematic effects?"

Her answer was to lick my nose with her warm tongue and then get up and ask to go out.

The ship had been modified to create a room with an absorbent surface to handle her urine, so we went with each other to take care of business, then went to the closest galley for col and dog food.

I filled Sasha's bowl and fed her. Halfway through ordering the col, Ming walked in and glared at me. "You're supposed to tell me when you start moving."

She was beautiful and smart, and sometimes funny, and I had become more used to her company as time passed. Still, this morning I wanted to be alone. I took a deep breath. "I need time to think. Can't you just follow me with cameras today?"

Annoyance flickered across her face. "Cameras won't save you from an attack. I can always walk behind you."

I grunted, sat at the bolted-down square table, and took a sip of the bitter brew I'd chosen for this morning. It tasted as bracing and awful as my dreams, perfectly appropriate. Her bowl empty, Sasha leaned against my calves.

Ming chose her own cup, something sweet. "You keep underestimating your value as a target."

"How is that possible? You remind me once a day."

Her lips thinned but she didn't bother to answer my question. Wisely. "You don't have any meetings today."

"The fleets are going to meet in three days. I need to study and see Chelo."

She stepped in front of me, standing while I sat, looking down. "You look terrible. Are you all right?"

"I slept badly." Although it took a great effort, I managed to smile at her. "Look, Ming. I really want to be left alone this morning. I'll meet you for lunch, and you can brief me on the security of the ship."

She wasn't having any of it. "Who can I send with you?"

I hadn't been her boss until just about a week ago. But if my dreams were true, I'd probably either die or kill myself in the next week, and then I wouldn't be her boss anymore. And I hated it, but she was right. I had become a high value target, a rich man with power and spaceships.

How the hell had Marcus been so cavalier about life? He had never seemed weighed down. I had never known how much power or credit he had. Still didn't. Although what he had given me was more than I had thought any one man could own.

I tried for a smile, mostly failed. "Let me have my breakfast, and then I'll decide."

She nodded and sat in the corner, looking more like the impartial bodyguard she said she was, but nonetheless radiating a faint air of feeling miffed. I had been right to save her, but I should have made her something besides my chief of security.

At least I trusted her.

The col helped, and so did thinking of Chelo, who would hate my bad mood. I ate a simple meal of crackers and protein paste. When I finished, I nodded at Ming. "I'm going to find Chelo and Mohami. Coming?"

She smiled and walked two steps behind me all the way to the door of Mohami's small complex of rooms. Her plan seemed to be to follow me in, but I shook my head at her. "Yes, you are my friend and my security chief, but this conversation is private." As soon as I'd said the words, I felt guilty for them, and then thought—again—about how I needed to be more forceful, to lead. The conflict left me unbalanced as I slid through the door and closed it behind me and Sasha.

Mohami's apartments were simple. About thirty people sat or stood in the largest room. Soft rugs softened the floor. Walls held colorful mandalas generated by mathematic equations and printed by our colorful schematic printers. The room could have been in a cave somewhere. Other than the computerized nature of the graphics, it could have existed in any time. The faint scent of a smoky incense completed the illusion.

Mohami sat on a square cushion, smiling and talking animatedly while people listened. I tried to ignore what must be the end of his talk. Chelo, Liam, Caro, and Lou were there. A security person who worked for Ming. Ulrika, my backup pilot. A handful of people I'd seen in uniform around the corridors, although everyone wore civvies here. *Mid-level shipmen*, I thought. A young mechanic I'd interacted with a few times on *Bryan's Hope*.

Mohami ended with "… even in war, there are moments of grace, and out of the pain of fighting we can build those moments. There is power in facing a fight with no fear and no hatred."

The group began to break up and I hung back, suddenly uncertain as to why my dreams had driven me here. Maybe everyone dreamed of war on the way to war. As Mohami's audience passed me by the door, I nodded and smiled, and greeted the few I knew by name.

Chelo smiled at me, approving of my politeness. She had been a pest lately about remembering names and greeting people. She called it acting like a Master.

Had Marcus done all these things Chelo kept insisting I do? I couldn't remember.

Liam clasped me on the shoulder as he went by, struggling with Caro, who obviously wanted to stay. This wouldn't be a good conversation for her. I leaned down and looked in her eyes. "I'll come find you later today if I get time. We can practice."

She nodded, although she still looked reluctant to leave.

Chelo stood beside Mohami, swaying as if she might fall asleep on her feet. She tilted her head and raised a hand, asking me if I wanted her to stay.

I nodded at her. *Stay.*

When we did fight, she would be beside me. I had grown up with her as my strength and my protection, and I would have died more than once if not for her steady presence. I had left her for more than a few days only once in my life, when I first flown the *New Making* to Silver's Home searching for my father. I had begun to miss her the moment we'd lifted off from the grass plains of Fremont, and I hadn't stopped missing her until we'd shared the same planet again.

Chelo's trust in Mohami had drawn me here. Maybe he could help me keep from breaking. I felt unexplainably shy as I addressed him. "Can … can we sit and talk?"

His smile came out as genuine as always. "Of course." He turned to address Kala, the acolyte he'd brought from Lopali. "Would you be so kind?"

Kala nodded and glided away. Her footsteps made no sound at all. She was never far from Mohami and seldom spoke. A pretty enough girl, sturdy and strong, she carried herself in a way that drew little notice.

Mohami sat, gesturing me down to his right and Chelo to his left. Sasha curled in a corner where she could watch us. I didn't wait for Kala's return, but said, "We will be at war soon. I am Master of three warships now, and part-owner of more."

Mohami nodded.

Chelo took my hand in hers, squeezed, let go.

"I will be expected to kill Islans."

Another fact, another nod.

I swallowed. "I did that once. It didn't go well." I paused. "I … you came with us, knowing we were going to war. Even though you always preach peace. Can we talk about that? About why you came?"

Kala glided in with a tray that held four cups of tea, some cookies, a fruit plate, and four small bowls of warm nuts. She took her share and faded back against the wall, almost immediately becoming invisible again. Part of her invisibility was the silent way she moved, and part was that her coloring was all shades of light brown, including her eyes and hair. I realized just then that another reason she seemed invisible was that she seldom met my eyes.

Mohami picked up his teacup, holding it, and Chelo picked up hers, so I picked mine up as well, all three of us holding the tea up, like an offering. Mohami raised his higher. "May we all speak and hear the truth."

Chelo raised hers. "May we all speak and hear the truth."

I did the same, and then Kala whispered the same words from her dark corner.

Mohami sipped and then put his cup down. "Thank you for coming to me." He met my eyes, and I felt like he was looking through mine and into my heart. "We all hope for peace. I hope for peace every day of my life. But I do so inside of a universe that thrives on creative tension."

I nodded. We each ate a few nuts, the noise of my teeth loud in my ears. The music stopped playing and Kala stroked something on the wall to restart it.

Chelo trusted this man. I took a deep breath and spoke. "The coming war is tearing me up inside. My dreams are riddled with fears and battles. The first time I killed people with my mind, it almost killed me to have done it. Not in the moment. In the moment, it felt like being a god. But after? I was physically sick. I wept for days."

Mohami sipped his tea, watching me.

My hand shook, and I gripped my teacup harder.

Chelo touched the back of my free hand. "Go on."

"That was a small ship with only a few people in it. Evil people. They tried to kill me and my family and the people I loved on Fremont. They succeeded in killing some that I loved very much." I held up my hands, picturing the faces of the dead. "The thing is, *I didn't have to kill them*. We'd already won, and it was unlikely that they would have killed anyone else. *So I didn't have to, but I did it anyway.*"

Mohami nodded. "You killed when you think you didn't have to, and it made you feel pain."

I felt like he was addressing a child who'd had a tantrum. "I have a lot of power. Marcus taught me I should use it for good."

Mohami smiled. "Stories say Marcus killed many people during his life."

I nodded. "I know. But I never saw him kill anyone."

Chelo spoke. "Aren't you doing his job now? He would have had to join the fight. He swore oaths. Like you."

"Yes. But he had more control." I turned my attention to Chelo. She had been on that ridge with me in Fremont, after all. "I lost control. I did that in a flick of anger. You saw it. They never had a chance." I looked at her and saw only calm. "Chelo, I'm stronger now. Ten times stronger, maybe more. The work we did on Lopali taught me a lot about focus. Marcus said I'm stronger than him. Other than Caro, I might be the strongest Wind Reader in both fleets." My voice was rising, shaking despite myself. "What if I kill people for no reason except that I can? How do I know what I must do versus what I can do?"

She turned to Mohami.

His hands were clasped in front of his chest, his cup on the ground, his face even calmer than Chelo's. "The people who were just in here? They all feel something like that, even though they will be cogs in a wheel of power that orders the killing. You will issue orders, but you will not make all of the decisions. Those will be made above you."

I nodded, although the words didn't sit well with me. After a moment I understood why. "No one but Marcus knows what I can do. And he's dead. That means I will be the one who chooses, at least at some level."

"Fair. But we are birthing a new world here, and we are doing it through war. This is the human way. Unfortunate. But we often grow and change through conflict."

Chelo's lips thinned, and I suspected there was a counterpoint stuck in her throat. But she kept it in.

Fear riffled through my throat. When I'd first seen this fleet, back in the cave on Lopali, I had known I would join this fight. Now that I was here, the immensity of the fleet and the complexity of the battle soured my stomach.

Mohami spoke. "Joseph."

I looked at him.

"What we can affect is what comes after the fight. You will have to survive it if you want to help on the other side."

I swallowed.

"If you like, come to me in the morning before your first shift starts. We'll spend half an hour a day together on this."

Did I have that much time?

My uncertainty must have shown on my face; Chelo whispered, "It might keep you sane."

I looked back at Mohami. He had left his position as Speaker of the Ways of Lopali—a position of great power—to come here. Maybe I could learn from him. "I will come every morning for a week. Then we should be in battle, and my time may not be available."

Mohami nodded and took a cookie. "Until the battle."

Chelo squeezed my hand and leaned over to kiss my face. She glanced at the tray of cookies. "And since we need time to eat all of those, can I share my latest campaign for positive creation with you?"

Chelo the stubborn. "Of course."

While I was worried about killing people, she was trying to save them from themselves, one at a time.

40
JOSEPH

That afternoon, Chelo, Ming, Captain Hill, and I held the first of a series of planned virtual meetings with the captains of my two new ships.

We started with the *Peacemaker*. Captain Shella Grundson greeted me enthusiastically and showed me around the *Peacemaker* herself, using a drone to video her face and showcase her ship. Nothing appeared out of place. Nothing.

We passed cleaning bots more than once. The hydroponics garden flourished with red tomatoes and perfect green carrot tops, ever-bearing berry bushes, multi-colored pepper bushes, and even edible flowers. Not one dead, dry leaf. "I'd like to visit that garden someday," I told her.

"You will. Marcus designed many of the plants, and his students designed others." Captain Grundson sounded proud of that.

The rest of *Peacemaker* lived up to the hydroponics. Neat repair bays for small ships and bots next to well-organized storage bays for the same. Comfortable crew quarters.

Her weapons were formidable. I suspected that was why, of all three of Marcus's ships—my ships—the *Peacemaker* was closest to the front of the fleet.

After the tour, she gave me a crisp little bow and said, "Thank you for visiting. Perhaps I will meet you in person one day."

"I'd like that." I would, too.

The captain of the *Sun's Orbit,* Li Zhao, called us exactly on time. He sat behind a desk with the ship's sigil behind him, a stylized sun with an arrow-shaped spacecraft flying in front of it. He'd been a ship's captain for twenty-five years, and the *Orbit's* captain for fifteen. He'd overseen her retrofit from a cargo ship into a carrier. I glanced down at the summary on my monitor. He and Marcus had worked for the Port Authority on Silver's Home together almost forty years ago.

If Marcus's death had shaken him, it didn't show. In fact, no emotion showed on his broad, unlined face as he said, "I'm sorry for your loss, and wish to congratulate you on your inheritance."

I swallowed, suddenly worried. Captain Grundson had immediately deferred to me, but I sensed a need to convince Li Zhao that I had authority. "Thank you for your kind words. Marcus left notes that said he considered you very capable."

Still no reaction.

"I'm honored to have you working for me." I meant it as a polite force.

I detected the slightest stiffening. A pause.

Chelo touched my back, telling me to stand straight.

Li Zhao waited a while before he said, "I trust Marcus's judgment."

"Good enough." That was what we were both doing.

"I'd like to introduce you to someone who will give you a tour of the fighting ships and small arms in the *Orbit's* hold."

A second man stepped forward, younger and broader. Even though he clasped his hands behind his back and stared evenly at the camera, he appeared more casual than his captain, more comfortable in his skin. Li Zhao lifted a hand toward him. "This is my Second. He will lead the fleet we carry inside of our belly when we fight, while I command the *Orbit* herself. Cy Littleton."

Cy's broad, easy smile filled his whole face beneath close-cropped, deep red hair accented by a tight-fitting blue uniform. I had studied him even more closely than Zhao. Cy was a Wind Reader who had taken on many of the characteristics of a strong. He was rumored to have a side hobby of physical fights he usually won. "Pleased to meet you," he said. "I understand you and I share some abilities."

I smiled back, hoping my smile looked as friendly. "I think we do. I look forward to meeting you some day."

Captain Zhao drew my attention back to him. "I've asked Cy to give you a tour of the *Orbit's* holds. He's got live camera implants, and also has a few videos to show you. I understand we have an hour?"

I sensed Captain Zhao withholding something but chose not to press him. Perhaps Cy would show it to me. "I'm ready when you are," I said.

Li Zhao nodded, and a faint smile touched his lips. He addressed Captain Hill. "Shall we talk in another room?"

"I'll transfer you to my office."

"Thank you."

Captain Hill turned to leave. We had known how the meeting would be choreographed, and I had expected to want to go with her. But I didn't.

Cy turned. A faint click came across the speaker. The viewscreen filled with an expansive view of an open space so big that the entire *Thorn* would probably fit inside it. Ships rested in berths all around the edges. Three larger ships were clamped carefully in the open space, near the top. Lights moved here and there, probably robots or transportation of some kind. It looked clean, industrial, and far larger than I'd expected.

Chelo took my hand, perhaps also a little awed. She leaned in, peering at the ships. "The one in the middle? That's big, isn't it?"

Although we could no longer see his face, I heard approval in Cy's voice. "It's special. We'll get there." He stepped into a small space with metal walls and small, rounded windows. The view smeared and then settled as he sat in a small craft, which he piloted. He pointed out several small fighters. "Intelligence says Islas has similar small fleets. We're trying to place the *Orbit* in position to neutralize those."

Fleets within fleets.

Because the cameras were basically near his eyes, watching the screen felt like being in a child's first-person game experience, and I felt dizzy as he pointed. "The ships on that wall might carry bombs to other ships. Some are manned, but most aren't. Over half the fleet is fully autonomous, so we won't be losing pilots every time we lose a ship."

"That's good." When I glanced at Chelo I could tell she approved.

By the time he docked with the large ship in the middle, I had decided that he was hyper-efficient and had an excellent memory, and also that I liked him.

He ducked in through the lock. "This is the *Lily Star*." I couldn't see his face, but his voice sounded excited, and as if he carried a secret.

"That's a curious name."

"She's a curious ship. I was looking forward to showing Marcus around her."

Chelo asked, "Did you know Marcus?"

"No. But who wouldn't have wanted to meet him?"

I had been lucky. Very lucky. "I understand."

"But you." Cy turned a corner and started down a short hallway toward a wide black door. "You're almost as famous."

I swallowed.

Cy opened the black doorway and stepped through into a wide hallway. A young woman dressed in white welcomed him, and he followed her through three turns and into an open place with a row of high metal walls made of bars down the middle.

Chelo whispered, "Cages?"

I waited for Cy to turn his head so that I could see inside.

When he finally looked directly into the cage closest to him, I could see that it went further back than I expected. Rocks. A pond. Crazy things to have in a spaceship.

Cy seemed to hear my questions. "The rocks are all bolted down. The pond is only four inches deep. We can drain it into sealed tanks in five minutes."

Chelo made a soft sound and her fingernails dug into my palm. "Is there something moving in there?"

"A glitter-dragon."

I leaned toward the monitor. "A what?"

"A glitter-dragon. It's manufactured. Came from the Water Lily Hunting Grounds."

I blinked. "I heard about them. Islands on Silver's Home where people hunt big game?"

Cy laughed. "Or it hunts them. Crazy, if you ask me. But people pay a lot for the opportunity to die by tooth and claw. Let's see if I can get you a better visual."

His cameras zoomed in until the display showed a long black and gray snake-like creature with a long snout. Its head moved like a bird. I squinted. "Is it really a snake? Does it have legs?"

"Short ones. And a wicked tail. A slap from the tail can kill a man —there are barbs on the back. Sunlight makes the scales glitter so they almost blind you. That's how it got its name. It's got teeth, too. Story is, it can kill you twenty ways, and then start in on the next person." He adjusted the cameras so I could see its eyes better. They looked … aware. More like human eyes than a reptile's eyes. Cy stepped back. "I don't want to get near the bars."

Chelo sounded incredulous as she asked, "Why would anyone design a creature that can kill a person?"

Cy zoomed a little closer, revealing how well-muscled the creature was. "Water Lily Hunting Grounds is a place where the rich and bored come to die or find new life. It is an honor to be killed by a wild beast on Silver's Home."

Chelo shivered.

"Why is it here?" I asked. "Why did Marcus want it on his ship?"

"It's an example. That creature? It's smart. Like a flier."

"But it kills people?" Chelo sounded incredulous. "Why not just send people to Fremont? There are plenty of animals that will kill you there. I just don't understand."

Cy pulled the cameras back to a more normal view. He turned and stepped to the next cage. This one was taller. No water. Well, a little. A small stream. And … redberry bushes? I held my breath.

Even after the dragon, which had been larger than a yellow snake, seeing a full-sized animal that looked so familiar shocked me. It stood half as tall as me, but of course with long legs and a long body, it wouldn't even need to get close to me to take me with its claws.

It paced.

"What the hell?" I whispered. "Did you bring demon dogs? Yellow snakes?"

"Just paw-cats." Cy said.

Chelo's face had turned to stone.

I asked him again. "Why are they here? Why did Marcus want to see them?"

Cy kept watching the paw-cat, which meant we did, too. He shook himself, smearing the visual again. "Let me introduce you to Keeper Romi."

A man stepped out from behind the paw-cat and started heading toward us. He wore black, head to toe, the opposite of the woman who had led us here.

I glanced at Chelo. She looked almost ill. She spoke in a broken whisper. "They have no right."

"We knew they'd taken some. The first time. When we were left behind."

"But …" She trailed off. "So they hunt paw-cats on purpose? And the paw-cats kill people? *And that's okay?*"

Cy's attention was still on the man coming toward us *with his back to the paw-cat*. Unreal. I told Chelo what I knew. "Marcus tried to help me understand. Silver's Home has no wild dangers, nothing like Fremont. Living forever has its downsides. People go to Water Lily Hunting Grounds to prove a point, to experience a real risk, and sometimes to die." I pulled my hand free of hers to slide my arm around her waist. "Silver's Home is even stranger than Lopali. It's full of powerful people, but only a few seem to be happy. Some of them go crazy. And this is how a few of them make that choice."

"I hate to interrupt," Cy said. The man was almost here. Up close, he looked slightly feminine, with hair almost as dark as his clothes and an awkward smile. "This is Romi. He is the Keeper of Fighting Animals here. He came with them from Water Lily." Cy switched the visual that fed our screen to an external camera, which showed me that Cy dwarfed Romi by a foot of height and maybe more than that across the shoulder. "Romi—meet Master Joseph Lee and his sister Chelo. Joseph won the first battle of this war, and now he owns the *Orbit*."

Romi nodded way too seriously. "Joseph."

He looked calm, like the Lopali Keepers. I wondered if there was a relationship. "That is a paw-cat, right?"

Romi smiled. "It started as pure Fremont stock. We made them bigger and gave them a few more brains. But we didn't have to do much. Fremont must have been … interesting."

Chelo balled her hands into fists and leaned in toward the camera, her voice tight with anger. "What are you doing with those beasts on a spaceship in a *war*? They could *die*! They belong in the sun under a twin tree. They belong on the Grass Plains, invisible in spite of their size. *They don't belong here.* Humans don't belong on starships, and animals certainly don't. That's cruel."

Her voice shook. She stepped away from me, so I took her hand again; her anger trembled through my palm, and she loosed her fists to grab my fingers, as if she didn't know what to do. All of that would be off-screen of course. Romi and Cy could see only our heads and shoulders.

Cy held up a hand to forestall any more commentary. "Marcus funded this."

Romi added, "These animals already have had a better life than they would have on Water Lily." He spread his arms wide. "They'd probably all be dead by now. Most of them only survive one to three fights. A few more. That would be weeks after they're put into rotation. These have been on the ship for months, living fairly sedate lives. They're here to use either as ambassadors, or as warriors. And what difference does it make if they are warriors on a star ship or an island?"

I nodded, trying to keep my face free of anger. "Who owns the *Lily Star*?"

"We do." Romi spoke carefully. "Water Lily Hunting Grounds owns the *Lily Star* and the animals in her. You pay us. Like mercenaries."

Why had Marcus allowed this? "Who decides how you are used?"

Cy answered. "I do. Through Captain Zhao's authority. And I guess through yours."

This was only getting worse. "How many animals do you have?"

Romi answered, "Almost fifty. We lost a constrictor on the way. Cy has a manifest he can send you." He spoke quickly, clearly trying to convince us wild animals belonged in a war. "I love my animals. They're smart, and they're sentient. Some of them, anyway. But they have no rights."

Which was what this fight was about. Chelo was shaking, and I wasn't sure what she'd say next. Maybe we'd seen enough for now. "Thank you. We have to go. I'll be in touch again. Good luck."

Cy's voice sounded clipped. "Thank you, Sir." The screen went black.

I leaned down and kissed Chelo on top of her head. "Who would have thought?"

41
CHELO

I found Liam in our bedroom. I told him about the *Lily Star* while I double-checked that drawers were latched and tucked a pair of dirty socks away. When I finished relating the facts—the size of the *Orbit*, the war ships, the animals on the *Lily Star*, I told him. "Seeing the paw-cats made me so angry."

Liam stopped in the middle of the room, his face a uniform white, lips thinned to a grimace. "What else did they have?"

"Snakes and animals with four legs. One that looked like a demon dog but wasn't—and didn't need a pack. Some kind of wolf. Romi told me they only brought animals that might survive on a ship. Nothing with hooves, for example. Scary stuff, though. Some, like the glitter-dragons, were just made. Created from goo. Like by combining DNA from a few things, tweaking stuff the way Joseph and Marcus …" I broke off, unable to sustain my anger. The way people with power did. Damn it.

When Liam touched my cheek, the tips of his fingers felt warm.

I looked directly into his blue eyes, which were cloudier than usual, and my voice shook. "They made them to be toys for hunters."

Liam blinked, looked away, and took a long breath. Then he smiled slightly. "Well, someone or something made the paw-cats."

He was trying to break my anger, but I really didn't want to give it up yet. "They made them to die!"

"We don't know that the animals on Fremont evolved on their own. We don't know that anything, ever, evolved. One of the women in our band was convinced everything, everywhere, was created by someone."

He was such an island of calm that the river of my anger bunched up against it, roiling. Not a leadership trait. It just felt good, right now, in this moment. A sign of how stressed heading into battle made me. I took a deep, fluttery breath and lightened my tone. "That makes no sense. Everything can't have been created. The first thing had to evolve even if nothing else did. So don't go deep philosopher on me."

He arched an eyebrow. "Deep?"

His voice teased, an attempt to continue to lighten my mood, so I play-slapped him.

He grabbed both of my hands, pulled me down, and we rolled together on the bed, a coming together that resulted in Liam telling the door to lock, and each of us undressing the other.

We hadn't missed many of the opportunities we got to share our bodies with each other, but it felt as if I was starved for him. If the bruising intensity of his kisses was a marker, he felt the same. We twisted and shook in each other's arms, part fight, part lovemaking, part scream.

When we both fell still at once, panting, my anger was gone. His arms felt warm and my skin tingled against his. Moments later, unexpected tears coursed down my cheeks.

Liam murmured nonsense into the top of my head. I didn't mind that I couldn't understand it.

There was exactly nothing I understood.

The cry took a long time to wring me dry. I stood up and poured us each a bulb of water, then found two washcloths and soaked them with warm water so we could wash. As I handed him one, I asked, "We're not going to live through this, are we?"

"No one does."

My calm, easy, truthful man. I spoke to keep myself from crying again. "I want the children to live through this. They should."

He started pulling on clothes. "Let's go find the kids. I heard we could be fighting in a few days."

"I thought we had five left."

"I heard four."

Not enough. Twenty minutes later, we were with the children and Kayleen. Kayleen and I made salads and an anise-flavored protein loaf, and everyone ate together at the table. Liam cleaned up, and then all three of us took turns reading until we finished a story about a dog like Sasha.

Caro didn't ask any inappropriate questions. Jherrel worked hard on his reading, puzzling out tough words on his own. Kayleen tickled the kids and talked too much. After we tucked the little ones into bed, we three sat quietly, watching them, and each other, and sometimes Kayleen hummed a little. After a long time, we closed the door on the kids and fell together in our big bed, tangling for a short while in comfortable sex and then drifting to uneasy sleep.

Every few hours, I checked that Caro and Jherrel still breathed.

42
JOSEPH

The alarm tugged me from a deep sleep. The room was still dark, and no alerts blared anywhere. I sighed and pushed Sasha gently off the bed so I could get up. "We have a briefing this morning, girl. Or I do. Only I didn't ask for it to be so early!"

Sasha looked unimpressed.

I managed to walk and feed her with time left to jog to my meeting, hungry but on time.

Paloma had the children. Chelo and Liam hadn't yet arrived, so I greeted Jenna and Tiala and then let most of my attention fall into the ship's data feeds.

There, I found Captain Hill, a determined presence in the data, seamlessly attuned to the ship. *I'm here. I see you*, she said.

I see you.

Her awareness danced through the feeds. She flowed like water through the ship's systems, somehow everywhere. I had been deeply connected with the *New Making*, but it was far smaller than the *Thorn*, with simpler systems and only a handful of people on board. The *Thorn*'s safety mechanisms were deeply layered and used tens of thousands of sensors. This was my third tour with the captain, and I was getting the hang of the complex ship.

Captain Hill spoke a message into the data for me. *No Caro?*

Not so far.

Can Paloma keep her out?

I don't think she knows about this meeting. Just in case, I asked Paloma to keep her busy.

I hope it works.

Me, too. As if Caro knew how much I wanted her out of this war, she continually asked to help, and I told her no every way I knew how. I had been a teenager deep in shared data feeds when my adoptive parents died in a rockfall on the High Road above Artistos on Fremont. Hearing their last breaths and last words had felt like having my soul ripped free of my body. What would feeling the death of another human be like for a six-year-old? *We can drug Caro if we have to. But I'd rather not. Chelo might eat me for lunch if I do that to Caro.*

Understood.

Are you ready? I asked her.

I imagined her laughing. *I'm ready to be done waiting.*

Me, too.

I had remained aware of the conference room. Still, as I switched most of my attention into my physical senses, the bright chatter shocked me a little. Speculation about the war. Bets about the time we had left. Col and berries and some kind of warmed nutbread had been set out on the table. I poured a cup and made a small plate.

Liam, Kayleen, Chelo, Jenna, Dianne, and two of the captain's senior staff sat around the table. Jenna leaned across it, peering at the monitors on the wall opposite her. Tiala was beside her, quietly watching both Jenna and the screens equally. Chelo, Liam, and Kayleen huddled in a family group, Kayleen in the middle. The captain sat on my left, every hair in place, her skin burnished brown as if she'd just stepped out of a high-end salon. She was so beautiful I had to force myself to look away. Seeing someone inside of data streams created an intimacy that was best handled carefully in the physical world.

The captain turned her head to smile at me, and I nodded.

She began. "Good morning."

People's attention swiveled to her.

"Welcome to our first war briefing. This briefing will occur at this hour every day until we finish fighting."

Liam looked thoughtful. Jenna smiled, once more a tiny bit feral, like the Jenna I knew as a child back on Fremont. "We'll help fight if you like," she told the captain. "We fought the mercenaries on Fremont."

"I know the story," Captain Hill said. "And I appreciate your abilities. But we have trained personnel who have drilled with the *Thorn* and her weapons for years. There will be work for you, but I will choose it. I will be in command for twelve hours a day. For the alternative twelve, it will be Master Joseph Lee. Each of us will have a backup." She nodded toward two of her senior staff. "Ulrika will be Joseph's, and Malto, mine."

Ulrika nodded at me, a supportive smile flittering across her narrow face before she turned her attention back to the Captain. Her uniform was slightly worn, and her hair caught back in a thin ponytail, both of which gave her a no-nonsense look. I'd been around her before. The crew respected her.

Malto, whose red hair and beard framed a round face, merely nodded.

Captain Hill raised her voice slightly. "The *Thorn* was designed to operate best with oversight from a powerful Wind Reader, and Joseph and I are the strongest on this ship."

She looked around the room, as if making sure everyone understood her command structure. "It would have been me and Marcus, but now it will be me and Joseph Lee. He has been in battles, which is more than many members of this fleet can say."

I sat as straight as I could and tried to look calm in spite of my fingers flexing with nervous energy under the table.

The captain switched to a spreadsheet view with lists of assignments. "Twelve-hour shifts require support. I will take mine from my crew, and Joseph will take his from his sister, and if she is not available, from the next in command below Ulrika." Her gaze swept the table, pausing at each person until some form of acknowledgement had been extracted.

Captain Hill touched her wrist, and every screen hummed to life.

Images of the two fleets flitted along the two long walls of the room while statistics scrolled on ribbons above them. There were one hundred seventy-one ships under one command in the Islan fleet. There were one hundred twenty in ours, but only seventy were Port Authority ships under direct unified command. The rest were like us, waiting to play parts when the Authority chose them for us.

Over half the Port Authority ships were near the front of the fleet, the others scattered throughout. None were very near us. Even the *Opportunity* had gone ahead of us, looking for her own glory.

Our position near the back might be punitive. The Authority had admired Marcus, but hadn't trusted him, nor he them. The *Unicorn* was in charge of our battle group, so Master Skulla and Captain Sawyer. If anything happened to the *Unicorn*, the *Black Star* would take over, then the *Highline*, then us.

It galled me to be last. If Marcus had lived ...

Captain Hill stood by the screen, turning her back on it and addressing us. "The fleets will fly through each other. We won't see the beginning of the action. But we will be ready for the Islan fleet to reach us, and we will faithfully follow any orders we receive."

She looked at Dianne. "You're from Islas. Can you tell us anything about the Islan ships?"

Dianne shook her head. "I was a mercenary. Most of us were. It was mandatory. But I don't know much about the military's ships. I don't see anything that looks like the mercenary fleet there."

I thought about the *Orbit*. "But they could be inside those ships, right? The bigger ones?"

She hesitated. "Maybe. I haven't been on Islas for twenty-two years. The mercenaries were never considered part of planetary defense. We were out to frustrate you and to gather information, and also—most often—to get rich. The Star Mercenaries did not report to the military then, and I bet they don't now."

"If you think of anything—observe anything—useful to us, will you let me know?"

The captain's question reminded me of what Caro had asked Dianne before we'd even reached the *Thorn*. I hadn't been there, but I'd heard about it. *Can you kill Islans?*

Caro was merely a child, but Chelo trusted Dianne, and Marcus had been close to her.

Dianne smiled broadly. "If we're lucky, there will be some use for my skills in diplomacy."

Captain Hill smiled back. "After the first round of fighting, we may need a lot of soft skills." Her smile faded into a more severe look. "There may only be hours until the leading edges of the fleets meet. Be ready."

I found Mohami on a prayer rug, hands folded, dressed in white robes trimmed in red and gold as if he were back on Lopali. Kala once again sat in the shadows.

They had, apparently, been waiting for me.

I greeted them both. This always seemed to surprise Kala. I had expected her to become accustomed to it, but once more her eyes widened, and a pleased grin flitted across her lips. Then she closed her eyes and fell into calm silence.

I sat in front of him, likewise cross-legged. This morning, there was no tea, no col, nothing. He must have known about the early meeting. He had an eerie way of knowing most things about the ship.

"How do you feel?" he asked.

"Frightened. Excited. Anticipatory. Part of me wants to fight, and wishes we were near the beginning of it. Feeling both at once is tearing me up. They don't go together."

"Don't they?"

"Fear of fighting and wanting to fight? Not really."

His smile was soft, yet it filled his whole face. "Contradictory feelings can signal a large change coming."

"A large change?"

"Close your eyes."

"Okay." I did.

"People will die. On both sides. This is one change." He paused, breathed audibly, sighed. Started again. "Beings that are like you will die. The stuff of their souls will be recycled, but they will no longer be accessible to you. So breathe deeply for a moment. Feel that. You can't help it. You cannot stop it."

I breathed. Counted. *One. Two. Three … ten.* The rug felt itchy and my ankle seemed determined to go to sleep.

"You may have to kill. You may die. Both of these things are possible."

My eyes opened.

"Close your eyes. Breathe. Life and death are possible for all of us, every day. They are constants. They come even though we are all connected.

"We are one.

"We and our enemies are not enemies, we are one. Silver's Home and the Islans. Made dragons, changed paw-cats, captains, gunners, and Masters. Engineers. Ships' AIs. We are all connected, all made of the same stars, the same history, the same future."

He had said many of these things to me before. At times they seemed mystical, and at times they made me want to laugh. I didn't know how to feel what he wanted me to feel, what Chelo wanted me to feel.

Still, I felt calmer for talking to Mohami and breathing in his strange beliefs. Every time I left here I felt … bigger.

"Breathe," he said softly. "Breathe."

I breathed.

Mohami held his silence. Kala's robes rustled faintly, then stilled.

My breath rattled in my throat, just the way he had taught me. A not-quite wheeze.

I imagined Captain Hall here, wondered what she would think of Mohami's lessons on inter-being. At least that was one thing he called it. When Mohami talked of the war, the two fleets floated together in my soul the way two halves of a whole did, rather than as two opposing forces. Outside of this room, I felt the fleets thrum with the energy of the coming fight, but inside of it, I watched two wings on the same butterfly.

I focused again on my breath. Counted three breaths.

A memory floated up. I had been thinking of it anyway for days.

The moment when I flung the ship into the sea on Fremont and killed everyone on her.

I couldn't have done that even half an hour before I did do it. I wouldn't have had the strength.

I had been strong enough because, for just a moment, everything I could touch had been one thing. All of the data on Fremont had been one thing, one vibrating energy, and all of the people had been one thing, one constellation of hearts, and I'd heard all of the hearts beating. They'd sounded the same. The heart of my enemy had beat like the heart of my family.

I had forgotten that, been bowled over by the guilt at how I had used that moment of oneness. I opened my eyes and stared at Mohami.

He watched me back.

I felt full. Peaceful. Clear of warring emotions.

"I'm ready," I said.

He smiled and bowed toward me, a thing he had never done before. "Breathe. When you need this moment, this memory, breathe."

43
ALICIA

Marti stood in front of me, her red wings hunched forward to keep the tips from trailing on the ground. I balanced on a stool, tugging a comb through her red hair. "Ouch!" She held her hand up. "That hurt." She leaned forward, risking another tug on her hair. "The fleets are close now."

I put my hands on her shoulders and rose to tiptoe so I could see the display over the curve of her wing. Just this morning, the metrics had switched from distance between us and the entirety of the two fleets to the distance between us and individual ships. The *Anvil* was fast. We were angling toward where the fleets would be, looking to join up near the center of the fleet from Silver's Home.

Tsawo had filed a flight plan with Fleet Admiral Mott's systems. They had given us coordinates, but no greeting. No special treatment. No *hello, welcome great ambassadors of Lopali.*

Marcus had told us we were the key to stopping or slowing the war, maybe even to winning.

The leaders of the fleet didn't appear to share his conviction.

I wasn't sure I wanted to see Marcus. I did want to see Joseph, so he could approve of my wings and tell me I was still beautiful to him.

I lowered my heels and started spinning black beads into Marti's thin braids. "I have no idea what ship Joseph is on."

She laughed. "Guess. What about *The Dark Arrow*?"

"Joseph thinks every glass is half full."

"*Arik's Bane*."

"What does that even mean?"

She laughed harder and leaned back a little into me. "That someone named Arik has an enemy. What about *Sunspire*?"

"Too upbeat."

Maybe laughter was her way of dumping stress. She kept it up, making it hard to finish her hair. *Dream Maker. Spinner. Maker's Thorn. Possibility Curve.* At least it was a good way to learn the names of the ships.

Hopefully they'd found the traitor. I threaded another bead. "Maybe we should develop a secret code language."

"Huh?"

"I can't tell Joseph about the traitor when I see him, not unless we can talk in private. It could be anyone but us six or Jenna." I hesitated. "Or Tiala. I can't imagine Tiala."

Marti rustled her wings. "I can't hold this pose anymore."

Wings were meant for flapping. Holding them open was hard. "Switch."

We did. "Secrets are hard to keep." She settled behind me.

She started fluffing my hair with her fingers. I found the most comfortable stance I could, which wasn't saying much. "I talked to Jagruti again this morning," I offered.

"She's a mean old woman."

"And you're treating her like you think that." I had grown surprisingly fond of her after seeing her almost every day, always in her quarters. "She thinks both sides are equally wrong. Joseph would say the same thing if he were here. And Chelo. That war is wrong."

She tugged a comb through a tangle.

"Ouch."

"Sorry."

"The Islans are wrong for wanting to tell everyone else to be like them, for wanting all the power."

Marti finished freeing the tangle and started in on another one. “They’re worse than the Makers. We wouldn’t exist under their regime.”

“Not unless we had a military use.”

Her laughter was edged. “It’s not funny. It’s true. And sad.”

I glanced at the screens in front of me. “I knew how many ships were in the fleets, but not how they would feel aimed at me.”

“Are you afraid to die?” she asked, her voice calm now.

“Of course. But mostly, I’m afraid I’ll die before I see Joseph again.”

The door opened behind us, and Tsawo came in.

He was beautiful this morning and smelled of perfumes and sweat. A dark angel with dark and lively eyes, well-defined cheekbones, black wings, and almost no adornment.

Why were the most attractive men utterly uninterested in relationships? I pursed my lips, staying quiet, listening. This wasn’t the time for acting out or adding risk. The coming battle fed my love for risk perfectly well, beating in my blood and releasing endorphins.

Tsawo’s voice snapped out, “The first shot has been fired.”

I leaned in, pulling a braid almost free of Marti’s hand and staring at the screen.

“You won’t be able to see it,” Tsawo said. “Unless it—”

A blinking red dot showed on one of the ships in front of our fleet. “What does that mean?”

“A hit.” He reached toward it, but before he could call up information, a second red dot appeared on the same ship. Well, on the image of the ship. The icons were small and stylized.

“There,” he pointed. “One of ours hit its target.”

A red dot obscured an Islan ship.

Marti stepped out from behind me, and I flapped my wings to settle them into a more comfortable position.

Tsawo pulled up newsfeeds.

“I’m glad we’re not there yet,” I said.

Another red dot appeared.

If only I knew Joseph’s ship. “Are people dying?” I asked, knowing the answer, but I needed the words anyway.

"It's war," Marti said.

"We all die," Tsawo said. He stared at the screen as if he were starved to be right there in the middle of it all, then turned to us and snapped, "Get into your crash bubbles."

"After all this work on our hair?"

He laughed. "Go."

Clearly, he was going to try to get closer faster.

Good.

44
JOSEPH

Uniformed crew filled the seats in the briefing room. Chelo and I leaned against the walls, inhaling the scents of fear and sweat. Captain Hill stood near us, watching Weapons Chief Fillip give the primary situation status. He was a small, compact man who seemed twice his size as he waved his arms and spoke in a booming voice. "Two of our ships were hit. A Port Authority flagship near the front, the *Authenticator*, held some of the tactical command staff. Destroyed with all hands lost. One shot pulverized the drive and another the life support systems. Not luck: tactics."

Chief Fillip paused.

People shifted, but no one spoke.

"A smaller gunship backed away from the fighting but is expected to re-enter after repairs. Two casualties." He frowned. "We hit one of their flagships twice, but it did not stop."

Hundreds of people had died today. Maybe more. Chelo's face had gone white.

"News will be posted on the boards." With that, the Weapons Chief hurried out the door.

Captain Hill stood by the door, thanking each crew member as they left. When the last one nodded at her, she took a deep breath and sat down. "This will get worse." She looked directly at me. "This is a slow-motion war until it's our turn, and then it won't feel that way."

I nodded.

She glanced around the room. "Dianne, Tiala, help monitor battle reports. Dianne—take first shift—that's this one. Tiala second. Jenna —rest so that you can support Joseph."

Jenna nodded, although my bet was that she'd spend three hours in the gym before she passed out from exhaustion.

Kayleen and Liam started discussing childcare, but Captain Hill interrupted. "Ask my mother and Paloma to help. You two should sleep now. We'll need you to help with the next shift."

Liam's surprised glance belied the banked anger I recognized in the set of his jaw. "Can we serve on different shifts so one of us can be available for the children any time?"

I could see the word "no" form itself on the captain's mouth, but before it escaped Liam said, "Caro."

The captain pursed her lips. "Very well. Kayleen is to stay on Joseph's shift."

Not what I would have done, but this wasn't the time to play the Master card. I hadn't been asked. Lou was a stronger Wind Reader than Kayleen, or at least more stable. She wouldn't go catatonic if Caro lost it. And I could look after Kayleen.

The captain stood. "Dismissed. Go about your business normally." She smiled at us as she added, "Stay out of my crew's way."

Everyone left but me and Chelo.

The calm on the captain's face morphed into something more like relaxed hunger. "Follow me. You'll shadow me and Singh for two hours and then go to sleep."

I obeyed. This was more my ship than the *New Making* had ever been, more than any ship, ever, but I was not her captain. Fate was a strange beast, indeed.

In the Command Room, Captain Hill addressed the ship's AI. "You have control. Wake me if fighting starts near us."

It replied in a formal, feminine voice. "Yes, Ma'am."

She strapped into her crash couch. A trusted advisor, Singh Rac, sat beside her.

Malto sat in a chair on her far side, in a place where he could hear anything she or Singh said, and could also interact with the other crew on the bridge.

At Singh's invitation, I strapped into the co-pilot's chair. Moments later, I followed Captain Hill down, once again marveling at how smoothly she moved through the ship's data.

An hour before my shift, Chelo and I stood side by side in a galley ordering up col and packing simple meals and water. I'd sent Sasha with Liam in hopes she would help distract Caro.

"We won't see battle today," I mused. "Probably. But the *Peacemaker* might."

Chelo suggested, "Maybe you should call Captain Grundson."

"A call from me might clutter up her neatly organized day."

Chelo laughed as she added napkins to her packed shift bag. She hummed softly under her breath, apparently in a good mood. "Remember the Joseph Chair?" I asked.

A smile crossed her lips. "I do."

Our adoptive father, Stephen, had made it for me before he died. "It was like a crash couch for my childhood self on Fremont." I had felt safe in that chair with Chelo beside me. "I couldn't do this without you," I told her. "No one else can know how frightened I am. Not even Mohami knows that."

"Sure he does."

The door burst open and Jenna flowed through it. She wore loose, comfortable clothes and soft shoes. Fighting clothes. "You'll be interested in one of the messages we got from the Fleet Admiral. The battle grouping with *Sun's Orbit* in it has added two ships. One is from Lopali."

"Alicia?" Chelo and I said in unison.

"I'm verifying. Probably. It may be grouped with the *Orbit*. Lopali has small attack ships like the *Lily Star*, and the fliers are almost as exotic as the paw-cats." Her mouth twisted into an ironic smile. "Keeps the weirdness away from the main fleet."

"Isn't that the weirdness we're fighting about?" Chelo asked.

Jenna cocked her head. "It's an embarrassing weirdness for the Authority. It wouldn't do to have the created beings we're fighting for the right to treat like slaves win the war for us."

The small, round ships the fliers had used to keep us safe in the skies above Lopali were effective at keeping small craft away from us, but they hadn't seemed like fighting ships, not even then. More like bubbles full of feathers. I swallowed, hoping it was Alicia and hoping it wasn't. "What's the name of the ship? Do you know anything about it?"

"The *Sky Anvil.* We have stats now. It's big, and fast. Faster than the *Thorn.*"

"Really?"

"Yes. It got here in less than half the time it took us. There are only about twelve people aboard her. Three are fliers."

I raised an eyebrow at her.

"She's almost got to be there. Leaving Lopali had to be a big risk. There are nine people who could be her, or maybe three if she did get wings." Chelo hesitated. "But it seems fast for that."

"It's been over a year since we left."

"It must take a long time to grow wings and learn to use them." Chelo let out a long, overplayed sigh. "But maybe. She's probably there."

"You're smiling."

"No I'm not."

She was. Chelo was just like Sasha. Our family's human herding dog. She'd love to have everyone close.

Jenna ducked back out of the door, and I leaned over Chelo. "Will you check on Caro? I don't want to get Sasha all excited."

"You mean will I take your dog to potty?"

I smiled. "Well, you're still my big sister."

She shoved the bag of food we'd been packing into my hands, took her bulb of col, saluted me with it, and said, "See you in a few."

I glanced at the two plates of potatoes and protein slices, and called for a delivery bot. When it arrived a few moments later, I stacked the plates in its belly, told it to go to the conference room, and then started after it. I needed a moment of time to think about Alicia returning. What did that mean?

I came up with exactly zero ideas of how to feel about Alicia on the way to Command. Captain Hill said, "Good evening. The fight is escalating, but we still have no direct orders except to stay our course and remain prepared." The thin line of her lips was all the indication she gave that she might not be happy with those orders.

"All right. Anything specific I should know?"

She shook her head. "Right after the briefing, I am to meet our local captains via video." We followed her into the briefing room. We were still being drubbed at two to one, and our fleet wasn't double the size of theirs.

The lines had lengthened, both fleets hoping to force the other to stay close while they moved ships outside where they could find unique angles of attack. The brightly colored icons for the fleets shifted like leaves blown by a chaotic wind. After her crew left and before she went to her meeting, Captain Hill said, "So far, neither fleet is playing three-dimensional chess. *But they will.* Watch for it. And so far, no sign of other Wind Readers."

She left before I thought to ask if she'd been referring to Caro, to friendly Wind Readers from our own compliment of ships, or to Islans. Any of the above were likely to try to dig into our data.

Chelo sat where she could read the monitors or her slate at will and still reach out a hand to touch my shoulder or rub my back. She leaned over and whispered in my ear. "Blood, and Bone, and Brain."

I wasn't the same child who had needed that chant from her back on Fremont, but it *did* sound good. So I closed my eyes, breathed, and dove.

After establishing a good connection with the pilot AI and reviewing the logs from the time when the captain and I had both been minimally connected to the *Thorn*, I started a sequence through the ship. Instead of following exactly what Captain Hill did, I chose my own path, but one that touched everything she did. Hydroponics. Security. The Bay of Ships where we kept the smaller ships. Robotics. Life Support. Security. Battle reports. Living quarters. Engines. Security. After I'd checked everything, I left some attention behind to collect alerts and came up for water and a snack. "Did you hear yet? Is it Alicia?"

She shook her head, handing me a bulb of water. "I sent the *Orbit* a message. They might know."

"Good."

"Do you want it to be Alicia?"

"Yes."

"After she left you?"

"Yes." And I didn't want to talk about it. "How is Caro?"

"Asleep."

"Good." While we watched war reports on the screen, I ate a handful of sweet fruit Chelo handed me. A small woman in a perfect uniform reported over three thousand dead on our side with a straight face. No emotion. In a little over twenty-four hours. Most had been on the first ship.

I hadn't felt them die. When the fighting neared us, I'd be in every feed I could, and I would feel the deaths in those feeds. It soured my stomach.

"Three thousand people is a lot of death. More, if we count the Islans. For what?"

"To make sure people can't create sentient beings like fliers out of humans, or out of engineering drawings and raw material—and own them."

Which they did for money. "It comes down to credit."

Chelo followed my thoughts. "No, power."

"Yes." One was the other, in my experience.

"I hate everything about war." Chelo tucked her knees in close to her and wrapped her arms around them, deeply troubled. "I hate war so much I wish we were anywhere else."

"I do too," I told her. "But we can't go home. And you hate Lopali.

You would hate Silver's Home. You would hate Islas. I suppose we could float around in a delivery ship for the rest of our lives."

"Not if I can help it. I want soil."

At least her voice wasn't shaking. I took a last sip of water and prepared. This time, I'd try and reach our sister ships, check on them, make sure they were ready to fight.

When I fell back down, I discovered that Caro wasn't asleep.

45

ALICIA

Marti, Tsawo, and I stood, slowly flexing our wings, bending our arms, and stretching our ankles in front of a full wall-sized display of battle statistics. "Will we get there in time to join the fight?"

Tsawo smiled, looking quite satisfied. "We did. That's just from the first few ships in each fleet fighting. We're going into the middle, joining a ship called the *Sun's Orbit*."

What a dumb name. Suns were the middle of systems, and planets orbited around them. Maybe someone from Lopali had named it. Although then it might have been the *Golden Majestic Orb of Transit*.

A picture of the *Sun's Orbit* showed a wide, squat ship that had clearly begun life as a cargo vessel. Statistics on the right side of the screen suggested it held hundreds of smaller ships and drones inside its holds.

Tsawo watched me closely. "Joseph owns it."

"He can't." The words came out as reflex.

"The nets say he does."

"You've got the right Joseph Lee?"

"There's a picture."

He looked more than a year older. Neat as a pin, too. The uniform in the picture was more formal than his old captain's coat. His face looked like he was starving. "When he left here, he didn't even own a skimmer."

The *Sun's Orbit* was so big the *Sky Anvil* would fit in her hold if it were empty. My heartbeat sped up. Joseph! "Is he there?"

"No. He's on another ship. *The Maker's Thorn*." He smiled. "But we do get to go visiting. We've been invited to the *Orbit* for a strategy session on the *Lily Star*."

That lifted my spirits. Someplace that wasn't Lopali or a small ship with only a few people on it. "What is the *Lily Star*?"

"I imagine it's a ship. Let's go see."

I had expected fanfare when we arrived, not a polite invitation to a meeting with strangers.

Marti and I looked at each other, and I had the sense that she felt as curious and slightly miffed as I did. "Shall we dress for dinner?"

"Yes. We have half an hour."

I touched a hand to my braided hair, which felt brittle from the dry air of the bubble. To assert our importance, we needed to look the part. "That's not enough!"

He smiled and raised an eyebrow.

I had emerged almost naked from the bubble. We all had. We needed more than clothes. This would be a first impression. "Can you get us fifteen more minutes?"

Tsawo dipped in an exaggerated bow that rustled his wings. "I know nothing about what I can do here, yet. But I will try."

I combed and re-braided my hair, highlighted my violet eyes with blue shadow, then ran out of time. I pulled on a black wrap, admiring the rather severe look of it against my mostly-black wings.

Marti matched me in black except for her red hair and wings.

Tsawo's blacks were all the blacks of deepest night and empty space. He had outdone us both.

Three of us barely fit in our biggest shuttle. It might have held ten humans, but wings made three feel crowded. The shuttle looked like a super-sized version of the crash balls—a large, mostly clear ship with benches that were a cross between massage tables and seats. We lay belly-down and canted at an upward angle on these couches with our feet on the floor. We each looked out in different directions, our wings touching lightly in the middle if we fluffed them. We probably looked like three butterflies stuck face-down in a snow-globe.

The *Sun's Orbit* had no trouble swallowing our round shuttle. We passed flight control to the *Orbit* and a door irised open for us, swallowed us smoothly, and then shut the stars out. A tunnel slid free of the far wall and a robot guided it to mate with our outer door and create an airlock.

I had to bend a little in the tunnel to keep the bottoms of my wings from touching the sides, and in front of me, Tsawo had to do the same.

A thickset man who reminded me vaguely of Bryan held his hand out. "I'm Cy, the Master of War for small ships here. You're assigned to me."

I looked more closely at him. He seemed friendly enough, and confident in the way Tsawo was—a little cocky.

Tsawo shook Cy's hand and introduced himself as a "Protector of Lopali," Marti as a "Flier of Lopali," and me as "related to Master Joseph Lee."

Cy raised an eyebrow at that. A smaller man stood just behind him, darker and far slighter, built for running. "I'm Romi, Master of the *Lily Star*, serving with permission of the board of Water Lily Hunting Grounds."

So formal. He sounded more important than us, although he wasn't.

"Isn't that where people go to fight paw-cats?" Marti asked.

He looked amused and slightly pained. A complex reaction. "Yes. Follow me."

They took us through the *Sun's Orbit* to the biggest ship inside of her hold, the *Lily Star*. A woman in white bowed as we entered and led us to a picnic table complete with perches that could have come from Lopali.

Tsawo asked, "Do you have other fliers on board?"

Cy shook his head. "No. Marcus designed this for fliers when he retrofitted it. He always dreamed that the fliers would join us in the war. That's probably why you were assigned here: The *Orbit* is one of a mere handful of ships that can accommodate fliers."

I settled onto a perch.

Cy smiled up at me. "Marcus would have liked to see you here."

I cocked my head. "Is he on board?"

Romi put a hand on my arm. I looked at him, and saw his eyes were troubled. "I'm sorry." He waited a moment. "Marcus died. His ship blew up."

Tsawo and Marti both looked as startled as I felt. That explained how Joseph had become Master of a ship. Maybe.

Cy repeated Romi's sentiments. "I'm sorry about Marcus."

Joseph would be heartbroken. I said, "Thank you." Perhaps I even sounded a little sincere.

The young woman in white brought us food, and as soon as we began eating Cy said, "I researched your abilities. We could be fighting as early as tomorrow, although more likely, there's another day." His eyes shone with excitement. "This will be the biggest part of the fight —the middle. The most ships. The closest infighting. That's why we put the *Orbit* here. We think there will be a call for fighters like you. You're all trained in your smaller bubble ships, right?"

What? Marti and I shared a glance. I didn't come here to fight directly! We were ambassadors!

But Tsawo grinned, "We're all good."

I shivered. Maybe. He had made us drill in simulators every day during the slower parts of our flight here. We'd also spent three hours outside two days ago, after we'd dumped most of our speed, but we'd still had to use part of our auxiliary fuel to catch back up to the *Anvil.*

"Well enough," Marti modified.

Cy narrowed his eyes at her, but she added nothing more, so he went on. "When the bigger battleships engage with each other, small fleets like ours can make a difference. Islas has some, too, but we think we have more." He leaned in and whispered theatrically. "We might be our fleet's greatest surprise."

The more we talked about battle, the more excited I felt, and the more alive.

We shared a plate of warm bread with cold berries, and nuts heated in small cups. Cy drilled us via tabletop exercises for ten different scenarios before he stood up. "You're not as ready as I'd like, but there's no time. Go home and rest."

It wasn't praise.

Tsawo sent the mechanics to double-check everything on the little round flying machines the three of us would go to battle in. He led us back into the simulators, which were smaller versions of the shuttle. Subtract space, add weapons, change the outside surfaces so they could look like rocks or space or be wide open and clear.

I dripped with sweat by the time we finished.

On our way back to our quarters, I asked Tsawo, "Can I call Joseph?"

"I tried. When he's on shift, he's not accessible. We can try again tomorrow."

We stopped in an alcove with a display of the stars that pretended to be a window. "Did you leave a message for him? Did you tell him I'm here?"

Tsawo began to pluck at Marti's feathers, fluffing them out the way a Keeper might. "I want to talk to him in person. More, I want to find out how this war is being run. Marcus had indicated he'd be able to give us a seat at the negotiating table. Maybe we got slotted here because of some command Marcus gave the *Sun's Orbit* about fliers, and so maybe there's some next step we don't know about."

Marti said, "Turn around," and started grooming my wings. I spread my shoulders, fluffing them some, making it easier.

"Joseph probably wants to know about Induan," I said.

"Take two steps forward," Marti told me.

I did. That put me closer to Tsawo, and so I started on the wing nearest me. Marti adjusted how she stood, and after a while we each found a reasonably comfortable way to work on the other. Tsawo's feathers were oilier than mine, and I liked the feel of them through my fingers.

Tsawo niggled with the thing that was still bothering me as well. "I expected to try and make a case to someone. To talk about being us. What if we die?"

Marti looked thoughtful. "The people we need to talk to are probably in front, and thus in the fight, or just out of it. We didn't arrive at the moment for making cases."

"I don't think we can get out of fighting," Tsawo mused.

I teased him, "The great protector, thinking of not fighting?"

"I'm not interested in fighting *for* the Wingmakers. If we could at least say we're here to fight for our freedom, then if we die, it might still matter."

"We could record something," I suggested.

Tsawo frowned. "Sleep in your crash couches. I'm going to sleep. We need to rest."

Marti said, "I'll follow you. Just let me finish Alicia's wing here."

As Marti worked on the last section of my other wing, I felt a soft release.

She grunted. "You've shed your first pinion."

I turned around and held out my hands, palm up.

She handed it to me, and I stared at it. Up close, the fine feathering near the shaft looked like dark fog, and the many tiny filaments stuck to each other in fine waves. As I tilted my hands to catch other angles of light, the feather changed from matte black to bright black and back to matte. "Maybe it's good luck."

Marti smiled. "Do you have your box?"

"In my room."

"I'll call for it," Tsawo said. "You should keep it safe."

Once it lay in the box, the feather looked like a sharp knife, or perhaps a sword. I felt inordinately proud of it, and then laughed at myself. It wasn't as if I'd had a child. But when I looked at the feather, I had trouble pulling my eyes away.

Tsawo must have noticed. He leaned down beside me. "Go to bed."

"I need to think a little."

"Okay." He watched me closely for a moment. "Remember to sleep in your crash couch."

"You already told me that."

He cupped my cheek. "You've been very brave. All the way through. I don't know if I ever told you how proud of you I am."

"Thank you."

He looked deeply into my eyes. "I mean it. I didn't think you had the grace to become a flier. But your soul proved me wrong. I thought you would be too selfish to join us, but you haven't been. You have been … beautiful. Now let's stay alive tomorrow and live to do more for this war."

I smiled. "That's the plan."

He leaned in and kissed me.

I kissed him back, the brief heat of it a fitting coda to a day spent talking of war.

After he and Marti left, I sat with the pinion feather on my lap in the open box and recorded a message for Joseph. I encrypted the message and left a second message for Jagruti, asking her to send it to Joseph immediately if I died.

Dear Joseph,

I am both in your war and on one of your ships.

One reason we came out here was to tell you we learned there is a traitor who flew with you on Bryan's Hope. *We don't know who that is.*

I am amazed at all you have become. I have achieved dreams as well, and now I just have to survive the fighting that may soon come our way. If perhaps I don't, please ask here for a gift from me. I will have some luck to pass on to you. It is in a long box.

Love always, Alicia.

I stopped just short of telling him I had wings, although he would see that if he received the feather box.

46
JOSEPH

Caro waited for me in the *Thorn*'s data. Her energy felt solemn and … what? Dutiful? *Caro?*

Yes, Uncle.

Why are you here?

You need me.

I have work to do. It's not work for a child.

It's not my fault I'm a child. She hesitated, as if thinking hard. *The work exists. I can do it.*

She couldn't possibly understand the things I might need to do when we joined the battle. *Your mom needs you.*

She's sleeping.

I didn't want to spend the first possible battle shift fighting with my niece. I tried persuasion. *Please, Caro. Go. I will worry about you, and then I might not be as safe. I need for you to watch your mom and help you with her tomorrow.*

You need my help now.

I hated all of my choices.

The *Thorn* signaled incoming news.

We had destroyed an Islan ship. They had destroyed three of ours. We had damaged two of their smaller ships.

Caro's attention followed mine. She stayed by my side, much like Sasha followed me from place to place in the real world. I had come to check on the *Thorn* and then on the *Unicorn*. I wanted to know I could reach and maybe even influence all the ships we flew with.

Caro said, *I can make you stronger.*

How?

Like we made each other stronger when we were looking for Mommy. You can visit the other ships. I will keep you from getting lost.

How?

I will link to you the way you and Lou linked to me. I'll make you stronger. I'll focus on you and not on what you see.

You can't Caro. You're too young.

You will need me.

A shock of anger almost drove me out of the data. Too bad I couldn't afford the time to disengage from my task, tie her up and tickle her, or slam a data shield over her and keep it there. She knew how to push my feelings. Love. Worry. Frustration. Pity. Not exactly pity. But something like it. No child should be able to do what she could do, or should have to do what she had already done.

Go, Uncle. Talk to the Unicorn *first.*

Guilt, need, duty, and curiosity blended badly. This was my first day of battle and I needed to do what Captain Hill had asked me to.

I ran a last check of the *Thorn*'s data. Then I *reached.*

I slid into the *Unicorn*'s data as easily as if I were on board. The move felt so smooth that it startled me, and I slid back to the *Thorn*. *What happened?*

I told you I could help.

She sounded proud of herself.

No time to explore that right now. *I love you. I'm going back.*

This time I expected the easy slide, and detected Caro's energy supporting me. Marcus had been that strong. I told her, *Thank you.*

The *Unicorn* seemed quiet. Tense, like we were, but waiting. Off-duty crew hung in their rooms or played games with each other in galleys. True to her word, Caro offered only support.

The *Highline* had some problems with her air scrubbers. Robots had already started working on them, so I didn't try to fix them. I set a monitor program to report back to me when they were done. The *Black Star* was harder to get into. After the second rebuff from her automated security systems, Caro sent me an idea. *Convince it you are one of its small ships.*

It worked.

I could control these ships.

So easy. I had been, maybe, half this strong the last time I had tried this. I had been with Marcus, but he had pointedly not helped. He and I had multiplied each other's strength on Lopali. All of the Wind Readers on Lopali had joined once, to save Kayleen. They had succeeded where Caro and I together had failed. Wind Readers could strengthen each other … even though we usually travelled alone.

I couldn't have done this so easily yesterday, or maybe at all for the *Black Star.*

Go further.

No. Not yet. This is what I promised Captain Hill. We must respect her.

No hesitation. *Okay.*

Good. She was obeying. Sliding back to the *Thorn* was easier as well. Was I stronger, or faster, or both? I was too tired to tell.

I checked on my family. Kayleen and Liam lay tangled together, her hair spread across his arms and his chin on her forehead. A twinge of jealousy ran through me before relief that they were both here and okay chased it away.

Thank you, I told Caro.

You're welcome.

I shouldn't allow this. It was evil. I was using my niece. She might want me to, but she was six. Six.

I came up and Chelo was there, waiting for me with nuts, cheese, and fine thin crackers glistening with pink salt. Before I took anything, even water, I said, "Caro."

"Is she okay?" Chelo leaned in toward me, took my hand. "Is she okay? Was she there?"

I swallowed. Words stuck in my chest until I drank some water. When they finally spilled out, I said, "She did what we did to get Kayleen." When I saw that she didn't understand, I added, "When we went after Kayleen, it was Caro who went, Caro who found her. Lou and I helped her." I paused, took a cracker. How could I even describe what we did to someone who was deaf to data? I nibbled at the cracker, savoring the salt. "We built and then maintained a bridge between her and us. That way she could go deeper into streams of data. It makes you thin to do that, spreads your *self* across a lot of inputs. Lou and I built a link that helped Caro stay sane and connected so she could get home. We made her stronger, and we maintained a trail for her."

Chelo frowned. "I think I understood that."

"I don't know how to be clearer."

She touched my cheek briefly, her fingers cool. "You're doing okay."

"Just now, it was the reverse. Caro made it so I could go farther, do more. She made me stronger. But that can't be okay."

Chelo fell silent for a long time, troubled. She stood and stretched before she turned to me. "Could you have stopped her?"

"Stopped her from helping me? Only by not doing what I needed to do. I might be able to build a way to shield from her, but that might be cruel."

"Eat." She pointed at the cracker, which I hadn't yet finished.

"I'm not hungry. And I'm not done. But she'll be there. She'll be waiting to help me."

"Eat."

"What if she gets hurt?"

Chelo's voice came out low. "I don't know. I don't know how to make her stop. We talked about drugging her." She reached for another cracker, spread some orange protein paste on it, and put it in my hand.

The edges felt sharp, and the smell of the salt snuck up my nostrils, gagging me. I choked. "We can't drug a child."

Chelo sat back in her seat. "Is it possible that she's safe with you? You and she are alike, and I don't know anyone else who is like you. Even Kayleen is not like you. Maybe you need each other?"

I put the cracker down and tried to think. I picked up a piece of faux cheese and tore it into little pieces, put it on the cracker. "She's strong, but she's a baby." I tasted a single piece of cheese. Smoky. "Would you let Jherrel do anything so dangerous?"

Chelo got up to refill my water glass. "How is it dangerous?"

I stood up, paced. "We're supposed to protect children."

"Can she be hurt doing this?"

"You know what might happen if she sees someone she loves die."

"I do." She kissed my cheek. "What are the chances of her being hurt if she's alone in the ship's data?"

I sat down and picked the cracker back up, nibbled at the edge. "High. Higher."

"Will it be easier for her to see death if you are beside her?"

"Maybe you don't understand. She makes me stronger. That feels … like using her."

"Is this about you or is it about her?"

"Both." I ate another bite, and another, the food making me queasy. "She's probably safer with me. It just feels wrong."

She put her hand over mine. "I'll talk to Kayleen tomorrow, and to Liam. It's possible that you need her, and she needs you."

I swallowed.

"You won't hurt her. I trust you."

"I love you."

"I know. Eat."

I shook my head. "I'll be sick." I glanced at the clock. Three hours of my shift remained. "I need to go."

"I know."

Caro waited for me. She could be eerily patient for a child. Or maybe she had been listening.

Did you take a break?

I got up and went to the bathroom and drank water.

You should eat on breaks.

You sound like Mommy. Next time. I'm only a little hungry.

Do you want something to eat now?

No.

Maybe I could set it up so Liam did for her what Chelo did for me. Or Jherrel. Or Lou. Someone needed to see that her needs were met.

The Thorn *is fine. I think you should look into the war.*

I didn't want to show her much of that. Not yet. Maybe I didn't want to see it either. *I'm going to find the* Sun's Orbit.

What's that?

Another ship like the Thorn.

Caro rattled off coordinates. *Look there.*

How did you do that?

I've been watching the databases about the fight.

Chelo was right. I needed to keep Caro busy. *Okay.* I glanced at the coordinates. It was far. I hadn't even thought to try that kind of distance before.

I set aside my dismay. *Thank you. I'm going now. Stay here and help, and be careful.*

I have to follow you to help. I'll stay safe.

I'm going now.

47
CHELO

After his first turn in the battle chair, Joseph barely spoke. He allowed me and Ming to support most of his weight on the way back to his room. Ming looked worried as we tucked him into bed.

"He'll be better after he sleeps," I told her. "You rest, too."

She left, still looking anxious.

With a blue coverlet tucked up next to his ear, he looked like the boy who had flown away from me all those years ago.

He had been near Caro's age when he'd first demonstrated his strange capabilities. Joseph's skills were utterly strange to us on Fremont. They had stolen his childhood, and I suppose, mine. We had been defined by his strangeness, which drove him, scarred him, and fascinated him. I had helped, but from outside of his strange world. Caro was inside. What was that like?

I needlessly straightened his blankets and checked that he had a bulb of fresh water locked into the holder on his bedside table. Hopefully he would sleep through the whole break. I couldn't.

I found Liam and Kayleen passed out in our big bed. Caro leaned on pillows in the corner, Jherrel sound asleep next to her.

She looked up as I walked in and held her arms out. "Hello, Momma Chelo."

I picked her up and took her to the shared galley closest to our living quarters. Thankfully, it was empty. She looked fine. Normal. Not even particularly tired. Amusing, that, and also slightly irritating. As I ordered up hot cereal with berries for breakfast, I tried to sound casual. "Did you have a good night?"

Her plump fingers twisted together in her lap. Surely, she knew Joseph had told me what she'd done. Apparently, she didn't want to talk about it. "Daddy promised he'd make me another cake."

I couldn't let her escape so easily. "Why did you find Joseph last night?"

"Because he's going to need me one day."

The bowls of oatmeal were almost ready. I poured tea for me, juice for her, and set the table. "Need you for what?"

"You know how you help him?"

"Yes." I froze.

"I do that for him inside the data."

I swallowed. I calmed Joseph's fears and kept him out of his own dark places. This was no work for Caro. "What do you mean?"

"I make him feel good and help him go farther. I help him stay connected to his body, too."

I set the bowls down and took my seat. "You might distract him, sweetheart. We need him to protect us."

Her eyes widened. "That's why I matter."

I took a few bites, buying time. "Do you know what war is?"

"It's killing." She smiled. "I have to be sure we don't get killed."

I found her smile disconcerting. "That's Joseph's job." I tried to soften the knives in my voice. "And Captain Hill's job. Would you like me to ask her if you can be assigned a job? Like watching the hydroponics garden? You could help us make sure our food supply is safe."

She shook her head and glared at me, her look so precious it was hard not to burst out laughing or scoop her into my arms. But this could mean her life or her health. "It's dangerous," I told her. "Being in war. Joseph says other Wind Readers could attack us. That's how he met Marcus. Marcus was trying to force Joseph's first ship to land. Did Joseph tell you that story?"

She nodded. "And then they became friends."

"It didn't have to end up that way." How was she always a step ahead of me? I leaned in. "Caro. You can't do this. It could hurt you," I whispered. "Sometimes Wind Readers get sick when they try too hard, and then they can't be Wind Readers anymore." I hesitated. But she knew. "Like your mother. She used to be stronger. I don't want that to happen to you."

She ate the rest of her cereal without looking at me, then carried her bowl to the sink.

I joined her in the kitchen. "Sometimes you're as stubborn as Alicia."

Caro looked up at me. "She's here. In the fleet. She came last night."

I stopped with my hand under the hot water. "Do you know that?"

She pushed my hand to safety. "I wouldn't say it if I didn't know it."

I took a deep breath. "How do you know Alicia's here?"

"I heard her talking. Joseph went to the *Orbit* last night, and I heard Alicia talking in the background. I know her voice."

"I know you do." The *Orbit*? It was so far! Joseph could get from here to the *Orbit*?

I pursed my lips. So did Caro.

"What did Alicia say?"

"She wants to know where we are." Caro closed her eyes. "She wants to know why there are cats on the *Orbit*. Can I see the cats? I couldn't see them, not the way Alicia could. She liked seeing them. And she wants to be a real person, so she wants to win the war."

A real person? That meant she had wings. I swallowed. "Did you see her?"

"Uncle Joseph makes me stay mostly here. I don't think he did either."

I wanted to ask more, but now, sitting across from my daughter, I understood Joseph's worries. Caro was six, and using her for our ends felt wrong, even though she offered things we truly needed.

I changed the subject to a review of her times tables, which she knew to the tens in her head. Of course, if I asked her to multiply seven-hundred-and-three by ninety-two she would just query the ship's

AI. But that wouldn't give her knowledge. She understood what the number sixteen meant, but not how many of anything 64,676 represented.

Liam interrupted the times table game before we finished breakfast. He must have wondered at the profound relief on my face when he showed up. He leaned down and kissed us both on the forehead and told Caro, "Time to go see Lou for lessons."

I glanced at the time. "I have to do something. Can you meet me in our rooms in an hour? With Kayleen?"

"You're supposed to be sleeping." Unsaid, *I'm* supposed to stay with Caro.

I picked Caro up and looked into her eyes. "You be good for Lou, and you sleep some. If you don't nap today, I will see that you eat something that makes you tired tonight."

She nodded, probably thinking I hadn't said anything direct because I was planning to keep her secrets.

Fat chance.

Liam started talking about a new book he'd downloaded for her, and I picked up our breakfast dishes and took off to find Mohami.

I stopped in the crowded corridor long enough to catch up on the battle statistics from last night on a wall screen. The Port Authority published new data every six hours, and always emphasized Islan losses more than ours. Today's numbers estimated ten thousand dead, seven thousand hurt. Eight ships lost.

The total turned my stomach to acid. More people than the entire population of Fremont had been killed or hurt in a day and a half of battle.

News blared from every galley. People in uniform moved fast. Off-shift crew wandered more slowly, talking animatedly and dodging serving and delivery bots.

Anger at the useless deaths hammered through me in dizzying waves. By the time I got to Mohami's I felt sick with it, sour and disgusted.

I found him alone, sitting on the floor, his hands on his bent knees. I sat cross-legged in front of him.

"Breathe." No hello. Just *breathe*.

I did.

"More."

By the time I felt calm enough to talk, twenty minutes of my hour had bled away.

He made me wait at least three breaths past the point where I felt fully ready before he opened his hands to invite me to tell him why I had come.

I spilled out the war statistics.

Mohami nodded, unsurprised. "It's plausible that half the fleet will die. Maybe we will die as well. War is a crucible. We have talked about that."

"Can we slow it down?"

"What will happen if you tell people not to fight right now?"

I swallowed, breathed some more. "They will be less effective."

He nodded. "And?"

"They will consider us traitors."

He shifted his posture slightly, sat a little straighter. "I have to tell you something you won't like. Are you ready to hear it?"

"Yes."

He cocked his head. "You should not be seen with me and the movement for now. Yes, you helped create it. But it will send a badly mixed message for you to be beside Joseph as he fights and then here preaching peace."

"I have to do both!"

He shook his head. "Supporting Joseph is crucial. He needs you, and we all need for him to survive."

I stretched my legs out in front of me, bounced them. "I don't have any trouble being both things. I understand."

His smile was faint but filled his eyes with warmth. "I know that. But it could confuse some, and as I said, Joseph needs you."

I felt empty and chilled, still slightly sick to my stomach. Sadness dripped from my response. "Okay."

"I will provide support for the people we've nurtured, but not recruit new ones. Not in the midst of battle. This place will be a quiet haven." He sounded sad. "I'm sorry that I cannot offer haven to you now. You will have to be your own strength."

How would I manage without him? I swallowed, sniffed, then sat up straighter. "I understand."

He didn't move, which meant he knew I wasn't finished. Already, I felt his pending absence from my days.

Kala brought us a tray with tea and biscuits on it. "This will help you be strong," she told me.

"Thank you."

She faded into the background.

We were all near edges. I sipped at the tea, recognized herbs Paloma might have put into a nightcap tea. Mint and something earthier I had no certain name for.

Mohami hadn't mentioned Kayleen or Caro. I told him about the night before, and Joseph's panic, and how I had felt. Then I added, "I am like a Keeper for Joseph. But I cannot do what he does. I cannot keep him safe inside of data, inside of where he will fight the war. But surely a child is not the right option. We have to stop Caro."

"Can you? Joseph is truly extraordinary. He is also young, and dangerously exhausted. The universe is asking much of him."

"Caro is younger. It's not fair!"

"How old were you when you began helping Joseph?"

Not fair. I had told him our story. "But we were being threatened with our lives!" Even as the words came out, I recognized the parallel and heat flushed my cheeks.

Mohami smiled at that. "Perhaps Joseph needs Caro's support so much that you cannot stop her. She is a great empath, you know."

I blinked. Caro? Empathic?

"You will see it when she is older. Six-year-olds are not closely tied to the world outside of themselves. But she is magnificent."

"But how can we keep her safe?"

"None of us is safe now." He stood.

I had ten minutes to get back, and no idea how to talk to the others about Caro. But it had to be done, and then I had to sleep, or I would not be able to wake in time to talk with Joseph before his shift.

Mohami offered me his hand.

I took it, and as I stood, he pulled me into a warm embrace that smelled of incense and tea over soft, dry skin.

I took a deep breath, swearing I would remember what he felt like, what he said, and, when I encountered new situations, the kinds of things he said. When the battle was over, I would sit at his feet again. "Can Caro come to you if she needs to?"

"If Paloma brings her. You and Joseph should stay away for now. I am sorry."

"I understand."

I did understand, but nevertheless when I got back to my bed to try and sleep, tears soaked my pillow.

48

JOSEPH

I dreamed of a winged Alicia flying circles around the sun and falling, falling into it. Dragging awake felt like crawling up a mud-slicked tunnel. Alicia. I had known she was here the moment I heard about the *Sky Anvil.* Her voice had pulled a string tight in my stomach. It didn't matter that she loved herself more than she could ever love anyone else, even me.

As hot water from the shower poured over my scalp and down my back, my head returned to the conundrum Caro presented.

If I could multiply my strength by as much as I had last night … could I afford to turn down the help?

What would she do if I refused her?

What if she saw someone we loved die?

What if she felt me die? Would that burn her the way my parents' deaths burned me?

I found Ming and Chelo near a table full of steaming col and fresh protein pancakes with sweet berry jam. Calories sharpened my twisting thoughts into knives. As soon as I pushed my plate away, Chelo said, "We should discuss Caro."

"I know." I started my second cup of col. Too sweet.

Chelo laughed at the face I made. "I added nutrient powder. You looked drained at the end of your shift."

"Thanks."

She leaned toward me. "You went to the *Orbit.* Caro says she heard Alicia."

That startled me so much I almost dropped my cup. "Caro told you?"

"Are you okay?" Chelo asked.

She meant about Alicia. "I'm worried about her."

"Did you talk to her?"

"No. I can't let anyone know I can reach so far."

Ming leaned forward. "Good. Did anyone notice you were there?"

"I don't think so."

Ming opened her palm so her knife-bladed nails extended and flashed in the overhead lights. "Could you have gotten to the *Orbit* without Caro?"

"No. Maybe. Probably no. She multiplies my strength. It's weird." I sipped more col, made another face, told Chelo, "It's like what you do for me, only stronger."

Chelo finished the last pancake on her plate. "Caro has been immersed in data fields since she left Fremont. All of her life, really."

I shrugged. "You think that makes her different?"

"It's dangerous," Ming stared at her extended fingers. "being so young and strong. I'm assigning her a guard. They'll wait outside the family quarters but will follow her in public. I'll assign guards to the rest of you, too. We'll say it is because of your wealth. I'll watch Caro myself today and leave three guards with you."

I stiffened. But my physical fighting prowess was bad on a good day. "We do need to protect Caro." Everything was getting harder. No point in saying that. "But why physical guards? Did something happen?"

Ming's lips thinned. "There's tension between the people of the Doctrine and the crew who just want war. If that's going to blow, it will be soon."

"Point." I reached out and touched Ming on the shoulder, a small thank you that drew a smile.

Chelo stood and took my empty drinking bulb. "Caro is safer with you than on her own. We want her to be with you."

I swallowed, happy and unhappy. It still felt wrong.

"Will she distract you too much?" Ming asked.

"Not yet, today. But when the battle comes here ..."

Chelo narrowed her eyes, an unspoken secret in them. I wasn't ready to force it from her, especially in front of Ming. "What happened while I slept? The other ships?"

"*Peacemaker* may see combat before you come off shift. She's got crew at battle stations and warm weapons. The *Sky Anvil* is with the *Orbit.* We did get a small-ship news report about fliers which said Alicia is there. It didn't name her as your sister, and it called her 'Alicia the Black.'"

I smiled at how much she would love a title like that. "Does she have wings?"

"I think so. Tsawo is there, too."

Were he and Alicia finally lovers? The thought stung even though I wanted her to be happy. I took a deep breath, steadied myself. "They'll fit in with the *Orbit*'s fleet of small fighters. Fliers have agile small-combat bubbles, and we'll all be doing that kind of fighting soon." I finished the inordinately-sweet col, and while I felt better for it, the taste made it harder to swallow with each sip.

Ming left to find Caro, and Chelo and I headed for Command. Sure enough, three guards peeled away from the wall outside and followed us. Two men and a woman. I waved at them to keep their distance, and the woman slid past us and walked ahead, leaving the two men to watch our backs.

It took a while to find an empty stretch in the crowded corridors to ask Chelo, "Are you okay?"

She took my hand and squeezed it. "What's not to like? I hate war and I'm on my way to a vast battle."

I enjoyed the warmth of her palm against mine. "I believe in the third way you have been crafting. I also think Mohami is right. The first pass through of the battle needs to happen. We need to survive that and be able to re-group on the other side."

Chelo sounded resigned. "People are so full of fear they can't back away."

"I don't hate these people. On Fremont, I hated the mercenaries for killing my family there. But I knew them. As individuals. I'd looked into their eyes."

"These are people from the same place," Chelo observed quietly.

"True. Maybe it's that this seems less personal."

We let go of each other's hands as we threaded through a busy corner. She turned to me. "What if the ships all keep turning back into one another until everyone is dead?"

"It's not like you to be so bleak."

"Fighting steals my soul."

I pulled her close enough to smell her shampoo. "I know."

We passed through the double doors into Command. The room hummed with activity. Captain Hill waited for us in a small quiet place in the center of the chaos with five chairs. "Good morning." She gestured to a seat near her.

We sat.

"Two Wind Readers watched me last night. One is on this ship. The other is from the *Black Star*." She smiled. "Neither is a six-year old."

"Caro was with me part of last night."

Captain Hill's lips thinned. "Is that wise?"

Chelo answered, "We've talked to her. Allowed it with rules. She can support Joseph, but she can't wander ahead of him. She can't touch weapons or communication systems. We told her we'll drug her if she does that."

Captain Hill raised an eyebrow and sat back, one thumb rubbing the heel of her opposite hand as if it hurt.

"What did they want?" I asked her. "The Wind Readers who were hacking in?"

"They were poking at the AI. The *Thorn* was able to block them—we have excellent security. So they got nowhere. But I wasn't able to lock them out. I have instructed my security crew to get that done, but you need to know. They represent a risk."

Like I did when I ran through other ship's systems. Some of this war would come down to what people like me could do, rather than to what people with triggers for big weapons could manage. "I'll be watchful."

"Good luck." She stood. "You have the *Thorn* for the next twelve hours."

"Thank you."

She hadn't said a thing about Caro. I knew her well enough now to understand that meant she was thinking about it.

Caro waited for me in the outer layers of the *Thorn*'s data. I took her on a tour of the *Thorn*'s sensors, testing her on their functions. She knew more than I'd expected her to. Understood it. Not like an engineer or anything, not even like I did, but the way a crewman who didn't work with the systems might. Which was a lot for a six-year old.

We'd been working together for an hour before the AI informed me the intruders were back.

Caro—do you see them?

Silence for a while. *Yes. I think so.*

Thorn*? Is she right?*

Yes.

Can you tell what they're trying to do? I asked Caro.

Learn.

Learn what?

How to control the Thorn. *They're afraid that we won't fight, and they want to take command when the battle gets here.*

That's absurd! Then, *How do you know?*

I followed their logs and figured out how they talk to each other.

I queried the ship. Thorn*?*

She did.

Caro felt appalled. *Don't you trust me?*

I do. But you are still six, and I still have to convince others you are telling the truth.

She didn't respond directly, but since she dropped the subject, I assumed she understood.

Thorn*? Do you know enough to stop them now?* I asked the AI.

With ninety-five percent accuracy.

Very good, Caro. Thank you.

I could have stopped them!

I want you to be our secret. If people are scared of you, they might hurt you.

Ming told me that. So did Mom and Dad. And Chelo. Like one wasn't enough. But I could have stopped them!

Someday you might have to. But do you promise to use the Thorn *and her security crew whenever you can? Will you be their secret weapon?*

A long silence. *I will.*

Thank you.

There was no way to know whether or not I would have been able to see what Caro saw. All I knew was that she saw it first, and she showed me. I had been able to tell that these were amateurs. But any day now, we might encounter whatever Islas had been training to throw at us. They hated Making, but they loved starships and, apparently, war. They had to use Wind Readers for pilots. Did they also use them as weapons?

Caro asked me a question. *Are they right? Will you keep us from fighting?*

Only if that's the right thing to do.

How will you know?

Sometimes you have to trust yourself. Caro? I'm going to go up and eat and talk to Chelo. You should come out of the data as well for a little bit, eat.

What if something happens?

Something probably will. We have Ulrika as backup. I will tell her we are taking a break. Neither of us can be here every moment. I will stay in touch with Thorn, *and it will tell me if I need to go back.*

I can stay.

Eat. Keep your strength up. Ulrika will do fine. I winced as I realized how much I sounded like Chelo. *Take care of yourself.*

Okay.

Chelo waited for me, her face calm but her eyes worried. "It's okay. Just a minute." I looked around and spotted Ulrika just a few feet away, staring at a stream of data. I called her over to me. "We're out of the *Thorn*'s data for the moment."

Ulrika nodded. "I'll send in someone else. I need to stay focused."

Ulrika didn't follow my orders easily. I suspected that was because while she would follow Captain Hill to the end of the Five Worlds, she still had no reason to trust me. I could force her, but to lead through that I would need to understand the task she didn't want to leave. She fidgeted, ready to be back in front of her screen. I told her, "Thank you," and she nodded and turned her back immediately.

Chelo asked, "Is Caro okay?"

"She is."

"Good." She pushed a plate toward me.

As I started in on the small feast of water, finger sandwiches, berries, and sweet cakes that she had laid out for me, I worried at the problem. "We found the intruders the captain mentioned, and Caro figured out how to keep them out. *Thorn* took care of it. Can you do some research for me?"

She cocked her head. "What?"

"I need to know what Islas can throw at us."

"Weapons?"

"Cyber. Well, everything, I think. But we've been briefed on their conventional weapons for weeks, as well as our own. But what else has Islas been working on? They have their mercenary fleet, which I suspect is here somewhere. By system law, they have to have Wind Readers as pilots, but are they backing them up with anything? Or worse, using AIs as primary and the Wind Readers just to meet the intent of the law?"

"*Islas* has to use Wind Readers for pilots?"

I often forgot that she had been on Fremont while I was learning about the Five Worlds. She had odd holes in her knowledge. "Sometime long before we were born, some ship's AIs took each other out. Lives were lost. AIs fighting AIs apparently did some scary things. Even I don't know what, although I'm sure it's in a record somewhere. Anyway, it's outlawed. Every ship has an AI, but they all must have human pilots. In fact, I suspect the ability to Read the Wind was engineered because of that rule."

She looked thoughtful.

I added, "But that doesn't mean they won't try to infect our AI with something."

"That's not outlawed?"

"It probably is. But so is some of what I'm doing, if I get caught."

She drew in a breath but didn't protest.

"This is war."

She let the breath out slowly. "I'll see what I can learn."

I took care of my body's needs and strapped back down in to the crash couch, my head whirling with worries about Caro.

Having her here focused me in strange ways. If I could keep her safe, I could keep the *Thorn* safe.

Chelo stood by my crash couch, her fingers massaging my scalp and my shoulders. She whispered, "It will be okay. You'll be okay. It will all be okay. That's the only outcome we can allow, the only one we can see."

Always hopeful, Chelo. I couldn't bear to tell her how precarious our situation felt.

The *Thorn* called to me, not with any purpose, but with the sweet siren of its data. I went, falling into the places where I worried about machines more than people, and where Caro was with me in spirit, like family inside the machine. She shared my love of ships, of data, of consistency.

As soon as she felt my presence, she asked, *What next?*

Support me? I'm heading for the Black Star.

You're going to look for the hackers there?

Maybe. I promised your mom you would not venture past the Thorn *right now.*

I promised her, too. I'll be able to see a little while I support you going there. Like when you went to the Orbit.

The *Black Star* was close, and to reach the *Orbit* I'd had to hop across three ships, leaving a bit of myself behind in each one like breadcrumbs. *Stay safe, Caro.*

I will.

I love you.

Thank you, Uncle Joseph.

If anyone hurt her, I would find a way to destroy them.

I came back from the *Black Star* after about an hour. I felt connected to Caro the whole time even though she was demonstrably wedged strongly in the *Thorn*'s data.

Are you okay?

Yes. I found the hackers on the Black Star.

More than one?

Two. I left them messages, so they know we know who they were, and that we had to fight together. I told them we'd report them if we caught them again.

Is that all? I thought they'd get in more trouble.

I had to get into the Black Star*'s systems to find them.*

She went silent for as long as it took me to tour the *Thorn*'s basic diagnostics. Finally she said, *Oh. You were doing what they were.*

Right.

Is that okay?

Let's have this conversation face to face. Later.

Okay.

We toured the other nearby ships. I kept an eye out for news from *Peacemaker*. I wanted to know when she went into battle. There was so much news though. She was my best warship, but she was still small compared to the great Port Authority ships and the Islan flagships.

I didn't learn anything until near the end of my shift. Captain Hill waited for me alongside Chelo. "The *Peacemaker* is fighting."

"What happened?"

"She was set upon by two smaller Islan ships and a torpedo round hit her."

Even as tired as I was, the news made me cold.

"She's okay. She'll pull out to the edge of the fleet. She's got a few holes to fix, but they didn't destroy her. I just thought you should know."

I glanced at Chelo. She reached for me. "Ten people died."

"The captain is okay?"

"Yes. But she lost her main Engineer and three lower officers. A few of the cleaning crew. She glanced at Chelo. "You'll want to send condolences."

Chelo took a note. "Okay."

I closed my eyes for a moment. The *Peacemaker* felt more like the ship I flew in my dreams than the *Thorn*. It would have seemed a bad omen if she'd been destroyed. "Did we shoot anyone? The *Peacemaker*, I mean?"

"Yes. The *Peacemaker* and the *Opportunity* took out an Islan flagship, the *Doni Mihalo*. I'm not sure who did it, but someone managed to blow her drives. There is a rescue operation underway."

"I hope they succeed."

Captain Hill smiled. "That's kind of you."

Chelo handed me a bulb of water and turned toward Captain Hill, her voice grim. "My brother is kind, but he can also be strong and terrible."

I smiled.

49

ALICIA

An alert siren startled me awake. I pulled my mask off and carefully slipped my arms free from their straps. I glanced at the pinion, smiled, and then looked at my wrist. Nothing. Did Joseph even know I was here? Why had I recorded that sappy message and not just said hello?

In the main galley, Tsawo paced in front of plates of fruit, nuts, protein bars, and cookies. "Three Islan ships are headed directly for the *Sun's Orbit*. That's two more than we'd expected. We appear to be a target."

Marti and I shared a worried glance. Why would the Islans direct three full-size battleships at an old retrofit like the *Orbit*?

Tsawo continued, "We could get the opportunity to fight some ships our size, one on one. We've been told to watch out for drone bombers, too."

A frisson of excitement ran through my nerves.

"And of course, the *Sun's Orbit* has autonomous weapons, too. So be careful of friendly fire. Our current orders are to get out there and stay near the ship."

He looked around to see if we shared his excitement.

I had been designed for risk. Fear felt good to me. Marti, however, looked frightened and a little ill.

Tsawo ended with, "That's all the orders we have now. We'll get more."

Jagruti bustled around the galley. She wore a flowing black Keeper's uniform, her hair coiled in fine, complex braids. She helped pull my helmet on and attached the breathing apparatus. Fliers couldn't wear full environment suits, so the little ships we flew were our atmosphere suits. The breathing equipment let me take in extra oxygen if I needed it and should keep me alive for a short time even in a vacuum. My flier's lungs were huge; I'd need to empty them fast in a breach. If I succeeded, the helmet and oxygen bottles would provide a little time, in spite of the horrors of vacuum. At least the ships were hard to breach.

My war bubble had room for one flier and one wingless. We didn't have any extra wingless humans on *Anvil*, so we would each fly solo.

Adrenaline buzzed through my nerves.

I settled into piloting position: legs shoulder-width apart, torso on a padded bench. My arms were each able to direct the ship with simple gestures. Supports took the weight of my wings.

Jagruti helped me tug thick gloves on. I had been forced to wear them in the simulator and knew my hands would sweat in the damned things. As Jagruti helped snug the buckles that would hold me fast to the bench, she leaned down and whispered, "Remember everyone does their best. There is no truth, but everyone strives for it." She touched my chest and the back of my neck and whispered something too low for me to understand.

A prayer?

Then she tightened a big, padded strap over my mid-back just below where my wings joined my back, and stepped out of the door, her face a mask of formality.

Tsawo stuck his head inside. "Stay safe."

The memory of his kiss tickled my nerves. "You, too."

His return smile was hot with adrenaline, his eyes shining.

The *Anvil* ejected me with a quick push.

I floated, waiting for the other two. Stars were startlingly clear points of light obscured on my right side by the angles and sharp planes of the *Anvil.*

It took ten minutes for Marti to join me.

Tsawo followed eight minutes after that.

We ran with low lights, hard to see. Induan would have approved.

I should have told Joseph we'd lost Induan. I whispered, "Look at me now," to her ghost and then tilted my hands to speed the craft ahead, following Tsawo.

A display in the far-right corner of my helmet showed our positions near each other.

With no further orders, Tsawo led us away from the bigger ships. His voice sounded tinny in my helmet speakers. "Cy is sending battle information to your HUD. Look to the right quadrant."

Amber light bloomed, with black figures against it. I flicked my gaze back and forth, watching the screen and the space in front of me while Cy's voice played in my ears. "The Islan ship *Wild Wind 3* is coming in from below you, targeting the *Sun's Orbit.*

One of the figures on the HUD blinked. The *Wild Wind 3* looked bigger than the *Sun's Orbit* and the *Sky Anvil* put together.

Cy's voice kept me from drifting past the current moment. "The *Star Speed 1* is also coming in, from a different angle."

The third ship, the *Space Soldier 7*, was farther away, but apparently close enough to pose a threat within a few hours.

Cy spoke to all of the human flying weapons he'd sent out. That included the three of us, but also a number of other manned ships, including the *Lily Star.* "Stay out of the way of the *Orbit*'s guns and stay invisible so you don't draw fire."

Thirty minutes passed.

I played with the bubble, named it *Cat* in my head, thinking of the paw-cats and the way they surprised, attacked, and then got away.

"Torpedo." Cy's voice.

A single line on my HUD showed it streaking in from above, which meant from *Star Speed 1*. I decided to call it *One*. So *One* fired a single torpedo, and the *Sun's Orbit* fired back.

The two missiles chased each other through the sky and then detonated together.

"Another … Another … Another."

Staccato.

Two of the incoming torpedo lines extended past the *Orbit*. One of those nicked the *Anvil*, which bucked but continued. The third torpedo put a hole in the *Orbit*.

A plume of gas leaked out but stopped quickly. Cy gave us no damage information for either ship. He simply called shots which were coming at us, and occasionally gave us navigation instructions to keep us clear of the *Orbit*'s own small ships. The *Orbit* seemed to be firing mostly defensively. But then, we were its primary offense, and there were no threats close enough for us to react to yet.

I practiced small maneuvers with *Cat* and kept a watchful eye on the enemy ships.

We lost three small manned ships. Only one of the pilots had time to curse.

The *Orbit* disgorged a swarm of small unmanned craft as the other Islan ships came closer.

We bobbed, waiting, trying not to be targets.

Cat was small and tight, and while I could stretch my wings, they were mostly in the way. Here I was, flying beautifully and faster than I'd ever flown, graceful as hell, but my wings themselves were cramped and in the way.

I blinked, told myself to focus.

A cloud of even smaller objects floated free of the *Wild Wind 3*.

Cy's voice. "Tsawo? Can you three help shoot at those?"

"What are they?"

"I don't know. But you might be able to kill them."

All three of us flowed toward the objects. They were small metal boxes with thrusters, maybe a quarter the size of the *Cat*.

"Cy?" Tsawo said. "I don't like these. I can't tell what they do."

"Are you close enough to shoot at one?"

"I'll try."

My fingers twitched, but I wasn't the one with the orders to shoot.

A tiny flash of light gave away Tsawo's position. The flying box darted at him, faster than I thought it should be able to.

Something hit the *Cat*, just above my head and slightly behind. A long metal claw appeared overhead.

50
CHELO

Joseph had passed out. Caro was sound asleep with Kayleen curled protectively around her, and as far as I could tell the rest of the ship was either actively on duty or asleep. I sat, listening to boots walking past, robots scuttling overhead, muffled commands coming over the comm system, and the usual creaks and moans of a metal ship.

Maybe that's how active warships were. Cold and noisy. The *Thorn* felt different than it had in the long days leading up to the battle.

I got up and roamed her corridors, humming to myself and trying to stay out of the way of bustling uniformed crew. A tall young man ghosted after me, looking as miffed at his guard duty as I felt about having a guard. I kept thinking of Caro, Kayleen, Joseph, and now Alicia.

Alicia. Surely she'd cause some kind of trouble.

Eventually, I let myself into the gardens. This late, I was the only flesh and blood being here except the plants themselves. I felt the strong, fuzzy leaves of the hybrid tomatoes and brought my fingers to my face, breathing in the earthy smell they left on my skin.

A string of pollinator bots whizzed by, startling me. They were bright red with blue wings, cute enough to force a smile from me.

I wanted to live somewhere with dirt and soil all the way to the core, and not the dirt of a hydro garden on a ship. Dirt full of worms and little pebbles and old rotting leaves.

The door opened. I turned. Liam. He looked almost as tired as Joseph, and I realized I'd never even asked what he had been doing on his last shift. "Are you okay?"

He folded me in his arms. "Of course not. I would fight a battle where I can see my enemy, but this is … unnatural. We're in tin cans with long range weapons. Half the people who die out here will die without knowing what's about to happen to them. Some might not even notice it then."

"I miss home."

"Which home? Akashi is going to step down next year, and he's appointed Merino to be his successor. They're already sharing duties."

If we were home, Liam would be stepping into Akashi's shoes. "How did you get news from Fremont?"

"Sky sent me a long message. It went to Lopali first, but it got shuttled up with some messages for Mohami."

"Any other news?"

"Sky had her second baby. I'll forward the message to you later."

I searched his face. He looked worried, but then he'd looked worried since we left Lopali. I folded him in my arms.

He rested his chin on the top of my head. "How did we get here?"

"I don't know."

"I'd give anything to go back. Even to our waterfall."

Where we'd been trapped, and every day I'd wanted to be back with the band. At least then home had been on the same planet, maybe days away at most. Now we were years away, and essentially banished. "Mohami says we always all end up where we need to be."

A short, bitter laugh escaped Liam. "Mohami says whatever helps keep us calm."

"Why not? We can think better when we're calm."

"And go like lambs to the slaughter."

"That's not like you. Mohami didn't lead us here. Joseph did. And Marcus."

"If this is ever over, I want to find a place for the five of us. If the others want to come, they can."

I pushed away and looked up into his face. "Me, too."

The door opened again. My guard, followed by a broader man who must be Liam's guard. They came straight toward us.

Liam stood up straight, pushing a little away from me. "What?"

My guard looked at us, the bored look completely erased. "You need to come with us."

Liam cocked his head. "Why?"

"We're taking you to a secure location. There have been threats on your lives."

Before I could think of what to say, my guard added, "Mostly against you," he nodded at me, "but we're taking all of you into temporary protective custody. The whole family."

Including Joseph? The children? My skin crawled. "Surely we're fine here. You're both armed." I swept my arm around at the gardens. "There's nothing here but a few gardening robots."

"Captain Hill gave the orders."

Captain Hill was on shift. To give these orders, she had to have been pulled away from worrying about the *Thorn* and about her work with the war.

"Come with us."

Liam and I shared a glance. He didn't look any happier than I felt. But he nodded. "We'll come."

As I walked out, I picked a ripe cherry tomato and stuck it in my mouth.

It tasted good, but not as good as tomatoes grown in dirt.

51
ALICIA

A second long, metal claw dropped into view, each wider than my hands. Together, they nearly blocked my vision on both sides. They splayed against the *Cat*'s rounded surface, inching around as if looking for something to hold onto.

I screeched, "What is that?"

Tsawo's reply came fast and loud. "There's something on me, too! Can you see it?"

The controls responded normally in spite of my visitor. But then weight or drag weren't really issues out here. Still, adrenaline drove my spin wide. After correcting, I spotted Tsawo's bubble.

My rider stayed with me, the frightening claws scraping lightly across the surface only at the greatest speed of my turns.

Sticky.

Another square started matching its trajectory to mine. It flared open, a flower of robotic arms trying to catch me in a second deadly hug.

I screamed and goosed the *Cat*, moving so fast I had to reorient toward Tsawo again. The thing on him had its back to me now. Slender, black arms, the back a simple disk that the arms attached to. It appeared strong and agile, and moved as if alive.

This might be the perfect way to destroy a fleet of small ships. Killer origami robots. The thought brought an edgy laugh, dampened my fear.

Risk.

The arms inched farther down the *Cat*'s front side and stole my view of Tsawo.

Before I could think of how to describe it, Marti said, "It's a mech. Six arms. All of them around your bubble. It's pressed against the side. They move like snakes."

I couldn't see her bubble. "Do you have one, too?"

"No. I'm heading toward you."

Cy's voice cut in. "One of those things just crushed a drone. Can you shake it?"

The claws in front of my face had stopped moving, but the arm above them flexed, changing the angle so a sharp edge like a metal fingernail touched the bubble. "I think it's going to try to crush *me*."

"We lost another drone. Move!"

I flicked the controls right so hard the *Cat* spun dizzyingly. I lost sight of Tsawo's bubble, and screamed at my HUD. "Find Tsawo! Visual contact."

The HUD parsed the command and the signup's computer stopped the *Cat* where I could once more see Tsawo's bubble.

Marti called, "I'm going to shoot at the one on you."

"Don't hit me!"

"I'll try not to. Tsawo, you okay?"

No answer.

The thing on my bubble jerked once, hard, and a scratch appeared on the surface near one of the claws. A claw flailed loose and for a moment I thought the whole monster would drop away, but then the loose arm swung down hard, rattling the outside of the bubble and causing the straps holding me down to strain to keep me in flight position.

"I did it!" Marti shouted, triumphant, then whispered, "It's still there."

My weapons weren't designed to hit something on me, not unless it decided to camp on top of one. Not likely.

The monster machine jerked again. "I got it harder," Marti said. "Trying for the brain."

The brain? Maybe where the legs came together. My breath sounded like a windstorm in my helmet, the glass fogging at the edges, stealing my peripheral vision.

What about my thrusters? The direction I'd turned hadn't hurt it, but what about the other way? I gave the *Cat* instructions to rotate left.

The claws in front of my face disappeared, simply and suddenly not there.

"I got it!" Marti yelled.

"Thank you."

"I'm going to Tsawo."

"Me, too."

"Go back to the *Anvil*," she said. "In case your ship is damaged."

Even after all this time, she clearly didn't know me well. I spun the *Cat* until I spotted Tsawo and his unexpected guest. Marti was already close to him, but I was not far behind her.

Another one of the machines drifted near her, uncurling. "Don't back up, Marti."

"Okay."

The thing bumped her and started opening.

I swallowed, checked my targeting, and fired.

I missed.

One of the huge clamps landed on Marti's bubble just as she fired at the robot on Tsawo's craft.

Her voice was high. "I got one on me!"

"You do. I missed. Hold still."

"Get closer." Marti steered closer to Tsawo's bubble, where the machine still hugged him like a lover.

"Hurry," Marti said.

I fired again, hit it near the center. It shivered.

Even with one on her, Marti fired at the monster that rode Tsawo's bubble again. It fell away. The bubble cleared, showing the black of Tsawo's wings. "I'm okay," he panted. "I'm okay."

The outside of Marti's bubble crumpled inward.

The claws dug into holes they had made.

"Blow your air out!" Tsawo yelled.

"Come on *Cat*," I whispered. "Let's do this." I struggled to aim, hesitated, waiting for a lock. No time. I fired.

Marti's bubble came apart.

Had I hit her instead of her monster? How could I tell? I screamed in anger.

The thing grabbed at her. She was still mostly inside, in spite of the fact that at least a quarter of the outside of her bubble had started streaming behind her, trailing cables and wires.

Tsawo nosed toward her.

The tip of a red wing was visible. It jerked about, signs of struggle. Maybe Marti trying to unstrap?

"Hang on!" Tsawo screamed.

Marti would still have on her helmet, still have air. We'd been trained for this. Jagruti's words played in my head. *Everyone does their best.* Marti had done her best to save us. She had done it, too. It had been enough. My own best hadn't saved her. Yet.

She'd have minutes if she'd been able to release most of her breath before the sudden loss of pressure.

A claw crept along the broken bubble that held her, questing for a way to reach in and grab her.

I gained a better angle. "I'm shooting it. Be careful." I took a deep breath to steady myself, whispered, "Careful," and pushed the button to shoot again.

Both monster and machine went one way, Marti another.

"I'll get her," Tsawo said. "Keep any more of those things away."

Marti's winged figure receded quickly, the bubble of her helmet hiding her face. She carried a small air bottle in one hand.

I took off after her. I had no idea what I was going to do, but losing sight of her wouldn't help with anything.

Tsawo's voice. "My bubble is alerting." I heard alarms screaming in the background, turned to look. Something vented from a hole near his feet.

"You're hurt. Go back!"

"But—"

I cut him off. "No point is risking all three of us. Go back to the *Anvil*."

"Good luck." Longing and pain choked his voice. "Don't die."

52

JOSEPH

Chelo wasn't in my room when I woke. My clothes hadn't been set out, and there was no cup of hot col waiting for me. I splashed water on my face and pulled on clothes. As soon as I opened the door I came face to face with Ming. She looked tired and slightly unkempt, and vaguely older. "Is everything okay?" I asked her.

"The fight's about to reach us. We've received threats against your family. Credible enough that Captain Hill asked that everyone be put into protective custody."

"The children?"

"All of you."

"You're not putting me in custody!"

She waved a hand in front of her face. "No. No. Your job is custody enough. Speaking of, the captain asked that you arrive twenty minutes early for your shift for an extra debriefing. I've got someone making you breakfast."

"I want to see my family."

"Of course you do." She started walking, using a gesture to pull me into step beside her.

Anger made me walk faster. "Are we going to my family?"

"There's no time. They're being kept near the ship's bay in case they

—or we—need to escape. The captain said you'd be able to check on them while you're on duty."

She meant in the data. "That's not the same as seeing them in person."

"The fighting will reach you this shift."

"Why didn't you wake me up?"

She glanced at me sideways in exasperation. But then, of all of the people I counted as my own, Ming and Dianne were the only two with military experience.

"All right. Work when you can, sleep when you can."

She smiled. The captain was the first one who'd said that to me, but Ming used the phrase more since she'd become my bodyguard. Off shift meant off shift. "Caro is there, too?"

"There're five guards. One is inside their new rooms to run information and errands, and two are stationed in each corridor."

I felt deeply unsettled, but we were moving too fast for me to think. My boots rang on the hard metal corridors. "Who made threats?"

"We're almost there."

Captain Hill paced alone inside the briefing room. She glanced at me when I came in, her face tense and worried. "Good morning."

Enough food, drink, and thankfully, col, for at least five people filled the conference table. I poured a bulb from a steaming carafe on the table and sat down. Chocolate. One thing was going right. "What happened?"

The captain sat, her face grave. "Early this shift, a fresh set of rumors hit the ship's social webs. They were … not complimentary. To you or your family. Then the rumors had babies, and the babies grew into new ones. Hopefully all lies." She gazed at me as if I could testify to that before I even knew what the rumors were about.

"So tell me," I demanded, anger roughing my nerves.

"Apparently you started this whole war on Fremont." She reached for her glass of water, started pouring. "And apparently you now want to finish it, make sure as many people as possible die, all in revenge for your family."

A laugh exploded from me before I got control. "You know neither is true."

Ming leaned back in her chair. "I told her that."

"That's not all. Theoretically, you killed Marcus in order to gain his fortune."

That one hurt. The first two were so absurd they didn't matter; no one but conspiracy nuts would believe them. Not that the *Thorn* and her sister ships didn't have a handful of those. But this? "I would never."

"There are videos circulating. We're trying to prove they're doctored."

I stared at her. Each word came out heavy and separated by space. "I did not kill Marcus."

Her features softened into a smile. "I know that. I met you when you came in after, and I saw the look on your face. I've also worked with you deep in data. So I *know* you didn't kill Marcus."

I nodded. Working together to keep the ship safe exposed us one to another. She would know if I were false, like I would know if she was.

She continued, "I already know—from Marcus—your version of the fight on Fremont. If anything, Islas started this."

I didn't look away from her steady gaze. "Do you trust me?"

"I do." She took a deep breath and refilled her water glass. "Two of my officers came to me this morning and asked me to remove you from duty until you can demonstrate innocence."

I blinked at her. "What did you tell them?"

"That we needed you. The captain of the *Sun's Orbit* also sent a message asking about it, so the rumor has gone through the fleet in less than eight hours, and that's while the *Orbit* has been fighting."

That felt like being hit with a board. "You do want me to take this shift?"

She hesitated for a fraction of a second. "Can you be effective?"

"Yes."

"I'm going to tell Ulrika to take front. She'll give commands. I need you to keep the *Thorn*'s systems safe. Ulrika will call you if the fighting gets bad enough to need you to back her." She sighed and met my eyes. "But my orders could change. This story is still new and evolving. We'll enter battle on the next shift. Fighters need to be led by someone they trust."

A tingle of mixed excitement and dread ran through me. "Tell me about the fighting."

"In a minute. First, I need to know that you will pull yourself off shift and hand the *Thorn* over to Ulrika if you feel that there's any reason you are not a hundred percent. *Any reason.* Rumors. Caro. Chelo. Anything in how you feel. *Any reason.*"

I took a deep breath. I'd sworn to protect the Port Authority and the ship above all other things. "I will."

Caro, of course, waited for me. There were no facial expressions in streams of data. I couldn't see her smile. But her energy was easy to locate. Young and curious and sincerely confident. She babbled on for a moment about moving, but apparently she didn't feel threatened. Good for Chelo and Liam. *Show me where you are in physical form? Where in the* Thorn*?*

She did. The captain had installed my family in a suite of rooms near the docking bay with a galley, a restroom, one bedroom, and a larger room with couches and a meeting table. It was probably designed for visiting pilots who docked ships inside the *Thorn*. There were plenty of camera feeds. Liam and Chelo were talking in the big room. Jherrel was sleeping with his head on Chelo's lap. Kayleen was on the bed beside Caro, stroking her shoulder and back, keeping her promise to stay out of the data while still supporting her daughter.

If only I could reach through and hug them all.

After Caro and I settled into work, I told her, *We might see some of the battle today. Will you obey me, no matter what I ask you?*

No. What if you ask me to hurt you?

I swallowed an inappropriate response and said, *Will you obey me if I ask to you to stop helping me and come back completely to the Thorn?*

Yes.

If I see something I don't want you to look at, will you look away?

If I can.

At least she was always honest. Stubborn, but honest. I loved her with all my heart, and I still hated the extra power she gave me. If only I could turn away from it.

Estimates suggested we wouldn't engage for five hours or more. Two enemy ships headed toward our group of five, and a few more could turn our way and might join. Battle, when it came, would be the larger and less maneuverable ships firing at each other where the fleets met, and hundreds of small battles between both manned and automated small craft.

As much as I wanted to focus on the *Thorn* to watch over my family here, this might be my only chance to check on Alicia. *Can you help me bridge to the Sun's Orbit again?*

I'll try. Some ships have moved.

Thank you. Tell me if I'm needed here.

I will.

It took an hour to jump carefully across three other ships to the *Orbit*. We went through the *Unicorn*, which was now easy to enter with data already flowing between the *Thorn* and her. Next, we bridged a newsfeed through the *Nebulae's Child*, which had such lousy security I doubted it would survive its first battle, and—with great effort—along a command string through the *Sky of Star Clouds*, which was as beautiful as the *Peacemaker*, and as well-tended. When Caro and I together bested her systems after six tries, I actually felt a twinge of guilt at breaching her.

For all three hops, it felt like I relied less on Caro, which was a relief. Maybe if I practiced enough, I wouldn't need her at all.

Not that the battle gave me any time.

The next hop was to the *Orbit*. *Caro—I'm going without you. There's damage reported. You stay here. This ship is safe.*

Do I have to?

I need you to be a strong anchor home.

Okay.

Good. That was one order obeyed.

The *Sky of Star Clouds* had too much security for me to talk with its AI, at least not without spending a lot of time doing it. News feeds suggested that fighting raged all around us. The big ships had passed, but as the fleets slid through each other, there was more than one opportunity to take or give damage for every ship, maybe many.

Visiting the *Orbit* would be safe enough for now.

It was easy to slide into her feeds. I'd been there before.

I checked my anchor to the *Sky of Star Clouds*, and to Caro. This supporting and anchoring was a thing I could not describe to anyone who had not done what I have. Part pathway, part scraps of self left behind, an effort that feels like stretching away from your heart, and taking crumbs of your soul with you.

I shall know how to return to myself, I chanted. Again. *I shall be able to return to myself. I shall be able to return to Caro.*

Caro must have heard me. *I will keep hold of you.*

She was six, and amazing. What would she be like at ten? At twenty? *Thank you.*

I turned my attention to the damaged *Orbit*.

Data flashed and flew throughout her systems, focusing on the breaks. I followed some of the fastest and most strident data streams to locate a hole in section of crew quarters. They'd retained life support in the rest of the ship. Repair bots scuttled everywhere, chattering to each other in broken streams of communication on overloaded circuits.

They used spare parts and welding-torch arms to make sure the hole didn't grow and to add a layer of protective coating to the parts of the ship that used to be inside but were now outside.

They didn't bother to salvage anything. So the ship's AI saw it as an emergency.

I drew back, headed for the great hold.

It was largely empty. So most of the small ships were out, fighting.

I found Cy stalking corridors, giving orders as he went. I verified he was okay. I didn't speak to him. No one needed to know I could get this far except Caro, Chelo, and Captain Hill.

Captain Zhao sat in his command chair, barking orders, his face concerned.

The *Lily Star* was gone. I searched through all of the cameras onboard quickly, a continuous blurring spin through empty rooms.

No sign of Alicia. No sign of any fliers, or anyone from Lopali. No Keepers. Nothing.

They had come in the *Sky Anvil.* Maybe they were there.

The *Anvil* was locked into a path near the *Orbit. Caro?*

Yes?

I'm going next door.

That will stretch you further.

I'll be careful.

The two ships already shared navigation data, which was a steady stream I could follow easily.

The *Anvil* was a deeply damaged beauty. She had been shot at by the same ship that had holed the Orbit. It had hit her twice. One person had died. A human male.

Not Alicia.

Surely she was okay.

Half the crew had lost access to their living quarters.

The *Anvil* had been assaulted by small robots. I hesitated, then stopped and took time to play back some of the history. The damage reports sent me the camera logs, where I got a decent look at the robots from some angles, and in other shots there were blurs or dots on the outside of the huge ship. They attached to whatever they bumped into and then started cutting and destroying. Determined more than subtle. Almost brutish. The *Anvil* reported robot damage to a communications antenna, two cameras, and two places on the ship where they had almost breached the hull. Based on the camera footage, it had taken two or three far smarter but weaker defense bots to remove each of the three robots that had attached themselves to the outside of the ship.

At least none had come in.

The list of personnel was more protected than the ship's basic hardware systems.

Not surprising.

I had been gone too long already, but I needed to know if Alicia was safe.

I kept at it, trying one assault on the personnel systems after another.

No luck.

I went to the medical records.

No luck.

The exercise records finally yielded some data. The three fliers were Tsawo, Marti, and Alicia.

She had gotten her wings.

No pictures, no way to know what she looked like now.

Still, armed with that much data, I flowed through the ship until I found the bay. There were records of three flier ships leaving. Each one held one flier and no one else, each with a single pilot.

I'd seen these little ships around Lopali. They looked like soap bubbles. Unsafe as hell. Fast and lethal and dangerous. They were part of the reason Marcus had imagined Lopali would make a difference in the outcome of the war. But he must have been imagining hundreds of them. Not three.

I watched the logs to the end.

Only one had returned.

Alicia hadn't come back. Neither had Marti.

I managed not to scream, but still I felt a brief probe from Caro. *Are you okay?*

I couldn't talk.

Are you okay?

She deserved an answer. *I can't find Alicia.*

I'm sorry. I need you to come back.

That startled me. *Why?*

Mommy's trying to pull me home. If I don't go, she'll come into the data.

I couldn't allow that. I could stay here even if Caro left, but I might get lost. Especially if anything happened to the *Anvil.* I wanted to stay here and explore, but the war didn't care what I wanted.

Give me a minute. Just one.

Hurry.

I searched the *Anvil*'s communication systems. Found a way to send a message to Tsawo. *This is Joseph. Tell me when Alicia is okay.*

I slid back to the *Orbit*, and then back to the *Sky of Star Clouds*, and then Caro pulled me back through the other two ships.

I let her. I drifted in data while allowing a child to tug me back to my body and my ship. But this might be my only moment to worry about Alicia, or even to think about her. What if she came all the way here, and I never saw her? What if I never knew what she looked like with her wings? She had left me for them, and I wanted to see her fly.

53

ALICIA

I kept my thumb on the accelerator button, leaned forward as far as I could, and squinted. Marti's bright red wings were nearly impossible to see against the black of space.

It had to have been two minutes already. Maybe more.

A small light bloomed in the spot where I thought she was.

Hope raced through my heart, tightened my thumb even further despite the fact that the *Cat* was going so fast that little red warning lights bloomed along the left edge of my HUD. "Calculate matched speed." Maybe the *Cat* would understand.

Numbers raced along the bottom of my HUD, and the amber words "Engage Autopilot Y/N?" stopped in front of my face, the slowly tumbling light of Marti's spinning body behind them.

"Yes." I lifted my thumb. "Open communication."

The *Cat* moved faster than I expected. I gripped the bench hard with my left hand to try and keep the straps from cutting me in two.

The *Cat* slowed suddenly, skewed left, and then passed Marti.

I caught a glimpse of her face inside her helmet, eyes wide.

She looked alive. "Marti!"

Nothing.

Now what? Marti's suit trailed wires behind it. Could I grab them?

With what? I looked around, wishing I knew this machine better.

A voice in my helmet. Marti's. Soft and punctuated. "No point."

How could I get her inside?

My heart stuttered with fear that I might have caught up to her just to watch her die.

The door?

An emergency evacuation process blew the door off. We'd been drilled on it. If I did that, I'd be like Marti, dependent on my one spare bottle of oxygen.

I had missed Marti when I needed to catch her, and still had to make it back to the *Anvil*. But I couldn't abandon her.

I gave the *Cat* another order. "Calculate distance and travel time to the *Anvil*."

"Five minutes, thirty-four seconds."

Too long. And it would only get worse. We had turned so we moved in the same direction as the *Anvil*, but now that I'd slowed, the distance grew steadily.

"Marti. I'm coming close to you. I'm staying in my seat. You need to grab the open door."

"Crazy."

"Yes."

My heart beat into a long silence before she said, "I can't."

"Why?"

Her voice sounded soft. "Tired. Going. It's okay."

Anger shot through me. I was going to save her. "Damnit Marti, grab the door!" I turned to the ship's comm channel. "Emergency operation. Remove door. Wait for my command. Calculate fastest trajectory to *Anvil*."

The door hinges clicked and whirred.

Back to communications. "Marti. Watch the door. I'll be right by you. Grab something if you can. Anything. Get to the door."

"Won't fit."

The door stopped making noise, and then clicked. My HUD began counting backward from ten. "We'll think of something." I blew every bit of air out of my lungs as fast as I could.

The door shot off of the *Cat*, disappeared almost immediately. Alarms went off in my head and everything on my HUD turned red.

My head and neck stayed warm from the helmet, but every other part of me screamed at the cold, begged for air and warmth, for life.

I tried to breathe. Air caught in my throat and I huffed a little, frightened, then my lungs took the air. Painfully, but they held on. This was how Marti was alive. No wonder she couldn't respond easily.

I looked through the door. She floated in space, bloated but in one piece, her wings still against the black sky.

I could still talk. "Calculate retrieval."

The *Cat*'s thrusters huffed and shot and she turned slightly, inching closer to Marti.

We had to miss her wings!

"Hold out your arms and legs."

I couldn't reach outside while I remained strapped in, but if I didn't, I'd be out there with Marti. A thick rubber strip of insulation clung to the metal opening where the door had been. I ripped at it, yanking.

I dangled the rubber outside the door, hoping it had enough strength to hold her. "Grab this."

I barely heard over the alarms, "Can't."

"Try again." The thrusters huffed again, bringing us close.

This was crazy. It would never work.

I was a fool.

"Try!" I screamed into my helmet.

Silence.

The rubber dangled like a fishing line in a stream back on Fremont with nothing to bite and no significant current. My fingers had started swelling with vacuum; my grip was loosening.

Please, I thought. *Please, please.*

I screamed, my voice blending with the high-pitched warnings from my HUD. My back arched and my head snapped back and my shoulders tried to beat my wings as if flying could save either of us, as if flying could work at all with my wings strapped into the *Cat*. I couldn't scream loud enough to drown out the unhappy sounds the *Cat* wailed in my ears.

My screams turned into a chant of Marti's name as I struggled to get the *Cat* to shift so I could see her.

From time to time I caught a flash of her brilliant red wings.

The rubber slid out of my fattened, cold fingers.

Marti's wings drooped. The bottle of oxygen floated free of her hand, a small cylinder still attached to her helmet.

She was gone.

54

JOSEPH

I began to feel more myself as Caro tugged me back toward the *Thorn*, as if I were a stretched rubber band slowly released. I set aside my worries for Alicia and the *Orbit*, letting myself shift to the center of my real job.

As we came back through the *Unicorn*'s systems, it was clear that they were on alert. I watched for any energies that might be other Wind Readers in her systems. As far as I could tell, they were clean.

The last hop went quickly.

We're home, Uncle Joseph.

Thank you, Caro.

I have to go now. I'm scaring Mommy.

I bet you are. Thank you.

Her energy was gone as quickly as that, nothing left behind. Hopefully everything was okay for her and Kayleen. So many distractions. The house arrest here. Alicia, lost. The fight starting around us.

I toured the *Thorn*'s systems quickly. Engines warm and purring. Directional thrusters all ready. Two torpedo bays open. The other six closed but manned. Crew flowed through the corridors, some even jogging. Everything felt hot and ready, but controlled. No viruses. No hostile Wind Readers. The AI on full alert, watching everything. A hand on my shoulder.

Chelo.

I opened my eyes.

She smiled at me, the smile her whole face, her eyes lit with relief. "You felt so far away."

"I made it."

"Caro, too," she said. "Kayleen nearly went crazy."

"Caro is amazing." Hunger and thirst slammed into me and I reached for water. "What's happening?"

She glanced at a monitor above my head. "Three ships headed toward us. They're all medium-sized battle ships, roughly the size of the *Thorn*. That makes it pretty even."

"I checked on the *Orbit*. It's damaged. Alicia is missing."

Her lips thinned.

"I had to come back. I didn't want to."

She caressed my cheek, bringing me even more solidly into the room. "No one has shot at us yet, but the *Thorn* is ready to shield and to fire. Ulrika is giving orders, but you can interrupt when you know enough."

Bless her, I could tell what she thought of the idea by the tone in her voice. "Please tell her I'm happy to trust her for the moment. She knows the *Thorn*. Tell her I'll stay on patrol." Then I asked, "Can Captain Hill do both? Keep track of the physical orders on the ship and yet still read all of the data?" The idea overwhelmed me.

Chelo shrugged and handed me a tube of protein paste. "She must."

I sat up straighter and ripped the ragged top off the tube, staring at the monitors and orienting myself to the story of the upcoming battle.

The big bay doors opened, pilots headed for their small ships, the tiniest drones—no bigger than a fist—streamed out like a flock of small birds.

The wall to my right displayed all of our ships. The *Thorn* and the *Unicorn* both in front, both sharp-nosed cylinders near the same size, the *Thorn* longer and thinner. The *Black Star* and the *Highline* strung behind us.

In unison, all four ships disgorged small ships to create a storm of targets and weapons.

The three Islan ships were doing no such thing yet, but surely they would. Or maybe we just couldn't read them?

Suddenly I hungered to try for the Islan data nets. I knew how to do that. I'd learned on Fremont.

Should I try?

55
ALICIA

I felt naked to space, inadequate for its cold heart. It didn't care about me; it was inexorable. My helmet attached to a rubber scarf, roughly four and half inches tall, tightened with clips and held on with two straps tied together. This made a great seal, but not a perfect one. An irritating little burble of runaway air ran down from beside my ear, just loud enough to be audible in spite of the alarms the *Cat* kept sending out.

My fingers and toes, calves and thighs fattened as the water in my body tried to escape.

The helmet held. Parts of my body were lightly protected with clothes that now felt like bands of restrictive material. If they didn't split, they would help.

The only small mercy was that the open door showed stars. Just stars. No receding battleships, no tumbling winged body, nothing but the colored points of light from suns. There were so many more stars out here than I'd ever seen from Fremont, Silver's Home, or Lopali.

I had ordered the *Cat* to take me back to the *Anvil.* We were gaining on the far larger ship, but couldn't reach her in the two to three minutes I had left. If I had that much left. Thinking felt hard, the voices in my head shrieking about cold and pain and alarms, all of them trying to keep me from acting.

My fingers toyed with the straps that held me down.

I gasped a little, taking in extra air from the bottle to make up for what leaked down my neck.

There was no survival out here. No risk I could take that would let me live.

I stared at the *Anvil* and thought of Joseph and Chelo, of Induan. I whispered, "I'm sorry," and then I gave the command. "Initiate emergency escape."

"Password?"

I gave it, closed my eyes, and prepared for a jolt.

None came. I looked. Thrusters spit out fuel, slowing the *Cat*.

I understood. Blowing even a small ship apart at top speed wasn't a good idea. Well, at least Tsawo wouldn't have to deal with my body. I would join Marti, and we could fly through the void together.

The straps dug into my back and shoulders.

I took in a sip of air, blew it out again, then took another deep breath and blew all of that out explosively, then squeezed my eyes shut again.

Still no jolt.

Maybe I just couldn't tell how fast we were going. Maybe the *Cat* was still slowing down.

The straps fell away. No jolt, no buzz, nothing. They just fell away.

I opened my eyes.

Protection fell away from me in pieces. A blue triangle near my right arm, a lump of metal with wires in front of me and to the left, a bit of the outer bubble near my feet.

The oxygen bottle was still attached by an umbilical. I reeled it in, held it in my hand the way I'd seen Marti hold it.

I floated.

Stars all around me, even brighter now that all of the lights of the *Cat* had winked off as it turned to space debris.

I spread my wings.

They barely moved, brittle with cold. Still, they felt light, like I had expected wings to feel, like silk kissed by the air and born through life on puffs of wind.

One of the blocks of monster robot floated by without touching me.

I started humming to mask the annoying hiss of the escaping air and began counting stars.

A great peace settled on me, and time began to lose the threads of understanding, of separateness, and I floated, flying lightly if at all, in a great void. The only pain came from my lungs, and I knew that was the pain of dying.

It was nothing next to the pain of becoming.

56
JOSEPH

As I stared at the battle display in front of me and Chelo, the idea that I could enter the Islan ships obsessed me. This fleet's communication protocols *must* be similar to the ones I had breached on Fremont. I had no permission from anyone, but the idea grew more demanding.

Chelo clutched my hand so tightly it hurt. She hated war. I did too, for all the same reasons and more. I was afraid of myself in battle. But Mohami had given me tools, so I breathed deeply into my stomach and felt for the balls of my feet. It helped, but the Islan ships still called to me.

Small icons moved across the screen. From time to time, a ship flared bright and disappeared.

The data came from a thousand feeds, the point-of-view on the screen as if we were on a ship far above the fleets instead of near the front of the back third of our fleet, and thus near the end of the first pass of battle. The two fleets mingled, the ragged and bruised heads of each fleet nearing the thin tails of the opposing fleets. Some of the scattered ships that already flown through each other floated freely, dead or dying, others moving away from the greater concentration of ships or looping back to join them.

We were losing. We wouldn't lose in the first pass, but if the math held, we would lose in the second or third pass. If it came to it, we would lose in a melee.

Captain Hill and Mohami had both insisted this first fight had to happen.

So what? Did it have to finish? Could I stop it now?

Chelo spoke, her voice broken and halting. "How many dead? A million on each side?"

I winced, thinking of Alicia. Had she made it home to the *Anvil*?

"Let me control the screen?"

Chelo handed me a palm-sized device. I rubbed my thumb around on the slick surface, feeling for the device's sensitivity, pressed to zoom in.

It took two minutes to find the *Anvil*. We had a tracker on the *Sun's Orbit*, so I started there. It was further away from the *Anvil* than I'd expected. Chelo pointed. "There."

On the screen, it was simply an icon with information next to it: *Sky Anvil. Class four cruising ship retrofitted to fighter level T2. Lopali registration*. A flash of hot light obliterated the icon, and then I blinked at a screen that included no information for it at all.

The *Anvil* had been destroyed.

I clutched Chelo's hand tighter.

She stuttered. "Did. Did. Did … was that Alicia's ship? Did it?" She drew in a sharp breath. "No!"

I clutched Chelo tightly to me. She grunted, either because I held her too tight or because she hurt like I did, or both. It didn't matter. I couldn't let go. I stood, holding Chelo and looking over her head at the screen, desperate for patterns, or some sign of a mistake. The *Orbit* was slow compared to the other ships near it. Drifting? I asked the machine, "Status on *Sun's Orbit*."

"Holed. All hands lost."

And even though I knew it, I asked, "Status, *Sky Anvil*."

"Destroyed."

I dropped the control and held Chelo closer. As I stroked her hair, anger nipped at my spine and quickened my breath.

"Sir?"

I glanced up to find Ulrika beside us, hand up, just about getting ready to say something. She closed her mouth and stared.

Our grief must have been evident. She licked her lips and touched her hair, clearly uncomfortable to have walked in on a personal moment. "Are you okay?"

"I am."

"The fighting will start soon. Do you want …"

I stepped into her hesitation, my voice stronger than I'd expected. "We just lost a family member. I need to breathe. Can you take the weapons systems? I'll take care of the *Thorn*, fight from inside the data."

She looked relieved. "Yes, Sir."

"Go on."

She backed out.

A message pinged on my wrist and hope surged. Alicia?

"What is it?" Chelo asked.

My voice shook. "Play message."

Alicia's voice. I smiled.

Dear Joseph,

I am both in your war and on one of your ships.

One reason we came out here was to tell you we learned the there is a traitor who flew with you on Bryan's Hope. *We don't know who that is.*

I am amazed at all you have become. I have achieved dreams as well, and now I just have to survive the fighting that may soon come our way. If perhaps I don't, please ask here for a gift from me. I will have some luck to pass on to you. It is in a long box.

Love always, Alicia.

The last line doubled me over.

A sob escaped Chelo. Her hand touched my shoulder and she whispered, "I'm sorry."

◎

Love always, Alicia.

◎

Her voice played in my head on a repeat tape until my breath finally slowed and deepened, and my spine grew even stiffer. I stepped back from Chelo, looked carefully at her face. Grief. Understanding. Resolve. No panic. She was so strong.

I whispered. “I have to go do my job.”

She stiffened. “Wait. What about the traitor?”

“What traitor?”

“Alicia said there is traitor on board here.”

“Well, isn’t that why our family is in lockup?”

“No.” Chelo spoke slowly. “Alicia’s note says the traitor came with us. We’re under guard because of things people who were already on the ship said about us.”

“I can’t deal with enemies inside the ship and enemies outside the ship all at once. The battle won’t wait for us to decide who hates us.” I stepped back and settled into the crash couch. “I have to go.”

Chelo fretted as she tightened the straps around me. “Stay aware of your body.” She leaned down and kissed my forehead. “Come back to me.”

I nodded stiffly, the best I could do. For a breath, I felt fear behind the anger. This wasn’t the way to go into the Islan nets. Not angry. I should do it with cool calm. The war wouldn’t wait for me to calm down. I buried the frisson of fear licking my heart and fell away from the Command Room, from Ulrika and her concerns, from my hurting sister, and let the familiarity of the ship’s lifeblood of data overtake my senses.

I flitted out of the *Thorn* and through the ships we flew with. The social nets on the *Black Star* thrummed with excitement, the *Unicorn* felt more modulated, the *Highline* something in between. Everywhere, nerves.

I jumped out a ship, skimming the surface of a small fighter heading toward an Islan ship.

Caro watched me.

Oh no, Caro! Go back!

I can make you stronger.

Guilt. I couldn't risk Caro. *You should not be out here. Go back. Help your mother.*

I have to help you.

I surrendered to the inevitability of it, to my anger, to the heat of the fight that engulfed us.

The *Unicorn* gave clipped orders. All four ships fired at rounds fired at them. I would need focus there soon. *Okay, Caro. Just lend your strength. Don't look.*

The rounds in the first salvo were all successfully knocked away or blown up. Score one for our side.

The small Islan fighter was close, and not much bigger than the ship that had attacked us on Fremont. I reached for my memories of that day, threaded through the pain and the horror of killing, remembered Chelo beside me on the ridge above Artistos.

Now that Caro amplified my strength, I knocked harder on the electronic doors of the Islan ship, but it threw up walls faster than I attacked. I slid down a level in the network architecture, looked for a sensor thread to ride in. Everything moved fast, we and the little ship hurtling toward each other. I kept having to account for vector. There was no visual help in this kind of data assault. I leaned on the *Thorn*'s AI for help with calculation.

I'm going to ask the Unicorn *to shoot at the ship.* Caro, determined.

Would they listen to Caro? Did she have the strength to support me and still send messages? She seemed to be getting stronger just like I was, the two of us amplifying each other.

I continued sliding around the ship's sensors, finally easing in the outer level of ping and report data now, but finding no way deeper in. I did verify that the communication style was the same as the other Islan ships I had penetrated.

Caro's strength still amplified my own, although I could tell most of her attention had gone elsewhere. Talking to Master Skulla?

I managed to extract the name of the ship. *War Wind 421.*

It probably wouldn't kill me to have part of my consciousness inside the *War Wind 421* if it took a direct hit, but it would surely weaken me. Could I make it need evasive maneuvers? And would that open a line to its parent ship and make a pathway into the *War Wind*?

I will see that it's fired on.

Thank you, Caro.

I watched the communications systems. Breathed. Waited.

Moments later, a missile locked onto the *War Wind 421*. Tight-beam data warned the other Islan ships of the danger. The hole was small, but enough that I slammed into the *War Wind 421*'s systems.

Now what?

The little ship had to try to deal with me while evading the missile.

I needed for it to dodge the missile, and then I needed to own it.

I needed for the human crew and AI to see the missile as a greater threat than me.

The *War Wind* sped up, twisted. A wash of telemetry data almost drowned out my hold on the communication systems.

Run! Caro shouted into the data.

I jerked back to the *Unicorn* just as the *War Wind 421* broke up in a silent and light-filled explosion.

Keep going. We can't stop. There's a bigger ship coming.

She was right. If we stopped, we might give them time to build defenses. If the *War Wind*'s AI had been able to communicate. We couldn't know. Machines sometimes lived longer than humans in space, and milliseconds could have been enough.

57
CHELO

When Joseph was young, he'd slipped into data for minutes or maybe an hour at a time. Now? He fell away from me for hours at a time.

I tried to meditate, but it was impossible. The idea that a traitor had come with us gnawed at me.

It wasn't me or Kayleen or Liam or Joseph. Not Paloma, who had adopted Kayleen as a child all those years ago and left Fremont, which she loved, to come with us. None of those choices would be bearable, so I set them aside as impossible.

Jenna wasn't possible. Neither was Tiala, surely. It would wound Jenna if we were harmed, and Tiala could not hurt Jenna, ever. Not if I understood her at all.

Mohami and Kala were utterly peaceful.

Ming? Joseph had told me how she'd left a Port Authority job to come with them when they'd come to Fremont to rescue me. She was head of Joseph's security, and often his bodyguard. It could be her. Someone could have given her orders to go to Fremont all that time ago, and she could have obeyed and stayed with us. But I didn't think so. She was so much her own person.

Joseph rolled and thrashed in his crash couch. His eyelids fluttered like Sasha's did when she dreamed. I let him be. I had made the mistake of forcing him back before when he'd worried me, and he had been groggy and on-edge for days, said it felt like being pulled out of a dream right before the climax and being unable to fully wake.

He kicked the light blanket that covered him off his feet. I tugged it back down.

If Ming was a Port Authority spy, then why would she have sent a message to the Islans?

Dianne was another possible bet. She was Islan, so she would be a rather obvious plant. Too obvious? She was a contained person. Even after spending so much time with her, I didn't know her well. She had talked to me about the power of stories on Lopali, how we were building a network of tales around Marcus and Joseph as a way to keep them safe. If all of her stories were lies, then it could be her.

But Marcus had truly loved her, and I had always felt that Marcus saw into our very souls.

Maybe it was some crew member who had come with us? But then how would they have had the information?

I dozed, as I often did at these times. I dozed the way Sasha did, always a little bit awake, ready in a moment to be there for Joseph if he needed me.

58

JOSEPH

After the *Unicorn* blew the *War Wind* into tiny pieces, Caro and I withdrew into the *Unicorn*'s data. *Are you okay?* I asked her.

Yes. Go! Just go. You need to go.

She pushed me toward a bigger Islan ship, shoving its picture at me.

I hesitated. How could I best help the *Thorn*? Keep Caro safe?

That's the Boom 12, Caro informed me.

Silly name.

Just go! Here are its statistics.

She was right. If I hesitated, the Islans might find a way to fight me. I reviewed the stats while I parsed for a path between the two ships. The *Boom 12* was one of the more common warship classes in the Islan fleet, well-armed and well-defended. She carried two hundred thirty-one people, and twelve small ships including *War Wind 420–434*. She had just lost one!

Don't revel in the deaths of others, I reminded myself. *Never again.*

Boom 12 had torpedoes, shields, autonomous drones, the small ships, and four large guns which wouldn't be much use to her in this kind of fighting, but an awesome defense if she waited behind a barrier for other ships to move toward her. Although with smart enough ammunition …

Fear I couldn't afford licked at my resolve.

I had to open a path from the *Unicorn*. I did, briefly, slamming the door shut behind me and riding a data probe and the standard hailing data that all ships used. They deflected the probe but not the hail. I arrived at the edges of her data, knocking, knocking. Communications streamed into *Boom 12* from three directions and out from her in more. I rode in, making myself as small and unimportant as possible. Once inside her defenses, I moved slowly.

She hadn't noticed me. She was a warship, so there wouldn't be much time. The *Thorn* wouldn't have allowed me to exist inside of her unnoticed for more than seconds.

I let myself flow with traffic, sipping from myriad communication streams. Many were encrypted, and I didn't dare to try and read them. Not yet. Some weren't. Even deep in data, I was human, not computer, and far slower than an AI. Still, I learned or verified much in just a few moments of objective time.

The Islan command structure was tighter than ours by far.

Islan news carried only stories of victory and propaganda (The fleet from Silver's Home was weak | The ships were flown by genetically mutated monsters | Silvers would force Islans to take modifications | Silvers made fortunes on the backs of slaves | Silvers' only goal was riches). The lists of our losses that they published was bigger than the last list I had seen.

The *Boom 12* had loosed four of her twelve fighting ships, and she had more ammunition in her hold than she could possibly use on this run.

She had destroyed at least five ships on her way here. One was the *Anvil.*

Emotions run muted when you're deep in data, but my anger swelled. If I let it loose, it would cloud my choices and dull my abilities. The *Anvil*! *Alicia!*

The *Boom* noticed me. First-level query programs tried to drag data out of me, and then to separate me from the ship. Marcus and I had drilled on every standard form of security. I recognized these and sent them away with the story that I was an acceptable string of data. I dug in, listening. At the center of the communications hubs, information flowed to and from other ships and internally between departments and crew members. I took in the stream of unencrypted chatter between crew, learning what normal sounded like so I'd recognize its opposite.

Caro was a soft, supporting energy. Distant. Good girl. I wanted her distant.

The *Boom* felt like *Thorn* had the last few days. Busy. Frenetic.

Any communication about the war would be encrypted. Physical systems might be a softer target.

Her torpedo bays were loaded. Telemetry data told me she already targeted the *Unicorn*.

Caro was there, a ghost in the *Unicorn's* data streams. If the *Unicorn* died, Caro could die with her.

I slammed into the systems and forced away the orders to fire.

Klaxons went off, the *Boom* immediately identifying a serious threat. Crew began to turn their heads, to focus. The navigator AI sent walls toward me, but amazingly, they fell easily.

How strong had I become?

I shut down system after system. The four big guns. The bays where new small fighting ships could leave the belly of the *Boom* and come after me and mine. Every system that could hurt us. I couldn't hurt the crew. Not with Caro there to see it.

I felt her awareness of my choices, sent her back a message. *Tell Master Skulla not to fire on the Boom 12. Tell him to pick something else.*

Okay.

Thank you.

I dug into the *Boom 12*'s AI and forced myself past layer after layer of defenses until I owned the AI. I forced the systems to loop so that no one could bring the weapons systems back up easily.

I wasn't finished.

I left a message from my sister in the heart of the ship's AI. *Peace. Look for the Doctrine of New Making!*

There were more ships out there and taking one out wouldn't win the larger battle. I had bought the *Thorn* a single additional moment of safety.

I felt strong. I could do more.

A soon as I made sure my orders would hold for a while, I gathered myself back together, questing for Caro. *Are you there? Safe?*

Yes, Caro finally said.

Did you pick another ship?

I could feel her satisfaction with the question. *The Boom 14 is close. And so is the Defender 17.*

Could I do two? I hesitated.

As she knew my thoughts, she said, *Let me think about two at once.*

I chose the *Boom 14*. She had just fired six torpedoes.

I ensured she'd fire no more.

Surely they'd identify me soon, find some way to close the holes I used. I slid into the next ship. The *Defender 17* was smaller. No torpedoes. Wicked guns, though. I stopped up communications with her gun bays and sent in some of the repair robots to dismantle key parts.

It felt sweet. Triumphant. Right. They couldn't hurt us, and I wasn't killing them to make it so. Marcus would have approved. Chelo would approve. I left the same message. *Peace. Look for the Doctrine of New Making.*

I returned to the *Unicorn*. *Caro, are you okay? Is Chelo okay?*

Everyone is okay. No shots hit the Thorn *or the* Unicorn. *The* Black Star *got hurt, and some people died. But the ship is still near us and can be fixed. The* Highline *is okay, too. I think she got hurt some by a little* War Wind *ship.*

Islas clearly designed in repetitive patterns. That might be how they were winning. We were a planet full of independents, and the rules of this battle favored centralized control.

The beginning of the fleet was past us now. But there would be more ships coming.

I had kept us alive! We had, Caro and I. But that was only so far.

I queried the *Thorn*'s AI. *Are there more threats to us?*

Not for an hour.

Relief. My body tugged gently at me, calling me back to care for it. I suddenly felt thin. I had an hour to gather energy. *Caro. Go back now. Take care of your body.*

Yes, Uncle!

Thank you.

She was already gone.

Chelo managed a smile as I opened my eyes. She reached forward to loosen the straps so I could sit up. "Are you okay?" she whispered.

"Tired. We stopped some Islan ships." I smiled back at her, proud of myself for it.

"You what?" She handed me water, always the first and best thing after time down. I glanced at the clock. It had been almost two hours. It felt like eight. Only a little more than an hour left of my shift. I blinked at the wall, thinking. If I stayed up here a whole hour, I would have to wait for the captain and tell her what I was doing.

Which she could forbid.

Was there any way I could prove I had saved the *Unicorn*? It surely wasn't something I could discuss with Master Skulla, not in the clear. I sipped the water slowly.

Chelo interrupted me. "How? How did you take over the ships?"

I drank the water; my cells rejoiced. "Remember Fremont?"

"Of course."

"I remembered how to talk to Islan nets. I got into some ships. Damaged their weapons systems, but not life support. I even left them a note—I told them we were killing their weapons, but we weren't killing them. I told them to look for the Doctrine of New Making."

A short smile touched her lips and fled.

"One of their ships was targeting the *Unicorn*, and probably would have hit it."

Her eyes widened; her sharp glance caught mine. "Did they see you?"

"Yes."

"Won't they target us? The *Thorn*?"

I stopped with the water bulb halfway to my mouth. "Maybe."

She sat still for a long moment. She looked as if she'd suffered a shock. But then, she had always hated war.

Idiot! I had to do what I'd done, but what if the Islans traced me back to the *Thorn*? The Star Mercenaries from Fremont had gone back to Islas with systems I had compromised. Did they have my signature? Would I even leave the same traces in the systems now that I had left then? On Fremont, I had been at best a half-formed student. After working with Marcus on Lopali, I was almost as strong as he was, and the boost Caro gave me helped me be … even more. Maybe much more.

What was I becoming?

Besides, what other choice had I had? I couldn't have allowed the *Unicorn* to be destroyed. Or the *Thorn*. I blew out a long breath and touched Chelo's temple, briefly brushing her hair. "I'll talk to the captain. In the meantime, I need to eat."

Chelo swallowed.

"There's something wrong," I told her. "isn't there? What aren't you telling me?"

"Do you remember Alicia's note about the traitor?"

"Yes. Did you find something?"

"I told Captain Hill about it, and she set the ship's AI to watch all incoming and outgoing communications carefully. The AI found a set of coded messages sent to two Islan ships. They haven't decoded everything, but your name is in both messages. Security thinks it warns the Islans about you."

And I had been running loose in Islan ships, doing damage, leaving cryptic notes. "What ships?"

She shook her head, her usually tidy hair falling into her eyes. "An Islan flagship and one of the ships that we will pass in a day or so, a destroyer-class ship named *Disciple's Peace 100*."

Disciple's Peace hardly sounded like a ship designed for battle. But surely it was. Something else was bothering her. "Are Liam and Kayleen and Jherrel okay? Caro is—she helped me."

Chelo's jaw tightened.

I knew her. "What is it?"

"The ship's AI reported that the messages it intercepted appear to have come from Mohami."

59

ALICIA

The stars faded even with my eyes open and I drifted, cold and swollen.

Maybe this was the end of my air? My fall into sleep?

I had become so much, but I hadn't yet really flown.

Tsawo would be the only ambassador left.

Something bumped my foot.

I grunted, opened my eyes, and tried vainly to twist around and see if it was a robot with six claws.

A piece of silver metal flashed in my poor peripheral vision. Then it came around, right in front of me. One of the battle drones from the *Lily Star*. It was the size I would be if I curled into a ball and cut off my wings.

What did it want?

It brushed against my hand.

Oh.

A rail would clearly serve as a handle. I reached for it with one hand, then rolled onto my belly as if I were swimming in air and grabbed it with my other hand as well. My fingers were bloated. They refused to curl far. Even a light grip made it feel like my skin wanted to split open.

I held on. My fingers burned.

The drone began moving.

I could see the *Anvil* now, behind the drone, way too far away.

The drone rotated, turning. The bulk of the far *Lily Star* obscured a swath of stars.

I smiled.

A voice trickled through my helmet, and I recognized the master of beasts, Romi. “Are you okay?”

“Yes.” My voice sounded thin. I said it again, louder. “Yes!”

“I’ll meet you in the hold. How much oxygen do you have?”

I glanced at the thin red line on my HUD. “A minute?”

A long moment of silence stretched inside of my short minute, and then Romi snapped, “Hold your breath when you have to.”

The drone pulled me through the void, my arms aching, my feathers trailing behind me. I focused on the pain of curled, fat fingers and the pain of each breath.

Romi waited in the open doorway of the *Lily Star*. As we came close, he took my arm and pulled me toward him, helping force my feet to the ground in the low gravity. He unzipped the empty oxygen bottle I still clutched in my right hand and twisted a new hose into place.

I tried breathing.

Nothing.

He held up a finger, then nodded.

Air flowed. Air. Beloved, sweet, painful air.

He backed into my distended stomach and bent over, pulling my arms over his shoulders. From there, he dragged me to a low cart and lay down on it on his back, pulling me on top of him. The cart zipped off.

I almost choked, shut my mouth, and fought the pain of moving this way.

The cart headed straight for a cargo airlock. Once we were inside, the door clanged shut. As the chamber filled with air, I lay there, cold and fat, new pains screaming for attention.

Air tasted golden. Sweet. Pressure was a gift of the gods. My skin hurt, my head throbbed, and I drifted in and out of regret and hope.

Romi slapped me. "Stay with me!"

I choked, and then laughed, and laughed, and laughed.

Life was the funniest thing in the universe, the best thing, the most whole and complete thing. I laughed because I had been saved, and when I could manage it, I clutched Romi to me.

60

JOSEPH

Chelo poked me. “Get up and move around.”

“Slave driver.” But she was right. I needed to talk to Captain Hill before I committed more single-handed warfare. I helped Chelo move our dishes to the sink, passing busy crew sitting heads-down, or standing and staring at air displays.

Funny how a room full of data for normal humans was full of pings and beeps and hums, and data immersion was a beautiful silence.

After we rinsed our dishes, I did ten deep squats, then stood and stretched my arms high. A few crew members looked up at the motion, but I kept going, swiveling right to left and back in spite of the quizzical looks a few of them gave me. It was crucial to cement my connection to my body so that I could find my way home. Marcus had told me over and over that Wind Readers who got separated from their bodies disappeared. Rumors that they lived somewhere in the machines of the world abounded, but Marcus thought whatever soul or personality stayed with us out riding streams of data became white noise in the systems, that we dissolved into the data itself until we lost coherence.

I suspected he was right. Too bad he hadn't had that chance, though. Maybe I'd have been able to find pieces of him somewhere.

Chelo walked ahead of me on the way back to the crash couches, her shoulders squared in spite of how tired and heartsore she must be over Mohami. Surely she needed to go to him, but she was as loyal to me as Sasha.

Captain Hill waited for us by our crash couches, the look on her face cold and assessing. "Let's debrief."

She was half an hour early. She was … never … half an hour early. It felt … dangerous? intrusive? I didn't know. Not that I had a good escape plan—be out deep in the data when she showed up to debrief? "Okay."

She waited.

"What can I answer for you?"

"Master Skulla called me on his private line. He thinks you can control Islan ships."

"I didn't know I could do it here until just now." The look on her face made me feel defensive. "I learned on Fremont, with the mercenary ships."

Her lips thinned, her jaw tight. In that moment, she looked more angry than beautiful, and she frightened me a little. "Can you show me?"

"I … I don't know. I need to go back out. There are more ships coming." I settled into my crash couch and started to strap in.

Chelo didn't come forward to help me.

The captain took a step toward me, looking down, fierce and frightening. She spoke slowly, as if to be certain I understood. She held up an index finger. "First, you may be the best weapon we have or could ever have." She touched her middle finger. "Second. You just did direct battle with the Islan fleet without permission. *You didn't even bother to notify Ulrika of your intentions.*" She touched her ring finger. "Last, you may be our best weapon, but you have deployed a frightening capability with no sense of strategy and given the Islans time to protect themselves against you."

Chelo took a step toward the captain, level-eyed and chin high, although it quivered with … something. Rage? Chelo? "And whoever the traitor is told them about this skill anyway. At roughly the same time."

The captain kept her eyes on me. "Do you understand any of that?"

"I have to go. Back. Now. Before they do figure out how to stop me."

"Lastly," she said, "You almost certainly directed most of the rest of the fleet toward this ship. My ship. I should kick you off."

"He owns it!" Chelo protested.

I tightened the buckles down and tried to be as honest as I could. "I wasn't sure I could do it. I was angry. They killed Alicia. On Fremont, they killed people I loved and after that, I broke into their systems. Who would have thought I could do it here?"

Captain Hill's scowl didn't flicker.

"I have to go. If I don't strike first, they will kill us." My fists clenched of their own accord, and I willed them to relax. "I will not lose my sister."

Chelo smiled for just a split second.

"I will not lose Caro or Kayleen or Liam or Jherrel. I'd like to keep you in one piece as well. You're a fine captain."

My words didn't move her.

"I have to go. I'm sorry. You can follow if you want, but you might be needed here."

Her lips thinned even more.

I closed my eyes. Chelo's hand fell on my shoulders, comforting. Telling me it was okay to go. She understood.

I took a deep breath and dove.

61

ALICIA

It amazed me that my brain worked. It worried at the fact that I hadn't saved Marti, had maybe accidentally killed her. If my shot had been bad. I'd never know. Any video footage had drifted into the depths of space. Poor Marti.

The joy of being alive made even that loss seem bearable.

The doctor on the *Lily Star* was a tiny woman with red hair that fell below her waist in a long braid. She wore casual black pants and a black turtleneck.

That wasn't right. She'd been wearing blue. Was she a twin?

She had installed me belly down on a hospital bed, my face supported on a padded circle which made it hard to see her as she muttered to herself and paced the room, consulting data streams and her own instruments. "I think you will be okay," she finally said. "You are stronger than I would have thought."

I lifted my head. My neck ached, the muscles sluggish. "I've always been strong," I said, still too pleased at being alive to feel much of anything else. The need to laugh had worn off, but a buoyancy remained in me, a sense of freedom.

My voice didn't work very well yet. Pain shot through my shoulders when I flexed my wings, but they moved the way they should. I managed to croak out, "I'm a little tired."

"They want you awake."

I frowned, contemplated asking who *they* were.

She frowned at me. "I've never worked on a flier. A human wouldn't have survived that ordeal."

I swallowed. "A human as opposed to a…?"

She had the good sense to blush. "Isn't it better to be a flier than a human? I mean you chose it, right?"

What a stupid question. Anger sparked my tired muscles into a shiver. "It's not possible to be both?"

Apparently, she didn't hear the question in my voice. She blathered on. "You should be fine. The sedatives gave you eleven hours of sleep, but they'll leave you groggy for a while. I need to unhook you before you can get up."

I gave up on talking to her.

It took ten minutes to free me of the wires and the catheter and rotate the bed so I could stand. She was awkward around my wings, maybe a little dangerous, so I moved as slowly as I could. I felt bruised all over.

She helped me turn sideways. The low ceiling, clicking machines, and air purifier all around crowded me. My feet didn't want to move. "I don't know if I can do this."

"I think you have to. There's no … time. This is war."

I hadn't forgotten.

The serious look slid back onto her face. "Some people want to see you. There are things you should know."

"Bad things?"

She shrugged, the move of a doctor who wasn't going to tell a patient the wrong thing at the wrong time.

"I'm Alicia."

That elicited a tiny smile. "I know."

"What's your name?"

"Doctor Gilli Hunt." She smiled and took my hand. "Can you take a step?"

In spite of her clear prejudices, the reassuring strength of her small, warm hand felt good. I felt as if lifting one foot would make me fall to my hands and knees. My skin and muscles felt like bruised liquid. I managed a single step, my knees shaking and my balance tenuous. The bottoms of my feet hurt as I picked them up an inch and put them back down.

"You won't fit in a wheelchair. I could wheel you into the meeting on the bed."

That wasn't going to happen. I took a step.

It took a long time, but I took enough steps.

Tsawo and Jagruti waited for me.

Relief thrummed through every nerve. They were okay.

Tsawo stood. "I'm sorry to make you come so far. There was no place else comfortable enough to hold two of us."

The doctor and Tsawo helped me settle on the lowest of the perches, my feet dangling a few inches above the ground. The soles had stopped hurting, but my knees still felt swollen. The sweet scent of flowers from the cages almost obscured the tang of scrubbed air. "Marti died."

"I know," Tsawo said. "I told you not to die."

"I didn't."

"Good." His face held still, but I could feel the press of emotion trying to escape from it. "I wish she had listened, too."

"I know."

The doctor looked from one to another of us, nodded, and left.

"How did you get here? What happened on the *Anvil*?"

A short silence gave me time to study them. Jagruti had a bruise on her right cheek, her braids were a tangled mess. Tsawo had dark circles under his eyes and puffy cheeks. Cy simply looked pissed, but I'd only met him once before and he'd looked a little pissed then. Romi had the calm I was used to seeing on Jagruti. But then, too, he was a Keeper.

"What happened?"

"The *Anvil*'s gone. They blew the power plant. There's a hole the size of the *Anvil* in the *Sun's Orbit*. We left it behind us. It's probably derelict."

"You could have died!"

Jagruti put her hand out and covered mine with it. "We thought we were going after your body. You and Marti. We didn't see how you could survive."

I licked my lips. "The doctor was surprised I did."

"So were we." She swallowed. "We were so sure we'd lost you that I sent your note to Joseph."

Oh. So he probably thought I had died.

My dismay must have been obvious to Jagruti. "I'm sorry," she said.

"You did what I asked you to."

She nodded. "I know. We all almost died. You in space. Tsawo out there with that thing on his ship, and then both of us on the *Anvil*. Luckily, we were already strapped into one of the smaller warships. We were on our way to try and come for your body when the alarms went off."

"What about the ship Joseph is on. The *Thorn*?"

Tsawo said, "They are still fighting back there. I don't know what's happening." He pulled up a display, squinted at it.

"Not now," Jagruti told him. "We'll look in a minute."

The display shrank to a little golden dot and hung in the air, ready for Tsawo to reactivate it.

"We need to decide how to matter," Tsawo said. "No one's even bothered to check on us. Even here, we're curiosities. Marcus planned for us, so there are rooms we can use and a perch here and there. But we have nothing now. No ships." He sounded bitter. "No one from the fleet has even sent a greeting."

Tsawo saw himself as a protector. Had he expected people from Silver's Home to recognize that in him? Or to even see him as human? He'd never been there, but I had. Fliers hadn't been treated badly, but they hadn't been *important*.

Jagruti spoke soothingly, her voice melodic and soft. "Maybe everyone is in shock." She smiled broadly. "I'm probably still in shock."

I nodded. "Did anyone die on the *Anvil*?"

Tsawo nodded. "Everybody but us and you."

My first pinion feather was there. Might still be there. What a silly thing to think about. But what was being alive if not luck? My hands started to shake, then my shoulders, which rattled my feathers against each other in a soft susurration.

A tear dropped onto the back of my right hand, then another one, then another.

Jagruti still held my hand.

Tsawo came up beside me and stood where he could slip an arm around my waist. He felt warm and alive and strong. He smelled like feather oil and sweat and strength.

Jagruti's gaze offered only love, the same look Induan had been developing, a look full of acceptance.

Everyone I'd met on the *Anvil* was gone. Marti. Marti was gone. Like Induan. Like Bryan. I bowed my head and cried.

I felt as if all of my losses, ever, flowed through the tears. Being reviled in Ruth's band on Fremont while Liam landed with Akashi, who loved him like a son. Joseph's abandonment when he did what he was born to do instead of what I needed him to. Tsawo's refusal to help me get wings. Bryan's death. Good, smart, angry, strong Bryan. My old self. My ability to run. Induan. Marti. It felt like a string of loss being pulled out through my heart, each loss a bead of pain.

Tsawo's arm tightened around me. Jagruti's hand felt warm and slippery and alive.

Eventually there was no more loss to feel afresh.

Jagruti, in the way of Keepers, began to hum, the sound filling the places that had just emptied. Tsawo joined her.

When I looked up to gasp for breath, Romi stood nearby, shifting uncomfortably on his feet. When he saw my face, he hurried off and fetched tissues and a washcloth. As he handed them to me, he smiled hopefully. Maybe he'd found the same part of him that gentled paw-cats.

That made me laugh.

We all stood, disentangling, breathing. Jagruti and Tsawo let the hum fall gently into the background and away. I began to notice the sounds of animals in cages around us, and then the creaks and hums of the ship.

I thought about the doctor. "These people don't see us as human.

How can they see us as important if they cannot do that? We need to go meet some of them."

Tsawo raised an eyebrow.

"We do. We need to know them and let them know us. Not as little pet birds on perches in Lopali." My voice rose. "But as warriors. As strong. As smart. We are all of those things, and we don't need to live as if someone was pulling our strings."

Jagruti smiled.

Tsawo's smile had emotions I had never seen in his eyes when he looked at me. Deep, thoughtful, and approving. In that moment, he looked more beautiful than he had ever looked before.

62

CHELO

After Joseph left me to go after the Islan ships, the captain and I stood on either side of his still form, looking down as if we could change his choices. We could, of course, force him awake and keep at least most of him here. But I had never kept him from doing what he felt he needed, not even when he was seven. I wouldn't stop him now.

Besides, if Joseph had the ability to stop or slow the Islans, well, nobody else seemed to. One glance at the situation status display on the screen showed me that.

"Captain Hill?"

She shook herself, as if trying to force herself awake. At least she hadn't chosen to try to follow Joseph. Maybe she didn't have the strength, or maybe her duties didn't allow it. Maybe both.

"Captain?"

"Who would have imagined?" she whispered. "Can he save us?"

"If anyone can. I need to go to Mohami. I need to understand. But I also need to be here."

Her eyes widened for just a moment in surprise. "Do you plan to tell Mohami what I told you? About the message?"

"I have to know."

She hesitated. She did that a lot around Joseph or me, or even Caro. Clearly we were not what she had expected. I had the sense she was quite unused to being questioned. But I did need to talk to Mohami. "I have to ask him. My whole—"

"I understand. I'll tell my security detail that you'll be talking to him. You'll have your own guards there, too."

"Mohami won't hurt me!"

"He may have just betrayed us all." She glanced down at Joseph. "Give me a minute to check on the state of the war, and to talk to my security detail. They are on the way to take him in. I'll see if I can buy you an hour."

She had barely met Mohami; she didn't know him at all.

I swallowed, glanced at Joseph. He was doing something big. "Can I call Liam to come? Joseph needs one of us."

She looked thoughtful. "He *is* coming on shift."

"Yes." She was so careful about shifts and schedules, about rules and discipline. I admired her control. She pursed her lips, clearly hesitating. "I suppose that's the best option. I was going to offer to keep Ulrika an extra hour and sit with him myself, but if Joseph can't save us from the Islans, or even one ship gets through, I'll be needed." Unexpectedly, she reached over and pulled me toward her, her hug brief but hard and genuine. It carried words of forgiveness I knew she wouldn't say.

"I'll send someone for Liam," she told me before she left.

I sat beside my brother and waited. From time to time his eyelids twitched or a finger moved, and once his whole body jumped. Alicia had died. Joseph had said so, and the note from her supported that. I should be mourning her.

I couldn't imagine it, somehow. She was one of our original six, and if she was dead now too, we were down to four.

Damn war in all of its permutations. A hatred of fighting was bred into me as much as love of risk was bred into Alicia. What had our designers been thinking?

Where was Joseph now? How far had he gone? Was Caro with him? I stood up and tapped Captain Hill's shoulder. She turned quickly, startled. "Is everything okay?"

"Can you ask whoever brings Liam to bring Caro, too?"

She narrowed her eyes.

"Liam usually watches over Caro. It might help them to be together."

She looked around the small space—the crash couch, a chair for me, a table, a little room, and then the next crash couch, which could be needed by whoever was captain if we had to maneuver sharply or speed up quickly.

"Caro will fit beside Joseph." Which meant I wouldn't. But there were other crash couches farther away if I needed them. More than enough here in Command.

Captain Hill nodded, clearly unhappy but granting the request. As she turned to relay the commands, I returned to Joseph's side. He had feared this moment. He had spoken of it more than once, of being forced into fighting and causing harm. So far, Joseph had refused to kill again. He had even left a message about the Doctrine of New Making.

But if Mohami was a spy, was the Doctrine pure? Would it work?

It took almost half an hour for Liam to come, escorted by two guards. Caro nestled in his arms, apparently asleep, one leg dangling against his side.

My brother had grown thin, and Caro was long and lanky for her age. I helped Liam tuck them in close to each other. Her arm circled Joseph's waist. He moved a little, making room for his niece.

Liam said, "I had to fight Lou and Kayleen on this. They wanted to watch her."

"Kayleen should sleep anyway."

"I know."

I realized he didn't know about the traitor or about Alicia. I told him, quickly, and then said, "I have to go. I want to hurry, so I can be back in case he needs me."

Liam nodded, leaned over for a kiss, and said, "I'll watch them both."

He smelled of Kayleen and Jherrel. I whispered, "I love you."

He smiled. "Always. Good luck."

My guard picked me up as I left Command. Gretchen. She seemed happy with her duty, smiling at me and walking with a lilt in her step. I sped to Mohami's as quickly as I could, dodging crewmen and robots as I jogged through the corridors.

The voices of people we passed in the corridors sounded edgy, and the looks I got as I jogged through them varied from curious to unfriendly.

Near Mohami's door, two armed crew members wearing the crossed arms of the security detail lounged against a wall. They nodded briefly at me.

I hesitated. What if he had done this thing? I took a deep breath and opened the door without knocking. Even though I had been forbidden to see him since the battle started, he had allowed me this courtesy in the past.

Gretchen came in behind me, and I gestured to her to stay just inside the door, hopefully out of earshot.

Mohami and Kala sat on low cushions, talking quietly. Two women sat near him, one tall and dark and the other small and fair. When the taller one turned to smile at me, I recognized her as mid-level crew who had been to a few of our Doctrine meetings. I nodded in greeting, and Mohami looked up. His eyes narrowed and he spoke to the women in a low tone. They got up to leave, both giving me curious looks.

Kala faded into the background, as usual.

As soon as I was as alone with Mohami as I was going to get, given Kala and the guard, I bowed to him. This was our signal that I needed to speak from a spiritual place.

He bowed back.

We both sat.

Kala arose from the place she had taken by the wall and disappeared toward the kitchen. We both waited for her to bring the tea and cakes that had become a ritual part of serious discussions. I breathed in and out, slowly, trying not to worry about Joseph and think about what to say all at once. It was difficult to ignore one thing and think about the other when they were so tangled together.

Mohami watched me, his beloved face utterly calm.

How could I doubt him?

As usual, by the time the tea appeared, I was ready to speak. Kala had an uncanny sense of timing about such things.

As soon as she backed away, Mohami and I raised our cups and sipped. The tea tasted more bitter than usual this morning, almost astringent. I looked directly into his eyes and said, "The ship's AI intercepted a message sent from this ship to one of the Islan flagships. It spoke of Joseph and his uncanny strength, and it mentioned that he had killed others in another Islan ship."

Mohami's eyes widened.

"This is a thing you knew, and I knew. I did not send that message." I swallowed, sucked in my stomach, and said, "The ship's AI traced the message to a terminal in these rooms."

He jerked a little. Guilt? Surprise? He took another sip of tea, which forced me to take one. Still bitter.

"Do you have the text of the message?" he asked.

"No." My voice shook and my hands quivered. "There are guards outside these rooms. I don't think you'll be allowed to leave."

Mohami kept his gaze on me. He looked thoughtful, and maybe a little sad. "Do you think that I could betray you?"

Not betray my brother, not betray Silver's Home, or even the *Thorn*. Betray me. I raised my tea, and he his. I took a long, slow sip, stilling the shaking cup against my bottom lip. I searched my body for answers. I could not hear guilt from him, or feel it in my heartbeat. All I felt was fear that this crime might be ascribed to him in spite of his innocence. But how could I know? When I set my cup down, I said, "No. I don't believe you could have done anything so cruel."

He looked past me, and when he did, I knew.

A great deal of pain and worry fled my body. It wasn't Mohami.

The traitor didn't move. She sat against the wall, still and small, as if her betrayal could yet go unnoticed.

Mohami gestured for her to join us.

She brought her tea, sat so we made a triangle. She sat simply, robes covering her knees, ankles crossed. She controlled her eyes and face, although a muscle twitched along her jawline.

Mohami raised his cup.

I raised mine, curious to see how the game played itself out.

We had spoken too quietly for the guards to hear. Still, they would be waiting for Mohami, prepared to take him into custody. We could give them Kala. But first, I wanted to know why she'd betrayed my brother. She took another breath, raised her cup, and said, "I serve the Wingmakers. You and I took the same vows."

Mohami said nothing, so I said nothing.

For a long time neither did Kala. Moments crawled by in awkward silence.

Gretchen started toward us, but I raised my hand and she stopped.

Kala swallowed and raised her tea cup, her gaze on me rather than on Mohami. "Your brother is strong enough to win this war. But he will not win it for Silver's Home. He doesn't support Makers." She shifted her gaze to Mohami. "If the fliers are freed, you will lose all you have built, and so will I. There will be no need for Keepers of the Ways." She sat straight, her voice pitched too low for the guard to hear.

Mohami set his cup down, and we did the same. The ritual seemed so odd here. Mohami's own voice was like hers, uncannily low and even warm. "Who helped you?"

"I did this myself."

"You did not."

"I gathered people to me. People who want to be pure."

It took a few breaths to calm myself and put the right question to her. "How many people are part of the insurrection against us?"

She smiled a little, though her eyes had gone sad. "There are many. I don't know how many. One makes three makes nine."

As rumors flew. "Give me names."

She looked at me, eyes wide, both stubborn and hopeful. "No."

So she thought she might have won …what? Dissension here? Poisoned rumors about the Doctrine?

The door opened and the security detail from outside poured in, followed by three others. Gretchen looked as surprised as I did. But then she had been assigned by Ming, and not by Security.

In moments, we were surrounded.

One of them took my arm and pulled me up. My foot kicked over the cup, spilling leftover tea onto the carpet.

There were two guards on Kala, two on Mohami, and only one holding me. He spoke near my ear. "You will come with us to security. After you are briefed, you may be allowed back out."

I felt dizzy. This couldn't be happening. I needed to go back to Joseph and Liam and Caro. "Captain Hill is expecting me."

"She is expecting us to interrogate you."

63

JOSEPH

When I fell back into the data to find more Islan ships, Caro waited for me. *Let me try to go further by myself,* I told her. Maybe I could keep her a tiny bit safer.

I will make you as strong as I can.

Good girl. Once more, I had to push guilt aside and let necessity ride the moment and take me to battle. Caro's presence had helped me control my anger and turn away from killing. I had managed to be the good uncle.

Could I do that to the whole damned fleet? Be the good uncle?

I checked the landscape of the battle. Three ships were close enough that I had to hurry. Behind them five more. Behind those, ships were turning away from their original trajectories, as if they thought it might take all of the combined might of the back half of the Islan fleet to defeat the *Thorn.*

Caro?

I see them. They're all coming for us.

She always spoke her truths. *If this gets too hard, Caro, save yourself. I'll find a way.*

I saw the way you spoke to the Islan ships. I can do it now, too. I can help you.

You could become a target. Just help me be strong.

If you are strong enough.

I will be. I had to be.

Strength meant to be like a paw-cat. To stalk my prey and disable them quickly. Perhaps like a family of cats. I would have to be in more than one ship at once. If I hesitated, if I doubted my own strengths for even a moment, I might lose my courage.

The closest ship had new algorithms. I pushed at them, hard, and it felt like stretching into a strong piece of rubber. I couldn't get through. But in three tries, I could. Every time I came out here, I was bigger and faster and better. More capable.

Caro was a battery.

It took seconds for the first ship to fall to me. Too long. But now I knew how they were laid out. It just took moments to sink into the patterns of this ship, and even as I began to give its weapons systems orders, I started to breach the next ship. I finished with the first ship before I reached for the third, again leaving a message about the Doctrine. This time, I left behind a few of Chelo's basic tenets. *No sentient being deserves to be owned. No Maker should make a thinking being without designing its freedom into its creation plan.*

When I was done with the first three ships, I had time to survey the system.

Thinking about paw-cats made me wonder about Romi. I found the *Lily Star* easily, plunging into her far more familiar systems.

Shock, then joy: Alicia lived! My elation thrummed through all the bits of me spread through every ship. Caro vibrated with happiness.

Alicia lived! Something dark and heavy lifted, the light of excitement and hope filling in behind it. From hope, power. I began to feel the edges of what I had felt on Fremont all those years ago. It began to take me, transform me. The interconnectedness of all life. Before I lost myself, I needed to get Alicia a message. Caro could do it.

Caro! Tell Alicia to go to the Peacemaker. She isn't safe out here, not in that little ship, not unless I prevail. Send the whole Lily Star. Tell them to go quickly.

Okay.

There was more. I had seen myself flying the Peacemaker. I had to be there, too. *Caro? Ask the captain to send my body there, and you. Send us all. You will have to go to be my anchor.* I needed Caro to understand how much this mattered. *We need to be together, and we need to be on the Peacemaker.*

Why?

Because I dreamed it.

I surrendered to the pull of unity, of oneness. I felt the ships coming for us, felt the *Unicorn* and the *Black Star* and the ships beyond that.

In the spaces between, I felt the drones.

They were. All. One.

Go Caro. Go with my body. Take it to the Peacemaker.

I will.

I love you.

If everything connected, if it all became one beating heart of data, would I be able to separate myself enough to keep the parts from destroying each other?

Would I even see destruction as wrong?

64
ALICIA

I perched outside the paw-cat enclosure, missing Marti. Missing Induan. They would both be alive if it weren't for me. Induan would still be on Silver's Home, or maybe somewhere else in this war, doing logistics. That was her skill—planning and making things happen. That was why I had brought her to Lopali—a planner to balance a risk-taker.

I had never expected to love her.

The cat must be near the back. There was no movement except for a desultory swinging of some kind of long, yellow leaves near a fan. What an oddness to have found something I loved from the planet I had hated way out here among the stars.

If I hadn't begged for wings, neither Marti nor Tsawo would be here. Marti would be alive, flying joyfully beside Amalo. Whether or not I had actually murdered her with a bad shot, I might as well have just shot her in cold blood.

This wasn't good thinking. I knew it wasn't, nor was it like me. Surely I would get over it soon.

The warm weight of a hand on my shoulder surprised me. The bangles on her wrists identified Jagruti.

"Sit." I gestured at one of the human chairs and sighed. "I could use some keeping."

She sat. "It's not your fault."

"How do you know what I was thinking?"

"Regret is written all over your face. So what else can you be thinking? You did not send robots to kill you all."

"I might have killed her. If I missed the robot."

She smiled. "All of you could have died. We're lucky we have you two."

"Do you know where Tsawo is?"

"Closeted with Cy. They're trying to decide our next move. The fight isn't past us yet, but we don't have a parent ship left. Tsawo still has some idea that he should be greeted like a power of some kind."

I sat back, staring vacantly at the paw-cat pen. Something moved near the back, dark, hard to see. Squinting, I made out two shapes. The big cat and Romi, walking side by side. The cat's haunches came almost to Romi's shoulders. It could turn and rip his throat out in one fast, fluid move.

He didn't seem worried. He patted the cat on the shoulder, which should have cost him a hand. The cat almost looked sad to see him slide through the gate and out of the pen. It could have been pathetic, except it wasn't. The cat didn't appear to be at all afraid of Romi, nor did it appear in any way domesticated.

If the most awesome predator I had ever met could be caged and yet respected, what did that mean for fliers? What, for that matter, did it mean for paw-cats?

Romi, who hardly looked like a man capable of gentling anything big and scary, walked quickly over to us. "I just spoke to Cy. He got a message from Joseph, who suggested we go to a ship called the *Peacemaker*."

We had to go somewhere. At least that ship was aptly named. And Joseph was alive!

Romi stepped back a pace, making room for us to stand up easily. "Cy and Tsawo want us to join them."

Tsawo and I spent the half hour before we started to burn for the *Peacemaker* in a conference room with Cy, staring at screens that showed what we knew about the trajectories and patterns of the slow-motion battle. The *Lily Star* had decent enough computers to create a historical re-enactment of the roughly week-old battle from the point the fleets came close enough to each other to matter.

It looked choreographed. "Why are the Islans fighting this way?" I asked. "Why so orderly?"

"Large starships don't turn quickly," Cy said. "And every starship in the system is required by law to broadcast its location. The fight couldn't happen near any of the five planets. This location was negotiated to allow for time—so the fleets had to gather and get here. That was mostly an advantage for Silver's Home, and what the Port Authority bargained for."

"That seems so stupid," I blurted out. "Why have so many rules?"

Cy ignored me. "The Islans wanted a frontal assault battle, since they saw themselves as better able to coordinate. The place and the rules of engagement were decided politically."

Without including fliers in the discussion, or as far as I knew, anyone from Lopali.

Tsawo raised his drinking bulb, full now of a medicinal tea Romi had promised would help us survive the day we'd spend in bubble crash couches. *Lily Star* was only designed for fliers to a point, but when Jagruti and Tsawo had fled here from the *Sky Anvil*, they'd brought the transport ship we'd used the first time we'd come here. That could keep us reasonably comfortable during acceleration. "So," Tsawo asked, "this battle is like a cage match in a way? Everyone needs to behave, and follow the rules, and the biggest guns win?"

"The smallest guns, I think. Both teams thought their fleets of small ships and drones and the like would win the war. That's what almost killed you two."

The chair was uncomfortable, so I stood, hunching over slightly to keep my wingtips from trailing on the ground. Why hadn't the damned Wingmakers figured out how to design us so we could just sit like normal humans?

Cy swiveled so he faced us both. "Each side planned to overwhelm the other with unexpected feints within the rules, and with sheer volume. The Islans expected their centralized communication would help them win. Up until a few hours ago, I thought the Islans were right. I figured we were on a suicide mission. Even more so after we lost the *Sun's Orbit* and the *Anvil.* I was planning a 'party before we die' event." He looked completely serious. "Because up until a few minutes ago, we were going to die out here."

I'd rather run us into an Islan ship and kill it than have a good party and wait to be shot out of the sky. A warrior who would give up on survival when the odds were against him bothered me.

As if he knew what I was thinking, Cy said, "There were three Islan ships bearing down on us. Three. They would have been here about two hours from now."

"How were you going to party?" Tsawo whispered.

"By loading up all the ammunition we could and picking a target."

That made me feel better.

"But all the targets just stopped heading for us." Tsawo stared at the simulation, which was slightly less than a day away from our current time.

Cy pointed. "See that? See the two ships headed toward the *Maker's Thorn* where Joseph is?"

I blinked.

Cy stood and touched the glowing images, making sure.

"Yes." I sipped my own drink. It tasted like something Paloma might have fed us, bitter and sweet both, but good for me.

"Watch that ship. See? It flies right past. It could have taken out the *Thorn*. Now watch these two."

I pursed my lips. They also flew through the small group of ships that included the *Thorn* without firing.

Cy stood up, speaking in an exaggerated tone. "Not only did they fly past the *Thorn* without firing, *but it did not fire at them.* Neither did the *Unicorn*, one of the other ships in the same battle group. The other two fired, but only one of them even hit any of the Islan ships." Cy looked triumphant, like he was showing us a miracle. "And ... watch for it ... as those three Islan ships continue through the fleet they don't fire at anything, even once. See here"—he pointed—"they're changing direction to avoid any other possible battles. If it was one ship, I'd say they lost a major system or something, just couldn't fire. But it's not. All three of them acted the same way." He leaned toward us and grinned. "Watch the last three hours closely."

I stared as a few Islan ships seemed to bend toward the *Maker's Thorn*. Then more. Then more.

None of them fired.

Joseph had done something like it on Fremont, but with one ship. One. A little one at that, a ship that would have fit inside the *Lily Star*. Which had fit inside the *Sun's Orbit*.

Suddenly, I desperately wanted to see him.

"Whoever, whatever," Cy smiled at us and put both of his hands on the table. "I think the battle is almost over."

He was so sure of himself a cold dread filled my chest. Joseph was fragile, far more fragile than most people thought. I knew that—I had been able to hurt him easily. Marcus's disapproval had almost frozen him more than once. Out here, at least one fleet would be fighting every move he made, and more likely, they'd both be fighting him. Hell, every ship out here might be fighting him. "I know Joseph. He gets scared, he gets angry, he feels uncertain. Any of those things could undo him. He's as human as the rest of us."

Cy burst out laughing, and it took me a moment to realize that I had said that, and I was no longer considered human, and that was why we were here. I laughed, too, but inside it coiled anger.

Tsawo looked as bitter as I felt. Cy had the same prejudices as everyone else. Why wouldn't he? Maybe this wasn't the moment for this battle, but damnit, I wasn't going to be still. Not now, not ever. I stood as straight as I could with my wings, which meant opening them a little even in the small space. "We are people. Both of us. Tsawo started as a flier, but he was a person then, and he is a person now. My wings are new, and I will tell you that I did not become less when I earned them. I became more." I leaned toward Cy. "This is *reality*. This is what is true. And this is what we will prove to all of you."

He leaned back, putting his hands up. "I didn't mean any harm."

Tsawo held his hands up as well, toward me, a gentling gesture.

What?! My voice rose in astonished response. "And you! You believe it. That you are less. You ..." My voice shook, now, the anger rattling all the way through my wings, unexpected, unwelcome, but righteous. It spread, beyond Tsawo, engulfing those who'd made us. "All the years of being told you are less have stuck to you. That is what you have heard since you were an infant. That you are both more—because you suffer—and less, because you are not fully human and have the rights of an object."

He stared at me in disbelief; whether at my anger or my words, I couldn't tell.

"You fight it. You have always fought it. You have tried to protect us all, and also yourself from the truth. You are as human as any other fighter out here. You are not less. And neither am I. It's time to stand up for who we are."

Disbelief turned to surprise. "Now?"

"No? When? We are about to go represent our race on the *Peacemaker*. Joseph is creating that for us." I knew it, beyond all question or doubt. The puzzle of all of us, of how we had been designed, and of our experiences, snapped together in my head. It was what Chelo had taught us, what Marcus had taught us, even what Tsawo had taught us. Joseph did the bidding of his sister, our greatest pacifist, and he was sending us to a place he had sworn we could go. I knew, knew *deeply*, how he was trying to end this war. He was breaking every one of its rules.

He had become something glorious and inhuman, something greater than himself. I could feel him at the edges of my consciousness, as if something in what I had become let me connect with him in ways I never had. If I wanted to help, I had to become bigger than I had ever been. He needed me. I had always needed him, but right now, he needed me.

More, we needed each other.

I stared at Tsawo.

He stepped back.

The next words I spoke came from the depths of my soul. "You will be my protector, and you will have my back. But *I* will represent us on the *Peacekeeper*. This is what the fire of Becoming created, what Induan's death created, and what Marti died for. This is the fruit of the pain of my childhood, of my adolescence, of my wings." My voice filled the space around us. Tsawo and Cy looked round-eyed and a little awed. "I will not waste the prices that have been paid for this. We will win."

Cy didn't matter. He wasn't us. But Tsawo did.

I lowered my voice. "This is what you made of me. I am no longer what I was, or who I was, when you met me. If anyone can sculpt a future for us, it will be me."

I saw the moment the balance of power finished shifting between us. His body shivered. Then he touched the single feather around his neck and said, "I will be your protector. I will make sure that you live, and that you thrive, and I will follow you."

Cy looked at each of us in turn, his eyes wide. "I didn't mean anything when I laughed. I'm sorry."

This time, my laugh was genuine.

As soon as I stopped, Cy said, "First, we have to get to the *Peacemaker.* Joseph appears to be controlling the big fleet, but I'm not at all sure that he has *all* of the autonomous fleet in his sphere of influence. Go. Get strapped in. I'll figure out how to get you there safely."

65
CHELO

I paced inside of the small room I had been locked up in. Back and forth. Back and forth.

I needed to be with Joseph!

After an hour in the small space, fear and fuming had just started to fade to resignation when the door opened and two guards came in, both male, and both fairly big. Given that I was a pacifist, the size of the guards was either miscalculation or overkill.

One of them wouldn't look me in the eye and the other one couldn't stop staring at me. Both of them seemed slightly spooked. They led me out of the security offices, one in front, one behind, trailed by the same female guard who had been in Mohami's rooms with me when Kala confessed her sins. As soon as I realized they were taking me to Command, I relaxed a little.

They didn't take me all the way to Joseph. I caught a glimpse of Liam's blond hair as we passed through the ship but couldn't spot Caro or Joseph. They led me to the small conference room. A single water glass and a pitcher graced the table.

Gretchen and one of the two hulking guards who had brought me stayed in the room with me.

I sat. Then stood. Then sat and stretched. I paced. I had returned to sitting when the door opened, and Captain Hill came in. Her hair had come partly loose from its braids, falling in kinks around her shoulders, and her captain's coat had developed wrinkles. Her face looked thinner than usual, her sharp cheekbones turned to shelves. She stood over me and snapped out a question. "What is your brother doing?"

"I don't know. I'm no Wind Reader."

"Every Islan ship near us appears to have been disarmed."

I felt the grin inside before it broke across my face. "Good news, right?"

"He's a *child.* Not a trained negotiator. *What do you know?*"

I gritted my teeth and tried to catch my breath and think. Joseph wasn't a child. None of us were. Three of us *had* children. I took two deep breaths, and the time I took to answer seemed to calm her a little. I told her, "My brother is strong. He's sweet and strong, and he is undoubtedly trying very hard to keep people from killing each other."

She sat. "Every Islan Wind Reader in the fleet is surely focused on him. That means they are focused on the *Thorn*. Right now. My battle team is on high alert. And you know what?"

"No."

Her voice rose. "There's nothing for them to do. No shots are being fired. And you expect me to believe you know almost nothing about it?" The fear in her voice was subtle, but this woman had never shown the slightest alarm in my presence. "What if they kill him? They'll kill us next. All of us. He's breaking rules of engagement that took months to negotiate!"

"Are there rules about stopping a battle with no shots fired?"

Her dark eyes hardened. "There are rules about cyber attacks!"

"My brother is not a computer program." I held my hand up to signal I wasn't taking her lightly. "I'm certain that if we pull him out, your bubble of safety *will* collapse."

She snapped at me. "Stop telling me things I know."

"Is he in contact with you at all?"

"No. I … I refused to give him permission to do this."

I took a deep breath and stood up so I was looking down at her.

"What would have happened if he hadn't done this? Weren't we already being attacked?"

"We were. And we might be dead." Her face fell in a little on itself, lost its certainty. "Maybe he is saving us. But we only had a few ships pointed at us before this and now, if Joseph's defenses fail, we cannot survive against the remaining Islan battleships. They'll all target us."

"Maybe they'll stop when they realize it won't do any good."

She stared at me for a long time before she stood up and walked out of the room.

I drank the water.

Just after I finished, the door opened again. Captain Hill looked five years older than she had ten minutes ago. "Joseph wants his body to be taken to the *Peacemaker*. He says Alicia is going there, and he and Caro need to go there, too. Without being disturbed."

It took a moment to digest all that. Alicia was alive. He wanted to be near her. He surely wanted me to go, as well. Caro. Thus, we should all go. "We'll have to bring his dog."

She shook her head, as if she'd expected me to say something else.

"It gets the attention away from you."

She paced a circle around me, clearly struggling with how to respond. A second circle. A third. And then she said something I didn't expect. "We'll take *Bryan's Hope*. It's been modified to be faster than its specs. It will be the best ship to get us there."

Her circling made me dizzy, but her word choice made me more so. "You'll leave the *Thorn*?"

"Someone has to fly you there. Joseph can't do it. The best way for me to protect my ship is to protect Joseph. And as much as I want to question him, and even tell him that he's wrong, or crazy, or something else entirely, he's the strongest Wind Reader I've ever seen. I could not do what he is doing." She smiled. "I will go."

"*Bryan's Hope* will hold us all."

Her smile grew. "Even Sasha."

66
ALICIA

As the *Lily Star* flew toward the *Peacemaker*, I reflected on the strange complement of beings aboard her. Fliers determined to change the world and wrest a place in society. A Keeper of the Ways of Lopali who had run from her job in horror, and a Keeper at Water Lily Hunting Grounds accompanied by a paw-cat from Fremont. A determined fighter, Cy, now in charge of the *Lily Star*'s defenses. Some number of robed acolytes. A dragon. A few other exotic animals.

Maybe it was time to see Jagruti. I knocked on her door, clutching a covered plate in one hand.

Her hair hung loose, flowing past her waist over a simple white robe. She looked almost like one of the *Lily Star*'s almost silent staff, except older and less deferential.

I decided she was happy to see me in spite of her severe expression; her eyes failed to hide a spark of delight. "Come in." She stepped aside. "What can I do for you?"

I hesitated for a breath. "Induan was my strategist. Will you help me?"

"What do you need help with?"

"I want to help Joseph create peace."

"Well." She smiled. "That is a very tall order." She sighed. "How much time do I have?"

Cy estimated a twelve-hour trip. If Joseph's eerie control of the Islan ships lasted that long, we might as well move boldly through the battlefield. I needed some sleep. "Two hours now. Then maybe two more later?"

"I'll make tea."

Bless her. I held out the plate. "I brought some food. They don't have much flier food; I cleaned them out of easy carbs. But there's day-old bread and berries to mash on it, and two protein bars."

"A full belly is a useful thing on the way to peace negotiations."

"What can you tell me about the Islans?"

"Nothing you don't know." She smiled. "You don't need more facts. You need more control. Let's start with control over your feelings."

I bit back a surge of irritation. But then, my anger itself proved that I needed what she was offering. I nodded.

She gestured to me to sit on a tall green chair with an ample darker-green cushion and rungs where I could rest my feet. She sat opposite me on a slightly lower brown stool. I set the plate on a round table between us, and she placed the two steaming cups of tea beside it. They smelled like honey and something bitter. "Did you put truth fruit in the tea?" I asked her.

"Would I need to for you to speak your truth to me?"

"Not now."

"That's what I thought." She sipped her tea, so I sipped mine, and for a moment we mirrored each other. "Now," she said. "Let's talk about anger."

67

CHELO

Marcus's retrofit of *Bryan's Hope* impressed me. He'd planned for Sasha, for fliers, and for more people than we had with us, even though Ming had insisted we bring two guards each.

Liam, Ming, and Jenna helped me carefully slide Joseph and Caro from the surface of the med-bot gurney to crash couches. Sasha was in the corner of the same room lying in a doggy crash-couch Marcus had included. It looked like a padded cave with a urine vacuum and stank a little. Sasha curled up tight, nose on paws, and watched Joseph and Caro. I scratched her nose to thank her, and then settled as close to my brother as I could get. I couldn't hear his breathing, or Caro's, but I could see her little right arm flung across her chest.

The small ship felt fragile. The rules of space travel meant anyone could know *Bryan's Hope* had come from the *Thorn*, and it might be possible to trace the ship all the way back to our escape from Lopali.

Five other ships would leave with us. One for a distant escort, and four as unmanned bait. All six floated out, one at a time, a string of metal boxes and cylinders leaving the safety of a full-sized warship for the vastness of space.

We hung below the *Thorn*'s long, cylindrical body for some time, carefully avoiding anyplace that maneuvering thrusters might fire from. The *Thorn* was a darkness in a star-lit sky, flying with no exterior lights. I knew we were free of her when the starfield opened up.

Captain Hill's voice came over the comm. "Prepare for thrust." Weight threw me back. I swallowed, already uncomfortable. I hated small ships like this even more than larger ones like the *Thorn*. Jherrel whimpered at the acceleration. Joseph and Caro didn't move and made no sound at all.

I tried to forget our danger. We were immobilized while our ship moved faster than other ships through the battlefield. We would draw attention and had to trust Joseph to keep us safe while doing whatever else he was up to. Dangerous debris cluttered the battlefield. I held my breath.

Hard thrust continued for an hour. Jherrel stopped whimpering and stared. The ship spoke stats regularly in a language full of acronyms I barely—or didn't—understand. Twice, the ship's maneuvering thrusters jogged our course slightly one way or another, making me nauseous.

Just when I thought I might scream, we slowed.

Captain Hill's voice shook. "Clear."

I snapped the restraints away and staggered to Jherrel. Liam beat me there by a step and gathered his son up, so I hugged them both and turned to stand beside Joseph. He was so still and white that he looked dead. Caro only looked ever-so-slightly pinker.

68

JOSEPH

I felt thin as fog and as big as both fleets. I began to connect to each of the ship's AIs. As I added them, one by one, the fog began to feel less diffuse.

I'm here, Caro reminded me.

It took a while to understand her simple statement. Like hearing a single raindrop in a hailstorm. Eventually, I sent back, *Good. Can you check on our bodies?*

Each AI added more computational power, but also more complexity. Each of them was both more and less than I. As I became the being they answered to, they made me stronger and gave me more tools, more skills. And pulled me thinner.

I didn't know how much more complexity I could hold.

Our bodies must be fine, Caro said. *There's no time. We have to do this.*

How are Alicia and Chelo? I asked her.

They are on their way. I will keep their path clear of dangers.

Be careful.

I will stay beside you.

Damn. No time. I erected a barrier between her and the web of

AIs. I let her see through it, but if I lost control I didn't want her to try and take it. Too dangerous.

My deepening connection to the ship's AIs rippled toward the *Opportunity*, who appeared to be headed toward the same region of space where the *Peacemaker* waited to accept my family. I hesitated. Lukas might be my enemy, but he could lead me to the people I needed to negotiate with.

I began to sort the ships into three fleets in my head. Lukas's *Opportunity* went with the fleet from Silver's Home. So did the other flagships. Sorting made the work slower, more exacting, and split my focus between three tasks. I kept each Islan weapon unarmed, increased my understanding of each ship and through them, each captain. I did my best to force the sort into a repeatable pattern so I could do more than one ship and captain at the time.

Ships were clearly from Islas or Silver's Home, but they were not clearly Third Fleet ships. Starting with the ships from Silver's Home, I placed a few into the Third Fleet list: those where the leadership seemed swayed by Chelo's Doctrine or philosophies that seemed close. I added a few who were clearly sick of the fighting to the list.

No Islan or Port Authority ships went to the Third Fleet list.

I observed myself choosing, acting, connecting. The me that watched felt separate from the me that kept his full focus on the fleet.

The center that held all of my various selves together was the small piece of my heart that kept Caro safe.

69
ALICIA

The *Peacemaker* opened double doors onto a huge open bay. A blinking red light led us into a berth. The orders from the larger ship to the *Lily Star* must have been issued by a human, but they were delivered by the ship's AI in an annoying electronic voice. "Bring your negotiating team. Bring two sets of clothes and all of the toiletries you need. My representative will meet you at the showers."

Romi swallowed and looked to me, his face almost pleading. "You might need a runner, or someone to record conversations or be an extra pair of hands."

"We might at that," I said. "Will the animals survive without you?

Romi smiled thinly. "I asked them not to eat the crew."

"Nice of you."

I led us off the *Lily Star*, stopping at the edge of the platform to look at the bay while the others followed me out of the ship. The berth we were in had been designed for something bigger. There were other empty berths, and many repair bots. A row of ten hooks just above us held two drone ships. The *Peacemaker* had fought, and she hadn't won. Nor had she been destroyed.

Tsawo followed behind me, Jagruti behind him, and Romi after Jagruti. The four of us barely fit in the airlock. The air coming in carried a distinct antiseptic smell. Maybe someone on board suspected us of being dangerous.

Once we stepped through the lock and into the *Peacemaker*, I decided they might simply hate dirt. Most starships looked worn and scratched, like old wagons, and showed repairs. The *Peacemaker*'s walls gleamed as if someone had polished them the way fancy hotels on Silver's Home polished their bathrooms.

A silver robot shaped like a table greeted us and suggested we put our bags on it and follow it. I did so. One of its wheels rattled a little, which I found subtly reassuring given how neat and well-maintained the corridors were. At least something imperfect existed here. That thought told me why the *Peacemaker* bothered me. It, like Lopali, was just a little too perfect.

The robot led us to a suite with a single shared galley and meeting room space that had been fitted with barstools for perches. Off of the shared space, a narrow hallway led to four rooms. Neither Tsawo nor I was likely to fit down the hallway or in through the bedroom doors.

Once the door closed behind the robot, we all looked at each other for some time. Then I shook my wings and laughed. "Well, we made it. This is our show. I suppose we had better get ready for it. Tsawo, shall I groom your feathers while Jagruti fixes my hair?" I glanced at Romi. "Can you find some way for us to wash up?"

Romi stiffened, blinked, then smiled broadly. "I did say I would do anything you needed."

Twenty minutes later we were ready. Many fliers were joyfully colorful, but Tsawo and I appeared like dark angels, black except for my violet eyes, the range of purples where my wings met my back, and the blood-red circles for Bryan's blood. I wore white, Tsawo black. Jagruti wore some of each, and I helped her weave colored jewels into her braids. Romi wore the simple white robes of his kind of Keeper, and when they parted, I noticed a black bodysuit beneath them.

Just as we finished, one of the walls revealed itself as a two-way screen into what looked like a command deck. A woman in a subtle golden captain's coat sat in a chair I wished I could try out. Gel-based armrests would allow her access to controls under almost any circumstance, the top could fold slightly over to either stream her commands or allow her to see video. She was slender and compact with short red hair, blue eyes, and long manicured fingers. Her uniform and coat appeared unwilling to suffer a single wrinkle. It included slender mag boots, and it appeared likely her bodysuit could double as part of an environment suit if necessary. She spoke pleasantly. "I am Captain Shella Grundson. Welcome aboard the *Peacemaker*."

I said, "Thank you. I am Alicia and this is Tsawo." I pointed to him. "We are emissaries from the fliers of Lopali. With me, I have Jagruti, who is a Keeper of the Ways of Lopali, and Romi, who is a Keeper for Water Lily Hunting Grounds on Silver's Home. We have arrived at your Master's request and look forward to joining the leadership of this conflict in conversation."

Her face gave away exactly zero. I saw no sign of a smile, no welcome in her eyes. Maybe there was a little curiosity.

I continued. "Thank you for the quarters. Do you have any word of Joseph?"

"He has not arrived yet." She leaned into the camera. "The war appears to have been stopped. What do you know about that?"

I sought the simplest explanation. "I suspect it has something to do with Joseph. But I have not yet seen him or spoken to him, so I don't know very much."

This time her face was easier to read. Suspicion.

"Honestly," I said. "I don't know. Surely you've traced our origin."

"The *Lily Star* came here from Silver's Home."

"And we came to the *Lily Star* from our ship, the *Sky Anvil*, which was destroyed." I smiled, forcing the sudden surge of anger down. I glanced at Jagruti, who gave me the barest nod of support, as if she recognized that I followed one of her instructions from earlier. *Stay calm. Calmness gives you power.* Staying calmer than Captain Grundson was going to require a miracle.

I tried. "We came from Lopali and arrived at the fleet just before the battle started near us. The *Lily Star* picked us up after the *Sun's Orbit* was lost. We know little about this fight. Would you be kind enough to brief us?"

She leaned forward. "What do you want to know?"

How the power structure was distributed and who made decisions. But I started with, "Tell me about this ship."

"Marcus built the *Peacemaker* for this war. We are fast, have excellent weapons, and one of the best AIs ever built. There are berths more appropriate to your physical body types, and we will move you there after access is restored."

"How long will that take?"

"A day. We took damage during our part of the fight, and while the bots have completed the hull repair, we have not finished testing yet." She smiled. "I'm sorry we cannot do better. Marcus planned for you, and we will offer the best hospitality we can. But I must see to preparations for others as well. Not only are Joseph and his family coming here, but the leaders of both fleets are on their way."

The screen went dark.

"Well," I mused to Tsawo. "That's interesting. Both leaders."

His smile looked slightly feral.

70
CHELO

The captain had Ulrika fly *Bryan's Hope* while she watched for dangers in the way she and Joseph had done on the *Thorn*. Which meant Captain Hill, like Joseph, appeared to be sleeping. Ulrika paced. I called up an illustrated story on my slate, placing it so that Jherrel could see it and read to me.

His small, halting voice kept my skin from crawling free of my body.

He had reached page three when Ulrika ordered, "Crash Couches! Now!" An alert screamed through the ship. I risked a brief glance toward Joseph and Caro. No change. No change in the captain either.

I buckled Jherrel in and Liam and I dove for own safe spaces.

Ulrika talked to other crew through her microphone, muttering about targeting and weapons. The *Hope* began to hum. Jherrel whined and Liam shushed him.

The ship jerked.

The tendons in Ulrika's neck stood out. Lips clamped, she listened, then spit out words in an intense whisper. She paced around our couches. Whatever was happening, she didn't seem to think *she* needed to be strapped in.

Something banged into the hull behind us and Ulrika spit more orders as three repair bots streamed past us and the sound of scuttling in the hallway suggested there were more. But no one started talking about environment suits, so whatever it was didn't affect life support.

The *Hope* jogged so hard my right side pressed into the gel. Then my left. My stomach did tiny twists. Jherrel screamed. Ulrika braced herself on a chair.

Nothing from any of the Wind Readers.

Something else hit us, the hull pinging.

Ulrika pulled up a window that showed a repair bot outside of the ship, one long limb clinging to a handhold and three feet splayed wide. Another bot crept into the view, broader. They approached each other. One pushed another off and then turned, was pushed away. A short battle started, a few blows of metal feet. After just seconds, only one remained.

Ulrika's face relaxed, which must mean ours had won.

Captain Hill stirred and sat up. "That was something."

Ulrika nodded. "Good work."

"What happened?" I asked.

"They threw all of the small debris they could at us. We lost part of a cargo bay and some supplies. Behind us." Ulrika jerked her thumb toward the place the largest of the bangs had come from. "But everyone is okay."

Captain Hill stretched. "For a while. It seems like the big ships are utterly unable to harm us. That was the available extra debris with brains, sent after us. We're probably clear."

I glanced at Jherrel. "How long?"

"An hour," Captain Hill said. "Stay strapped in. I think it's those two"—she pointed toward Joseph and Caro—"who are keeping us safe."

"I need to give them water."

Her brows narrowed. "How?"

"Do you have a washcloth or a rag? And a water bulb?"

I climbed out of my couch and spent the last part of the ride twisting water from a rag onto Joseph's lips. I had to prop Caro up to do the same. I wasn't sure which still form frightened me the most. My beloved brother, white as snow and limp in my arms, refusing to participate actively in drinking, or Caro, who sucked at the rag like a favorite childhood bottle but didn't react to my voice at all.

I remembered Joseph's worry about letting her help him and stroked her fine hair and watched her small chest rise and fall and her long-lashed lids rest against her cheek.

What if she never woke up?

71

JOSEPH

C*helo is inside the Peacemaker*, Caro reported.

Are we?

Of course. Alicia, too.

No one was hurt?

I didn't let anyone get hurt.

Only the smallest part of me conversed with Caro, but the relief of it spread through my distributed selves. It was becoming like that, as if one being controlled access to a thousand, and some of those to others.

I felt stacked and thin and yet … marvelous. It was harder to sort ships since they blurred together, all of humanity in this sector of space like one beating heart. It was … beautiful.

I resisted falling completely away. It was time for the end to begin, and I needed to tell Caro something. What was it?

Oh.

Oh.

The ships and hearts and lives all spread around me, the possibilities for the next steps almost endless.

Caro?

Yes?

Tell Chelo she and Alicia have to do this together. I will do my job, but I cannot negotiate. They must.

Can I come back?

After you eat and drink and after you tell them—and after you sleep.

After I tell them and eat and drink.

So headstrong. But then we were both good at disobedience. A last thing. *I love you.*

I love you, too. Don't get lost.

I… and then I left her for the seductive, fractal strings and swoops of a fleet's worth of data. I couldn't help myself.

72

CHELO

As soon as the *Hope* nestled safely inside of the *Peacemaker*, Liam went to Jherrel and I to Caro. She stirred, one small hand lifting from her Uncle Joseph's side and rubbing at her eyes.

"Caro," I whispered. "Caro, are you okay?"

Her eyes opened and her hands rose, asking me to hold her. The gesture of a young child, but the look in her eyes was older, a little bit calculating and a little bit defiant.

It didn't matter. I picked her up and cradled her close, feeling her thin legs dangling along my thighs, her feet kicking my knees and her fingers clutching at my neck. If only I had some way to understand what they went through. I murmured in her ear, "I'm here. I love you. We're on the *Peacemaker*."

"I know where we are," she mumbled into my neck, then pushed back and away. "Joseph told me you and Alicia must negotiate. He can't. He can do what he is doing."

"What is he doing?"

She hesitated. "Making the fleet one."

That didn't help me understand, but I liked the way it sounded. We had ridden *Bryan's Hope* to the *Peacemaker* and Joseph was *making the fleet one*. Damned if I knew what that meant I needed to do, but it felt right.

"I should go with you," Caro said. "But I must be able to sleep. Pretend I'm sick."

She didn't mean sleep. But maybe we would need a conduit to Joseph. I frowned. "Really?"

"Yes."

Maybe she knew more than I did. "Come with me where?"

"To talk to the admirals. There are two."

"They're here?"

"Joseph made them come here."

"He made them?"

"He can tell them what to do. If they don't obey, he can blow up their ships." She screwed her little face up for a moment, her eyes rolling up into her head. She jerked twice, so hard that for a second I thought she might be seizing. Then she whispered against my shoulder. "Leave Uncle Joseph here in case he needs to fly away."

Fear shivered along my spine and shoulders and chilled my heart. Both fleets must be throwing every resource they had at destroying my brother.

Caro let me feed her protein cakes and a tube of vitamin gel. She remained solemn and quiet, at best distracted and at worst like she was moving through a fog. Still, she drank her fill of water and took care of her body's needs. She moved slower than normal, every step and gesture deliberate. While Liam washed her face and she submitted to a complete change of clothes, I found a simple cart and built her a nest of blankets and pillows. I stacked an extra change of clothes and some snacks on the lower shelf of the cart. Liam let her go, his face as worried as mine surely was. Caro sleepwalked over to her younger brother and kissed Jherrel on the cheek once. Right after that, she let me lift her onto the nest, curled up, and closed her eyes. I felt certain she had gone back to my brother rather than to dreams.

Captain Hill and I sorted people. Ulrika, Dianne, Tiala, Liam, Jherrel, and Paloma, the rest of the crew, and most of the security people stayed behind. They would care for and defend Joseph, and Tiala would bring us news if there was anything we needed to know.

The captain led our delegation off *Bryan's Hope*, followed by Ming, Jenna, Kayleen, and Mohami. I pushed the cart with a makeshift bed on it for Caro. It looked like I was wheeling a doll to a meeting. The same female guard who had been there when the captain arrested me and Mohami walked behind us. Gretchen.

The boundary between the *Hope* and the *Peacemaker* was identifiable by smell (fear to antiseptic) and look (ragged to spotless). I liked the orderly feel of the larger ship. A rolling escort robot met us just outside our door and led us through two corridors, up an elevator, and stopped in front of a set of double doors. They slid open.

I took a deep breath. I was about to see Alicia, who had hurt my brother; Alicia who had abandoned us. I told myself, again, that it was okay, that she was too selfish to know what she was doing, but she had needed that to survive. Of all of us, Alicia's childhood had been the hardest.

At first, I was occupied with angling Caro's rolling bed through the door without hitting anyone. After I made it in, the room awed me. It was large and businesslike with a much higher ceiling than I'd expected inside of a spaceship. The walls displayed art, but I was certain they could display data or news feeds.

Across the room, I spotted two fliers. Tsawo was instantly recognizable. The female beside him had to be Alicia. For a heartbeat I froze, staring. She had been re-made into a slender, dark-winged goddess. Of course she had chosen dark wings. Or maybe they had been formed around her personality. The rounded arc of the tops of the wings rose up from her back and framed her face. Purple accents matched and even outshone her eyes, and near the ends of her ebony feathers, maroon highlights gleamed in the bright lights.

I pushed Caro in front of me, stopping a few feet away from Alicia as the extent of her physical change sunk in. There was no mistaking her for anyone else, but her limbs were longer, her face shaped differently, her eyes bigger. She had become a work of art.

Surely she saw the admiration in my eyes. I could tell by the tilt of her head, the slight smile that made her look both proud and distant. Something had matured in her. She felt ... calm, almost spiritual. As if perhaps the old Alicia had taken a little bit of Mohami into her.

I turned to look for him, and when I found him, I saw a smile on his face. I had thought it was about Alicia, but then I saw him heading toward a woman I had seen a few times on Lopali but couldn't even put a name to. They were both smiling, like old friends.

I turned back to Alicia. None of the anger or worry I had expected surfaced. The only feeling that seemed possible in the moment was awe. When I grew close enough, I nodded at her. "You did it." It was really the only thing to say, the only way to start.

She smiled. "I did." And then she did the strangest thing for Alicia. She asked about someone else. "Is that Caro? Is she okay?"

"Uh ..." She had thrown me for a loop. How safe were we here? "She's a little ill, and I wanted her to be where I could see her."

Alicia nodded. It felt like she understood the subtleties of the moment, the way I couldn't say what was really going on. Her mouth silently formed Joseph's name.

I nodded as slightly as I could and made sure she saw the gesture. I suddenly wanted to tell her everything, to pour out my worries for Joseph and Caro, for all of us, and also how proud I was of them. I wanted to talk with her about the Doctrine. But whatever strange spell seeing her again had dropped over me lifted when Captain Grundson walked into the room and said, "The two fleet admirals will join us in about twenty minutes. I've ordered food for all to be served in our largest conference room. I will broker these negotiations."

Alicia's expression hardened into determination. She scanned the room like a professional politician. She glanced down at me, gestured me close, and whispered, "Did you find the spy?"

"Mohami's assistant was sending messages to the Islans."

She looked relieved.

Sound and movement drew my attention to crewmembers who bolted sandy blue chairs down with quick, precise flicks of their hands. The floor design allowed almost any configuration. Other than a single podium, the chairs made everyone equal.

Carafes of col and trays of small sandwiches and carrots covered tables by the wall. The captain and crew had done an expert job on short notice. I remembered that she worked for us, for Joseph, and looked up at Alicia. "Can I leave Caro with you for a moment?"

She glanced down at me, eyes wide with surprise. "Sure."

As I passed Kayleen, she took my hand. "Alicia looks amazing."

"I know. Go talk to her. I left Caro there."

Kayleen nodded. "Good luck."

As I crossed the room some inner clock pushed me to move quickly. The two captains stood side by side in a corner, whispering together. Both were thin and striking, Captain Hill dark with her long and multicolored coat and Captain Grundson more compact and more stylish, but not more beautiful. They broke off their conversation as I came up.

I held my hand out to Captain Grundson. "Hello, I'm Chelo Lee, Joseph's sister. You've done a fabulous job here. Thank you."

Her smile was professional. "Pleased to meet you."

I straightened and focused on sounding confident. "These negotiations are not between two sides. My brother is not buying a win for Silver's Home, but a win for all."

Captain Grundson's eyes widened, and Captain Hill looked like she was hiding a smile that made me wonder what the two women had been talking about before I got here.

I continued. "I will speak for Joseph and for many others spread throughout this fleet and the planets it represents." That sounded pretentious. I went with it, holding my head up. "Alicia and Tsawo will speak for the fliers." There hadn't been time to ask Alicia, and maybe she hadn't changed enough to make this a good idea, but surely they came all this way to say something.

Ming separated from a conversation with Jenna and floated over to my side, giving me her *you should think harder about security* look. I nodded to thank her for coming, and again held my hand out to Captain Grundson.

She took it, looking like she wanted to resist, then she blew out a sharp breath and said, "Very well."

I began to tell them how to arrange the seating. This was my chance to advocate for peace, and for a different way. I was going to take it.

73
JOSEPH

The fleet took more space than three planets complete with moons and orbiting spaceports. I felt the size, the massiveness. Different protocols no longer slowed me. I could move from ship to ship in the deeper languages meant to be understood by metal and silicon and other parts.

I exerted myself only a little, told them where to go, kept them separate from one another but inside of the huge battlefield. Most listened easily. Three did not. Small parts of me negotiated, nudging them into doing what I needed them to do. The AIs all had code designed to keep them from destroying humans, and all I wanted was for all of the humans in each ship to stay safe. Nudging was possible.

Wind Readers fluttered around the edges of my consciousness. I didn't allow them in. A few tried to group up, at best able to perform a tiny version of what Caro and I could do together. For now, I let them be, focusing on my ability to work with the AIs to direct the movement of the ships.

Ever so slowly.

I began to negotiate the ships into locations too far away from each other for any one to fire on any other.

A voice called me. *Joseph?*

Who? I should know. I did know but couldn't quite grasp it.

Joseph!

That was me. I said it. *I am Joseph.*

They are going to talk soon. I can hear. What do you need?

I kept focusing on what I knew. I was Joseph. I was keeping the fleet ships one from another. I was keeping the other Wind Readers one from another. I was Joseph.

Uncle Joseph!

What?

74

CHELO

I stood where I planned to sit for negotiations after I managed to get the room arranged the way I wanted it. Had I made good decisions?

Even the two captains seemed content to let me lead. But then, why not? My brother had caused this meeting, and he held us all hostage to his will.

They must believe I knew what he planned.

If only. There was no time to think too hard about him or Caro. I had to trust. This was a thing Mohami had been teaching me. Trust the universe, trust yourself, trust the hearts of humans.

So hard!

I placed Alicia to my left with Tsawo next to her and then Jagruti and the strange and lithe little man, Romi, next to her. On my right, I kept Mohami closest to me, then Jenna, then Captain Hill. The eight of us occupied half of the circle, and the other half was left open. That would leave the two warring admirals close to each other. That might be interesting.

This whole exercise was about trust, but I didn't trust Alicia enough to leave her across the room from me.

Silver's Home's Fleet Admiral Mott came in first. I had studied him for months, but never met him. He was a career Port Authority pilot promoted to admiral during the run-up to the war. He had distinguished himself stopping pirates trying to steal Silver's Home's intellectual property. The Port Authority was the closest thing Silver's Home had to a planetary government, and he was two heartbeats away from the top position.

A powerful man, indeed.

Admiral Mott stopped just inside the door. Pictures had identified him as tall and broad, but he bulked larger in person than he had on the screen. Standing in the doorway, very little light from the corridor slipped around him. Dark brown hair curled just above his shoulders, and his eyes were nearly as dark as Alicia's wings. He wore a complex captain's coat or, I supposed, admiral's coat shot through with silver and gold data threads and decorated with multiple insignia I couldn't read. He was clearly part strong and surely also a competent Wind Reader since he had been a pilot and a captain. Undoubtedly more. He would have my innate ability to lead and far more experience using it, enhanced vision and hearing, and maybe more mods. He assessed the room, and then headed toward the seat I stood behind.

Good. He'd done his homework. He stopped in front of me, the table separating us. The look in his eyes made me wish the table was wider. I felt fury inside of him, perfectly controlled and kept like a pet in his chest so he could pull it out and wipe me from existence if he chose.

Ming, behind me, stepped closer. The edge of her coat brushed my shoulder.

His retinue ranged around the floor behind him. Two women in uniform, three men and a woman who wore stunners on their belts and clothing that could conceal other weapons. Lukas, dressed in black and standing behind the rest.

Admiral Mott didn't hold out his hand, but stood, waiting.

I contemplated, then dropped my head into a very slight acknowledgement of his power and held out my hand, speaking deliberately and loud enough for those around to hear. "I am Chelo Lee. I am sister to Joseph Lee, who has stopped this battle."

Irritation flashed in the admiral's eyes.

Lukas stepped forward. "Your brother swore the oaths of a Master, which included obeying the will of the admiral."

Really? I wanted to ask if the admiral was hoping that the Islan ships would start shooting at his ships again. But surely this was merely a test to see how we would react. I ignored Lukas for the moment and spoke to Admiral Mott. "In order to manage the negotiations in here fairly, I am requesting that there be four people per delegation. The remainder of your team will have a private room assigned, and should we recess, we will each be able to meet with our full teams during that time."

He cocked his head slightly to the right, as if contemplating. I wondered if he was going to follow up on Lukas's suggestion, but apparently he had decided to follow my lead and ignore him. "Then there will be eight of us in formal talks."

Surely admirals could count chairs. I kept my cool. "Sixteen. You will have four, Islas will have four, the fliers will have four, and the Doctrine of New Making will have four."

He blinked, once. Otherwise he was still.

The lack of puzzlement told me he had heard of the Doctrine. Had his security forces brought him information, or had we infected the Authority ships?

Was Joseph spreading it further?

Everyone with the admiral also waited, even Lukas. Lukas leaked anger, visible in his stance and the set of his jaw. He might be beautiful if he weren't angry, but it made him look petty. Lukas's anger felt sharper and less dangerous than the deeper anger I sensed in the leashed admiral.

To my surprise, when Admiral Mott spoke, he did not reject the Doctrine. He kept his eyes on me, and thus not on Alicia who was next to me, as he said, "Fliers belong to Silver's Home. We will represent their interests."

Beside me, Alicia took in a quick breath, but managed to bite her tongue. Surprising. Either she trusted me or wings gave her patience.

"This war is as much about the fliers as it is about anything else." I leaned slightly toward Alicia, and by extension, toward Tsawo. "Allow me to introduce my sister, Alicia, and the leader of the Protectors of

Lopali, Tsawo." I made that title up for him on the spot, but hopefully it was close enough.

Admiral Mott slowly turned his head, reviewing the room and its set up. He stopped and settled his gaze on Captain Grundson for long seconds, and she offered him the slightest shrug. It seemed to say, *I understand and there's not a thing I can do about it.*

A predatory smile touched his face, then disappeared. He extended a hand. "Pleased to meet you, Chelo Lee. Perhaps this will be an enjoyable day." His handshake was business-like and strong. From me, he turned to Alicia, moving around the room to introduce himself.

When Lukas crossed in front of my table on his way to follow his admiral, he and Ming exchanged a look that might have been the wariness of two people who considered themselves predators. It might have been something else entirely, something only the two of them understood. It made me shiver.

I forced myself to let it go. Ming had abandoned a post in security for the Port Authority when she'd left Silver's Home to follow us to Lopali. She and Lukas had history. My brother had forced the admirals here, I supposed with a command, and that must worry or maybe even frighten Lukas. Still, Admiral Mott looked like he expected to win.

In spite of my convictions and my brother's strength, the admiral could win.

I turned toward Caro to find one eye open, the pupil fluttering as if some bright light blinked directly in it.

Kayleen knelt beside her so that she could look directly into that one eye that saw nothing here. A tear fell down her cheek.

Would we all be destroyed before this was over? The powers arranged against us seemed so much larger after just one admiral had entered the room.

I turned to wait for the other.

The Islan admiral, Gregory Kipple, didn't stop in the door. He arrowed toward Admiral Mott, ignoring everyone else in the room. He was only about three-quarters of the larger man's size, but his voice boomed through the whole room. "What is the meaning of this? We agreed on how this fight would proceed, and how we would choose the winner, and you have broken your agreements!"

The room quieted completely.

Admiral Mott answered calmly, but loud enough for me to hear him easily. "I helped you determine those rules of engagement. I know what they are. I did not break them." He nodded toward me. "Ask her."

The two men were most of the way across the room from me, and I couldn't cross directly because of the layout of the tables.

These two would love to return to fighting. I didn't for a minute think that either would surrender to the other. Rather, they would delight in destroying us and returning to the script they had been following. "Admiral Kipple," I called out.

He turned toward me. "Yes."

"I'm Chelo Lee. My brother is Joseph Lee. We are not fans of war."

Admiral Kipple offered the simplest response possible. "Then why are you here?"

A reasonable question that drew a smile from me. I turned toward Alicia and Tsawo. "This is my sister, Alicia, and Tsawo, both Fliers of Lopali." In that moment, I didn't even remember the title I had given Tsawo moments before. This was no time to stutter. "They are creations of Silver's Home who are legally owned. It is time for that to stop."

Admiral Kipple raised an eyebrow. "We agree."

Was this the moment to launch into the Doctrine? "As I understand, you would like to stop the making of fliers."

"That is one of our demands." He shifted his balance. "There are more." He glanced at Admiral Mott. "We know what we are fighting for. And why. And even how. But I don't know what you want."

Well, that was a challenge if I had ever heard one. "We are each working with a team of four and meeting to discuss that. Do you have your four?"

The two admirals shared a look that made my nerves flutter. I could see the moment they rejected my plans in subtle changes of the way they stood. Admiral Mott said, "We demand that you return autonomous control to each of the fleet members. You are in violation of every rule set up for this combat, and risking death or—if you are lucky—being locked up for the rest of your lives."

He was trying to exert the power of his position, and I felt it weighing on me.

Captains Hill and Grundson watched me.

75
JOSEPH

I am Joseph. I am Joseph.

You ARE Joseph. I am Caro. You need to help.

Help with what? I am Joseph. Two ships moved inside of me, headed away from each other. One began to near a third ship, and I made it move away. And on. And on. The fleet was effectively suspended as long as I could hold them inside the space of my being.

Or something.

It was so hard to understand what had happened between me and the universe of the battle's data. I and the battle were a union of different sets, a sideways mashup of things that could not be one but were, as if a living being, no – a type of being – that had not existed before had been born in the vast space occupied by the fleets.

Everyone is in one place. Alicia and Chelo and me. The admirals that you sent. What do you want people to do?

I moved ships around, talked with AIs, learned. There was so much complexity, so much creativity in this one tiny fleet. So many points of view, and feelings. Anger. Apprehension. Even peace. If only Marcus were here to share this with!

Uncle Joseph!

I am Joseph!

Uncle Joseph! Help.

See? There is the world of becoming, the knowledge of all that we all are.

I was supposed to keep her safe. I knew that. Keep her out, or at least only let her help me some. Did I still need her help?

It was so hard to isolate a single thread of thought. *Caro. You are Caro and I am Joseph. We need to tell all of the ships about what Mohami taught to Chelo.*

And what he taught to you, she shot back.

You studied with him a long time. Chelo had taken her every morning for the whole long journey here. I remembered that, although not any one morning.

It felt like Caro giggled. *I can help.*

Could I let her help?

I can help.

She was stating a fact. Not requesting. She was a child. But who other than a child might understand the power of Reading the Wind? She had never been afraid of it like I had. Marcus had been there for her. I had been there for her. Wind Readers on Lopali had been there for her. Mohami had been there. She had grown up believing in the melding of man and the data of machines.

Still. Could I let her help?

76

ALICIA

The two admirals clearly detested each other, but they hated the situation they were in more. Joseph had forced everyone together, but he hadn't shown any sign of participation now that we were here.

Chelo was drunk with hope. There clearly wasn't going to be a sweet little meeting where people negotiated in fours as if they were playing table games.

I flapped my wings, drawing attention. The rippling of muscles along my back and shoulders reminded me of what I had been through. From my perch, I could look down on all of them. I spoke in the voice I had been taught to use with seekers and pilgrims. "You are unable to control your own fleets right now. Either of you." I looked from man to man. Neither responded, but at least they'd both stopped talking. I raised my voice, wanting everyone in the room to hear. "You have been shooting at each other for days and nothing has changed. But it's time for change." I let a quick beat pass, continued. "This war is, at its heart, about us and others like us. We will speak. We will no longer be owned." I glanced at Chelo, who was watching me, her face a mask of rigid control. "We are only one created being. There are others. Some are even on this ship."

I let that sink in.

No one said anything.

A thin smile danced across Jagruti's mouth.

"You will not meet with each other to wrestle in this room. There's no point. You need to wrestle with your governments and come back with a plan that allows for the making of beings, of art, of all things that we humans have the ability to create." I liked that. We humans. I was never going to sell myself as anything less, or refer to myself as anything less, or allow anyone else to refer to me as anything less. Never. "I would not trade my wings for breath." I paused. Good line. I smiled, feeling momentum taking me. "But I *should not have to* trade them for my freedom, and I will not do so. It is time for fliers to be free. For all of the modified sentients to be free."

I turned from Admiral Mott, the target of most of that messaging, and fixed my attention on Admiral Kipple. I knew some of what drove Islas from the pilgrims I'd answered questions for. Hopefully it would be enough. "Silver's Home will not be told what to do. I'm sure you are not willing to accept their way of life on your planet. But you are about to lose your people's loyalty. They see what Silver's Home is capable of, and they want some of that freedom. *But you are right.* It can be destructive. Talk to your advisors and government and tell us how you will hold onto your values *and* allow for ingenuity and creation."

The Islan Admiral looked offended. Maybe by my very existence. Maybe by my words. He said, "I don't need to consult with anyone. I have my orders. They do not include taking orders from you."

Captain Grundson watched the two admirals closely.

Chelo stood straighter, watching me. We shared a glance, and I felt certain we understood each other. She cleared her throat, drawing some of the attention back to her. I closed my wings and let myself settle.

Chelo announced, "We will all take a one-hour break. I suggest you follow Alicia's instructions, although you can choose to spend your time however you like. We will meet back in here."

Captain Grundson spoke. "I am honored by your presence. Please enjoy our hospitality and take food back to your assigned rooms. I have crew waiting in the corridor to escort you."

Captain Hill must have been watching the data. Neither Chelo nor I were Wind Readers, but the captains were. She said, "As soon as you get to your rooms, I suggest you check on the location of your fleets."

The admirals left, and as soon as the room was clear of both of them with their outsized egos and over-fancy captain's coats, Chelo stood on tiptoe and quietly said, "Thank you."

"I wonder if we should have sent them away for two hours, or two days, or maybe forever."

She gave her head a soft shake. "Joseph appears to be holding the entire fleet in his mind, and Caro is helping him. She ate today and moved around some. But he hasn't come out of what amounts to a coma for two days now. He can't do this forever."

Kayleen looked over at me. "Caro did something really weird a few minutes ago. Her eyes rolled up and down in her head, really, really fast. One of them. She twitched. I'm afraid."

Chelo frowned. "How is she now?"

Kayleen leaned down to check. There were dark circles under her eyes, and her hair needed washing. A comb wouldn't hurt her either. "She looks good."

"Is Liam okay?" I asked them both.

Kayleen answered. "He's back in our room. With Joseph. What about Induan?"

Loss made the words hard to utter. "She was killed."

Chelo's eyes widened. "Like Bryan?"

Ming turned toward me, as if the name drew her. She and Bryan had probably been lovers. She was with him when he died.

I shook my head. "Not like Bryan. We can fill each other in later. Now, we need to decide how to get through the rest of the day, and what we want to happen."

Chelo looked uncertain. "I stated we're speaking for two different people. Should we all meet together?"

So she could still be obtuse. "Chelo—they're talking to each other. Besides, this is war. Even if that's what you're trying to stop, stopping a war might take acting like we're in one. Don't worry about breaking rules you made."

She winced but held her tongue.

Good.

Chelo glanced at Captain Grundson, who had drifted over near us. "Can we send a message to all of the ships?"

No hesitation. "Of course. Are you ready now?"

"It will come from Mohami." She turned to him. "Can you sort through what we need to say? The same simpler parts of the Doctrine we've sent out before. Fifteen minutes?"

I added, "Jagruti can help."

Mohami nodded and the two Keepers walked off to a nearby table together, talking animatedly and calling data displays up out of the air around them.

Captain Grundson left too, speaking orders to her staff as she went. She stopped beside Captain Hill, and the two of them bent their heads together.

I spoke to Chelo. "We had better agree on an outcome."

She looked distracted. "I have to check on Joseph. Mohami knows what we are trying to do."

"Keepers can't speak for us. They work for the people who keep us as pets."

Her eyes narrowed. "Mohami left because he couldn't stand what the Keepers were doing to you."

"And Jagruti for the same reason. But I cannot allow them to speak for us."

"You still don't trust anyone else, do you?"

"That's not it! We have to speak for ourselves." It came to me how to calm her, and that it was the truth. "I trust you."

She smiled at that, looking a little surprised.

I couldn't go closet myself with the Keepers. Someone had to think about the admirals, and I couldn't leave all of that to Chelo. I also needed a favor from Romi. I glanced at Tsawo, who stood ready but had not spoken a word to anyone other than greetings since he'd entered the room. "Can you work on the message? And be sure it is something we can communicate throughout this room as well?"

Tsawo nodded.

Chelo said, “I need to check on Joseph.”

Of course she did. “I’ll work on strategy with the Captains.” I still didn’t understand the power structure here, or how Chelo had so much power, or what exactly Joseph was doing. It felt like operating in a dimly lit room full of monsters. “Do you need to ask them to work with me?”

“Good question.” She glanced at me on my perch, pursed her lips, and crossed the room to the captains.

I gestured to Romi and asked him a question. When he nodded, I sent him off.

Chelo came back with the captains and told the three of us, “I need all of you. Strategy.” Clearly, she had been talking to them on the way here. “Half an hour. I’ll come back and hear what you think, what has been sent out to the ships, and prepare.” She glanced at Mohami and Jagruti. “I don’t have to approve what they say. I trust them.” Her glance toward me underlined the word *trust*.

There wasn’t time to argue the point. Eleven minutes had already passed. I should have kept the admirals away for at least two hours. “Okay.”

Chelo hurried away, Ming and two guards by her side.

77
JOSEPH

The Islan and Authority ships tried to override my controls together, fighting the commands I gave them. Not one at a time, or even two or three, or just one fleet at a time: all of them, except a few that were in my Third Fleet list. They swelled and stretched, straining against my control.

I pushed back. Holding. It felt like straining every muscle against a weight machine at once, like I held my breath and gave all of me to the fight. As I struggled, I started to feel overtaken by the nature of all things, which desired to be separate in spite of their oneness. Strange thoughts, thoughts I couldn't have found words for if I needed to, thoughts that were feelings that were heart. Truths of being.

I dove into the detail of the data, looking for the cause.

Each admiral had issued orders to all their ships to continue fighting. Most tried to obey. Those who didn't were added to my Third Fleet list and a few others dropped. The lists had lives of their own now, the algorithms managing them in the back of my head nearly autonomic.

I counted. Twenty-three Third Fleet ships. Not enough. I needed to make more. In the meantime, I sent each of the twenty-three a thank you and asked them to stand prepared as I would need them soon.

My focus snapped to the ships fighting me. There were so many.

A voice, again. *I can help!*

Four of the Islan ships slipped out of my control and moved toward the *Unicorn* and the *Thorn*.

I can help.

I needed help. The owner of the voice was like me but not me. Almost the same in this strange state of being. Still, I worried. *Be careful. See what I see?*

Yes. Her awe made me feel my own more acutely.

Two more ships slipped free. They also headed toward the *Unicorn*. I couldn't simultaneously chase them and braid Caro more fully into the weave that held the fleet. I knew her now. Caro. My brilliant niece. The baby. But I had seen her soul and knew to include her.

I had to lose some of the totality to come back and show her the blocks from which the grand wholeness was built.

It would weaken me for a moment.

It was impossible to know whether we would be fast enough to save the *Unicorn*. *See?* I told her. *Look here. Feel along* this *thread to* that *ship?*

I do.

And this one? Here is how an Islan ship feels.

78

CHELO

Jenna walked beside me. Ming and two guards trailed five steps behind us. Everyone else stayed behind in the main room, even Caro. Time pressed, and Kayleen could watch over her.

Jenna walked beside me. "What do you think?" I asked her.

She shrugged, but her eyes looked wary. "I think they want to wipe you out of existence. They know where you are, and they are far better armed."

From right behind me, Ming added, "I agree."

I swallowed. "All true. But the Fleet Admirals are here, too."

Jenna said, "That must be to keep the fleets from destroying this ship."

"Oh."

Jenna continued, "He has twice …" She hesitated. "More, some exponential more, power than Marcus had. But he has a fraction of Marcus's subtlety or sense of strategy. We'd be in a better position if we weren't all together in one place."

I couldn't blame her. I didn't feel safe, but I trusted my little brother. He was strong, and I loved him, and I had always trusted him. Still, the admirals frightened me.

"You are doing better than I'd expected," Jenna continued. She offered a tense smile. "I remain dubious about the idea that love and light and interbeing are going to save the worlds from this war."

Ming's footsteps brought her closer. "It'll take more than an idea to save the world."

She truly had gotten more martial since Joseph had made her head of security. She used to be a dancer. But she had also been one of Marcus's lovers. "Don't you believe we're right?" I asked her.

She hesitated, and her voice cracked as she said, "I used to be certain. I know the Islans can't be allowed to win. Can we stop that?"

"We're trying."

"Winning is always possible." Jenna sounded like she was rebuking Ming.

She had protected us since we were children on Fremont. She knew us like we knew ourselves, sometimes even better. I asked Jenna, "What do you think of the new Alicia?"

She was so silent for so long I thought she hadn't heard me. Then she said the same thing I was thinking. "She is herself, and better at choosing risks. And at least now she seems to be picking the right enemies. Otherwise, I don't know."

"Ming?" I asked.

She must have been listening. She took a few steps closer, walking just behind my left shoulder. "She read the generals right. Don't let them have their heads."

I had come to the same conclusion but hadn't expected Ming to point out my mistake so clearly. Still, you wanted the people who worked for you to tell you about mistakes. Marcus had taught me that, and Mohami. So I said, "You're right. She did seem to handle them better than I did. They scare me. I'll do better next time."

"None of us have dealt with them before, or even met them." Jenna wasn't apologizing for my weakness, and her tone was musing. "We have them caged, or rather Joseph does, and caged men can be dangerous. The fact that we share the cage may work for us, but be very careful."

We turned the corner, and I opened the door that led to my brother's still form. Liam stood over Joseph with a small kitchen funnel in one hand and a glass of vitamin slurry in the other. He was dribbling the slurry so that it landed in the corner of Joseph's mouth through the funnel, just a few drops at a time. I waited until I saw Joseph swallow, and then came up near Liam. Joseph stank of vitamins and sweat. "How is he?"

"I've gotten three forms of nutrients down him one drop at a time. But he looks like he's lost ten pounds in two days. He must be burning an incredible amount of energy."

"I can't even imagine. Has he woken up at all?"

"No." Liam looked drawn. "Caro is okay?"

"Better than Joseph. So there's that."

"I hate this."

I turned away from Joseph and drew Liam a few steps to the side, desperate for just a moment of connection and strategy.

He looked back at Joseph but let himself be led. "Did everyone see the light and decide to stop dying for stupid causes?"

"Not so far. But you should see Alicia!" I glanced back toward Joseph. Ming stood beside him, her back to me. "Well, you'll have to wait to see her. Joseph needs you. But she's strong. She was … helpful."

Liam was beside us on Fremont when Alicia threatened to blow up the entire Town Council. He knew how volatile she could be, how dangerous. He raised an eyebrow.

"She assessed a situation better than I did, helped me. She's … politic? Maybe something healed in her. She has a Keeper of the Ways with her, a woman. Mohami knows her. I haven't had time to—"

Sasha barked, high and sharp.

She never barked.

A flash of movement right behind us made us both snap around. Jenna had pushed Ming.

Ming's footing faltered, but she didn't fall. Her nails were out, the small knives glinting in the overhead light.

Jenna's face twisted in a snarl I hadn't seen since we'd left Fremont. She lunged toward Ming, her blow a blur.

In spite of Jenna's speed, Ming danced away, light and fast.

Jenna nearly fell. As she caught her balance, her eyes grazed mine.

Predatory. Warning. She stepped backward, maybe trying to draw Ming to her.

Ming twisted and rushed toward Joseph's bedside.

I moved close enough to see blood running down his cheeks from her nails.

Liam rushed her from the side, slamming into Ming with a grunt. Momentum drove him past her, and almost into Paloma.

Ming stumbled and Jenna tried to drive her down. Ming twisted, kept her balance, and raked Jenna's face.

Blood ran down Jenna's cheek.

I bolted to Joseph's side.

Behind me, Ming grunted as someone hit her, but I couldn't stop to look.

Sasha kept barking, her face as close to the wire grate on the crate as she could get.

I leaned over Joseph. He lay still, four small puncture marks from Ming's hands in his throat. Blood trickled down his neck. I turned his head, checked the other side. Nothing.

She hadn't hit the major arteries. Jenna had saved him.

What could possibly have kept him from waking up through that? I placed a flat palm on his chest to feel for his heartbeat. Before I found it, someone ran into me from the side. The new guard that Ming had brought, trying to tear me away from my brother.

I braced, resisted.

Gretchen screamed and expertly flipped her weapon, targeting the man who held me. She fired and he fell, stunned.

Behind me, Jenna growled like a beast. A boot hit flesh somewhere, followed by an exhaled grunt and a wrenching cough.

Someone screamed. "No!"

Fury focused me; everything seemed louder, faster. I leaped back to Joseph's side and stood facing out, daring anyone else to threaten him, breathing fast. Paloma and Tiala headed toward the downed guard, probably intending to tie him up.

Ming skated backward in response to something Jenna had done and fell, tripping over the stunned body of her guard. She was right in front of me. I slammed my foot down on her belly, felt it sink in.

Ming grabbed my calf, jerking me off my feet and throwing me to the floor.

Jenna threw herself on Ming, pinning her so she couldn't get to any weapon except her hands and those vicious nails.

Claws extended, Ming jabbed at Jenna's scalp and shoulders.

Liam came in from behind and yanked Ming's right hand back, twisting so Ming couldn't move without breaking her wrist. Ming screeched in frustration.

Gretchen held out wrist restraints. "Here!"

Liam clapped them on Ming's right wrist, put his knee into Ming's back, and reached for her other arm. She raked holes in his pants, but he got her chained. Paloma and Tiala were scrambling up from beside the guard.

For a moment, stunned silence reigned, replaced motion and energy. I turned to Joseph and listened. He still breathed. Low and slow and fine.

How could he possibly be okay and not have reacted to being hurt? To the fight?

"Washcloth!" I called, and Tiala raced to the sink while Paloma came and stood beside me.

"Thank you," I told Paloma; my voice shook. "Keep giving him nutrients. Don't stop. Not for one minute. Clean him up as you go."

Paloma nodded, eyes wide.

I turned toward Ming. "Why?" I demanded. "Why?"

79
ALICIA

Tsawo didn't move as the captains approached. Both wore the same expression: a base layer of shock, and on top of that, resolution. Underneath that, they both looked afraid. Not in any way I could pinpoint, and not in a way that anyone five feet away could have possibly seen. Maybe it was something I smelled.

Tsawo cleared his throat to draw attention, then asked Captain Grundson, "Are your people all loyal to you?"

Captain Grundson's lips thinned, but she didn't hesitate. "Most of them."

"The *Maker's Thorn* was mostly loyal." Captain Hill grimaced. "Not all. I had to lock up your brother's family for their own safety."

That was a story I wanted to hear some time.

Captain Grundson laughed out loud, a slight nervous edge worrying me. "Loyalty for loyalty's sake is not a common trait on Silver's Home except in the Authority. Even there, it's less than perfect."

Marcus had been disloyal to the Authority. I suspected both of these women knew that, but this was a dangerous path to go further down. "Are the admirals your prisoners?" I asked both captains.

Two sets of eyes grew perceptibly wider, although neither of them reacted as much as I'd hoped. Captain Hill spoke slowly and calmly, "We pledged loyalty to Admiral Mott when this war started."

Captain Grundson added, "He can say a word and remove us." She glanced at the door the admirals had left through. "If he issues orders, I might obey them. You need to know that. Everyone is dancing to Joseph's melody, but you can be sure no one likes it."

And neither did she. Captain Hill, however, winced. She saw me notice and controlled her features.

Tsawo lowered his voice. "What do you know about Joseph's plan?"

Captain Hill stretched, looked thoughtful, and then said, "I believe he is hoping that we will all talk—every side. And that every side will listen."

A political answer. Not very helpful. I took a deep breath and once again spread my wings. "We won't accept anything that leaves us bound."

Tsawo followed my lead, his wings wide and ever-so-slightly protective. "We assert our rights."

Captain Hill whispered, almost too low to hear. "Some people are looking for a middle way where no one loses, even if no one exactly wins."

I could imagine Chelo championing such a horrid idea. I glanced toward the door, hoping she would walk through it. I needed ten minutes of conversation with her. We had lost Marti to come out here and talk. We were going to get something in trade for it.

Bright light illuminated Captain Hill's high, thin cheekbones and dark skin, making her as beautiful as Induan had been, if dark rather than fair. I watched as she glanced toward Mohami and Jagruti, side by side a few tables over, heads bent close. She knew more than she was saying, and I wondered, briefly, if she worried about the message they were crafting.

"The middle way is not necessarily acceptable," I told her. "Is there anything else that I need to know to represent Lopali?"

Captain Hill looked thoughtful. The smaller woman, who had been less exposed to Joseph and his incredible skills, said, "Our laws don't give you a voice. Accept the miracle that you are here, and with luck everyone will get to talk."

I swallowed an arrow of anger. I took a deep breath, glanced toward Jagruti., took another breath and looked back at the two captains. "We won't be deterred by your unwillingness to see us as people."

Captain Grundson's face hardened, and I thought of the doctor earlier. Prejudice ran deep here if a woman who worked for Marcus shared any of it. I hadn't loved Marcus, but he had known fliers were human.

Captain Hill said, "If you'll excuse us?"

She didn't need to be polite, or to ask. "Of course. Thank you."

I hoped she was about to take Captain Grundson to task.

They left and I turned to Tsawo. He had chosen to pull the Protector mask over his face, and I suddenly realized that was how he protected *himself*. What a strange time to learn such a critical, simple thing. "What do you think?" I asked him.

"I don't like any of this." He glanced toward the door. "We don't have much time."

Caro cried out, a high shrieking wail. Kayleen leaned over her, her dark curls falling like a curtain in front of the child's face.

Caro took in a sobbing breath and screamed, "Uncle Joseph!"

80
JOSEPH

Caro learned quickly. I barely noticed my body. That was another theory about the Wind Burned who never came back, that they lost the last tie to their bodies in order to move at the speed of light.

So many ways to die or lose yourself in data when you stretched too far.

There were no stories that suggested anyone had stretched as far as we were going. I couldn't let Caro devolve. I showed her, block by block, ship by ship, thread by thread, how to see what I could now see easily, slid her into the communication streams with ships in all three groups. She picked them up one by one, handling the ever-growing knot of data streams with flexibility.

We were far stronger together than I could have been alone.

Still, time slipped past and I had to wait for her to have some grasp on the whole before I took back the four ships that had broken away. If the Islans were learning how to fight us, I couldn't let them regain control of a critical mass of ships to fight us with, or to demonstrate that it was possible to escape the net we had built.

A few ships tried to force their AIs to refuse our orders, or to fly on their own with no AI. Each failed, but making them fail took energy and focus. Those four original Islan ships stayed free of us, and each time I tried to get close to them I slid off like water touching an oiled surface.

I described the movements to Caro as the raveling and the unravelling. Only four Islan ships remained in the unravelling, unavailable to me.

The ships I identified as Third Fleet did not fight us. For them, for the ones who wanted peace like we did, I streamed loops of appreciation and requests to wait, to trust. There were more of them now, mostly from Silver's Home but two from Islas.

I sent something Mohami had said to me to every ship in the Third Fleet list: *Trust is the foundation for vulnerability. Vulnerability is the opening through which we can know one another. Knowing each other is the door to peace. Trust me, and I will lead you to peace.*

How many people would die if I failed?

This list of Third Fleet ships was not public, but I would use it soon. I would need a physical demonstration.

Caro. Stay and keep track of the other ships. I will help you. I have to see about the four that are resisting us.

Okay.

The four Islan ships bound for the *Unicorn* and the *Thorn* were over halfway there.

They had not started from the same place, but they were close together now.

I needed more focus.

I struggled to draw pieces of myself back and yet keep the remaining part of the fleet in control. It felt like pulling myself through myself, like breathing in and out at once.

It took too long, too long, but I formed a coherent and driven part of me that felt strong. With that self, I slid from ship to ship in the myriad data streams that watched for meteors and torpedoes alike, that photographed and monitored large bubbles of space around each fighting ship. Reading the Wind depended on being in the way of the wind of data. Sometimes I had to double back along paths and choose new ones.

I felt time passing, felt the danger to my body, to Caro, to this whole effort.

Each second was my mortal enemy.

I neared the four ships.

It felt like a wall surrounded them. They were impenetrable the way the *Unicorn* had been before Caro and I had learned to work together; walls of blackness with no entry point.

I began to probe.

One wall enveloped all four ships. A shield.

I should have come before they were so near each other.

I tried to get through.

Nothing.

I withdrew, puzzled, and checked more closely on the state of our little war. The web of ships was fine, which meant Caro was fine. I didn't have the energy to go back to the *Peacemaker*.

Funny. I had always thought I'd fight from the deck of the *Peacemaker*. In my dreams it had been me piloting the ship and using physical weapons. Instead, I slept deeply inside of the ship's hold, my body guarded by people I loved.

But then, when had my best weapons ever been physical? I wasn't even much of a fighter.

The distractions of that thought plucked at me, the remembrance of dreams, a sign that I was becoming tired.

I needed to be *now*.

I refocused. There was a good chance my enemies thought my body was on board the *Thorn*. I refocused and found a path to the *Unicorn*. Once there, I left a message for Master Skulla. *Four Islan ships heading toward you. I am trying to stop them. Be prepared for physical assault. Warn the Maker's Thorn and anyone else close.*

I watched the four ships. Why couldn't I reach them? Data flowed to them, but I couldn't get through. Could whatever tool they were using spread through more of the fleet?

I leapt toward the ship, pointing more of my energy at it, more focus.

A great wall of energy rushed out and met me. The combined minds of a hundred Islan Wind Readers working together. They had been bending the streams of data to create a space I could not enter.

Together, they could not do anything like what I could do, but they had been able to build an effective wall.

I could let them go, allow the attack. But that would show I had a weakness, and endanger the *Unicorn* and the *Thorn.* I couldn't abandon them.

The longer I waited, the harder this would be, and the stronger they would become.

A hundred Wind Readers. Maybe more. They must have gathered them using small ships or already planned them as a weapon. A dirty trick, in case they were losing. Before me, they'd stayed inside the lines of the agreed-upon rules of the battle. Conjecture. It seemed likely. If so, they would be attuned to working together, and formidable. I had seen the power of combined teams when Wind Readers saved Kayleen in the cave on Lopali.

A capable enemy.

I gathered what strength I had, thin and tired as I was, and arrowed hard and fast toward the ships.

An opening appeared, a river of data. As fast as I recognized it for the baited trap it was, I had slid down the river. The weight of a hundred Wind Readers pecked at the edges of my consciousness.

At the same time, pain—physical, sharp—slammed across the distance between me and my body, demanding my return.

81

ALICIA

Every head turned toward Caro. Kayleen lifted her, cradling her close. Kayleen's right hand stroked her daughter's hair, and even at this distance I could see her shoulders shaking.

Mohami and Jagruti turned toward Caro, eyes wide and startled.

"Kayleen!" I called. "Bring her here."

She obeyed me, carrying Caro. The girl's limbs were stiff, and she murmured something into Kayleen's neck. She turned her head toward me as they neared, and her mouth opened when she saw me. "Alicia?"

"Caro, is Joseph okay?"

"No."

"Is he alive?"

She hesitated, and I held my breath, fear and worry beating inside of me. Then she said. "Yes. I have to go back. I didn't mean to come here."

With that, she fell against her mother's breast, unmoving except for the slight rise and fall of her breath.

Kayleen's eyes widened in a startled stare, and then she sank to the ground and curled protectively around Caro.

I glanced at the clock. Fifteen minutes left.

"Take her back and stay beside her." Poor little thing. Children could endure much. I had.

Mohami stepped over and held his arms out to Kayleen, taking Caro. He carried her carefully back to her nest of blankets. Kayleen trailed behind, holding Caro's hand the whole way.

"Protect her," I told them. "See if you can get her to drink something."

Kayleen snapped, "I know how to take of my daughter."

I laughed at that, a short laugh, part release of tension and part happiness that Kayleen had demonstrated spine.

In the meantime, the room buzzed with talk and most eyes followed Kayleen and Caro. If I hadn't seen her assist Joseph on Lopali, I would have bought Chelo's simple story that she was ill and Chelo wanted to watch over her. But the whole room had heard her scream Joseph's name. I lifted my wings and spread them, flapping once, sending a breeze through the room.

Beside me, Tsawo did the same.

That shifted attention from Kayleen and Caro to us.

"The child is asleep again. A bad dream. Illness can cause that."

A few heads nodded. Some faces still looked skeptical. Mohami put a hand on Jagruti's shoulder and whispered something in her ear.

I kept talking. "We have much to do. Chelo will be back in a moment, and then the admirals, and we will persevere." Not that I had a clear idea how.

No one asked.

82

JOSEPH

The energy of a hundred brilliant and driven humans tore at me. Bits of my energy and self-awareness popped away one by one, fast, like sand in a beach storm.

Data that I reached for had been poisoned, filled with lies, layers on layers of lies. Pieces of me that clung to better data—I don't know how else to describe this, that's not correct, but it's close—pieces of me were isolated and then destroyed.

I couldn't take a deep breath; I couldn't connect back to my body as a way to calm myself.

Something had happened to my body. I didn't know what, couldn't take time to try and tell.

I didn't dare reach out to Caro.

Surely, she knew.

It was all I could do to maintain an opening back away from these ships, a slender line to the *Unicorn*.

I reached for my name, found I still had it. *I am Joseph Lee. I am Joseph Lee.*

I tried to build defenses, but each time I made a shred of progress someone noticed and called for help, and the weight of multiple minds cut me off.

I am Joseph Lee.

Messages came back to me, swarms of lies. *You are weak. You are traitor. You are death. You are evil. You are broken. You are dying. You are enemy!*

I didn't want to hurt any of them, but there were too many. So far I had kept my promise to myself: I hadn't killed any ships, any people, anything at all. I had used my power for peace.

That had been the way to save Caro. Maybe to save myself.

You are evil. You are broken. You have failed. There were so many Wind Readers thinning me.

Joseph Lee. Joseph Lee. Joseph …

I could let myself go. It wouldn't hurt. I would just … diminish.

Caro. Caro would try to save me, or they would learn this technique worked, and they would hunt her down. Caro would die if I died.

Caro taken down to the sand of her soul and scattered. Caro and I, together as sand, indistinguishable from one another, part of the greater whole, never to be ourselves again.

One of the wraiths in the machine repeated, *You are evil.*

And I became evil and smothered that one's connection back to his body, forcing him out into the void, feeling disassociation steal his center. He screamed into the data, fought me, poured a desire to live all over me.

We struggled, he and I. Desperate, he called for help.

The wind of my life scattered him with a single burst of strength.

Maybe others would go and save him?

They chose not to.

I took another, and another. Each loss drove regret like a knife into my heart, and yet each made me stronger, more myself. I fought my way to the ships' AIs and began to command them. *Go! Go!*

83

CHELO

Ming lay on the ground where Liam had cuffed her, her mouth a thin line beneath oddly sorrowful eyes. "Why?" I asked again.

She shook her head. A drop of blood rested on her cheek, probably Jenna's. "Hope doesn't beat power."

"That's not an answer," I snapped.

"It's the truth." She stared up at me. "I wouldn't have hurt him if I didn't have to. I couldn't let him succeed." She grimaced. "I never thought he could succeed. I thought he was safe."

If I had answered, I would have screamed at her. There was no time to extract more information. "Jenna? Will you contain her someplace?" I glanced at the stunned guard, who would surely begin to move soon. "And him? Put them in separate places."

Jenna's grin looked feral. "My pleasure."

I glanced toward Paloma and Tiala. "Take care of Joseph."

Paloma said, "It's time to go back. Do you have a plan?"

Did I? "The Doctrine should already be being broadcast. Caro told me Joseph has been documenting the members of the third fleet."

Jenna looked up from Ming's side, where she was checking her bonds. "If you expose them, you put them all at risk. Is this the time?"

"I don't know yet. I need to talk to Joseph, but if that attack didn't bring him back here, he can't come back. Not right now." Or maybe ever. Maybe he had gone with Marcus into the void. Maybe he would fail, and I would lose my brother. Ming's words ricocheted in my head. *Hope doesn't beat power.*

My thoughts tangled as I waited for Jenna to finish containing the captives. I had hope. Joseph had power. We needed both. We had built up to this day carefully, but it was moving beyond my control. Everything seemed to be happening at once.

Alicia. Of all the people in the world, who would have expected help from Alicia?

Jenna returned, most of the blood washed from her cheek. I asked, "Do you see a way to get Joseph closer to us, closer to Caro?"

"That puts him at too much risk."

She was right. The admirals could kill him themselves. I let out a long breath, trying to slow my thoughts. I needed to ground him somehow, and maybe give him a line back to his body.

Sasha. She loved him unconditionally, and she had just saved his life. Without her barking, Ming might have killed him before we saw her. "Let his dog out."

Jenna only hesitated for a moment. Then she turned toward the crate.

Another thing had changed. Jenna expected me to lead, and she to follow.

I stepped up on the closest chair, made sure of my balance, and clapped to get attention. It only took a moment for everyone to look toward me—most were already watching. I glanced at the clock, pushed down panic. "The attack is over. We need to get back to the conference room." I glanced around at their faces, and then down at my hands. Blood stained one of them. "Take two minutes to clean up. No one should look like there was a fight. We will not discuss it in there. We will not give whoever ordered this attack a moment of satisfaction. Meet at the door."

I scrubbed my hands and glanced toward Paloma and Tiala to make sure Joseph was fine. I managed to catch the moment Paloma lifted Sasha up into the bed so that she could settle in next to Joseph.

She burrowed under one of his arms, tail wagging. Liam had already drifted to his side as well, Jherrel in his arms. The smile Liam gave me assured me I'd chosen right to let Sasha out.

I went to the door.

Five minutes later, we were back in the big room with only ten minutes until the admirals were due back.

If they came back.

Alicia and Tsawo were still on their perches, and Mohami and Jagruti stood below them, talking. I went to them and leaned over Mohami's shoulder. "Were you able to broadcast?"

He smiled. "Yes." He gestured toward Caro. "See to your child."

I rushed to the makeshift bed and noticed Caro's eyes were open. "Joseph got hurt," she told me.

"I know. Ming hurt him."

Her hair stuck to her scalp with sweat in spite of the normal temperature in the conference room. "No. Maybe." She paused, as if searching for how to tell us something. "Inside the data." She closed her eyes and opened them again, and this time they were clearer. "There was an attack on him, by pilots. He sent me out to tell you. It was hard to come here." Her eyes looked slightly unfocused. She clenched her fists. "I went back, and he won. Over them all. No one is trying to hurt him anymore."

So they had been attacking him on two fronts. Anger stiffened my spine, and then eased as Caro's words registered. He was okay. The Wind Readers had been stopped, and we had stopped Ming.

Caro rolled her eyes up in her head and fell back under the blankets. Was I sacrificing this child of my heart for my brother, both of them for everyone in the Five Worlds?

Or was there some way this could still be okay?

We hadn't even gotten any food in her.

We had five more minutes. The attack on Joseph had flooded my body with adrenaline, and now that had drained away, leaving me shaky. I poured a cooling cup of col from the table and took a small sandwich of ship's bread and protein paste with a fresh tomato in the center. The tomato tasted like candy.

I took my place at the head of our table, and slowly everyone else began to take their assigned places.

I glanced at the clock and then at the door.

The time for the admirals to come back passed.

Five more minutes passed.

It would have to be up to Joseph for now. None of us had the authority to force either admiral into the room.

I paced.

84

JOSEPH

The death of the last of the Wind Readers left me feeling like the charred webwork of struts from a burned-out Roamer wagon. If I had a stomach or could feel the one I had—if I were in that moment, fully human—I would retch.

I had sworn not to kill.

The whispers. They were true. *Evil. Losing.*

Warmth spread through me, a download of dopamine. I took a moment to check back into my body. Not to go all the way back, not to wake, not to eat or to move. But just to verify that the thread between me and my body existed.

It did. Thin and ragged, but unbroken.

Whatever was happening on the ship, Sasha was by my side.

My dog loved me. She did not see me as evil.

Caro!

I felt for her, found her.

These two were worth saving. Chelo. Liam. Paloma. Jenna. Tiala.

I slid back down the data thread to the *Unicorn*, curling into the rich data that created an ecosystem around the outside of the ship.

A Wind Reader came to meet me. Master Skulla, recognizable because of his diction and focus of his energy.

I felt too tired to form words, but managed to tell him, *I always wondered whether or not you were a Wind Reader.*

Marcus undersold you. I should never have questioned you. You are magnificent.

He sounded utterly sincere. *I'm tired. I have to do a thing. I have to threaten the whole Islan Fleet.*

Are you asking me if I agree?

Not really. But I might want to know if you don't.

I see no other path. Threats are not always real.

This will be real.

I mean you may not have to execute your threat. You just demonstrated great strength.

Hope bloomed for a moment. *Is it possible that is enough?*

It's unlikely.

For all my power, I didn't have his experience, or Marcus's. I didn't understand the politics, and that one weakness might doom us. *I'm grateful you came out here to counsel me.*

He spoke simply. *I came to thank you.*

And I am grateful for that, and for your advice.

I wanted to drop into my body and have tea with him and hug him. But then, I felt thin and shaky and I wanted to do anything except what I had to do next. *Wish me luck.*

Luck!

I regretted leaving him behind. But Master Skulla had his own ship and people to care for, and unlike me, his ship wasn't a recently acquired surprise. It was his life. I had known this from the moment I met him.

I slid back through the ships of the fleet, slowly spreading back out to contain the whole in the me that I paid attention to. All was well in the combined fleets. I found Caro. I had not wanted her to see fighting, or death. But surely she had seen what had happened to the Wind Readers who had attacked me.

It couldn't be undone, and it had saved her.

As I contacted ships, I left instructions with the AIs, and in the case of the Third Fleet ships, I left instructions to execute if they wanted to help me win the war. I also left them the choice.

It felt odd to ask those who wanted peace to prepare to fire on other ships. But they had come out here to do that in the first place, even if battle or my sister or some other force had changed their minds. I had sworn not to kill anyone, and I had failed.

Maybe peace always failed.

85

CHELO

I refused to let anyone leave. Caro appeared to be peaceful and continued to breathe. She and Joseph were out there doing something, and I was going to let them keep doing it. After the first half hour, the two captains began to pace around the room and I stood quietly beside Caro.

Alicia sat with her head bent toward Tsawo, talking about who knows what, and periodically fluffing her wings as if all she really wanted was to fly.

Well, I wanted to see her fly. Surely she was beautiful in the air of Lopali. Every flier I'd seen there was breathtaking, and it was possible she was even prettier than Tsawo. But as big as it was, this room was no place to fly. She'd have five wingbeats of length, but not quite two of height.

Kayleen looked exhausted. How much could she have left to give?

I wondered if anyone could sing, or if perhaps there was a band among the crew who we could induce to come in and play for us.

Captain Grundson came up to my side, Captain Hill trailing her. "We have something to show you."

I followed her. Better to see something, anything, than to simply wait for the truly powerful to fail to do my bidding. They led me to a small conference room off the main room, small enough to fill with only the three of us. A window opened up toward the main room, so I could watch people moving around restlessly.

A screen showed the fleet. It didn't look that different. "What?" I squinted at it. "Are some of the ships getting closer?"

"They are." Captain Grundson waved her hand toward the screen and the picture changed. All of the ships became one of two colors. The Islan ships glowed red, the Authority ships a dark blue. The ships from Silver's Home, like the *Peacemaker* and the *Thorn*, were a softer shade of blue. Altogether, there were more red ships. Maybe twenty percent more? Twenty-five? They had started out with a bigger fleet and taken fewer losses. Among the blue, a few more were the lighter shade. "So there are more of them than us. Nobody is shooting at each other."

"Now look."

A third color, a bright green, swept across over half of the light blue ships. It touched three of the darker blue that indicated Authority ships. To my surprise, it touched five red ships. It lay like a slightly smaller image in the same shape, so it was possible to tell the original colors of the ships which had turned green. It was slightly less than a third of the ships.

I whispered, "The Third Fleet."

Captain Grundson said, "What?"

Awe muffled my voice. "The Third Fleet." Joseph was out there, alive. He was winning. He was okay.

Captain Grundson stepped between me and the monitor. "He turned us green!"

I burst out laughing.

She glared at me and I struggled to contain myself. Maybe finding someone to sing was still a good idea.

Captain Hill was moved to neither laughter nor irritation. But I stopped laughing when she said, "Almost all of the ships in green are moving toward the other ships, and their weapons systems appear to be warming up."

Ah. My brother was the only single force that could move the Third Fleet as one body. *Oh Joseph, I hope you know what you're doing.*

I explained Joseph's strategy to Alicia, Tsawo, Mohami, and Jagruti. As if they sensed something important, almost everyone else in the room drifted nearer except for the two captains. They stayed in the smaller room, probably arguing about the wisdom of the Third Fleet. But it wasn't as if they could change anything, any more than the admirals could. I chose not to worry about them.

Just as I finished and before we could start any real discussion on the subject, the outer door opened and Admiral Mott again filled it. I glanced at Alicia and Tsawo. "I guess they saw Joseph's message, too."

Tsawo straightened on his perch, his attention focused on the admiral. I had heard Alicia tease Tsawo about being a protector, and in that moment, he looked like one. Alicia smiled, at the admiral, a charming raptor entranced with her prey.

I crossed the big room to him and held out my hand, pretending that he was exactly on time to a dinner party. "Thank you so much for coming back. Please take your seat."

His face was set in stone. Somehow, in spite of what I was certain he had seen, he hadn't yet given up. "Tell your brother his strength is impressive. Thank him for managing the fleets to allow us this time to take a break." He loomed over me. "And tell him it is time for him to transfer control to me."

Most of the Third Fleet used to be under this man's command. Still, he clearly didn't understand what was happening. Maybe he couldn't imagine the mutiny that a Third Fleet suggested. Maybe he couldn't image a peaceful loss of command, or the end of a fight he had geared up for his whole life.

I stood my ground and thought hard about how to answer him.

From behind me, Alicia spoke. "You lost."

Admiral Mott stood up and looked at her.

She fluffed her black wings and twisted a braid of her hair in her hands for a moment. "You lost. There are ships out there who did not want war any more than we do. Joseph has allowed those ships access to their weapons. No one else has access to weapons. Not even us. And certainly not you."

I could almost see the words he wasn't saying. *But some of those are my ships!*

Once more, I silently thanked Alicia for her directness. I asked the admiral, "Shall we sit down and talk?"

His eyes twitched. His fists made a few half-hearted attempts at clenching, quelled each time. He looked like he wanted to pick me up and rend me into small pieces. In spite of all that, he stood still for almost a minute before he said, "Yes, I'll sit."

That wasn't quite as good as "I'll negotiate," but I chose to take it and led him to his seat, offering him water.

I was almost back with a full bulb for him when Admiral Kipple came in. Tellingly, he held his coat over his arm. He glanced at Admiral Mott and offered a quick nod, then simply stood, as if waiting for instruction. He didn't appear to have the same need to understand what was happening. Instead, he looked both broken and proud at once.

I led him to his chair. He sat down, threw his beautiful coat over the chair next to him, and sighed audibly.

I looked around the room, making sure everyone was where I expected them to be. Then I began. "I want to be clear that we are negotiating for peace."

86

ALICIA

Chelo had been talking awhile, then listening. All of the talk was excruciating fluff. Chelo's as well. And then, she got it. She stood in front of Admiral Mott, her back straight and her face full of banked fire. "Which ship do you want to sacrifice to prove that my brother can destroy your fleet with your fleet?"

Admiral Mott, already a pale man, paled further.

We had been arguing about nothing for ten minutes, and I had been about to interrupt when Chelo finally took a risk. Good for her. As far as I knew, she didn't have any way in the world to contact Joseph, or to carry through on the threat she had just made.

Admiral Mott spit out his acquiescence. "No demonstration required."

Good. Now we could deal with real issues.

Chelo turned the floor over to the Keepers. It's not what I would have done, but I had to admit that the renegade Keepers looked pretty good at the podium. They were both small, unassuming, dressed in fancy robes, and burning with purpose.

Mohami began. "There is a Third Fleet out there. Those are ships where the majority of people, or at least the majority of people in power, do not worship the money and power that has controlled

Silver's Home for the last few generations. They don't support the unbridled economization of *everything* that can be made. They want to celebrate our abilities in a way that adds value to the whole of our culture rather than granting riches to the few." He glanced at Admiral Mott. "Although everyone does believe in rewards to the Makers."

Admiral Mott sat stone-faced.

"After all," Mohami continued, "as Joseph has just demonstrated, Makers can make peace." Mohami shifted his attention to the Islan Admiral. "No one in Silver's Home is likely to submit to being told they can't continue to create and evolve life. That is a thing we do, like breathing."

"Go on," Admiral Kipple said, his arms crossed over his stomach.

Mohami nodded. "Just as there is a Third Fleet, there is a third way. People can create whatever they want if they take responsibility for it, including helping whatever they create become independent."

No one responded.

I stretched and cleared my throat. "And we who have been created demand our own rights. The Fliers of Lopali demand that we be named fully human."

Admiral Mott looked away from me but said nothing.

I watched the door.

Romi came through, electronic leash in one hand, walking stick in the other. A prop, given that he could walk perfectly well without it. Maybe even a weapon. Following behind him, the paw-cat walked through the door. Four legs as long as mine, and stronger. A sleek body, built so its back was higher than Romi's belly button and the top of its head would come to my shoulder. Old scars marred its right flank and nose. In spite of the scars, or maybe because of them, it was a stunning animal.

It smelled like Fremont.

I liked that. I would have been disappointed if it had smelled like a tamed thing.

It came up beside Romi, tawny tail twitching and dark eyes surveying the room as if it were choosing dinner.

Both admirals stood.

I smiled. "That animal could kill you easily. It has already killed fifteen Hunters on the Island of Water Lily Hunting Grounds." I spoke to Admiral Kipple. "Are you familiar with the hunting grounds?"

He nodded. "I am."

"Then you know that this is not a tame animal, regardless of the control it is choosing to demonstrate now."

Admiral Kipple took a step back.

"I demand freedom for all sentient made things. That includes most of the Hunted on Water Lily."

Now Admiral Mott found words. "That's ridiculous. You want us to let bioengineered killers loose on Silver's Home?"

Romi spoke, the casualness of his tone a sharp contrast to the animal he stood beside. "Of course not. The predators may even choose to do what they do now—kill off the stupid who want a fabulous way to die by tooth and claw and fang."

I hid a smile.

Romi continued. "But they will have rights. A Hunter who breaks the rules might be thrown in jail. The Hunted who survive might be allowed to live out their lives."

"Are you trying to say they are sentient enough to make choices?" The admiral almost sounded curious.

"They are smart enough to beat humans at complicated hunting games."

"That's instinct!"

"Do you think it is instinct that allows me to fly?" I asked.

He had no answer for that. I myself was a little uncertain of a bioengineered paw-cat's claim to sentience, but I saw no reason for the cat to be enslaved to humans. Someone else could decide where to put that line, and they could draw it all the way to houseplants if they wanted.

I had more to say. "The Fliers of Lopali will still fly as humans, and we may even still work with seekers. Perhaps that work will be more authentic than it is today."

Admiral Mott tried a different approach. "It will take weeks to communicate back home and work all of this out. The entire—"

Chelo interrupted him even before I could. "You would be agreeing to worse things if Islas won. Which they were about to do."

Admiral Kipple smiled.

Admiral Mott, on the other hand, scowled. "I have to consult with my government."

This time I spoke up. "If you had lost the war, you would have negotiated the best peace possible. And since you did lose the war, that's what you should do."

Chelo's eyes widened ever so slightly.

This is what I was born for. To push the edges of evil until better choices got made. Unlike Chelo, I didn't feel any particular need to do it carefully.

87

JOSEPH

Feeling about as substantial as a spiderweb, I still stopped in at each of the Third Fleet ships and thanked them. I was spread so thinly I could do many at once, but not all, of course. It took time.

The exhale of winning left me floating and soft, partly carried on Caro's younger energy and also directing her.

Maybe we could do anything. But the negotiations included me promising never to control Islan or Authority Ships again, at least after they agreed to terms. This did not bother me. I had no desire to ever control more than one ship at a time. Whichever one I was flying.

There were still a few details to work out, but who would have expected five young people from backward Fremont to change the outcome of an interplanetary war?

I felt good.

As I slid carefully inside myself, the act of becoming smaller cost me the sense of vastness I had enjoyed. But it was replaced by the slick swipe of Sasha's tongue and a burbled hello from Jherrel—and the most intense hug of my life from my sister.

Each of these things also contained multitudes.

Chelo carefully fed me vitamin-charged water, making me take it in slowly.

Liam carried Caro over and set her in my lap. She was big enough that her feet almost touched the ground as her head lolled against my shoulder. I whispered into the data, *Thank you.*

I love you, Uncle Joseph.

And I love you. Sleep.

Okay.

And she did. Just like that, the sleep of the innocent and the young and the heroic.

Captain Hill came over and held out her hand. Her face looked more relaxed than I had ever seen it, and her smile wider. "You did well."

"Thank you."

She cocked her head. "Do you know my nickname?"

I smiled. "Marcus told me what he called you once."

She smiled again. "Rose. You can call me Rose."

"Thank you."

EPILOGUE

The end of the story of Chelo Lee, dated December 23rd Year 222, Fremont Standard, as brought to the Academy of New World Historians …

Immediately after the Making War ended, Joseph and Caro slept for weeks, during which time the admirals could have easily taken the Third Fleet. But either they did not know that, or in their heart of hearts they knew that the Doctrine of New Making promised great rewards.

You know, of course, what happened next. The world changed. The economy lagged then flourished under the Doctrine, and so did trade between Islas and Silver's Home. Even today, the Islans like to control their population, and the Silvers hate being told what to do. Gloriously, there are nearly eighty species in the Book of Life. The year the Making War ended there were two—humans and fliers.

Alicia returned to Lopali, since it was designed for her, and rose to power there. I think some of the other fliers may love her. Liam and Kayleen and the children and I returned to Fremont, although Caro joined Joseph in a new ship, which I will not name, as soon as she became an adult. Sometimes they visit. Neither has ever seemed quite human. I will never understand what they did to save us, and I have little idea what they do with their time now. Perhaps they are designing whole new worlds, or perhaps they are playing card games.

Neither of them has ever married or had children, but they do run an organization that helps the Wind Burned.

Sasha lived for seven more years. Joseph brought her back here to our farm near Artistos the year she died, and we buried her near the waterfall on Islandia where we'd once lived. She did well for a skinny stray.

That is enough detail for you. I told you when we started this that I would speak of all the things that led to the Making War, and of the war itself, and that the rest of our lives is our own.

ACKNOWLEDGMENTS

Thanks to John Pitts for supporting this series from the beginning. Fly free, my friend.

Thanks to two people in particular who read the manuscript all the way through and helped me cut tens of thousands of unnecessary words and found multiple small problems. Darragh Metzger, thank you for reading every one of these in manuscript and for continually telling me you wanted more scenery, more character reaction, and more emotion. I know you didn't get enough, but there was that 20,000-plus word cut exercise … Also to Danielle Ackley-McPhail who has been my publisher, my editor, and my friend, and a long-time supporter of this series.

Speaking of publishers, this book, book four, is only in your hands because of Kevin J. Anderson's support. I appreciate KJA and the staff at WordFire Press more than anyone can know. They brought out beautiful 10th anniversary editions of *The Silver Ship and the Sea*, *Reading the Wind*, and *Wings of Creation*. My agent, Eleanor Wood, helped me sell the first three of these books to Tor many years ago. I am grateful to Tor for giving me my first chance in publishing.

Thanks to my wife, Toni, and to the dogs. Sasha, upon whom the dog Sasha in this story is modeled, passed on long ago. But she lives on a little in this story. As always, thank you to my father for always telling me I could do anything.

The most important thanks go to you, as readers. Thank you for your time and attention. I hope the these characters and ideas gave you pleasure .

ABOUT THE AUTHOR

Brenda Cooper is the author of twelve science fiction and fantasy books.

She is the winner of the 2007 and 2016 Endeavor Awards for "a distinguished science fiction or fantasy book written by a Pacific Northwest author or authors." Her work has also been nominated for the Phillip K. Dick and Canopus awards.

A technology professional, Brenda is the Director of Information Technology for Lease Crutcher Lewis, a premier Pacific Northwest builder.

Brenda earned a BA in Management Information Systems at California State University, Fullerton. She also has an MFA in fiction from StoneCoast, a program of the University of Southern Maine.

Brenda lives in Woodinville, Washington, with her family and four dogs.

IF YOU LIKED ...

If you liked *The Making War*, you might also enjoy:

Selected Stories: Science Fiction, Volume 1
by Kevin J Anderson

Walking on a Sea of Clouds
by Gray Rinehart

Phule's Company
by Robert Asprin

OTHER WORDFIRE PRESS TITLES BY BRENDA COOPER

The Silver Ship and the Sea
Reading the Wind
Wings of Creation

Our list of other WordFire Press authors and titles is always growing.
To find out more and to see our selection of titles, visit us at:
wordfirepress.com